The Life Everlasting

A Reality of Romance

The Life Everlasting

A Reality of Romance

Marie Corelli

THE LIFE EVERLASTING
A REALITY OF ROMANCE

Published in the United States by IndyPublish.com
McLean, Virginia

ISBN 1-4043-1294-3 (hardcover)
ISBN 1-4043-1295-1 (paperback)

CONTENTS

AUTHOR'S PROLOGUE

In the Gospels of the only Divine Friend this world has ever had or ever will have, we read of a Voice, a 'Voice in the Wilderness.' There have been thousands of such Voices;—most of them ineffectual. All through the world's history their echoes form a part of the universal record, and from the very beginning of time they have sounded forth their warnings or entreaties in vain. The Wilderness has never cared to hear them. The Wilderness does not care to hear them now.

Why, then, do I add an undesired note to the chorus of rejected appeal? How dare I lift up my voice in the Wilderness, when other voices, far stronger and sweeter, are drowned in the laughter of fools and the mockery of the profane? Truly, I do not know. But I am sure that I am not moved by egotism or arrogance. It is simply out of love and pity for suffering human kind that I venture to become another Voice discarded—a voice which, if heard at all, may only serve to awaken the cheap scorn and derision of the clowns of the piece.

Yet, should this be so, I would not have it otherwise, I have never at any time striven to be one with the world, or to suit my speech pliantly to the conventional humour of the moment. I am often attacked, yet am not hurt; I am equally often praised, and am not elated. I have no time to attend to the expression of opinions, which, whether good or bad, are to me indifferent. And whatever pain I have felt or feel, in experiencing human malice, has been, and is, in the fact that human malice should exist at all,—not for its attempted wrong towards myself. For I, personally speaking, have not a moment to waste among the mere shadows of life which are not Life itself. I follow the glory,—not the gloom.

So whether you, who wander in darkness of your own making, care to come towards the little light which leads me onward, or whether you prefer to turn away from me altogether into your self-created darker depths, is not my concern. I cannot force you to bear me company. God Himself cannot do that, for it is His Will and Law that each human soul shall shape its own eternal future. No one mortal can make the happiness or salvation of another. I, like yourselves, am in the 'Wilderness,'—but I know that there are ways of making it blossom like the rose! Yet,—were all my heart and all my love outpoured upon you, I could not teach you the Divine transfiguring charm,—unless you, equally with all your hearts and all your love, resolutely and irrevocably WILLED to learn.

Nevertheless, despite your possible indifference,—your often sheer inertia—I cannot pass you by, having peace and comfort for myself without at least offering to share that peace and comfort with you. Many of you are very sad,—and I would rather you were happy. Your ways of living are trivial and unsatisfactory—your so-called 'pleasant' vices lead you into unforeseen painful perplexities—your ideals of what may be best for your own enjoyment and advancement fall far short of your dreams,—your amusements pall on your over- wearied senses,—your youth hurries away like a puff of thistledown on the wind,—and you spend all your time feverishly in trying to live without understanding Life. Life, the first of all things, the essence of all things,—Life which is yours to hold and to keep, and to RE-CREATE over and over again in your own persons,—this precious jewel you throw away, and when it falls out of your possession by your own act, you think such an end was necessary and inevitable. Poor unhappy mortals! So self-sufficient, so proud, so ignorant! Like some foolish rustic, who, finding a diamond, sees no difference between it and a bit of glass, you, with the whole Universe sweeping around you in mighty beneficent circles of defensive, protective and ever re-creative power,—power which is yours to use and to control- - imagine that the entire Cosmos is the design of mere blind unintelligent Chance, and that the Divine Life which thrills within you serves no purpose save to lead you to Death! Most wonderful and most pitiful it is that such folly, such blasphemy should still prevail,—and that humanity should still ascribe to the Almighty Creator less wisdom and less love than that with which He has endowed His creatures. For the very first lesson in the beginning of knowledge is that Life is the essential Being of God, and that each individual intelligent outcome of Life is deathless as God Himself.

The 'Wilderness' is wide,—and within it we all find ourselves,— some wandering far astray—some crouching listlessly among shadows, too weary to move at all—others, sauntering along in idle indifference, now and then vaguely questioning how soon and where the journey will end,—and few ever discovering that it is not a 'Wilderness' at all, but a garden of sweet sights and sounds, where every day should be a glory and every night a benediction. For when the veil of mere Appearances has been lifted we are no longer deceived into accepting what Seems for what Is. The Reality of Life is Happiness;—the Delusion of Life, which we ourselves create by improper balance and imperfect comprehension of our own powers, must needs cause Sorrow, because in such self-deception we only dimly see the truth, just as a person born blind may vaguely guess at the beauty of bright day. But for the Soul that has found Itself, there are no more misleading lights or shadows between its own everlastingness and the everlastingness of God.

All the world over there are religions of various kinds, more or less suited to the various types and races of humanity. Most of these forms of faith have been evolved from the brooding brain of Man himself, and have nothing 'divine,' in them. In the very early ages nearly all the religious creeds were mere methods for terrorising the ignorant and the weak—and some of them were so revolting, so bloodthirsty and brutal, that one cannot now read of them without a shudder of repulsion. Nevertheless, from the very first dawn of his intelligence, man appears always to have felt the necessity of believing in something stronger and more last-ing than himself,—and his first gropings for truth led him to evolve desperate notions of something more cruel, more relentless, and more wicked than himself, rather than ideals of something more beautiful, more just, more faithful and more loving than he could be. The dawn of Christianity brought the first glimmering suggestion that a gospel of love and pity might be more serviceable in the end to the needs of the world, than a ruthless code of slaughter and vengeance- -though history shows us that the annals of Christianity itself are stained with crime and shamed by the shedding of innocent blood. Only in these latter days has the world become faintly conscious of the real Force working behind and through all things—the soul of the Divine, or the Psychic element, animating and inspiring all visible and invisible Nature. This soul of the Divine—this Psychic element, however, is almost entirely absent from the teaching of the Christian creed to-day, with the result that the creed itself is losing its power. I venture to say that a very small majority of the millions of persons worshipping in the various forms of the Christian Church really and truly believe what they publicly profess. Clergy and laity alike are tainted with this worst of all hypocrisies—that of calling God to witness their faith when they know they are faithless. It may be asked how I dare to make such an assertion? I dare, because I know! It would be impossible to the people of this or any other country to honestly believe the Christian creed, and yet continue to live as they do. Their lives give the lie to their avowed religion, and it is this daily spectacle of the daily life of governments, trades, professions and society which causes me to feel that the general aspect of Christendom at the present day, with all its Churches and solemn observances, is one of the most painful and profound hypocrisy. You who read this page,—(possibly with indig-nation) you call yourself a Christian, no doubt. But ARE you? Do you truly think that when death shall come to you it is really NOT death, but the simple transition into another and better life? Do you believe in the actual immortality of your soul, and do you realise what it means? You do? You are quite sure? Then, do you live as one convinced of it? Are you quite indifferent to the riches and purely material advantages of this world?—are you as happy in poverty as in wealth, and are you independent of social esteem? Are you bent on the very highest and most unselfish ideals of life and conduct? I do not say you are not; I merely ask if you ARE. If your answer is in the affirmative, do not give the lie to your creed by your daily habits, conversation and manners; for this is what thousands of professing Christians do, and the clergy are by no means exempt.

I know very well, of course, that I must not expect your appreciation, or even your attention, in matters purely spiritual. The world is too much with you, and you become obstinate of opinion and rooted in prejudice. Nevertheless, as I said before, this is not my concern. Your moods are not mine, and with your prejudices I have nothing to do. My creed is drawn from Nature—Nature, just, invincible, yet tender—Nature, who shows us that Life, as we know it now, at this very time and in this very world, is a blessing so rich in its as yet unused powers and possibilities, that it may be truly said of the greater majority of human beings that scarce one of them has ever begun to learn HOW to live.

Shakespeare, the greatest human exponent of human nature at its best and worst,—the profound Thinker and Artist who dealt boldly with the facts of good and evil as they truly are,—and did not hesitate to contrast them forcibly, without any of the deceptive 'half-tones' of vice and virtue which are the chief stock-in-trade of such modern authors as we may call 'degenerates,'—makes his Hamlet exclaim:—

> "What a piece of work is man!—how noble in
> reason!—how infinite in faculty!—in form and moving
> how express and admirable!—in action how like an
> angel!—in apprehension how like a god!"

Let us consider two of these designations in particular: 'How infinite in faculty!'—and 'In apprehension how like a god!' The sentences are prophetic, like so many of Shakespeare's utterances. They foretell the true condition of the Soul of Man when it shall have discovered its capabilities. 'Infinite in faculty'—that is to say—Able to do all it shall WILL to do. There is no end to this power,—no hindrance in either earth or heaven to its resolute working—no stint to the life-supplies on which it may draw unceasingly. And—'in apprehension how like a god!' Here the word 'apprehension' is used in the sense of attaining knowledge,—to learn, or to 'apprehend' wisdom. It means, of course, that if the Soul's capability of 'apprehending' or learning the true meaning and use of every fact and circumstance which environs its existence, were properly perceived and applied, then the 'Image of God' in which the Creator made humanity, would become the veritable likeness of the Divine.

But, as this powerful and infinite faculty of apprehension is seldom if ever rightly understood, and as Man generally concentrates his whole effort upon ministering to his purely material needs, utterly ignoring and wilfully refusing to realise those larger claims which are purely spiritual, he presents the appearance of a maimed and imperfect object,—a creature who, having strong limbs, declines to use the same, or who, possessing incalculable wealth, crazily considers himself a pauper. Jesus Christ, whom we may look upon as a human Incarnation of Divine Thought, an outcome and expression of the 'Word' or Law of God, came to teach us our true position in the scale of the great Creative and Progressive Purpose,— but in the days of His coming men would not listen,—nor will they listen even now. They say with their mouths, but they do not believe with their hearts, that He rose from the dead,—and they cannot understand that, as a matter of fact, He never died. seeing that death for Him (as for all who have mastered the inward constitution and commingling of the elements) was impossible. His real LIFE was not injured or affected by the agony on the Cross, or by His three days' entombment; the one was a torture to His physical frame, which to the limited perception of those who watched Him 'die,' as they thought, appeared like a dissolution of the whole Man,—the other was the mere rest and silence necessary for what is called the 'miracle' of the Resurrection, but which was simply the natural rising of the same Body, the atoms of which were re-invested and made immortal by the imperishable Spirit which owned and held them in being. The whole life and so-called 'death' of Christ was and is a great symbolic lesson to mankind of the infinite power of THAT within us which we call SOUL,—but which we may perhaps in these scientific days term an eternal radio-activity,—capable of exhaustless energy and of readjustment to varying conditions. Life is all Life. There is no such thing as Death in its composition,— and the intelligent comprehension of its endless ways and methods of change and expression, is the Secret of the Universe.

It appears to be generally accepted that we are not to know this Secret,—that it is too vast and deep for our limited capacities,— and that even if we did know it, it would be of no use to us, as we are bound hard and fast by certain natural and elemental laws over which we have no control. Old truisms are re-stated and violently asserted—namely, that our business is merely to be born, to live, breed and arrange things as well as we can for those who come after us, and then to die, and there an end,—a stupid round of existence not one whit higher than that of the silkworm. Is it for such a monotonous, commonplace way of life and purpose as this, that humanity has been endowed with 'infinite faculty'? Is it for such poor aims and ends as these that we are told in the legended account of the beginning of things, to 'Replenish the earth and subdue it'? There is great meaning in that command—'Subdue it!' The business of each one of us who has come into the knowledge and possession of his or her own Soul, is to 'subdue' the earth,—that is, to hold it and all it contains under subjection,—not to allow Its forces, whether interior or exterior, to subdue the Soul. But it may perhaps be said:—"We do not yet understand all the forces with which we have to contend, and in this way they master us." That may be so,—but if it is so with any of you, it is quite your own fault. Your own fault, I say,—for there is no power, human or divine, that compels you to remain in ignorance. Each one of you has a master—talisman and key to all locked doors. No State education can do for you what you might do for yourselves, if you only had the WILL. It is your own choice entirely if you elect to live in subjection to the earth, instead of placing the earth under subjection to your dominance.

Then, again, you have been told to 'Replenish the earth'—as well as to subdue it. In these latter days, through a cupidity as amazing as criminal, you are not 'replenishing' so much as impoverishing the earth, and think you that no interest will be exacted for your reckless plunder? You mistake! You complain of the high taxes imposed upon you by your merely material and ephemeral Governments,- -but you forget that the Everlasting Government of all Worlds demands an even higher rate of compensation for such wrong or injurious uses as you make of this world, which was and is intended to serve as a place of training for the development and perfection of the whole human race, but which, owing to personal greed and selfishness, is too often turned into a mere grave for the interment of faulty civilisations.

In studying the psychic side of life it should be well and distinctly understood that THERE IS AN EVER LIVING SPIRIT WITHIN EACH ONE OF US;—a Spirit for which there is no limited capacity and no unfavourable surroundings. Its capacity is infinite as God,—and its surroundings are always made by Itself. It is its own Heaven,— and once established within that everlasting centre, it radiates from the Inward to the Outward, thus making its own environment, not only now but for ever. It is its own Life,—and in the active work of perpetually re-generating and re-creating itself, knows nothing of Death.

* * *
* *
*

I must now claim the indulgence of those among my readers who possess the rare gift of patience, for anything that may seem too personal in the following statement which I feel it almost necessary to make on the subject of my own "psychic" creed. I am so often asked if I believe this or that, if I am "orthodox," if I am a sceptic, materialist or agnostic, that I should like, if possible, to make things clear between myself and these enquirers. Therefore I may say at once that my belief in God and the immortality of the Soul is absolute,—but that I did not attain to the faith I hold without hard training and bitter suffering. This need not be dwelt upon, being past. I began to write when I was too young to know anything of the world's worldly ways, and when I was too enthusiastic and too much carried away by the splendour and beauty of the spiritual ideal to realise the inevitable derision and scorn which are bound to fall upon untried explorers into the mysteries of the unseen; yet it was solely on account of a strange psychical experience which chanced to myself when I stood upon the threshold of what is called 'life' that I found myself producing my first book, "A Romance of Two Worlds." It was a rash experiment, but it was the direct result of an initiation into some few of the truths behind the veil of the Seeming Real. I did not then know why I was selected for such an 'initiation'—and I do not know even now. It arose quite naturally out of a series of ordinary events which might happen to anyone. I was not compelled or persuaded into it, for, being alone in the world and more or less friendless, I had no opportunity to seek advice or assistance from any person as to the course of life or learning I should pursue. And I learned what I did learn because of my own unwavering intention and WILL to be instructed.

I should here perhaps explain the tenor of the instruction which was gradually imparted to me in just such measures of proportion as I was found to be receptive. The first thing I was taught was how to bring every feeling and sense into close union with the spirit of Nature. Nature, I was told, is the reflection of the working-mind of the Creator—and any opposition to that working-mind on the part of any living organism It has created cannot but result in disaster. Pursuing this line of study, a wonderful vista of perpetual revealment was opened to me. I saw how humanity, moved by gross egoism, has in every age of the world ordained laws and morals for itself which are the very reverse of Nature's teaching—I saw how, instead of helping the wheel of progress and wisdom onward, man reverses it by his obstinacy and turns it backward even on the very point of great attainment—and I was able to perceive how the sorrows and despairs of the world are caused by this one simple fact—Man working AGAINST Nature—while Nature, ever divine and invincible, pursues her God-appointed course, sweeping her puny opponents aside and inflexibly carrying out her will to the end. And I learned how true it is that if Man went WITH her instead of AGAINST her, there would be no more misunderstanding of the laws of the Universe, and that where there is now nothing but discord, all would be divinest harmony.

My first book, "A Romance of Two Worlds," was an eager, though crude, attempt to explain and express something of what I myself had studied on some of these subjects, though, as I have already said, my mind was unformed and immature, and, therefore, I was not permitted to disclose more than a glimmering of the light I was beginning to perceive. My own probation—destined to be a severe one—had only just been entered upon; and hard and fast limits were imposed on me for a certain time. I was forbidden, for example, to write of radium, that wonderful 'discovery' of the immediate hour, though it was then, and had been for a long period, perfectly well known to my instructors, who possessed all the means of extracting it from substances as yet undreamed of by latter-day scientists. I was only permitted to hint at it under the guise of the word 'Electricity'—which, after all, was not so much of a misnomer, seeing that electric force displays itself in countless millions of forms. My "Electric Theory of the Universe" in the "Romance of Two Worlds" foreran the utterance of the scientist who in the "Hibbert Journal" for January, 1905, wrote as follows:—"The last years have seen the dawn of a revolution in science as great as that which in the sphere of religion overthrew the many gods and crowned the One. Matter, as we have understood it, there is none, nor probably anywhere the individual atom. The so-called atoms are systems of ELECTRONIC corpuscles, bound together by their mutual forces too firmly for any human contrivance completely to sunder them,—alike in their electric composition, differing only in the rhythms of their motion. ELECTRIC-ITY is all things, and all things are ELECTRIC."

THIS WAS PRECISELY MY TEACHING IN THE FIRST BOOK I EVER WROTE. I was ridiculed for it, of course,—and I was told that there was no 'spiritual' force in electricity. I differ from this view; but 'radio-activity' is perhaps the better, because the truer term to employ in seeking to describe the Germ or Embryo of the Soul, for— as scientists have proved—"Radium is capable of absorbing from surrounding bodies SOME UNKNOWN FORM OF ENERGY which it can render evident as heat and light." This is precisely what the radio-activity in each individual soul of each individual human being is ordained to do,—to absorb an 'unknown form of energy which it can render evident as heat and light.' Heat and Light are the composition of Life;—and the Life which this radio-activity of Soul generates IN itself and OF itself, can never die. Or, as I wrote in "A Romance of Two Worlds "—"Like all flames, this electric (or radiant) spark can either be fanned into a fire, or allowed to escape in air,—IT CAN NEVER BE DESTROYED." And again, from the same book: "All the wonders of Nature are the result of LIGHT AND HEAT ALONE." Paracelsus, as early as about 1526, made guarded mention of the same substance or quality, describing it thus:—"The more of the humour of life it has, the more of the spirit of life abounds in that life." Though truly this vital radio-active force lacks all fitting name. To material science radium, or radium chloride, is a minute salt crystal, so rare and costly to obtain that it may be counted as about three thousand times the price of gold in the market. But of the action of PURE radium, the knowledge of ordinary scientific students is nil. They know that an infinitely small spark of radium salt will emit heat and light continuously without any combustion or change in its own structure. And I would here quote a passage from a lecture delivered by one of our prominent scientists in 1904. "Details concerning the behaviour of several radio-active bodies were detected, as, for example, their activity was not constant; it gradually grew in strength, BUT THE GROWN PORTION OF THE ACTIVITY COULD BE BLOWN AWAY, AND THE BLOWN AWAY PART RETAINED ITS ACTIVITY ONLY FOR A TIME. It decayed in a few days or weeks,— WHEREAS THE RADIUM ROSE IN STRENGTH AGAIN AT THE SAME RATE THAT THE OTHER DECAYED. And so on constantly. It was as if a NEW FORM of matter was constantly being produced, and AS IF THE RADIO-ACTIVITY WAS A CONCOMITANT OF THE CHANGE OF FORM. It was also found that radium kept on producing heat de novo so as to keep itself always a fraction of a degree ABOVE THE SURROUNDING TEMPERATURE; also that it spontaneously PRODUCED ELECTRICITY."

Does this teach no lesson on the resurrection of the dead? Of the 'blown away part' which decays in a few days or weeks?—of the 'Radia' or 'Radiance' of the Soul, rising in strength again AT THE SAME RATE that the other, the Body, or 'grown portion of the activity,' decays? Of the 'new form of matter' and the 'radio-activity as a concomitant of the CHANGE OF FORM'? Does not Science here almost unwittingly verify the words of St. Paul:—"It is sown a natural body; it is raised a spiritual body. There is a natural body, and there is a spiritual body"? There is nothing impossible or 'miraculous' in such a consummation, even according to modern material science,—it is merely the natural action of PURE radio- activity or that etherical composition for which we have no name, but which we have vaguely called the SOUL for countless ages.

To multitudes of people this expression 'the Soul' has become overfamiliar by constant repetition, and conveys little more than the suggestion of a myth, or the hint of an Imaginary Existence. Now there is nothing in the whole Universe so REAL as the Vital Germ of the actual Form and Being of the living, radiant, active Creature within each one of us,—the creature who, impressed and guided by our Free Will, works out its own delight or doom. The WILL of each man or woman is like the compass of a ship,—where it points, the ship goes. If the needle directs it to the rocks, there is wreck and disaster,—if to the open sea, there is clear sailing. God leaves the WILL of man at perfect liberty. His Divine Love neither constrains nor compels. We must Ourselves learn the ways of Right and Wrong, and having learned, we must choose. We must injure Ourselves. God will not injure us. We invite our own miseries. God does not send them. The evils and sorrows that afflict mankind are of mankind's own making. Even in natural catastrophes, which ruin cities and devastate countries, it is well to remember that Nature, which is the MATERIAL EXPRESSION of the mind of God, will not tolerate too long a burden of human iniquity. Nature destroys what is putrescent; she covers it up with fresh earth on which healthier things may find place to grow.

I tried to convey some hint of these truths in my "Romance of Two Worlds." Some few gave heed,—others wrote to me from all parts of the world concerning what they called my 'views' on the subjects treated of,—some asked to be 'initiated' into my 'experience' of the Unseen,—but many of my correspondents (I say it with regret) were moved by purely selfish considerations for their own private and particular advancement, and showed, by the very tone of their letters, not only an astounding hypocrisy, but also the good opinion they entertained of their own worthiness, their own capabilities, and their own great intellectuality, forgetful of the words:— "Except ye become as little children, ye shall not enter into the Kingdom of Heaven."

Now the spirit of a little child is receptive and trustful. It has no desire for argument, and it is instinctively confident that it will not be led into unnecessary difficulty or danger by its responsible guardians. This is the spirit in which, if we are sincere in our seeking for knowledge, we should and must approach the deeper psychological mysteries of Nature. But as long as we interpose the darkness of personal doubt and prejudice between ourselves and the Light Eternal no progress can be made,—and every attempt to penetrate into the Holy of Holies will be met and thrust back by that 'flaming Sword' which from the beginning, as now, turns every way to guard the Tree of Life.

Knowing this, and seeing that Self was the stumbling-block with most of my correspondents, I was anxious to write another book at once, also in the guise of a romance, to serve as a little lamp of love whereby my readers might haply discover the real character of the obstacle which blocked their way to an intelligent Soul-advancement. But the publisher I had at the time (the late Mr. George Bentley) assured me that if I wrote another 'spiritualistic' book, I should lose the public hearing I had just gained. I do not know why he had formed this opinion, but as he was a kindly personal friend, and took a keen interest in my career, never handing any manuscript of mine over to his 'reader,' but always reading it himself, I felt it incumbent upon me, as a young beginner, to accept the advice which I knew could only be given with the very best intentions towards me. To please him, therefore, and to please the particular public to which he had introduced me, I wrote something entirely different,—a melodramatic tale entitled: "Vendetta: The Story of One Forgotten." The book made a certain stir, and Mr. Bentley next begged me to try 'a love-story, pur et simple' (I quote from his own letter). The result was my novel of "Thelma," which achieved a great popular success and still remains a favourite work with a large majority of readers. I then considered myself free to move once more upon the lines which my study of psychic forces had convinced me were of pre- eminent importance. And moved by a strong conviction that men and women are hindered from attaining their full heritage of life by the obstinate interposition of their merely material Selves, I wrote "Ardath: The Story of a Dead Self." The plan of this book was partially suggested by the following passages from the Second Apocryphal Book of Esdras:—

"Go into a field of flowers where no house is builded. And pray unto the Highest continually, then will I come and talk with thee. So I went my way into the field which is called Ardath, like as he commanded me, and there I sat among the flowers."

In this field the Prophet sees the vision of a woman.

"And it came to pass while I was talking with her, behold her face upon a sudden shined exceedingly and her countenance glistened, so that I was afraid of her and mused what it might be. And I looked, and behold the woman appeared unto me no more, but there was a city builded, and a large place showed itself from the foundations."

On this I raised the fabric of my own "Dream City," and sought to elucidate some of the meaning of that great text in Ecclesiastes which contains in itself all the philosophy of the ages: "That which Hath Been is Now; and that which is To Be hath already Been; and God requireth that which is Past."

The book, however, so my publisher Mr. Bentley told me in a series of letters which I still possess, and which show how keen was his own interest in my work, was 'entirely over the heads of the general public.' His opinion was, no doubt, correct, as "Ardath" still remains the least 'popular' of any book I have ever written. Nevertheless it brought me the unsought and very generous praise of the late Poet Laureate, Alfred Lord Tennyson, as well as the equally unsought good opinion and personal friendship of the famous statesman, William Ewart Gladstone, while many of the better-class literary journals vied with one another in according me an almost enthusiastic eulogy. Such authorities as the "Athenaeum" and "Spectator" praised the whole conception and style of the work, the latter journal going as far as to say that I had beaten Beckford's famous "Vathek" on its own ground.

Whatever may now be the consensus of opinion on its merits or demerits, I know and feel it to be one of my most worthy attempts, even though it is not favoured by the million. It does not appeal to anything 'of the moment' merely, because there are very few people who can or will understand that if the Soul or 'Radia' of a human being is so forgetful of its highest origin as to cling to its human Self only (events the hero of "Ardath" clung to the Shadow of his Former Self and to the illusory pictures of that Former Self's pleasures and vices and vanities) then the way to the eternal Happier Progress is barred. There is yet another intention in this book which seems to be missed by the casual reader, namely,—That each human soul is a germ of SEPARATE and INDIVIDUAL spiritual existence. Even as no two leaves are exactly alike on any tree, and no two blades of grass are precisely similar, so no two souls resemble each other, but are wholly different, endowed with different gifts and different capacities. Individuality is strongly insisted upon in material Nature. And why? Because material Nature is merely the reflex or mirror of the more strongly insistent individuality of psychic form. Again, psychic form is generated from a divinely eternal psychic substance,—a 'radia' or emanation of God's own Being which, as it progresses onward through endless aeons of constantly renewed vitality, grows more and more powerful, changing its shape often, but never its everlasting composition and quality. Therefore, all the experiences of the 'Soul' or psychic form, from its first entrance into active consciousness, whether in this world or in other worlds, are attracted to itself by its own inherent volition, and work together to make it what it is now and what it will be hereafter.

That is what "Ardath: The Story of a Dead Self" seeks to explain, and I have nothing to take back from what I have written in its pages. In its experimental teaching it is the natural and intended sequence of "A Romance of Two Worlds," and was meant to assist the studies of the many who had written to me asking for help. And despite the fact that some of these persons, owing to an inherent incapacity for concentrated thought upon any subject, found it too 'difficult' as they said, for casual reading, its reception was sufficiently encouraging to decide me on continuing to press upon public attention the theories therein set forth. "The Soul of Lilith" was, therefore, my next venture,—a third link in the chain I sought to weave between the perishable materialism of our ordinary conceptions of life, and the undying spiritual quality of life as it truly is. In this I portrayed the complete failure that must inevitably result from man's prejudice and intellectual pride when studying the marvellous mysteries of what I would call the Further World,—that is to say, the 'Soul' of the world which is hidden deeply behind its external Appearance,—and how impossible it is and ever must be that any 'Soul' should visibly manifest itself where there is undue attachment to the body. The publication of the book was a very interesting experience. It was and is still less 'popular' than "Ardath"—but it has been gladly welcomed by a distinctly cultured minority of persons famous in art, science and literature, whose good opinion is well worth having. With this reward I was perfectly content, but my publisher was not so easily pleased. He wanted something that would 'sell' better. To relieve his impatience, therefore, I wrote a more or less 'sensational' novel dealing with the absinthe drinkers of Paris, entitled "Wormwood," which did a certain amount of good in its way, by helping to call public attention to the devastation wrought by the use of the pernicious drug among the French and other Continental peoples—and after this, receiving a strong and almost imperative impetus towards that particular goal whither my mind was set, I went to work again with renewed vigour on my own favourite and long studied line of argument, indifferent alike to publisher or public. Filled with the fervour of a passionate and proved faith, I wrote "Barabbas: A Dream of the World's Tragedy,"—and this was the signal of separation from my excellent old friend, George Bentley, who had not the courage to publish a poetic romance which introduced, albeit with a tenderness and reverence unspeakable, so far as my own intention was concerned, the Crucifixion and Resurrection of Christ. He wrote to me expressing his opinion in these terms:—"I can conscientiously praise the power and feeling you exhibit for your vast subject, and the rush and beauty of the language, and above all I feel that the book is the genuine outcome of a fervent faith all too rare in these days, but—I fear its effect on the public mind." Yet, when urged to a given point in the discussion, he could not deny that 'the effect on the public mind' of the Passion Play at Ober-Ammergau is generally impressive and helpful, while he was bound to admit that there was something to be said for the introduction of Divine personages in the epic romances of Milton and Dante. What could be written in poetic verse did not, however, seem to him suitable for poetic prose, and I did not waste words in argument, as I knew the time had come for the parting of the ways. I sought my present publisher, Mr. Methuen, who, being aware, from a business point of view, that I had now won a certain reputation, took "Barabbas" without parley. It met with an almost unprecedented success, not only in this country but all over the world. Within a few months it was translated into every known European language, inclusive even of modern Greek, and nowhere perhaps has it awakened a wider interest than in India, where it is published in Hindustani, Gujarati, and various other Eastern dialects. Its notable triumph was achieved despite a hailstorm of abuse rattled down upon me by the press,—a hailstorm which I, personally, found welcome and refreshing, inasmuch as it cleared the air and cleaned the road for my better wayfaring. It released me once and for all from the trammels of such obligation as is incurred by praise, and set me firmly on my feet in that complete independence which to me (and to all who seek what I have found) is a paramount necessity. For, as Thomas a Kempis writes: "Whosoever neither desires to please men nor fears to displease them shall enjoy much peace."

I took my freedom gratefully, and ever since that time of unjust and ill-considered attack from persons who were too malignantly minded to even read the work they vainly endeavoured to destroy, have been happily indifferent to all so-called 'criticism' and immune from all attempts to interrupt my progress or turn me back upon my chosen way. From henceforth I recognised that no one could hinder or oppose me but myself—and that I had the making, tinder God, of my own destiny. I followed up "Barabbas" as quickly as possible by "The Sorrows of Satan," thus carrying out the preconceived intention I had always had of depicting, first, the martyrdom which is always the world's guerdon to Absolute Good,—and secondly, the awful, unimaginable torture which must, by Divine Law, for ever be the lot of Absolute Evil.

The two books carried their message far and wide with astonishing success and swiftness, and I then drew some of my threads of former argument together in "The Master Christian," wherein I depicted Christ as a Child, visiting our world again as it is to-day and sorrowfully observing the wickedness which men practise in His Name. This book was seized upon by thousands of readers in all countries of the world with an amazing avidity which proved how deep was the longing for some clear exposition of faith that might console as well as command,—and after its publication I decided to let it take its own uninterrupted course for a time and to change my own line of work to lighter themes, lest I should be set down as 'spiritualist' or 'theosophist,' both of which terms have been brought into contempt by tricksters. So I played with my pen, and did my best to entertain the public with stories of everyday life and love, such as the least instructed could understand, and that I now allude to the psychological side of my work is merely to explain that these six books, namely: "A Romance of Two Worlds," "Ardath: The Story of a Dead Self," "The Soul of Lilith," "Barabbas," "The Sorrows of Satan" and "The Master Christian" ARE THE RESULT OF A DELIBERATELY CONCEIVED PLAN AND INTENTION, and are all linked together by the ONE THEORY. They have not been written solely as pieces of fiction for which I, the author, am paid by the publisher, or you, the reader, are content to be temporarily entertained,—they are the outcome of what I myself have learned, practised and proved in the daily experiences, both small and great, of daily life.

You may probably say and you probably WILL say—"What does that matter to us? We do not care a jot for your 'experiences'—they are transcendental and absurd—they bore us to extinction." Nevertheless, quite callous as you are or may be, there must come a time when pain and sorrow have you in their grip—when what you call 'death' stands face to face with you, and when you will find that all you have thought, desired or planned for your own pleasure, and all that you possess of material good or advantage, vanishes like smoke, leaving nothing behind,—when the world will seem no more than a small receding point from which you must fall into the Unknown—and when that "dread of something after death, The undiscovered country from whose bourn No traveller returns, PUZZLES THE WILL." You have at present living among you a great professing scientist, Dr. Oliver Lodge, who, wandering among mazy infinities, conceives it even possible to communicate with departed spirits,— while I, who have no such weight of worldly authority and learning behind me, tell you that such a thing is out of all natural law and therefore CAN NEVER BE. Nature can and will unveil to us many mysteries that seem SUPER-natural, when they are only manifestations of the deepest centre of the purest natural—but nothing can alter Divine Law, or change the system which has governed the Universe from the beginning. And by this Divine Law and system we have to learn that the so-called 'dead' are NOT dead—they have merely been removed to fresh life and new spheres of action, under which circumstances they cannot possibly hold communication with us in any way unless they again assume the human form and human existence. In this case (which very frequently happens) it takes not only time for us to know them, but it also demands a certain instinctive receptiveness on our parts, or willingness to recognise them. Even the risen Saviour was not at first recognised by His own disciples. It is because I have been practically convinced of this truth, and because I have learned that life is not and never can be death, but only constant change and reinvestment of Spirit into Form, that I have presumed so far as to allude to my own faith and experience,—a 'personal' touch for which I readily apologise, knowing that it cannot be interesting to the majority who would never take the trouble to shape their lives as I seek to shape mine. Still, if there are one or two out of a million who feel as I do, that life and love are of little worth if they must end in dark nothingness, these may perhaps have the patience to come with me through the pages of a narrative which is neither 'incidental' nor 'sensational' nor anything which should pertain to the modern 'romance' or 'novel,' and which has been written because the writing of it enforced itself upon me with an insistence that would take no denial.

Perhaps there will be at least one among those who turn over this book, who will be sufficiently interested in the psychic—that is to say the immortal and, therefore, the only REAL side of life—to give a little undivided attention to the subject. To that one I address myself and say: Will you, to begin with, drop your burden of preconceived opinions and prejudices, whatever they are? Will you set aside the small cares and trifles that affect your own material personality? Will you detach yourself from your own private and particular surroundings for a space and agree to THINK with me? Thinking is, I know, the hardest of all hard tasks to the modern mind. But if you would learn, you must undertake this trouble. If you would find the path which is made fair and brilliant by the radiance of the soul's imperishable summer, you must not grudge time. If I try, no matter how inadequately, to show you something of the mystic power that makes for happiness, do not shut your eyes in scorn or languor to the smallest flash of light through your darkness which may help you to a mastery of the secret.

I say again—Will you THINK with me? Will you, for instance, think of Life? What is it? Of Death? What is it? What is the primary object of Living? What is the problem solved by Dying? All these questions should have answer,—for nothing is without a meaning,— and nothing ever HAS BEEN, or ever WILL BE, without a purpose?

In this world, apparently, and according to our surface knowledge of all physical and mental phenomena, it would seem that the chief business of humanity is to continually re-create itself. Man exists- -in his own opinion—merely to perpetuate Man. All the wonders of the earth, air, fire and water,—all the sustenance drawn from the teeming bosom of Nature,—all the progress of countless civilisations in ever recurring and repeated processional order,— all the sciences old and new,—are solely to nourish, support, instruct, entertain and furnish food and employment for the tiny two-legged imp of Chance, spawned (as he himself asserts) out of gas and atoms.

Yet,—as he personally declares, through the mouth of his modern science,—he is not of real importance withal. The little planet on which he dwells would, to all seeming, move on in its orbit in the same way as it does now, without him. In itself it is a pigmy world compared with the rest of the solar system of which it is a part. Nevertheless, the fact cannot be denied that his material surroundings are of a quality tending to either impress or to deceive Man with a sense of his own value. The world is his oyster which he, with the sword of enterprise, will open,— and all his natural instincts urge him to perpetuate himself in some form or other incessantly and without stint. Why? Why is his existence judged to be necessary? Why should he not cease to be? Trees would grow, flowers would bloom, birds would sing, fish would glide through the rivers and the seas,—the insect and animal tribes of field and forest would enjoy their existence unmolested, and the great sun would shine on ever the same, rising at dawn, sinking at even, with unbroken exactitude and regularity if Man no longer lived. Why have the monstrous forces of Evolution thundered their way through cycles of creation to produce so infinitesimal a prodigy?

Till this question is answered, so long must life seem at its best but vague and unsatisfactory. So long over all things must brood the shadow of death made more gloomy by hopeless contemplation. So long must Creation appear something of a cruel farce, for which peoples and civilisations come into being merely to be destroyed and leave no trace. All the work futile,—all the education useless,—all the hope vain. Only when men and women learn that their lives are not infinitesimal but infinite—that each of them possesses within himself or herself an eternal, active, conscious individual Force,— a Being—a Form—which in its radioactive energy draws to itself and accommodates to its use, everything that is necessary for the accomplishment of its endeavours, whether such endeavours be to continue its life on this planet or to remove to other spheres; only then will it be clearly understood that all Nature is the subject and servant of this Radiant Energy—that Itself is the god-like 'image' or emanation of God, and that as such it has its eternal part to perform in the eternal movement towards the Eternal Highest.

I now leave the following pages to the reader's attentive or indifferent consideration. To me, as I have already stated, outside opinion is of no moment. Personally speaking, I should perhaps have preferred, had it been possible, to set forth the incidents narrated in the ensuing 'romance' in the form of separate essays on the nature of the mystic tuition and experience through which some of us in this workaday world have the courage to pass successfully, but I know that the masses of the people who drift restlessly to and fro upon the surface of this planet, ever seeking for comfort in various forms of religion and too often finding none, will not listen to any spiritual truth unless it is conveyed to them, as though they were children, in the form of a 'story.' I am not the heroine of the tale—though I have narrated it (more or less as told to me) in the first person singular, because it seemed to me simpler and more direct. She to whom the perfect comprehension of happiness has come with an equally perfect possession of love, is one out of a few who are seeking what she has found. Many among the world's greatest mystics and philosophers have tried for the prizes she has won,—for the world possesses Plato, the Bible and Christ, but in its apparent present ways of living has learned little or nothing from the three, so that other would-be teachers may well despair of carrying persuasion where such mighty predecessors have seemingly failed. The serious and REAL things of life are nowadays made subjects for derision rather than reverence;—then, again, there is unhappily an alarmingly increasing majority of weak-minded and degenerate persons, born of drunken, diseased or vicious parents, who are mentally unfit for the loftier forms of study, and in whom the mere act of thought-concentration would be dangerous and likely to upset their mental balance altogether; while by far the larger half of the social community seek to avoid the consideration of anything that is not exactly suited to their tastes. Some of our most respected social institutions are nothing but so many self-opinionated and unconscious oppositions to the Law of Nature which is the Law of God,—and thus it often happens that when obstinate humanity persists in considering its own ideas of Right and Wrong superior to the Eternal Decrees which have been visibly presented through Nature since the earliest dawn of creation, a faulty civilisation sets in and is presently swept back upon its advancing wheels, and forced to begin again with primal letters of learning. In the same way a faulty Soul, an imperfect individual Spirit, is likewise compelled to return to school and resume the study of the lessons it has failed to put into practice. Nevertheless, people cannot bear to have it plainly said or written down, as it has been said and written down over and over again any time since the world began, that all the corrupt government, wars, slaveries, plagues, diseases and despairs that afflict humanity are humanity's own sins taking vengeance upon the sinners, 'even unto the third and fourth generation.' And this not out of Divine cruelty, but because of Divine Law which from the first ordained that Evil shall slay Itself, leaving room only for Good. Men and women alike will scarce endure to read any book which urges this unalterable fact upon their attention. They pronounce the author 'arrogant' or 'presuming to lay down the law';—and they profess to be scandalised by an encounter with honesty. Nevertheless, the faithful writer of things as they Are will not be disturbed by the aspect of things as they Seem.

Spirit,—the creative Essence of all that is,—works in various forms, but always on an ascending plane, and it invariably rejects and destroys whatever interrupts that onward and upward progress. Being in Itself the Radiant outflow of the Mind of God, it is the LIFE of the Universe. And it is very needful to understand and to remember that there is nothing which can properly be called SUPER- natural, or above Nature, inasmuch as this Eternal Spirit of Energy is in and throughout all Nature. Therefore, what to the common mind appears miraculous or impossible, is nevertheless actually ordinary, and only seems EXTRA-ordinary to the common mind's lack of knowledge and experience. The Fountain of Youth and the Elixir of Life were dreams of the ancient mystics and scientists, but they are not dreams to-day. To the Soul that has found them they are Divine Realities.

MARIE CORELLI

"There is no Death,
What seems so is transition."

I

THE HEROINE BEGINS HER STORY

It is difficult at all times to write or speak of circumstances which though perfectly at one with Nature appear to be removed from natural occurrences. Apart from the incredulity with which the narration of such incidents is received, the mere idea that any one human creature should be fortunate enough to secure some particular advantage which others, through their own indolence or indifference, have missed, is sufficient to excite the envy of the weak or the anger of the ignorant. In all criticism it is an understood thing that the subject to be criticised must be UNDER the critic, never above,—that is to say, never above the critic's ability to comprehend; therefore, as it is impossible that an outsider should enter at once into a clear understanding of the mystic Spiritual- Nature world around him, it follows that the teachings and tenets of that Spiritual-Nature world must be more or less a closed book to such an one,—a book, moreover, which he seldom cares or dares to try and open.

In this way and for this reason the Eastern philosophers and sages concealed much of their most profound knowledge from the multitude, because they rightly recognised the limitations of narrow minds and prejudiced opinions. What the fool cannot learn he laughs at, thinking that by his laughter he shows superiority instead of latent idiocy. And so it has happened that many of the greatest discoveries of science, though fully known and realised in the past by the initiated few, were never disclosed to the many until recent years, when 'wireless telegraphy' and 'light-rays' are accepted facts, though these very things were familiar to the Egyptian priests and to that particular sect known as the 'Hermetic Brethren,' many of whom used the 'violet ray' for chemical and other purposes ages before the coming of Christ. Wireless telegraphy was also an ordinary method of communication between them, and they had their 'stations' for it in high towers on certain points of land as we have now. But if they had made their scientific attainments known to the multitude of their day they would have been judged as impostors or madmen. In the time of Galileo men would not believe that the earth moved round the sun,—and if anyone had then declared that messages could be sent from one ship to another in mid-ocean without any visible means of communication, he would probably have been put to torture and death as a sorcerer and deliberate misleader of the public. In the same way those who write of spiritual truths and the psychic control of our life-forces are as foolishly criticised as Galileo, and as wrongfully condemned.

For hundreds of years man's vain presumption and belief in his own infallibility caused him to remain in error concerning the simplest elements of astronomy, which would have taught him the true position of the sphere upon which he dwells. With precisely equal obstinacy man lives to-day in ignorance of his own highest powers because he will not take the trouble to study the elements of that supreme and all-commanding mental science which would enable him to understand his own essential life and being, and the intention of his Creator with regard to his progress and betterment. Therefore, in the face of his persistent egotism and effrontery, and his continuous denial of the 'superhuman' (which denial is absurdly incongruous seeing that all his religions are built up on a 'superhuman' basis), it is generally necessary for students of psychic mysteries to guard the treasures of their wisdom from profane and vulgar scorn,—a scorn which amounts in their eyes to blasphemy. For centuries it has been their custom to conceal the tenets of their creed from the common knowledge for the sake of conventions; because they would, or might, be shut out from such consolations as human social intercourse can give if their spiritual attainments were found to be, as they often are, beyond the ordinary. Thus they move through the world with the utmost caution, and instead of making a display of their powers they, if they are true to their faith, studiously deny the idea that they have any extraordinary or separate knowledge. They live as spectators of the progress or decay of nations, and they have no desire to make disciples, converts or confidants. They submit to the obligations of life, obey all civil codes, and are blameless and generous citizens, only preserving silence in regard to their own private beliefs, and giving the public the benefit of their acquirements up to a certain point, but shutting out curiosity where they do not wish its impertinent eyes.

To this, the creed just spoken of, I, the writer of this present narrative, belong. It has nothing whatever to do with merely human dogma,—and yet I would have it distinctly understood that I am not opposed to 'forms' of religion save where they overwhelm religion itself and allow the Spirit to be utterly lost in the Letter.

For 'the letter killeth,—the spirit giveth life.' So far as a 'form' may make a way for truth to become manifest, I am with it,—but when it is a mere Sham or Show, and when human souls are lost rather than saved by it, I am opposed to it. And with all my deficiencies I am conscious that I may risk the chance of a lower world's disdain, seeing that the 'higher world without end' is open to me in its imperishable brightness and beauty, to live in both NOW, and for ever. No one can cast me out of that glorious and indestructible Universe, for 'whithersoever I go there will be the sun and the moon, and the stars and visions and communion with the gods.'

And so I will fulfil the task allotted to me, and will enter at once upon my 'story'—in which form I shall endeavour to convey to my readers certain facts which are as far from fiction as the sayings of the prophets of old,—sayings that we know have been realised by the science of to-day. Every great truth has at first been no more than a dream,—that is to say, a thought, or an instinctive perception of the Soul reaching after its own immortal heritage. And what the Soul demands it receives.

At a time of year when the indolent languors of an exceptionally warm summer disinclined most people for continuous hard work, and when those who could afford it had left their ordinary avocations for the joys of a long holiday, I received a pressing invitation from certain persons whom I had met by chance during one London season, to join them in a yachting cruise. My intending host was an exceedingly rich man, a widower with one daughter, a delicate and ailing creature who, had she been poor, would have been irreverently styled 'a tiresome old maid,' but who by reason of being a millionaire's sole heiress was alluded to with sycophantic tenderness by all and sundry as 'Poor Miss Catherine.' Morton Harland, her father, was in a certain sense notorious for having written and published a bitter, cold and pitiless attack on religion, which was the favourite reading of many scholars and literary men, and this notable performance, together with the well accredited reports of his almost fabulous wealth, secured for him two social sets,—the one composed of such human sharks as are accustomed to swim round the plutocrat,—the other of the cynical, listless, semi-bored portion of a so-called cultured class who, having grown utterly tired of themselves, presumed that it was clever to be equally tired of God. I was surprised that such a man as he was should think of including me among his guests, for I had scarcely exchanged a dozen words with him, and my acquaintance with Miss Harland was restricted to a few casual condolences with her respecting the state of her health.

Yet it so chanced that one of those vague impulses to which we can give no name, but which often play an important part in the building up of our life-dramas, moved both father and daughter to a wish for my company. Moreover, the wish was so strong that though on first receiving their invitation I had refused it, they repeated it urgently, Morton Harland himself pressing it upon me with an almost imperative insistence.

"You want rest,"—he said, peering at me narrowly with his small hard brown eyes—"You work all the time. And to what purpose?"

I smiled.

"To as much purpose as anyone else, I suppose,"—I answered—"But to put it plainly, I work because I love work."

The lines of his mouth grew harder.

"So did I love work when I was your age,"—he said—"I thought I could carve out a destiny. So I could. I have done it. But now it's done I'm tired! I'm sick of my destiny,—the thing I carved out so cleverly,—it has the stone face of a Sphinx and its eyes are blank and without meaning."

I was silent. My silence seemed to irritate him, and he gave me a sharp, enquiring glance.

"Do you hear me?" he demanded—"If you do, I don't believe you understand!"

"I hear—and I quite understand,"—I replied, quietly, "Your destiny, as you have made it, is that of a rich man. And you do not care about it. I think that's quite natural."

He laughed harshly.

"There you are again!" he exclaimed—"Up in the air and riding a theory like a witch on a broomstick! It's NOT natural. That's just where you're wrong! It's quite UN-natural. If a man has plenty of money he ought to be perfectly happy and sat-isfied,—he can get everything he wants,—he can move the whole world of com-merce and speculation, and can shake the tree of Fortune so that the apples shall always fall at his own feet. But if the apples are tasteless there's something wrong."

"Not with the apples," I said.

"Oh, I know what you mean! You would say the fault is with me, not with Fortune's fruit. You may be right. Catherine says you are. Poor mopish Catherine!—always ailing, always querulous! Come and cheer her!"

"But"—I ventured to say—"I hardly know her."

"That's true. But she has taken a curious fancy to you. She has very few fancies nowadays,—none that wealth can gratify. Her life has been a complete disillusion. If you would do her and me a kindness, come!"

I was a little troubled by his pertinacity. I had never liked Morton Harland. His reputation, both as a man of wealth and a man of letters, was to me unenviable. He did no particular good with his money,—and such literary talent as he possessed he squandered in attacking nobler ideals than he had ever been able to attain. He was not agreeable to look at either; his pale, close-shaven face was deeply marked by lines of avarice and cunning,—his tall, lean figure had an aggressive air in its very attitude, and his unkind mouth never failed, whether in speaking or smiling, to express a sneer. Apparently he guessed the vague tenor of my thoughts, for he went on:—

"Don't be afraid of me! I'm not an ogre, and I shan't eat you! You think me a disagreeable man—well, so I am. I've had enough in my life to make me disagreeable. And"—here he paused, passing his hand across his eyes with a worried and impatient gesture—"I've had an unexpected blow just lately. The doctors tell me that I have a mortal disease for which there is no remedy. I may live on for several years, or I may die suddenly; it's all a matter of care—or chance. I want to forget the sad news for a while if I can. I've told Catherine, and I suppose I've added to her usual burden of vapours and melancholy—so we're a couple of miserable wretches. It's not very unselfish of us to ask you to come and join us under such circumstances—"

As he spoke my mind suddenly made itself up. I would go. Why not? A cruise on a magnificent steam yacht, replete with every comfort and luxury, was surely a fairly pleasant way of taking a holiday, even with two invalids for company.

"I'm sorry," I said, as gently as I could—"very sorry that you are ill. Perhaps the doctors may be mistaken. They are not always infallible. Many of their doomed patients have recovered in spite of their verdict. And—as you and Miss Harland wish it so much—I will certainly come."

His frowning face lightened, and for a moment looked almost kind.

"That's right!" he said—"The fresh air and the sea will do you good. As for our-selves, sickly people though we are, we shall not obtrude our ailments upon your attention. At least _I_ shall not. Catherine may—she has got into an unfortunate habit of talking about her aches and pains, and if her acquaintances have no aches and pains to discuss with her she is at a loss for conversation. However, we shall do our best to make the time go easily with you. There will be no other compa-ny on board—except my private secretary and my attendant physician,—both decent fellows who know their place and keep it."

The hard look settled again in his eyes, and his ugly mouth closed firmly in its usual cruel line. My subconscious dislike of him gave me a sharp thrust of regret that, after all, I had accepted his invitation.

"I was going to Scotland for a change,"—I murmured, hesitatingly.

"Were you? Then our plans coincide. We join the yacht at Rothesay— you can meet us there. I propose a cruise among the Western isles— the Hebrides—and possibly on to Norway and its fjords. What do you say?"

My heart thrilled with a sudden sense of expectant joy. In my fancy I already saw the heather-crowned summits of the Highland hills, bathed in soft climbing mists of amethyst and rose,—the lovely purple light that dances on the mountain lochs at the sinking of the sun,—the exquisite beauty of wild moor and rocky fore-land,—and almost I was disposed to think this antipathetic millionaire an angel of blessing in disguise.

"It will be delightful!" I said, with real fervour—"I shall love it! I'm glad you are going to keep to northern seas."

"Northern seas are the only seas possible for summer," he replied— "With the winter one goes south, as a matter of course, though I'm not sure that it is always advisable. I have found the Mediterranean tiresome very often." He broke off and seemed to lose himself for a moment in a tangle of vexed thought. Then he resumed quickly:— "Well, next week, then. Rothesay bay, and the yacht 'Diana.'"

Things being thus settled, we shook hands and parted. In the interval between his visit and my departure from home I had plenty to do, and I heard no more of the Harlands, except that I received a little note from Miss Catherine expressing her pleasure that I had agreed to accompany them on their cruise.

"You will be very dull, I fear,"—she wrote, kindly—"But not so dull as we should be without you."

This was a gracious phrase which meant as much or as little as most such phrases of a conventionally amiable character. Dulness, however, is a condition of brain and body of which I am seldom conscious, so that the suggestion of its possibility did not disturb my outlook. Having resolved to go, I equally resolved to enjoy the trip to the utmost limit of my capacity for enjoyment, which— fortunately for myself—is very great. Before my departure from home I had to listen, of course, to the usual croaking chorus of acquaintances in the neighbourhood who were not going yachting and who, according to their own assertion, never would on any account go yachting. There is a tendency in many persons to decry every pleasure which they have no chance of sharing, and this was not lacking among my provincial gossips.

"The weather has been so fine lately that we're sure to have a break soon,"—said one—"I expect you'll meet gales at sea."

"I hear," said another, "that heavy rains are threatening the west coast of Scotland."

"Such a bore, yachting!" declared a worthy woman who had never been on a yacht in her life—"The people on board get sick of each other's company in a week!"

"Well, you ought to pity me very much, then!"—I said, laughing— "According to your ideas, a yachting cruise appears to be the last possible form of physical suffering that can be inflicted on any human being. But I shall hope to come safely out of it all the same!"

My visitors gave me a wry smile. It was quite easy to see that they envied what they considered my good fortune in getting a holiday under the most luxurious circumstances without its costing me a penny. This was the only view they took of it. It is the only view people generally take of any situation,—namely, the financial side.

The night before I left home was to me a memorable one. Nothing of any outward or apparent interest happened, and I was quite alone, yet I was conscious of a singular elation of both mind and body as though I were surrounded by a vibrating atmosphere of light and joy. It was an impression that came upon me suddenly, seeming to have little or nothing to do with my own identity, yet withal it was still so personal that I felt eager to praise for such a rich inflow of happiness. The impression was purely psychic I knew,—but it was worth a thousand gifts of material good. Nothing seemed sad,— nothing seemed difficult in the whole Universe—every shadow of trouble seemed swept away from a shining sky of peace. I threw open the lattice window of my study and stepping out on the balcony which overhung the garden, I stood there dreamily looking out upon the night. There was no moon; only a million quivering points of light flashing from the crowded stars in a heaven of dusky blue. The air was warm, and fragrant with the sweet scent of stocks and heliotrope,—there was a great silence, for it was fully midnight, and not even the drowsy twitter of a bird broke the intense quiet. The world was asleep—or seemed so—although for fifty living organisms in Nature that sleep there are a thousand that wake, to whom night is the working day. I listened,—and fancied I could hear the delicate murmuring of voices hidden among the leaves and behind the trees, and the thrill of soft music flowing towards me on the sound-waves of the air. It was one of those supreme moments when I almost thought I had made some marked progress towards the attainment of my highest aims,—when the time I had spent and the patience I had exercised in cultivating and training what may be called the INWARD powers of sight and hearing were about to be rewarded by a full opening to my striving spirit of the gates which had till now been only set ajar. I knew,—for I had studied and proved the truth,—that every bodily sense we possess is simply an imperfect outcome of its original and existent faculty in the Soul,- -that our bodily ears are only the material expressions of that spiritual hearing which is fine and keen enough to catch the lightest angel whisper,—that our eyes are but the outward semblance of those brilliant inner orbs of vision which are made to look upon the supernal glories of Heaven itself without fear or flinching,— and that our very sense of touch is but a rough and uncertain handling of perishable things as compared with that sure and delicate contact of the Soul's personal being with the etheric substances pertaining to itself. Despite my eager expectation, however, nothing more was granted to me then but just that exquisite sensation of pure joy, which like a rain of light bathed every fibre of my being. It was enough, I told myself—surely enough!—and yet it seemed to me there should be something more. It was a promise with the fulfilment close at hand, yet undeclared,—like a snow- white cloud with the sun behind it. But I was given no solution of the rapturous mystery surrounding me,—and—granting my soul an absolute freedom, it could plunge no deeper than through the immensity of stars to immensities still more profound, there to dream and hope and wait. For years I had done this,—for years I had worked and prayed, watching the pageant of poor human pride and vanity drift past me like shadows on the shore of a dead sea,— succeeding little by little in threading my way through the closest labyrinths of life, and finding out the beautiful reasons of living;—and every now and then,—as to-night,—I had felt myself on the verge of a discovery which in its divine simplicity should make all problems clear and all difficulties easy, when I had been gently but firmly held back by a force invisible, and warned, 'Thus far, and no farther!' To oppose this force or make any personal effort to rebel against it, is no part of my faith,—therefore at such moments I had always yielded instantly and obediently as I yielded now. I was not allowed to fathom the occult source of my happiness, but the happiness remained,—and when I retired to rest it was with more than ordinary gratitude that I said my usual brief prayer:—For the day that is past, I thank Thee, O God my Father! For the night that has come, I thank Thee! As one with Thee and with Nature I gratefully take the rest Thou hast lovingly ordained. Whether I sleep or wake my body and soul are Thine. Do with them as Thou wilt, for Thy command is my joy. Amen.

I slept as soundly and peacefully as a child, and the next day started on my journey in the brightest of bright summer weather. A friend travelled with me—one of those amiable women to whom life is always pleasant because of the pleasantness in their own natures; she had taken a house for the season in Inverness-shire, and I had arranged to join her there when my trip with the Harlands was over, or rather, I should say, when they had grown weary of me and I of them. The latter chance was, thought my friend, whom I will call Francesca, most likely.

"There's no greater boredom,"—she declared—"than the society of an imaginative invalid. Such company will not be restful to you,—it will tire you out. Morton Harland himself may be really ill, as he says—I shouldn't wonder if he is, for he looks it!—but his daughter has nothing whatever the matter with her,—except nerves."

"Nerves are bad enough,"—I said.

"Nerves can be conquered,"—she answered, with a bright smile of wholesome conviction—"Nerves are generally—well!—just selfishness!"

There was some truth in this, but we did not argue the point further. We were too much engrossed with the interests of our journey north, and with the entertainment provided for us by our fellow-travellers. The train for Edinburgh and Glasgow was crowded with men of that particular social class who find grouse-shooting an intelligent way of using their brain and muscle, and gun-cases cumbered the ground in every corner. It wanted yet several days to the famous Twelfth of August, but the weather was so exceptionally fine and brilliant that the exodus from town had begun earlier than was actually necessary for the purposes of slaughter. Francesca and I studied the faces and figures of our companions with lively and unabated interest. We had a reserved compartment to ourselves, and from its secluded privacy we watched the restless pacing up and down in the adjacent corridor of sundry male creatures who seemed to have nothing whatever to think about but the day's newspaper, and nothing to do but smoke.

"I am sure," said Francesca, suddenly—"that in the beginning of creation we were all beasts and birds of prey, eating each other up and tearing each other to pieces. The love of prey is in us still."

"Not in you, surely?" I queried, with a smile.

"Oh, I am not talking or thinking of myself. I'm just—a woman. So are you—a woman—and something more, perhaps—something not like the rest of us." Here her kind eyes regarded me a trifle wistfully." I can't quite make you out some-times,—I wish I could! But—apart from you and me—look at a few of these men! One has just passed our window who has the exact physiognomy of a hawk,—cruel eyes and sharp nose like a voracious beak. Another I noticed a minute ago with a perfectly pig-like face,—he does not look rightly placed on two legs, his natural attitude is on four legs, grunting with his snout in the gutter!"

I laughed.

"You are a severe critic, Francesca!"

"Not I. I'm not criticising at all. But I can't help seeing resemblances. And some-times they are quite appalling. Now you, for instance,"—here she laid a hand ten-tatively on mine—"you, in your mysterious ideas of religion, actually believe that persons who lead evil lives and encourage evil thoughts, descend the scale from which they have risen and go back to the lowest forms of life—"

"I do believe that certainly"—I answered—"But—"

"'But me no buts,'"—she interrupted—"I tell you there are people in this world whom I see IN THE VERY ACT OF DESCENDING! And it makes me grow cold!"

I could well understand her feeling. I had experienced it often. Nothing has ever filled me with a more hopeless sense of inadequacy and utter uselessness than to watch, as I am often compelled to watch, the deplorable results of the determined choice made by certain human beings to go backward and downward rather than forward and upward,—a choice in which no outside advice can be of any avail because they will not take it even if it is offered. It is a life- and-death matter for their own wills to determine,—and no power, human or divine, can alter the course they elect to adopt. As well expect that God would revert His law of grav-itation to save the silly suicide who leaps to destruction from tower or steeple, as that He would change the eternal working of His higher Spiritual Law to rescue the resolved Soul which, knowing the difference between good and evil, deliber-ately prefers evil. If an angel of light, a veritable 'Son of the Morning' rebels, he must fall from Heaven. There is no alternative; until of his own free-will he choos-es to rise again.

My friend and I had often talked together on these knotty points which tangled up what should be the straightness of many a life's career, and as we mutually knew each other's opinions we did not discuss them at the moment.

Time passed quickly,—the train rushed farther and farther north, and by six o'clock on that warm, sunshiny afternoon we were in the grimy city of Glasgow, from whence we went on to a still grimier quarter, Greenock, where we put up for the night. The 'best' hotel was a sorry affair, but we were too tired to mind either a bad dinner or uncomfortable rooms, and went to bed glad of any place wherein to sleep. Next morning we woke up very early, refreshed and joyous, in time to see the sun rise in a warm mist of gold over a huge man-o'-war outside Greenock harbour,—a sight which, in its way, was very fine and rather suggestive of a Turner picture.

"Dear old Sol!" said Francesca, shading her eyes as she looked at the dazzle of glory—"His mission is to sustain life,—and the object of that war-vessel bathed in all his golden rays is to destroy it. What unscrupulous villains men are! Why cannot nations resolve on peace and amity, and if differences arise agree to settle them by arbitration? It's such a pagan and brutal thing to kill thousands of innocent men just because Governments quarrel."

"I entirely agree with you,"—I said—"All the same I don't approve of Governments that preach peace while they drain the people's pockets for the purpose of increasing armaments, after the German fashion. Let us be ready with adequate defences,—but it's surely very foolish to cripple our nation at home by way of preparation for wars which may never happen."

"And yet they MAY happen!" said Francesca, her eyes still dreamily watching the sunlit heavens—"Everything in the Universe is engaged in some sort of a fight, so it seems to me. The tiniest insects are for ever combating each other. In the very channels of our own blood the poisonous and non-poisonous germs are constantly striving for the mastery, and how can we escape the general ordainment? Life itself is a continual battle between good and evil, and if it were not so we should have no object in living. The whole business is evidently intended to be a dose conflict to the end."

"There is no end!" I said.

She looked at me almost compassionately.

"So you imagine!"

I smiled.

"So I KNOW!"

A vague expression flitted over her face,—an expression with which I had become familiar. She was a most lovable and intelligent creature, but she could not think very far,—the effort wearied and perplexed her.

"Well, then, it must be an everlasting skirmish, I suppose!" she said, laughingly,— "I wonder if our souls will ever get tired!"

"Do you think God ever gets tired?" I asked.

She looked startled,—then amused.

"He ought to!" she declared, with vivacity—"I don't mean to be irreverent, but really, what with all the living things in all the millions of worlds trying to get what they ought not to have, and wailing and howling when they are disappointed of their wishes, He ought to be very, very tired!"

"But He is not,"—I said;—"If He were, there would indeed be an end of all! Should the Creator be weary of His work, the work would be undone. I wish we thought of this more often!"

She put her arm round me kindly.

"You are a strange creature!" she said—"You think a great deal too much of all these abstruse subjects. After all, I'm glad you are going on this cruise with the Harland people. They will bring you down from the spheres with a run! They will, I'm sure! You'll hear no conversation that does not turn on baths, medicines, massage, and general cure-alls! And when you come on to stay with me in Inverness-shire you'll be quite commonplace and sensible!"

I smiled. The dear Francesca always associated 'the commonplace and sensible' together, as though they were fitted to companion each other. The complete reverse is, of course, the case, for the 'commonplace' is generally nothing more than the daily routine of body which is instinctively followed by beasts and birds as equally as by man, and has no more to do with real 'sense' or pure mentality than the ticking of a watch has to do with the enormous forces of the sun. What we call actual 'Sense' is the perception of the Soul,- -a perception which cannot be limited to things which are merely material, inasmuch as it passes beyond outward needs and appearances and reaches to the causes which create those outward needs and appearances. I was, however, satisfied to leave my friend in possession of the field of argument, the more readily as our parting from each other was so near at hand.

We journeyed together by the steamer 'Columba' to Rothesay, where, on entering the beautiful bay, crowded at this season with pleasure craft, the first object which attracted our attention was the very vessel for which I was bound, the 'Diana,' one of the most magnificent yachts ever built to gratify the whim of a millionaire. Tourists on board our steamer at once took up positions where they could obtain the best view of her, and many were the comments we heard concerning her size and the beauty of her lines as she rode at anchor on the sunlit water.

"You'll be in a floating palace,"—said Francesca, as we approached Rothesay pier, and she bade me an affectionate adieu—"Now take care of yourself, and don't fly away to the moon on what you call an etheric vibration! Remember, if you get tired of the Harlands to come to me at once."

I promised, and we parted. On landing at Rothesay I was almost immediately approached by a sailor from the 'Diana,' who, spying my name on my luggage, quickly possessed himself of it and told me the motor launch was in waiting to take me over to the yacht. I was on my way across the sparkling bay before the 'Columba' started out again from the pier, and Francesca, standing on the steamer's deck, waved to me a smiling farewell as I went. In about ten minutes I was on board the 'Diana,' shaking hands with Morton Harland and his daughter Catherine, who, wrapped up in shawls on a deck chair, looked as though she were guarding herself from the chills of a rigorous winter rather than basking in the warm sunshine of a summer morning.

"You look very well!"—she said, in tones of plaintive amiability— "And so wonderfully bright!"

"It's such a bright day,"—I answered, feeling as if I ought somehow to apologise for a healthy appearance, "One can't help being happy!"

She sighed and smiled faintly, and her maid appearing at that moment to take my travelling bag and wraps, I was shown the cabin, or rather the state-room which was to be mine during the cruise. It was a luxurious double apartment, bedroom and sitting-room together, divided only by the hanging folds of a rich crimson silk curtain, and exquisitely fitted with white enamelled furniture ornamented with hand-wrought silver. The bed had no resemblance whatever to a ship's berth, but was an elaborate full-sized affair, canopied in white silk embroidered with roses; the carpet was of a thick softness into which my feet sank as though it were moss, and a tall silver and crystal vase, full of gorgeous roses, was placed at the foot of a standing mirror framed in silver, so that the blossoms were reflected double. The sitting-room was provided with easy chairs, a writing-table, and a small piano, and here, too, masses of roses showed their fair faces from every corner. It was all so charming that I could not help uttering an exclamation of delight, and the maid who was unpacking my things smiled sympathetically.

"It's perfectly lovely!" I said, turning to her with eagerness— "It's quite a little fairyland! But isn't this Miss Harland's cabin?"

"Oh dear no, miss,"—she replied—"Miss Harland wouldn't have all these things about her on any account. There are no carpets or curtains in Miss Harland's rooms. She thinks them very unhealthy. She has only a bit of matting on the floor, and an iron bedstead— all very plain. And as for roses!—she wouldn't have a rose near her for ever so!—she can't bear the smell of them."

I made no comment. I was too enchanted with my surroundings for the moment to consider how uncomfortable my hostess chose to make herself.

"Who arranged these rooms?" I asked.

"Mr. Harland gave orders to the steward to make them as pretty as he could,"— said the maid—"John" and she blushed—"has a lot of taste."

I smiled. I saw at once how matters were between her and "John." Just then there was a sound of thudding and grinding above my head, and I realised that we were beginning to weigh anchor. Quickly tying on my yachting cap and veil, I hurried on deck, and was soon standing beside my host, who seemed pleased at the alacrity with which I had joined him, and I watched with feelings of indescrib-able exhilaration the 'Diana' being loosed from her moorings. Steam was up, and in a very short time her bowsprit swung round and pointed outward from the bay. Quivering like an eager race-horse ready to start, she sprang forward; and then, with a stately sweeping curve, glided across the water, catting it into bright wavelets with her sword-like keel and churning a path behind her of opalescent foam. We were off on our voyage of pleasure at last,—a voyage which the Fates had deter-mined should, for one adventurer at least, lead to strange regions as yet unexplored. But no premonitory sign was given to me, or suggestion that I might be the one chosen to sail 'the perilous seas of fairy lands forlorn'—for in spiritual things of high import, the soul that is most concerned is always the least expectant.

II

THE FAIRY SHIP

I was introduced that evening at dinner to Mr. Harland's physician, and also to his private secretary. I was not greatly prepossessed in favour of either of these gentlemen. Dr. Brayle was a dark, slim, clean-shaven man of middle age with expressionless brown eyes and sleek black hair which was carefully brushed and parted down the middle,—he was quiet and self-contained in manner, and yet I thought I could see that he was fully alive to the advantages of his position as travelling medical adviser to an American millionaire. I have not mentioned till now that Morton Harland was an American. I was always rather in the habit of forgetting the fact, as he had long ago forsworn his nationality and had naturalised himself as a British subject. But he had made his vast fortune in America, and was still the controlling magnate of many large financial interests in the States. He was, however, much more English than American, for he had been educated at Oxford, and as a young man had been always associated with English society and English ways. He had married an English wife, who died when their first child, his daughter, was born, and he was wont to set down all Miss Catherine's mopish languors to a delicacy inherited from her mother, and to lack of a mother's care in childhood. In my opinion Catherine was robust enough, but it was evident that from a very early age she had been given her own way to the fullest extent, and had been so accustomed to have every little ailment exaggerated and made the most of that she had grown to believe health of body and mind as well-nigh impossible to the human being. Dr. Brayle, I soon perceived, lent himself to this attitude, and I did not like the covert gleam of his mahogany-coloured eyes as he glanced rapidly from father to daughter in the pauses of conversation, watching them as narrowly as a cat might watch a couple of unwary mice. The secretary, Mr. Swinton, was a pale, precise-looking young man with a somewhat servile demeanour, under which he concealed an inordinately good opinion of himself. His ideas were centred in and bounded by the art of stenography,—he was an adept in shorthand and typewriting, could jot down, I forget how many crowds of jostling words a minute, and never made a mistake. He was a clock-work model of punctuality and dispatch, of respectfulness and obedience,—but he was no more than a machine,— he could not be moved to a spontaneous utterance or a spontaneous smile, unless both smile and utterance were the result of some pleasantness affecting himself. Neither Dr. Brayle nor Mr. Swinton were men whom one could positively like or dislike,—they simply had the power of creating an atmosphere in which my spirit found itself swimming like a gold-fish in a bowl, wondering how it got in and how it could get out.

As I sat rather silently at table I felt, rather than saw, Dr. Brayle regarding me with a kind of perplexed curiosity. I was as fully aware of his sensations as of my own,—I knew that my presence irritated him, though he was not clever enough to explain even to himself the cause of his irritation. So far as Mr. Swinton was concerned, he was comfortably wrapped up in a pachydermatous hide of self-appreciation, so that he thought nothing about me one way or the other except as a guest of his patrons, and one therefore to whom he was bound to be civil. But with Dr. Brayle it was otherwise. I was a puzzle to him, and—after a brief study of me—an annoyance. He forced himself into conversation with me, however, and we interchanged a few remarks on the weather and on the various beauties of the coast along which we had been sailing all day.

"I see that you care very much for fine scenery," he said—"Few women do."

"Really?" And I smiled. "Is admiration of the beautiful a special privilege of men only?"

"It should be,"—he answered, with a little bow—"We are the admirers of your sex."

I made no answer. Mr. Harland looked at me with a somewhat quizzical air.

"You are not a believer in compliments," he said.

"Was it a compliment?" I asked, laughingly—"I'm afraid I'm very dense! I did not see that it was meant as one."

Dr. Brayle's dark brows drew together in a slight frown. With that expression on his face he looked very much like an Italian poisoner of old time,—the kind of man whom Caesar Borgia might have employed to give the happy dispatch to his enemies by some sure and undiscoverable means known only to intricate chemistry.

Presently Mr. Harland spoke again, while he peeled a pear slowly and delicately with a deft movement of his fruit knife that suggested cruelty and the flaying alive of some sentient thing.

"Our little friend is of a rather strange disposition," he observed- -"She has the indifference of an old-world philosopher to the saying of speeches that are merely socially agreeable. She is ardent in soul, but suspicious in mind! She imagines that a pleasant word may often be used to cover a treacherous action, and if a man is as rude and blunt as myself, for example, she prefers that he should be rude and blunt rather than that he should attempt to conceal his roughness by an amiability which it is not his nature to feel." Here he looked up at me from the careful scrutiny of his nearly flayed pear. "Isn't that so?"

"Certainly,"—I answered—"But that's not a 'strange' or original attitude of mind."

The corners of his ugly mouth curled satirically.

"Pardon me, dear lady, it is! The normal and strictly reasonable attitude of the healthy human Pigmy is that It should accept as gospel all that It is told of a nature soothing and agreeable to Itself. It should believe, among other things, that It is a very precious Pigmy among natural forces, destined to be immortal, and to share with Divine Intelligence the privileges of Heaven. Put out by the merest trifle, troubled by a spasm, driven almost to howling by a toothache, and generally helpless in all very aggravated adverse circumstances, It should still console Itself with the idea that Its being, Its proportions and perfections are superb enough to draw down Deity into a human shape as a creature of human necessities in order that It, the Pigmy, should claim kinship with the Divine now and for ever! What gorgeous blasphemy in such a scheme!—what magnificent arrogance!" I was silent, but I could almost hear my heart beating with suppressed emotion. I knew Morton Harland was an atheist, so far as atheism is possible to any creature born of spirit as well as matter, but I did not think he would air his opinions so openly and at once before me the first evening of my stay on board his yacht. I saw, however, that he spoke in this way hoping to move me to an answering argument for the amusement of himself and the other two men present, and therefore I did what was incumbent upon me to do in such a situation—held my peace. Dr. Brayle watched me curiously,—and poor Catherine Harland turned her plaintive eyes upon me full of alarm. She had learned to dread her father's fondness for starting topics which led to religious discussions of a somewhat heated nature. But as I did not speak, Mr. Harland was placed in the embarrassing position of a person propounding a theory which no one shows any eagerness to accept or to deny, and, looking slightly confused, he went on in a lighter and more casual way—

"I had a friend once at Oxford,—a wonderful fellow, full of strange dreams and occult fancies. He was one of those who believed in the Divine half of man. He used to study curious old books and manuscripts till long past midnight, and never seemed tired. His father had lived by choice in some desert corner of Egypt for forty years, and in Egypt this boy had been born. Of his mother he never spoke. His father died suddenly and left him a large fortune under trustees till he came of age, with instructions that he was to be taken to England and educated at Oxford, and that when he came into possession of his money, he was to be left free to do as he liked with it. I met him when he was almost half-way through his University course. I was only two or three years his senior, but he always looked much younger than I. And he was, as we all said, 'uncanny '—as uncanny as our little friend,"—here indicating me by a nod of his head and a smile which was meant to be kindly—"He never practised or 'trained' for anything and yet all things came easily to him. He was as magnificent in his sports as he was in his studies, and I remember—how well I remember it!—that there came a time at last when we all grew afraid of him. If we saw him coming along the 'High' we avoided him,—he had something of terror as well as admiration for us,—and though I was of his college and constantly thrown into association with him, I soon became infected with the general scare. One night he stopped me in the quadrangle where he had his rooms—"

Here Mr. Harland broke off suddenly.

"I'm boring you,"—he said—"I really have no business to inflict the recollections of my youth upon you."

Dr. Brayle's brown eyes showed a glistening animal interest.

"Pray go on!" he urged—"It sounds like the chapter of a romance."

"I'm not a believer in romance,"—said Mr. Harland, grimly—"Facts are enough in themselves without any embroidered additions. This fellow was a Fact,—a healthy, strong, energetic, living Fact. He stopped me in the quadrangle as I tell you,—and he laid his hand on my shoulder. I shrank from his touch, and had a restless desire to get away from him. 'What's the matter with you, Harland?' he said, in a grave, musical voice that was peculiarly his own—'You seem afraid of me. If you are, the fault is in yourself, not in me!' I shuffled my feet about on the stone pavement, not knowing what to say—then I stammered out the foolish excuses young men make when they find themselves in an awkward corner. He listened to my stammering remarks about 'the other fellows' with attentive patience,—then he took his hand from my shoulder with a quick, decisive movement. 'Look here, Harland'—he said—'You are taking up all the conventions and traditions with which our poor old Alma Mater is encrusted, and sticking them over you like burrs. They'll cling, remember! It's a pity you choose this way of going,—I'm starting at the farther end—where Oxford leaves off and Life begins!' I suppose I stared—for he went on—'I mean Life that goes forward,—not Life that goes backward, picking up the stale crumbs fallen from centuries that have finished their banquet and passed on. There!—I won't detain you! We shall not meet often—but don't forget what I have said,—that if you are afraid of me, or of any other man, or of any existing thing,—the fault is in yourself, not in the persons or objects you fear.' 'I don't see it,' I blurted out, angrily—'What of the other fellows? They think you're queer!' He laughed. 'Bless the other fellows!' he said—'They're with you in the same boat! They think me queer because THEY are queer—that is,- -out of line—themselves.' I was irritated by his easy indifference and asked him what he meant by 'out of line.' 'Suppose you see a beautiful garden harmoniously planned,' he said, still smiling, 'and some clumsy fellow comes along and puts a crooked pigstye up among the flower beds, you would call that "out of line," wouldn't you? Unsuitable, to say the least of it?' 'Oh!' I said, hotly—'So you consider me and my friends crooked pigstyes in your landscape?' He made me a gay, half apologetic gesture. 'Something of the type, dear boy!' he said—'But don't worry! The crooked pigstye is always a most popular kind of building in the world you will live in!' With that he bade me good-night, and went. I was very angry with him, for I was a conceited youth and thought myself and my particular associates the very cream of Oxford,—but he took all the highest honours that year, and when he finally left the University he vanished, so to speak, in a blaze of intellectual glory. I have never seen him again—and never heard of him—and so I suppose his studies led him nowhere. He must be an elderly man now,—he may be lame, blind, lunatic, or what is more probable still, he may be dead, and I don't know why I think of him except that his theories were much the same as those of our little friend,"—again indicating me by a nod—"He never cared for agreeable speeches,—always rather mistrusted social conventions, and believed in a Higher Life after Death."

"Or a Lower,"—I put in, quietly.

"Ah yes! There must be a Down grade, of course, if there is an Up. The two would be part of each other's existence. But as I accept neither, the point does not matter."

I looked at him, and I suppose my looks expressed wonder or pity or both, for he averted his glance from mine.

"You are something of a spiritualist, I believe?"—said Dr. Brayle, lifting his hard eyes from the scrutiny of the tablecloth and fixing them upon me.

"Not at all,"—I answered, at once, and with emphasis. "That is, if you mean by the term 'spiritualist' a credulous person who believes in mediumistic trickery, automatic writing and the like. That is sheer nonsense and self-deception."

"Several experienced scientists give these matters considerable attention,"—suggested Mr. Swinton, primly.

I smiled.

"Science, like everything else, has its borderland," I said—"from which the brain can easily slip off into chaos. The most approved scientific professors are liable to this dire end of their speculations. They forget that in order to understand the Infinite they must first be sure of the Infinite in themselves."

"You speak like an oracle, fair lady!"—said Mr. Harland—"But despite your sage utterances Man remains as finite as ever."

"If he chooses the finite state certainly he does,"—I answered—"He is always what he elects to be."

Mr. Harland seemed desirous of continuing the argument, but I would say no more. The topic was too serious and sacred with me to allow it to be lightly discussed by persons whose attitude of mind was distinctly opposed and antipathetic to all things beyond the merely mundane.

After dinner, Miss Catherine professed herself to be suffering from neuralgia, and gathering up her shawls and wraps asked me to excuse her for going to bed early. I bade her good-night, and, leaving my host and the two other men to their smoke, I went up on deck. We were anchored off Mull, and against a starlit sky of exceptional clearness the dark mountains of Morven were outlined with a softness as of black velvet. The yacht rested on perfectly calm waters, shining like polished steel,—and the warm stillness of the summer night was deliciously soothing and restful. Our captain and one or two of the sailors were about on duty, and I sat in the stern of the vessel looking up into the glorious heavens. The tapering bow-sprit of the 'Diana' pointed aloft as it were into a woven web of stars, and I lost myself in imaginary flight among those glittering unknown worlds, oblivious of my material surroundings, and forgetting that despite the splendid evidences of a governing Intelligence in the beauty and order of the Universe spread about them every day, my companions in the journey of pleasure we were undertaking together were actually destitute of all faith in God, and had less perception of the existing Divine than the humblest plant may possess that instinctively forces its way upward to the light. I did not think of this,—it was no use thinking about it as I could not better the position,—but I found myself curiously considering the story Mr. Harland had told about his college friend at Oxford. I tried to picture his face and figure till presently it seemed as if I saw him,—indeed I could have sworn that a man's shadowy form stood immediately in front of me, bending upon me a searching glance from eyes that were strangely familiar. Startled at this wraith of my own fancy, I half rose from my chair—then sank back again with a laugh at my imagination's too vivid power of portrayal. A figure did certainly present itself, but one of sufficient bulk to convince me of its substantiality. This was the captain of the 'Diana,' a cheery-looking personage of a thoroughly nautical type, who, approaching me, lifted his cap and said:

"That's a wonderfully fine yacht that has just dropped anchor behind us. She's illuminated, too. Have you seen her?"

"No," I answered, and turned in the direction he indicated. An involuntary exclamation escaped me. There, about half a mile to our rear, floated a schooner of exquisite proportions and fairy-like grace, outlined from stem to stern by delicate borderings of electric light as though decorated for some great festival, and making quite a glittering spectacle in the darkness of the deepening night. We could see active figures at work on deck—the sails were dropped and quickly furled,— but the quivering radiance remained running up every tapering mast and spar, so that the whole vessel seemed drawn on the dusky air with pencil points of fire. I stood up, gazing at the wonderful sight in silent amazement and admiration, with the captain beside me, and it was he who first spoke.

"I can't make her out,"—he said, perplexedly,—"We never heard a sound except just when she dropped anchor, and that was almost noiseless. How she came round the point yonder so suddenly is a mystery! I was keeping a sharp look-out, too."

"Surely she's very large for a sailing vessel?" I queried.

"The largest I've ever seen,"—he replied—"But how did she sail? That's what I want to know!"

He looked so puzzled that I laughed.

"Well, I suppose in the usual way,"—I said—"With sails."

"Ay, that's all very well!"—and he glanced at me with a compassionate air as at one who knew nothing about seafaring—"But sails must have wind, and there hasn't been a capful all the afternoon or evening. Yet she came in with crowded canvas full out as if there was a regular sou'wester, and found her anchorage as easy as you please. All in a minute, too. If there was a wind it wasn't a wind belonging to this world! Wouldn't Mr. Harland perhaps like to see her?"

I took the hint and ran down into the saloon, which by this time was full of the stifling odours of smoke and whisky. Mr. Harland was there, drinking and talking somewhat excitedly with Dr. Brayle, while his secretary listened and looked on. I explained why I had ventured to interrupt their conversation, and they accompanied me up on deck. The strange yacht looked more bewilderingly brilliant than ever, the heavens having somewhat clouded over, and as we all, the captain included, leaned over our own deck rail and gazed at her shining outlines, we heard the sound of delicious music and singing floating across the quiet sea.

"Some millionaire's toy,"—said Mr. Harland—"She's floating from the mysterious yacht." It was a music full of haunting sweetness and rhythmic melody, and I was not sure whether it was evolved from stringed instruments or singing voices. By climbing up on the sofa in my sitting-room I could look out through the port-hole on the near sea, rippling close to me, and bringing, as I fancied, with every ripple a new cadence, a tenderer snatch of tune. A subtle scent was on the salt air, as of roses mingling with the freshness of the scarcely moving waters,—it came, I thought, from the beautiful blossoms which so lavishly adorned my rooms. I could not see the yacht from my point of observation, but I could hear the music she had on board, and that was enough for immediate delight.

Leaving the port-hole open, I lay down on the sofa immediately beneath it and comprised myself to listen. The soft breath of the sea blew on my cheeks, and with every breath the delicate vibrations of appealing harmony rose and fell—it was as if these enchanting sounds were being played or sung for me alone. In a delicious languor I drowsed, as it were, with my eyes open,—losing myself in a labyrinth of happy dreams and fancies which came to me unbidden,— till presently the music died softly away like a retreating wave and ceased altogether. I waited a few minutes—listening breathlessly lest it should begin again and I lose some note of it,—then hearing no more, I softly closed the port-hole and drew the curtain. I did this with an odd reluctance, feeling somehow that I had shut out a friend; and I half apologised to this vague sentiment by reminding myself of the lateness of the hour. It was nearly midnight. I had intended writing to Francesca,—but I was now disinclined for anything but rest. The music which had so entranced me throbbed still in my ears and made my heart beat with a quick sense of joy,- children—there may be several inoffensive reasons for his lighting up, and he may think no more of advertisement than you or I."

"That's true,"—assented Dr. Brayle, with a quick concession to his patron's humour. "But people nowadays do so many queer things for mere notoriety's sake that it is barely possible to avoid suspecting them. They will even kill themselves in order to be talked about." "Fortunately they don't hear what's said of them,"— returned Mr. Harland—"or they might alter their minds and remain alive. It's hardly worth while to hang yourself in order to be called a fool!"

While this talk went on I remained silent, watching the illuminated schooner with absorbed fascination. Suddenly, while I still gazed upon her, every spark with which she was, as it were, bejewelled, went out, and only the ordinary lamps common to the watches of the night on board a vessel at anchorage burned dimly here and there like red winking eyes. For the rest, she was barely visible save by an indistinct tracery of blurred black lines. The swiftness with which her brilliancy had been eclipsed startled us all and drew from Captain Derrick the remark that it was 'rather queer.'

"What pantomimists call a 'quick change'"—said Mr. Harland, with a laugh— "The show is over for to-night. Let us turn in. To-morrow morning we'll try and make acquaintance with the stranger, and find out for Captain Derrick's comfort how she managed to sail without wind!"

We bade each other good-night then, and descended to our several quarters.

When I found myself alone in the luxurious state-room 'suite' allotted to me, the first thing I did was to open one of the port- holes and listen to the music which still came superbly built,— sailing vessels are always more elegant than steam, though not half so useful. I expect she'll lie becalmed here for a day or two."

"It's a wonder she's got round here at all,"—said the captain— "There wasn't any wind to bring her."

Mr. Harland looked amused.

"There must have been SOME wind, Derrick,"—he answered—"Only it wasn't boisterous enough for a hardy salt like you to feel it."

"There wasn't a breath,"—declared Derrick, firmly—"Not enough to blow a baby's curl."

"Then how did she get here?" asked Dr. Brayle.

Captain Derrick's lifted eyebrows expressed his inability to solve the enigma.

"I said just now if there was a wind it wasn't a wind belonging to this world—"

Mr. Harland turned upon him quickly.

"Well, there are no winds belonging to other worlds that will ever disturb OUR atmosphere,"—he said—"Come, come, Derrick, you don't think that yacht is a ghost, do you?—a sort of 'Flying Dutchman' spectre?"

Captain Derrick smiled broadly.

"No, sir—I don't! There's flesh and blood aboard—I've seen the men hauling down canvas, and I know that. But the way she sailed in bothers me."

"All that electric light is rather ostentatious,"—said Dr. Brayle— "I suppose the owner wants to advertise his riches."

"That doesn't follow," said Mr. Harland, with some sharpness—"I grant you we live in an advertising age, but I don't fancy the owner of that vessel is a Pill or a Plaster or even a Special Tea. He may want to amuse himself—it may be the birthday of his wife or one of his and a warm atmosphere of peace and comfort came over me when at last I lay down in my luxurious bed, and slipped away into the land of sleep. Ah, what a land it is, that magic Land of Sleep!—a land 'shadowing with wings,' where amid many shifting and shimmering wonders of darkness and light, the Palace of Vision stands uplifted, stately and beautiful, with golden doors set open to the wanderer! I made my entrance there that night;—often and often as I had been within its enchanted precincts before, there were a million halls of marvel as yet unvisited,—and among these I found myself,—under a dome which seemed of purest crystal lit with fire,—listening to One invisible, who,—speaking as from a great height, discoursed to me of Love."

III

THE ANGEL OF A DREAM

The Voice that spoke to me was silvery clear, and fell as it were through the air, dividing space with sweetness. It was soft and resonant, and the thrill of tenderness within it was as though an angel sang through tears. Never had I heard anything so divinely pure and compassionate,—and all my being strove to lift itself towards that supernal height which seemed to be the hidden source of its melodious utterance.

"O Soul, wandering in the region of sleep and dreams!" said the Voice,—"What is all thy searching and labour worth without Love? Why art thou lost in a Silence without Song?"

I raised my eyes, seeking for the one who thus spoke to me, but could see nothing.

"In Life's great choral symphony"—the Voice continued—"the keynote of the dominant melody is Love! Without the keynote there can be no music,—there is dumbness where there should be sound,—there is discord where there should be harmony. Love!—the one vibrant tone to which the whole universe moves in tune,—Love, the breath of God, the pulsation of His Being, the glory of His work, the fulfilment of His Eternal Joy,—Love, and Love alone, is the web and texture and garment of happy Immortality! O Soul that seekest the way to wisdom and to power, what dost thou make of Love?"

I trembled and stood mute. It seemed that I was surrounded by solemn Presences whose nearness I could feel but not see, and unknowing who it was that spoke to me, I was afraid to answer.

"Far in the Past, thousands of ages ago," went on the Voice—"the world we call the Sorrowful Star was a perfect note in a perfect scale. It was in tune with the Divine Symphony. But with the sweep of centuries it has lagged behind; it has fallen from Light into Shadow. And rather than rise to Light again, it has made of itself a discord opposed to the eternal Harmony. It has chosen for its keynote Hate,—not Love! Each nation envies or despises the other,— each man struggles against his fellow-man and grudges his neighbour every small advantage,—and more than all, each Creed curses the other, blasphemously calling upon God to verify and fulfil the curse! Hate, not Love!—this is the false note struck by the pitiful Earth-world to-day, swinging out of all concordance with spherical sweetness!—Hate that prefers falsehood to truth, malice to kindness, selfishness to generosity! O Sorrowful Star!—doomed so soon to perish!—turn, turn, even in thy last moments, back to the Divine Ascendant before it is too late!"

I listened,—and a sense of hopeless fear possessed me. I tried to speak, and a faint whisper crept from my lips. "Why,"—I murmured to myself, for I did not suppose anyone could or would hear me—"why should we and our world perish? We knew so little at the beginning, and we know so little now,—is it altogether our fault if we have lost our way?"

A silence followed. A vague, impalpable sense of restraint and captivity seemed closing me in on every side,—I was imprisoned, as I thought, within invisible walls. Then all at once this density of atmosphere was struck asunder by a dazzling light as of cloven wings, but I could see no actual shape or even suggestion of substance—the glowing rays were all. And the Voice spoke again with grave sweetness and something of reproach.

"Who speaks of losing the way?" it asked—"when the way is, and has ever been, clear and plain? Nature teaches it,—Law and Order support it. Obey and ye shall live: disobey and ye shall die! There is no other ruling than this out of Chaos! Who is it that speaks of losing the way, when the way is, and has been and ever shall be, clear and plain?"

I stretched out my hands involuntarily. My eyes filled with tears.

"O Angel invisible!" I prayed—"Forgive my weakness and unwisdom! How can the world be saved or comforted by a Love it never finds!"

Again a silence. Again that dazzling, quivering radiance, flashing as in an atmosphere of powdered gold.

"What does the world seek most ardently?" it demanded—"The Love of God?—or the Love of Self? If it seeks the first, all things in heaven and earth shall be added to its desire—if the second, all shall be taken from it, even that which it hath!"

I had, as I thought, no answer to give, but I covered my weeping eyes with both hands and knelt before the unseen speaker as to some great Spirit enthroned.

"Love is not Love that loves Itself,"—went on the Voice—"Self is the Image, not the God. Wouldst thou have Eternal Life? Then find the secret in Eternal Love!—'Love, which can move worlds and create universes,—the love of soul for soul, angel for angel, god for god!"

I raised my head, and, uncovering my eyes, looked up. But I could see nothing save that all-penetrating light which imprisoned me as it were in a circle of fire.

"Love is that Power which clasps the things of eternity and makes them all its own,"—said the Voice in stronger tones of deeper music—"It builds its solar system, its stars, its planets with a thought!—it wakes all beauty, all delight with a smile!—it lives not only now, but for ever, in a heaven of pure joy where every thousand years is but one summer day! To Love there is no time, no space, no age, no death!—what it gives it receives again,—what it longs for comes to it without seeking—God withholds nothing from the faithful soul!"

I still knelt, wondering if these words were intended only for me or for some other listener, for I could not now feel sure that I was without a companion in this strange experience.

"There is only one Way of Life,"—went on the Voice—"Only one way— the Way of Love! Whosoever loves greatly lives greatly; whosoever misprizes Love is dead though living. Give all thy heart and soul to Love if thou wouldst be immortal!—for without Love thou mayst seek God through all Eternity and never find Him!"

I waited,—there was a brief silence. Then a sudden wave of music broke upon my ears,—a breaking foam of rhythmic melody that rose and fell in a measured cadence of solemn sound. Raising my eyes in fear and awe, I saw the lambent light around me begin to separate into countless gradations of delicate colour till presently it resembled a close and brilliant network of rainbow tints intermingled with purest gold. It was as if millions of lines had been drawn with exquisite fineness and precision so as to cause intersection or 'reciprocal meeting' at given points of calculation, and these changed into various dazzling forms too brilliant for even my dreaming sight to follow. Yet I felt myself compelled to study one particular section of these lines which shone before me in a kind of pale brightness, and while I looked it varied to more and more complex 'moods' of colour and light, if one might so express it, till, by gradual degrees, it returned again to the simpler combination.

"Thus are the destinies of human lives woven and interwoven,"—said the Voice—"From infinite and endless points of light they grow and part and mingle together, till the destined two are one. Often they are entangled and disturbed by influences not their own—but from interference which through weakness or fear they have themselves permitted. But the tangle is for ever unravelled by Time,— the parted threads are brought together again in the eternal weaving of Spirit and Matter. No power, human or divine, can entirely separate the lives which God has ordained shall come together. Man's ordainment is not God's ordainment! Wrong threads in the weaving are broken—no matter how,—no matter when! Love must be tender yet resolved!—Love must not swerve from its given pledge!—Love must be All or Nothing!"

The light network of living golden rays still quivered before my eyes, till all at once they seemed to change to a rippling sea of fine flame with waves that gently swayed to and fro, tipped with foam-crests of prismatic hue like broken rainbows. Wave after wave swept forward and broke in bright amethystine spray close to me where I knelt, and as I watched this moving mass of radiant colour in absorbed fascination, one wave, brilliant as the flush of a summer's dawn, rippled towards me, and then gently retiring, left a single rose, crimson and fragrant, close within my reach. I stooped and caught it quickly—surely it was a real rose from some dewy garden of the earth, and no dream!

"One rose from all the roses in Heaven!" said the mystic Voice, in tones of enthralling sweetness—"One—fadeless and immortal!—only one, but sufficient for all! One love from all the million loves of men and women—one, but enough for Eternity! How long the rose has awaited its flowering,—how long the love has awaited its fulfilment—only the recording angels know! Such roses bloom but once in the wilderness of space and time; such love comes but once in a Universe of worlds!"

I listened, trembling; I held the rose against my breast between my clasped hands.

"O Sorrowful Star!" went on the Voice—"What shall become of thee if thou forsakest the way of Love! O little Sphere of beauty and delight, why are thy people so blind! O that their eyes were lifted unto Heaven!—their hearts to joy!—their souls to love! Who is it that darkens life with sorrow?—who is it that creates the delusion of death?"

I found my speech suddenly.

"Nay, surely,"—I said, half whispering—"We must all die!"

"Not so!" and the mystic Voice rang out imperatively—"There is no death! For God is alive!—and from Him Life only can emanate!"

I held my peace, moved by a sudden sweet awe.

"From Eternal Life no death can come,"—continued the Voice—"from Eternal Love flows Eternal Joy. Change there is,—change there must be to higher forms and higher planes,—but Life and Love remain as they are, indestructible—'the same yesterday, to-day, and for ever!'"

I bent my face over the rose against my breast,—its perfume was deliciously soft and penetrating, and half unconsciously I kissed its velvet petals. As I did this a swift and dazzling radiance poured shower-like through the air, and again I heard mysterious chords of rhythmic melody rising and falling like distant waves of the sea. The grave, tender Voice spoke once again:

"Rise and go hence!" it said, in tones of thrilling gentleness— "Keep the gift God sends thee!—take that which is thine! Meet that which hath sought thee sorrowing for many centuries! Turn not aside again, neither by thine own will nor by the will of others, lest old errors prevail! Pass from vision into waking!—from night to day!— from seeming death to life!—from loneliness to love!—and keep within thy heart the message of a Dream!"

The light beating about me like curved wings slowly paled and as slowly vanished—yet I felt that I must still kneel and wait. This atmosphere of awe and trembling gradually passed away,—and then, rising as I thought, and holding the mystic rose with one hand still against my breast, I turned to feel my way through the darkness which now encompassed me. As I did this my other hand was caught by someone in a warm, eager clasp, and I was guided along with an infinitely tender yet masterful touch which I had no hesitation in obeying. Step by step I moved with a strange sense of happy reliance on my unseen companion—darkness or distance had no terrors for me. And as I Went onward with my hand held firmly in that close yet gentle grasp, my thoughts became as it were suddenly cleared into a heaven of comprehension—I looked back upon years of work spread out like an arid desert uncheered by any spring of sweet water—and I saw all that my life had lacked—all to which I had unconsciously pressed forward longingly without any distinct recognition of my own aims, and only trusting to the infinite powers of God and Nature to amend my incompleteness by the perfection of the everlasting Whole. And now—had the answer come? At any rate, I felt I was no longer alone. Someone who seemed the natural other half of myself was beside me in the shadows of sleep—I could have spoken, but would not, for fear of breaking the charm.

And so I went on and on, caring little how long the journey might be, and even vaguely wishing it might continue for ever,—when presently a faint light began to peer through the gloom—I saw a glimmer of blue and grey, then white, then rose-colour—and I awoke- -to find nothing of a visionary character about me unless perhaps a shaft of early morning sunshine streaming through the port-hole of my cabin could be called a reflex of the mystic glory which had surrounded me in sleep. I then remembered where I was,—yet I was so convinced of the reality of what I had seen and heard that I looked about me everywhere for that lovely crimson rose I had brought away with me from Dreamland—for I could actually feel its stem still between my fingers. It was not to be seen—but there was delicate fragrance on the air as if it were blooming near me—a fragrance so fine that nothing could describe its subtly pervading odour. Every word spoken by the Voice of my dream was vividly impressed on my brain, and more vivid still was the recollection of the hand that had clasped mine and led me out of sleep to waking. I was conscious of its warmth yet,—and I was troubled, even while I was soothed, by the memory of the lingering caress with which it had been at last withdrawn. And I wondered as I lay for a few moments in my bed inert, and thinking of all that had chanced to me in the night, whether the long earnest patience of my soul, ever turned as it had been for years towards the attainment of a love higher than all earthly attraction, was now about to be recompensed? I knew, and had always known, that whatsoever we strongly WILL to possess comes to us in due season; and that steadily resolved prayers are always granted; the only drawback to the exertion of this power is the doubt as to whether the thing we desire so ardently will work us good or ill. For there is no question but that what we seek we shall find. I had sought long and unwearyingly for the clue to the secret of life imperishable and love eternal,—was the mystery about to be unveiled? I could not tell—and I dare not humour the mere thought too long. Shaking my mind free from the web of marvel and perplexity in which it had been caught by the visions of the night, I placed myself in a passively receptive attitude—demanding nothing, fearing nothing, hoping nothing—but simply content with actual Life, feeling Life to be the outcome and expression of perfect Love.

IV

A BUNCH OF HEATHER

It was a glorious morning, and so warm that I went up on deck without any hat or cloak, glad to have the sunlight playing on my hair and the soft breeze blowing on my face. The scene was perfectly enchanting; the mountains were bathed in a delicate rose-purple glow reflected from the past pomp of the sun's rising,—the water was still as an inland lake, and every mast and spar of the 'Diana' was reflected in it as in a mirror. A flock of sea-gulls floated round our vessel, like fairy boats—some of them rising every now and then with eager cries to wing their graceful flight high through the calm air, and alight again with a flash of silver pinions on the translucent blue. While I stood gazing in absorbed delight at the beauty which everywhere surrounded me, Captain Derrick called to me from his little bridge, where he stood with folded arms, looking down.

"Good morning! What do you think of the mystery now?"

"Mystery?" And then his meaning flashed upon me. "Oh, the yacht that anchored near us last night! Where is she?"

"Just so!" And the captain's look expressed volumes—"Where is she?"

Oddly enough, I had not thought of the stranger vessel till this moment, though the music sounding from her deck had been the last thing which had haunted my ears before I had slept—and dreamed! And now—she was gone! There was not a sign of her anywhere.

I looked up at the captain on his bridge and smiled. "She must have started very early!" I said.

The captain's fuzzy brows met portentously.

"Ay! Very early! So early that the watch never saw her go. He must have missed an hour and she must have gained one."

"It's rather strange, isn't it?" I said—"May I come on the bridge?"

"Certainly."

I ran up the little steps and stood beside him, looking out to the farthest line of sea and sky.

"What do you think about it?" I asked, laughingly, "Was she a real yacht or a ghost?"

The captain did not smile. His brow was furrowed with perplexed consideration.

"She wasn't a ghost," he said—"but her ways were ghostly. That is, she made no noise,—and she sailed without wind. Mr. Harland may say what he likes,—I stick to that. She had no steam, but she carried full sail, and she came into the Sound with all her canvas bellying out as though she were driven by a stormy sou'wester. There's been no wind all night—yet she's gone, as you see—and not a man on board heard the weighing of her anchor. When she went and how she went beats me altogether!"

At that moment we caught sight of a small rowing boat coming out to us from the shore, pulled by one man, who bent to his oars in a slow, listless way as though disinclined for the labour.

"Boat ahoy!" shouted the captain.

The man looked up and signalled in answer. A couple of our sailors went to throw him a rope as he brought his craft alongside. He had come, so he slowly explained in his soft, slow, almost unintelligible Highland dialect, with fresh eggs and butter, hoping to effect a sale. The steward was summoned, and bargaining began. I listened and looked on, amused and interested, and I presently suggested to the captain that it might be as well to ask this man if he too had seen the yacht whose movements appeared so baffling and inexplicable. The captain at once took the hint.

"Say, Donald," he began, invitingly—"did you see the big yacht that came in last night about ten o'clock?"

"Ou ay!" was the slow answer—"But my name's no Tonald,—it's just Jamie."

Captain Derrick laughed jovially.

"Beg pardon! Jamie, then! Did you see the yacht?"

"Ou ay! I've seen her mony a day. She's a real shentleman."

I smiled.

"The yacht?"

Jamie looked up at me.

"Ah, my leddy, ye'll pe makin' a fule o' Jamie wi' a glance like a sun-sparkle on the sea! Jamie's no fule wi' the right sort, an' the yacht is a shentleman, an' the shentleman's the yacht, for it's the shentleman that pays whateffer."

Captain Derrick became keenly interested.

"The gentleman? The owner of the yacht, you mean?"

Jamie nodded—"Just that!"—and proceeded to count out his store of new-laid eggs with great care as he placed them in the steward's basket.

"What's his name?" "Ah, that's ower mickle learnin',"—said Jamie, with a cunning look- -"I canna say it rightly."

"Can you say it wrongly?" I suggested.

"I wadna!" he replied, and he lifted his eyes, which were dark and piercing, to my face—"I daurna!"

"Is he such a very terrible gentleman, then?" enquired Captain Derrick, jocosely.

Jamie's countenance was impenetrable.

"Ye'll pe seein' her for yourself whateffer,"—he said—"Ye'll no miss her in the waters 'twixt here an' Skye."

He stooped and fumbled in his basket, presently bringing out of it a small bunch of pink bell-heather,—the delicate waxen type of blossom which is found only in mossy, marshy places.

"The shentleman wanted as much as I could find o' this,"—he said— "An' he had it a' but this wee bittie. Will my leddy wear it for luck?"

I took it from his hand.

"As a gift?" I asked, smiling.

"I wadna tak ony money for't,"—he answered, with a curious expression of something like fear passing over his brown, weather- beaten features—"'Tis fairies' making."

I put the little bunch in my dress. As I did so, he doffed his cap.

"Good day t'ye! I'll be no seein' ye this way again!"

"Why not? How do you know?"

"One way in and another way out!" he said, his voice sinking to a sort of meditative croon—"One road to the West, and the other to the East!—and round about to the meeting-place! Ou ay! Ye'll mak it clear sailin'!"

"Without wind, eh?" interposed Captain Derrick—"Like your friend the 'shentleman'? How does he manage that business?"

Jamie looked round with a frightened air, like an animal scenting danger,—then, shouldering his empty basket, he gave us a hasty nod of farewell, and, scrambling down the companion ladder without another word, was soon in his boat again, rowing away steadily and never once looking back.

"A wild chap!" said the captain—"Many of these fellows get half daft, living so much alone in desolate places like Mull, and seeing nothing all their time but cloud and mountain and sea. He seems to know something about that yacht, though!"

"That yacht is on your brain, Captain!" I said, merrily—"I feel quite sorry for you! And yet I daresay if we meet her again the mystery will turn out to be very simple."

"It will have to be either very simple or very complex!" he answered, with a laugh—"I shall need a good deal of teaching to show me how a sailing yacht can make steam speed without wind. Ah, good morning, sir!"

And we both turned to greet Mr. Harland, who had just come up on deck. He looked ill and careworn, as though he had slept badly, and he showed but faint interest in the tale of the strange yacht's sudden exit.

"It amuses you, doesn't it?"—he said, addressing me with a little cynical smile wrinkling up his forehead and eyes—"Anything that cannot be at once explained is always interesting and delightful to a woman! That is why spiritualistic 'mediums' make money. They do clever tricks which cannot be explained, hence their success with the credulous."

"Quite so"—I replied—"but just allow me to say that I am no believer in 'mediums.'"

"True,—I forgot!" He rubbed his hand wearily over his brows—then asked—"Did you sleep well?"

"Splendidly! And I must really thank you for my lovely rooms,—they are almost too luxurious! They are fit for a princess."

"Why a princess?" he queried, ironically—"Princesses are not always agreeable personages. I know one or two,—fat, ugly and stupid. Some of them are dirty in their persons and in their habits. There are certain 'princesses' in Europe who ought to be washed and disinfected before being given any rooms anywhere!"

I laughed.

"Oh, you are very bitter!" I said.

"Not at all. I like accuracy. 'Princess' to the ingenuous mind suggests a fairy tale. I have not an ingenuous mind. I know that the princesses of the fairy tales do not exist,—unless you are one."

"Me!" I exclaimed, in amazement—"I'm very far from that—"

"Well, you are a dreamer!" he said, and resting his arms on the deck rail he looked away from me down into the sunlit sea—"You do not live here in this world with us—you think you do,—and yet in your own mind you know you do not. You dream—and your life is that of vision simply. I'm not sure that I should like to see you wake. For as long as you can dream you will believe in the fairy tale;—the 'princess' of Hans Andersen and the Brothers Grimm holds good—and that is why you should have pretty things about you,—music, roses and the like trifles,—to keep up the delicate delusion."

I was surprised and just a little vexed at his way of talking. Why, even with the underlying flattery of his words, should he call me a dreamer? I had worked for my own living as practically as himself in the world, and if not with such financially successful results, only because my aims had never been mere money-spinning. He had attained enormous wealth,—I a modest competence,—he was old and I was young,—he was ill and miserable,—I was well and happy,—which of us was the 'dreamer'? My thoughts were busy with this question, and he saw it.

"Don't perplex yourself,"—he said,—"and don't be offended with me for my frankness. My view of life is not yours,—nor are we ever likely to see things from the same standpoint. Yours is the more enviable condition. You are looking well,—you feel well—you are well! Health is the best of all things." He paused, and lifting his eyes from the contemplation of the water, regarded me fixedly. "That's a lovely bit of bell-heather you're wearing! It glows like fiery topaz."

I explained how it had been given to me.

"Why, then, you've already established a connection with the strange yacht!" he said, laughing—"The owner, according to your Highland fellow, has the same blossoms on board,—probably gathered from the same morass!—surely this is quite romantic and exciting!"

And at breakfast, when Dr. Brayle and Mr. Swinton appeared, they all made conversation on the subject of my bunch of heather, till I got rather tired of it, and was half inclined to take it off and throw it away. Yet somehow I could not do this. Glancing at my own reflection in a mirror, I saw what a brilliant yet dainty touch of colour it gave to the plain white serge of my yachting dress,—it was a pretty contrast, and I left it alone.

Miss Catherine did not get up to breakfast, but she sent for me afterwards and asked if I would mind sitting with her for a while. I did mind in a way,—for the day was fair and fine,—the 'Diana' was preparing to pursue her course,—and it was far pleasanter to be on deck in the fresh air than in Miss Catherine's state-room, which, though quite spacious for a yacht's accommodation, looked rather dreary, having no carpet on the floor, no curtains to the bed, and no little graces of adornment anywhere,—nothing but a few shelves against the wall on which were ranged some blue and black medicine bottles, relieved by a small array of pill-boxes. But I felt sorry for the poor woman who had elected to make her life a martyrdom to nerves, and real or imaginary aches and pains, so I went to her, determined to do what I could to cheer and rouse her from her condition of chronic depression. Directly I entered her cabin she said:

"Where did you get that bright bit of heather?"

I told her the whole story, to which she listened with more patience than she usually showed for any talk in which she had not first share.

"It's really quite interesting!" she said, with a reluctant smile— "I suppose it was the strange yacht that had the music on board last night. It kept me awake. I thought it was some tiresome person out in a boat with a gramophone."

I laughed.

"Oh, Miss Harland!" I exclaimed—"Surely you could not have thought it a gramophone! Such music! It was perfectly exquisite!"

"Was it?" And she drew the ugly grey woollen shawl in which she was wrapped closer about her sallow throat as she sat up in her bed and looked at me—"Well, it may have been, to you,—you seem to find delight in everything,—I'm sure I don't know why! Of course it's very nice to have such a happy disposition—but really that music teased me dreadfully. Such a bore having music when you want to go to sleep."

I was silent, and having a piece of embroidery to occupy my hands I began to work at it.

"I hope you're quite comfortable on board,"—she resumed, presently- -"Have you all you want in your rooms?"

I assured her that everything was perfect.

She sighed.

"I wish I could say the same!" she said—"I really hate yachting, but father likes it, so I must sacrifice myself." Here she sighed again. I saw she was really convinced that she was immolating herself on the altar of filial obedience. "You know he is very ill,"—she went on—"and that he cannot live long?"

"He told me something about it,"—I answered—"and I said then, as I say now, that the doctors may be wrong."

"Oh no, they cannot be wrong in his case," she declared, shaking her head dismally—"They know the symptoms, and they can only avert the end for a time. I'm very thankful Dr. Brayle was able to come with us on this trip."

"I suppose he is paid a good deal for his services?" I said.

"Eight hundred guineas"—she answered—"But, you see, he has to leave his patients in London, and find another man to attend to them during his absence. He is so very clever and so much sought after—I don't know what I should do without him, I'm sure!"

"Has he any special treatment for you?" I asked.

"Oh yes,—he gives me electricity. He has a wonderful battery—he has got it fitted up here in the next cabin—and while I hold two handles he turns it on and it runs all over me. I feel always better for the moment—but the effect soon passes."

I looked at her with a smile.

"I should think so! Dear Miss Harland, do you really believe in that way of administering electricity?"

"Of course I do!" she answered—"You see, it's all a question of what they call bacteriology nowadays. Medicine is no use unless it can kill the microbes that are eating us up inside and out. And there's scarcely any drug that can do that. Electricity is the only remedy. It gives the little brutes a shock;"—and the poor lady laughed weakly—"and it kills some, but not all. It's a dreadful scheme of creation, don't you think, to make human beings no better than happy hunting grounds for invisible creatures to feed upon?"

"It depends on what view you take of it,"—I said, laying down my work and trying to fix her attention, a matter which was always difficult—"We human beings are composed of good and evil particles. If the good are encouraged, they drive out the evil,—if the evil, they drive out the good. It's the same with the body as the soul,— if we encourage the health-working 'microbes' as you call them, they will drive out disease from the human organism altogether."

She sank back on her pillow wearily.

"We can't do it,"—she said—"All the chances are against us. What's the use of our trying to encourage 'health-working microbes'? The disease-working ones have got the upper hand. Just think!—our parents, grandparents and great-grandparents are to blame for half our evils. Their diseases become ours in various new forms. It's cruel,—horrible! How anyone can believe that a God of Love created such a frightful scheme passes my comprehension! The whole thing is a mere business of eating to be eaten!"

She looked so wan and wild that I pitied her greatly.

"Surely that is not what you think at the bottom of your heart?" I said, gently—"I should be very sorry for you if I thought you really meant what you say."

"Well, you may be as sorry for me as you like"—and the poor lady blinked away tears from her eyes—"I need someone to be sorry for me! I tell you my life is a perfect torture. Every day I wonder how long I can bear it! I have such dreadful thoughts! I picture the horrible things that are happening to different people all over the world, nobody helping them or caring for them, and I almost feel as if I must scream for mercy. It wouldn't be any use screaming,—but the scream is in my soul all the same. People in prisons, people in shipwrecks, people dying by inches in hospitals, no good in their lives and no hope—and not a sign of comfort from the God whom the Churches praise! It's awful! I don't see how anybody can do anything or be ambitious for anything—it's all mere waste of energy. One of the reasons that made me so anxious to have you come on this trip with us is that you always seem contented and happy,—and I want to know why? It's a question of temperament, I suppose—but do tell me why!"

She stretched out her hand and touched mine appealingly. I took her worn and wasted fingers in my own and pressed them sympathetically.

"My dear Miss Harland,"—I began.

"Oh, call me Catherine"—she interrupted—"I'm so tired of being Miss Harland!"

"Well, Catherine, then,"—I said, smiling a little—"Surely you know why I am contented and happy?"

"No, I do not,"—she said, with quick, almost querulous? eagerness— "I don't understand it at all. You have none of the things that please women. You don't seem to care about dress though you are always well-gowned—you don't go to balls or theatres or race- meetings,—you are a general favourite, yet you avoid society,— you've never troubled yourself to take your chances of marriage,— and so far as I know or have heard tell about you, you haven't even a lover!"

My cheeks grew suddenly warm. A curious resentment awoke in me at her words—had I indeed no lover? Surely I had!—one that I knew well and had known for a long time,—one for whom I had guarded my life sacredly as belong-ing to another as well as to myself,—a lover who loved me beyond all power of human expression,—here the rush of strange and inexplicable emotion in me was hurled back on my mind with a shock of mingled terror and surprise from a dead wall of stony fact,—it was true, of course, and Catherine Harland was right—I had no lover. No man had ever loved me well enough to be called by such a name. The flush cooled off my face,—the hurry of my thoughts slackened,—I took up my embroidery and began to work at it again.

"That is so, isn't it?" persisted Miss Harland—"Though you blush and grow pale as if there was someone in the background."

I met her inquisitive glance and smiled.

"There is no one,"—I said—"There never has been anyone." I paused; I could almost feel the warmth of the strong hand that had held mine in my dream of the past night. It was mere fancy, and I went on—"I should not care for what mod-ern men and women call love. It seems very unsatisfactory."

She sighed.

"It is frequently very selfish,"—she said—"I want to tell you my love-story—may I?"

"Why, of course!" I answered, a little wonderingly, for I had not thought she had a love-story to tell.

"It's very brief,"—she said, and her lip quivered—"There was a man who used to visit our house very often when I first came out,—he made me believe he was very fond of me. I was more than fond of him- -I almost worshipped him. He was all the world to me, and though father did not like him very much he wished me to be happy, so we were engaged. That was the time of my life—the only time I ever knew what happiness was. One evening, just about three months before we were to be married, we were together at a party in the house of one of our mutual friends, and I heard him talking rather loudly in a room where he and two or three other men had gone to smoke. He said something that made me stand still and wonder whether I was mad or dreaming. 'Pity me when I'm married to Catherine Harland!' Pity him? I listened,—I knew it was wrong to listen, but I could not help myself. 'Well, you'll get enough cash with her to set you all right in the world, anyhow,'—said another man, 'You can put up with a plain wife for the sake of a pretty fortune.' Then he,—my love!— spoke again—'Oh, I shall make the best of it,' he said—'I must have money somehow, and this is the easiest way. There's one good thing about modern life,—husbands and wives don't hunt in couples as they used to do, so when once the knot is tied I shall shift my matrimonial burden off my shoulders as much as I can. She'll amuse herself with her clothes and the household,—and she's fond of me, so I shall always have my own way. But it's an awful martyrdom to have to marry one woman on account of empty pockets when you're in love with another.' I heard,—and then—I don't know what happened."

Her eyes stared at me so pitifully that I was full of sorrow for her.

"Oh, you poor Catherine!" I said, and taking her hand, I kissed it gently. The tears in her eyes brimmed over.

"They found me lying on the floor insensible,"—she went on, tremulously—"And I was very ill for a long time afterwards. People could not understand it when I broke off my engagement. I told nobody why—except HIM. He seemed sorry and a little ashamed,—but I think he was more vexed at losing my fortune than anything else. I said to him that I had never thought about being plain,—that the idea of his loving me had made me feel beautiful. That was true!—my dear, I almost believe I should have grown into beauty if I had been sure of his love."

I understood that; she was perfectly right in what to the entirely commonplace person would seem a fanciful theory. Love makes all things fair, and anyone who is conscious of being tenderly loved grows lovely, as a rose that is conscious of the sun grows into form and colour.

"Well, it was all over then,"—she ended, with a sigh, "I never was quite myself again—I think my nerves got a sort of shock such as the great novelist, Charles Dickens had when he was in the railway accident—you remember the tale in Forster's 'Life'? How the carriage hung over the edge of an embankment but did not actually fall,—and Dickens was clinging on to it all the time. He never got over it, and it was the remote cause of his death five years later. Now I have felt just like that,—my life has hung over a sort of chasm ever since I lost my love, and I only cling on."

"But surely,"—I ventured to say—"surely there are other things to live for than just the memory of one man's love which was not love at all! You seem to think there was some cruelty or unhappiness in the chance that separated you from him,—but really it was a special mercy and favour of God—only you have taken it in the wrong way."

"I have taken it in the only possible way,"—she said—"With resignation."

"Oh, do you call it resignation?" I exclaimed—"To make a misery of what should have been a gladness? Think of the years and years of wretchedness you might have passed with a man who was a merely selfish fortune-hunter! You would have had to see him grow colder and more callous every day—your heart would have been torn, your spirit broken—and God spared you all this by giving you your chance of freedom! Such a chance! You might have made much of it, if you had only chosen!"

She looked at me, but did not speak.

"Love comes to us in a million beautiful ways,"—I went on, heedless of how she might take my words—"The ordinary love,—or, I would say, the ordinary mating and marriage is only ONE way. You cannot live in the world without being loved—if you love!"

She moved on her pillows restlessly.

"I can't see what you mean,"—she said—"How can I love? I have nothing to love!"

"But do you not see that you are shutting yourself out from love?" I said—"You will not have it! You bar its approach. You encourage your sad and morbid fancies, and think of illness when you might just as well think of health. Oh, I know you will say I am 'up in the air' as your father expresses it,—but it's true all the same that if you love everything in Nature—yes, everything!—sunshine, air, cloud, rain, trees, birds, blossom,—they will love you in return and give you some of their life and strength and beauty."

She smiled,—a very bitter little smile.

"You talk like a poet,"—she said—"And of all things in the world I hate poetry! There!—don't think me cross! Go along and be happy in your own strange fanciful way! I cannot be other than I am,—Dr. Brayle will tell you that I'm not strong enough to share in other people's lives and aims and pleasures,—I must always consider myself."

"Dr. Brayle tells you that?" I queried—"To consider yourself?"

"Of course he does. If I had not considered myself every hour and every day, I should have been dead long ago. I have to consider everything I eat and drink lest it should make me ill."

I rose from my seat beside her.

"I wish I could cure you!" I murmured.

"My dear girl, if you could, you would, I am sure,"—she answered— "You are very kind-hearted. It has done me good to talk to you and tell you all my sad little history. I shall get up presently and have my electricity and feel quite bright for a time. But as for a cure, you might as well try to cure my father."

"None are cured of any ailment unless they resolve to help along the cure themselves," I said.

She gave a weary little laugh.

"Ah, that's one of your pet theories, but it's no use to me! I'm past all helping of myself, so you may give me up as a bad job!"

"But you asked me," I went on—"did you not, to tell you why it is that I am contented and happy? Do you really want to know?"

A vague distrust crept into her faded eyes.

"Not if it's a theory!" she said—"I should not have the brain or the patience to think it out."

I laughed.

"It's not a theory, it's a truth"—I answered—"But truth is sometimes more difficult than theory."

She looked at me half in wonder, half in appeal.

"Well, what is it?"

"Just this"—and I knelt beside her for a moment holding her hand— "I KNOW that there are no external surroundings which we do not make for ourselves, and that our troubles are born of our own wrong thinking, and are not sent from God. I train my Soul to be calm,— and my body obeys my Soul. That's all!"

Her fingers closed on mine nervously.

"But what's the use of telling me this?" she half whispered—"I don't believe in God or the Soul!"

I rose from my kneeling attitude.

"Poor Catherine!" I said—"Then indeed it is no use telling you anything! You are in darkness instead of daylight, and no one can make you see. Oh, what can I do to help you?"

"Nothing,"—she answered—"My faith—it was never very much,—was taken from me altogether when I was quite young. Father made it seem absurd. He's a clever man, you know—and in a few words he makes out religion to be utter nonsense."

"I understand!"

And indeed I did entirely understand. Her father was one of a rapidly increasing class of men who are a danger to the community,— a cold, cynical shatterer of every noble ideal,—a sneerer at patriotism and honour,—a deliberate iconoclast of the most callous and remorseless type. That he had good points in his character was not to be denied,—a murderer may have these. But to be in his company for very long was to feel that there is no good in anything- -that life is a mistake of Nature, and death a fortunate ending of the blunder—that God is a delusion and the 'Soul' a mere expression signifying certain intelligent movements of the brain only.

I stood silently thinking these things, while she watched me rather wistfully. Presently she said:

"Are you going on deck now?"

"Yes."

"I'll join you all at luncheon. Don't lose that bit of heather in your dress,—it's really quite brilliant—like a jewel."

I hesitated a moment.

"You're not vexed with me for speaking as I have done?" I asked her.

"Vexed? No, indeed! I love to hear you and see you defending your own fairy ground! For it IS like a fairy tale, you know—all that YOU believe!"

"It has practical results, anyway!"—I answered—"You must admit that."

"Yes—I know,—and it's just what I can't understand. We'll have another talk about it some day. Would you tell Dr. Brayle that I shall be ready for him in ten minutes?"

I assented, and left her. I made for the deck directly, the air meeting me with a rush of salty softness as I ran up the saloon stairway. What a glorious day it was! Sky, sea and mountains were bathed in brilliant sunshine; the 'Diana' was cutting her path swiftly through waters which marked her course on either side by a streak of white foam. I mentally contrasted the loveliness of the scene around me with the stuffy cabin I had just left, and seeing Dr. Brayle smoking comfortably in a long reclining chair and reading a paper I went up to him and touched him on the shoulder.

"Your patient wants you in ten minutes,"—I said.

He rose to his feet at once, courteously offering me a chair, which I declined, and drew his cigar from his mouth.

"I have two patients on board,"—he answered, smiling—"Which one?"

"The one who is your patient from choice, not necessity,"—I replied, coolly.

"My dear lady!" His eyes blinked at me with a furtive astonishment— "If you were not so charming I should say you were—well!—SHALL I say it?—a trifle opinionated!"

I laughed.

"Granted!" I said—"If it is opinionated to be honest I plead guilty! Miss Harland is as well as you or I,—she's only morbid."

"True!—but morbidness is a form of illness,—a malady of the nerves—"

I laughed again, much to his visible annoyance.

"Curable by outward applications of electricity?" I queried—"When the mischief is in the mind? But there!—I mustn't interfere, I suppose! Nevertheless you keep Miss Harland ill when she might be quite well."

A disagreeable line furrowed the corners of his mouth.

"You think so? Among your many accomplishments do you count the art of medicine?"

I met his shifty brown eyes, and he dropped them quickly.

"I know nothing about it,"—I answered—"Except this—that the cure of any mind trouble must come from within—not from without. And I'm not a Christian Scientist either?"

He smiled cynically. "Really not? I should have thought you were!"

"You would make a grave error if you thought so," I responded, curtly.

A keen and watchful interest flashed over his dark face.

"I should very much like to know what your theories are"—he said, suddenly—"You interest me greatly."

"I'm sure I do!" I answered, smiling.

He looked me up and down for a moment in perplexity—then shrugged his shoulders.

"You are a strange creature!" he said—"I cannot make you out. If I were asked to give a 'professional' opinion of you I should say you were very neurotic and highly-strung, and given over to self- delusions."

"Thanks!"—and I made him a demure little curtsy. "I look it, don't I?"

"No—you don't look it; but looks are deceptive."

"There I agree with you,"—I said—"But one has to go by them sometimes. If I am 'neurotic,' my looks do not pity me, and my condition of health leaves nothing to desire."

His brows met in a slight frown. He glanced at his watch.

"I must go,"—he said—"Miss Harland will be waiting."

"And the electricity will get cold!" I added, gaily. "See if you can feel my 'neurotic' pulse!"

He took the hand I extended—and remained quite still. Conscious of the secret force I had within myself I resolved to try if I could use it upon him in such a way as to keep him a prisoner till I chose to let him go. I watched him till his eyes began to look vague and a kind of fixity settled on his features,—he was perfectly unconscious that I held him at my pleasure,—and presently, satisfied with my experiment, I relaxed the spell and withdrew my hand.

"Quite regular, isn't it?" I said, carelessly.

He started as if roused from a sleep, but replied quickly:

"Yes—oh yes—perfectly!—I had almost forgotten what I was doing. I was thinking of something else. Miss Harland—"

"Yes, Miss Harland is ready for you by this time"—and I smiled. "You must tell her I detained you."

He nodded in a more or less embarrassed manner, and turning away from me, went rather slowly down the saloon stairs.

I gave a sigh of relief when he was gone. I had from the first moment of our meeting recognised in him a mental organisation which in its godless materialism and indifference to consequences, was opposed to every healthful influence that might be brought to bear on his patients for their well-being, whatever his pretensions to medical skill might be. It was to his advantage to show them the worst side of a disease in order to accentuate his own cleverness in dealing with it,—it served his purpose to pamper their darkest imaginings, play with their whims and humour their caprices,—I saw all this and understood it. And I was glad that so far as I might be concerned, I had the power to master him.

V

AN UNEXPECTED MEETING

To spend a few days on board a yacht with the same companions is a very good test of the value of sympathetic vibration in human associations. I found it so. I might as well have been quite alone on the 'Diana' as with Morton Harland and his daughter, though they were always uniformly kind to me and thoughtful of my comfort. But between us there was 'a great gulf fixed,' though every now and again Catherine Harland made feeble and pathetic efforts to cross that gulf and reach me where I stood on the other side. But her strength was not equal to the task,—her will-power was sapped at its root, and every day she allowed herself to become more and more pliantly the prey of Dr. Brayle, who, with a subconscious feeling that I knew him to be a mere medical charlatan, had naturally warned her against me as an imaginative theorist without any foundation of belief in my own theories. I therefore shut myself within a fortress of reserve, and declined to discuss any point of either religion or science with those for whom the one was a farce and the other mere materialism. At all times when we were together I kept the conversation deliberately down to commonplaces which were safe, if dull,— and it amused me not a little to see that at this course of action on my part Mr. Harland was first surprised, then disappointed and finally bored. And I was glad. That I should bore him as much as he bored me was the happy consummation of my immediate desires. I talked as all conventional women talk, of the weather, of our minimum and maximum speed, of the newspaper 'sensations' and vulgarities that were served up to us whenever we called at a port for the mails,—of the fish that frequented such and such waters, of sport, of this and that millionaire whose highland castle or shooting-box was crammed with the 'elite' whose delight is to kill innocent birds and animals,—of the latest fool-flyers in aeroplanes,—in short, no fashionable jabberer of social inanities could have beaten me in what average persons call 'common-sense talk,'—talk which resulted after a while in the usual vagueness of attention accompanied by smothered yawning. I was resolved not to lift the line of thought 'up in the air' in the manner whereof I had often been accused, but to keep it level with the ground. So that when we left Tobermory, where we had anchored for a couple of days, the limits of the yacht were becoming rather cramped and narrow for our differing minds, and a monotony was beginning to set in that threatened to be dangerous, if not unbearable. As the 'Diana' steamed along through the drowsy misty light of the summer afternoon, past the jagged coast of the mainland, I sat quite by myself on deck, watching the creeping purple haze that partially veiled the mountains of Ardnamurchan and Moidart, and I began to wonder whether after all it might not be better to write to my friend Francesca and tell her that her prophecies had already come true,— that I was beginning to be weary of a holiday passed in an atmosphere bereft of all joyousness, and that she must expect me in Inverness-shire at once. And yet I was reluctant to end my trip with the Harlands too soon. There was a secret wish in my heart which I hardly breathed to myself,—a wish that I might again see the strange vessel that had appeared and disappeared so suddenly, and make the acquaintance of its owner. It would surely be an interesting break in the present condition of things, to say the least of it. I did not know then (though I know now) why my mind so persistently busied itself with the fancied personality of the unknown possessor of the mysterious craft which, as Captain Derrick said, 'sailed without wind,' but I found myself always thinking about him and trying to picture his face and form.

I took myself sharply to task for what I considered a foolish mental attitude,— but do what I would, the attitude remained unchanged. It was helped, perhaps, in a trifling way by the apparently fadeless quality of the pink bell-heather which had been given me by the weird-looking Highland fellow who called himself Jamie, for though three or four days had now passed since I first wore it, it showed no signs of withering. As a rule the delicate waxen bells of this plant turn yellow a few hours after they are plucked,—but my little bunch was as brilliantly fresh as ever. I kept it in a glass without water on the table in my sitting-room and it looked always the same. I was questioning myself as to what I should really do if my surroundings remained as hopelessly inert and uninteresting as they were at present,—go on with the 'Diana' for a while longer on the chance of seeing the strange yacht again—or make up my mind to get put out at some point from which I could reach Inverness easily, when Mr. Harland came up suddenly behind my chair and laid his hand on my shoulder.

"Are you in dreamland?" he enquired—and I thought his voice sounded rather weak and dispirited—"There's a wonderful light on those hills just now."

I raised my eyes and saw the purple shadows being cloven and scattered one after another, by long rays of late sunshine that poured like golden wine through the dividing wreaths of vapour,— above, the sky was pure turquoise blue, melting into pale opal and emerald near the line of the grey sea which showed little flecks of white foam under the freshening breeze. Bringing my gaze down from the dazzling radiance of the heavens, I turned towards Mr. Harland and was startled and shocked to see the drawn and livid pallor of his face and the anguish of his expression.

"You are ill!" I exclaimed, and springing up in haste I offered him my chair—"Do sit down!"

He made a mute gesture of denial, and with slow difficulty drew another chair up beside mine, and dropped into it with an air of heavy weariness.

"I am not ill now,"—he said—"A little while ago I was very ill. I was in pain— horrible pain! Brayle did what he could for me—it was not much. He says I must expect to suffer now and again—until— until the end."

Impulsively I laid my hand on his.

"I am very sorry!" I said, gently—"I wish I could be of some use to you!"

He looked at me with a curious wistfulness.

"You could, no doubt, if I believed as you do,"—he replied, and then was silent for a moment. Presently he spoke again.

"Do you know I am rather disappointed in you?"

"Are you?" And I smiled a little—"Why?"

He did not answer at once. He seemed absorbed in troubled musings. When he resumed, it was in a low, meditative tone, almost as if he were speaking to himself.

"When I first met you—you remember?—at one of those social 'crushes' which make the London season so infinitely tedious,—I was told you were gifted with unusual psychic power, and that you had in yourself the secret of an abounding exhaustless vitality. I repeat the words—an abounding exhaustless vitality. This interested me, because I know that our modern men and women are mostly only half alive. I heard of you that it did people good to be in your company,—that your influence upon them was remarkable, and that there was some unknown form of occult, or psychic science to which you had devoted years of study, with the result that you stood, as it were, apart from the world though in the world. This, I say, is what I heard—"

"But you did not believe it,"—I interposed.

"Why do you say that?" he asked, quickly.

"Because I know you could not believe it,"—I answered—"It would be impossible for you."

A gleam of satire flashed in his sunken eyes.

"Well, you are right there! I did not believe it. But I expected—"

"I know!" And I laughed—"You expected what is called a 'singular' woman—one who makes herself 'singular,' adopts a 'singular' pose, and is altogether removed from ordinary humanity. And of course you are disappointed. I am not at all a type of the veiled priestess."

"It is not that,"—he said, with a little vexation—"When I saw you I recognised you to be a very transparent creature, devoted to innocent dreams which are not life. But that secret which you are reported to possess—the secret of wonderful abounding exhaustless vitality—how does it happen that you have it? I myself see that force expressed in your very glance and gesture, and what puzzles me is that it is not an animal vitality; it is something else."

I was silent.

"You have not a robust physique,"—he went on—"Yet you are more full of the spirit of life than men and women twice as strong as you are. You are a feminine thing, too,—and that goes against you. But one can see in you a worker—you evidently enjoy the exercise of the accomplishments you possess—and nothing comes amiss to you. I wonder how you manage it? When you joined us on this trip a few days ago, you brought a kind of atmosphere with you that was almost buoyant, and now I am disappointed, because you seem to have enclosed yourself within it, and to have left us out!"

"Have you not left yourselves out?" I queried, gently. "I, personally, have really nothing to do with it. Just remember that when we have talked on any subject above the line of the general and commonplace your sole object has been to 'draw' me for the amusement of yourself and Dr. Brayle—"

"Ah, you saw that, did you?" he interrupted, with a faint smile.

"Naturally! Had you believed half you say you were told of me, you would have known I must have seen it. Can you wonder that I refuse to be 'drawn'?"

He looked at me with an odd expression of mingled surprise and annoyance, and I met his gaze fully and frankly. His eyes shifted uneasily away from mine.

"One may feel a pardonable curiosity," he said, "And a desire to know—"

"To know what?" I asked, with some warmth—"How can you obtain what you are secretly craving for, if you persist in denying what is true? You are afraid of death—yet you invite it by ignoring the source of life! The curtain is down,—you are outside eternal realities altogether in a chaos of your own voluntary creation!"

I spoke with some passion, and he heard me patiently.

"Let us try to understand each other," he said, after a pause— "though it will be difficult. You speak of 'eternal realities.' To me there are none, save the constant scattering and re-uniting of atoms. These, so far as we know of the extraordinary (and to me quite unintelligent) plan of the Universe, are for ever shifting and changing into various forms and clusters of forms, such as solar systems, planets, comets, star-dust and the like. Our present view of them is chiefly based on the researches of Larmor and Thomson of Cambridge. From them and other scientists we learn that electricity exists in small particles which we can in a manner see in the 'cathode' rays,—and these particles are called 'electrons.' These compose 'atoms of matter.' Well!—there are a trillion of atoms in each granule of dust,—while electrons are so much smaller, that a hundred thousand of them can lie in the diameter of an atom. I know all this,—but I do not know why the atoms or electrons should exist at all, nor what cause there should be for their constant and often violent state of movement. They apparently always HAVE BEEN, and always WILL be,—therefore they are all that can be called 'eternal realities.' Sir Norman Lockyer tells us that the matter of the Universe is undergoing a continuous process of evolution—but even if it is so, what is that to me individually? It neither helps nor consoles me for being one infinitesimal spark in the general conflagration. Now you believe—"

"In the Force that is BEHIND your system of electrons and atoms"—I said—
"For by whatever means or substances the Universe is composed, a mighty
Intelligence governs it—and I look to the Cause more than the Effect. For even I
am a part of the whole,—I belong to the source of the stream as much as to the
stream itself. An abstract, lifeless principle without will or intention or intelligence could not have evolved the splendours of Nature or the intellectual capabilities of man—it could not have given rise to what was not in itself."

He fixed his eyes steadily upon me.

"That last sentence is sound argument," he said, as though reluctantly admitting
the obvious,—"And I suppose I am to presume that 'Itself' is the well-spring from
which you draw, or imagine you draw, your psychic force?"

"If I have any psychic force at all," I responded,—"where do you suppose it
should come from but that which gives vitality to all animate Nature? I cannot
understand why you blind yourself to the open and visible fact of a Divine
Intelligence working in and through all things. If you could but acknowledge it
and set yourself in tune with it you would find life a new and far more dominant
joy than it is to you now. I firmly believe that your very illness has arisen from
your determined attitude of unbelief."

"That's what a Christian Scientist would say," he answered, with a touch of
scorn,—"I begin to think Dr. Brayle is right in his estimate of you."

I held my peace.

"Have you no curiosity?" he demanded—"Don't you want to know his opinion?"

"No,"—and I smiled—"My dear Mr. Harland, with all your experience of the
world, has it never occurred to you that there are some people whose opinions
don't matter?"

"Brayle is a clever man,"—he said, somewhat testily, "And you are merely an
imaginative woman."

"Then why do you trouble about me?" I asked him, quickly—"Why do you want
to find out that something in me which baffles both Dr. Brayle and yourself?"

It was now his turn to be silent, and he remained so for some time, his eyes fixed
on the shadowing heavens. The waves were roughening slightly and a swell from

the Atlantic lifted the 'Diana' curtsying over their foam-flecked crests as she ploughed her way swiftly along. Presently he turned to me with a smile.

"Let us strike a truce!"—he said—"I promise not to try and 'draw' you any more! But please do not isolate yourself from us,—try to feel that we are your friends. I want you to enjoy this trip if possible,—but I fear that we are proving rather dull company for you. We are making for Skye at good speed and shall probably anchor in Loch Scavaig to-night. To-morrow we might land and do the excursion to Loch Coruisk if you care for that, though Catherine is not a good walker." I felt rather remorseful as he said these words in a kindly tone. Yet I knew very well that, notwithstanding all the strenuous efforts which might be made by the rules of conventional courtesy, it would be impossible for me to feel quite at home in the surroundings which he had created for himself. I inwardly resolved, however, to make the best of it and to try and steer clear of any possibilities or incidents which might tend to draw the line of demarcation too strongly between us. Some instinct told me that present conditions were not to remain as they were, so I answered my host gently and assured him of my entire willingness to fall in with any of his plans. Our conversation then gradually drifted into ordinary topics till towards sunset, when I went down to my cabin to dress for dinner. I had a fancy to wear the bunch of pink bell-heather that still kept its fresh and waxen-looking delicacy of bloom, and this, fastened in the lace of my white gown, was my only adornment.

That night there was a distinct attempt on everybody's part to make things sociable and pleasant. Catherine Harland was, for once, quite cheerful and chatty, and proposed that as there was a lovely moonlight, we should all go after dinner into the deck saloon, where there was a piano, and that I should sing for them. I was rather surprised at this suggestion, as she was not fond of music. Nevertheless, there had been such an evident wish shown by her and her father to lighten the monotony which had been creeping like a mental fog over us all that I readily agreed to anything which might perhaps for the moment give them pleasure.

We went up on deck accordingly, and on arriving there were all smitten into awed silence by the wonderful beauty of the scene. We were anchored in Loch Scavaig—and the light of the moon fell with a weird splendour on the gloom of the surrounding hills, a pale beam touching the summits here and there and deepening the solemn effect of the lake and the magnificent forms of its sentinel mountains. A low murmur of hidden streams sounded on the deep stillness and enhanced the fascination of the surrounding landscape, which was more like the landscape of a dream than a reality. The deep breadths of dense darkness lying lost among the cavernous slopes of the hills were broken at intervals by strange rifts of light arising as it were from the palpitating water, which now and again showed gleams of pale emerald and gold phosphorescence,—the stars looked large and white like straying bits of the moon, and the mysterious 'swishing' of slow ripples heaving against the sides of the yacht suggested the whisperings of uncanny spirits. We stood in a silent group, entranced by the grandeur of the night and by our own loneliness in the midst of it, for there was no sign of a fisherman's hut or boat moored to the shore, or anything which could give us a sense of human companionship. A curious feeling of disappointment suddenly came over me,—I lifted my eyes to the vast dark sky with a kind of mute appeal—and moon and stars appeared to float up there like ships in a deep sea,—I had expected something more in this strange, almost spectral-looking landscape, and yet I knew not why I should expect anything. Beautiful as the whole scene was, and fully as I recognised its beauty, an overpowering depression suddenly gripped me as with a cold hand,—there was a dreary emptiness in this majestic solitude that seemed to crush my spirit utterly.

I moved a little away from my companions, and leaned over the deck rail, looking far into the black shadows of the shore, defined more deeply by the contrasting brilliance of the moon, and my thoughts flew with undesired swiftness to the darkest line of life's horizon- -I had for the moment lost the sense of joy. How wretched all we human creatures are!—I said to my inner self,—what hope after all is there for us, imprisoned in a world which has no pity for us whatever may be our fate,—a world that goes on in precisely the same fashion whether we live or die, work or are idle? These tragic hills, this cold lake, this white moon, were the same when Caesar lived, and would still be the same when we who gazed upon them now were all gone into the Unknown. It seemed difficult to try and realise this obvious fact—so difficult as to be almost unnatural. Supposing that any towns or villages had ever existed on this desolate shore, they had proved useless against the devouring forces of Nature,—just as the splendid buried cities of South America had proved useless in all their magnificence,—useless as the 'Golden Age of Lanka' in Ceylon more than two thousand years ago. Of what avail then is the struggle of human life? Is it for the many or only for the few? Is all the toil and sorrow of millions merely for the uplifting and perfecting of certain individual types, and is this what Christ meant when He said 'Many are called but few are chosen'? If so, why such waste of brain and heart and love and patience? Tears came suddenly into my eyes and I started as from a bad dream when Dr. Brayle approached me softly from behind.

"I am sorry to disturb your reverie!"—he said—"But Miss Harland has gone into the deck saloon and we are all waiting to hear you sing."

I looked up at him.

"I don't feel as if I could sing to-night,"—I replied, rather tremulously—"This lonely landscape depresses me—"

He saw that my eyes were wet, and smiled.

"You are overwrought," he said—"Your own theories of health and vitality are not infallible! You must be taken care of. You think too much."

"Or too little?" I suggested.

"Really, my dear lady, you cannot possibly think too little where health and happiness are concerned! The sanest and most comfortable people on earth are those who eat well and never think at all. An empty brain and a full stomach make the sum total of a contented life."

"So YOU imagine!" I said, with a slight gesture of veiled contempt.

"So I KNOW!" he answered, with emphasis—"And I have had a wide experience. Now don't look daggers at me!—come and sing!"

He offered me his arm, but I put it aside and walked by myself towards the deck saloon. Mr. Harland and Catherine were seated there, with all the lights turned full on, so that the radiance of the moon through the window was completely eclipsed. The piano was open. As I came in Catherine looked at me with a surprised air.

"Why, how pale you are!" she exclaimed—"One would think you had seen a ghost!"

I laughed.

"Perhaps I have! Loch Scavaig is sufficient setting for any amount of ghosts. It's such a lonely place,"—and a slight tremor ran through me as I played a few soft chords—"What shall I sing to you?"

"Something of the country we are in,"—said Mr. Harland—"Don't you know any of those old wild Gaelic airs?"

I thought a moment, and then to a low rippling accompaniment I sang the old Celtic 'Fairy's Love Song'—

"Why should I sit and sigh,
Pu'in' bracken, pu'in' bracken,
Why should I sit and sigh,
On the hill-side dreary—
When I see the plover rising,
Or the curlew wheeling,
Then I know my mortal lover
Back to me is stealing.

When the day wears away
Sad I look adown the valley,
Every sound heard around
Sets my heart a-thrilling,—
Why should I sit and sigh,
Pu'in' bracken, pu'in' bracken,
Why should I sit and sigh
All alone and weary!

Ah, but there is something wanting,
Oh but I am weary!
Come, my true and tender lover,
O'er the hills to cheer me!
Why should I sit and sigh,
Pu'in' bracken, pu'in' bracken,
Why should I sit and sigh,
All alone and weary!"

I had scarcely finished the last verse when Captain Derrick suddenly appeared at the door of the saloon in a great state of excitement.

"Come out, Mr. Harland!" he almost shouted—"Come quickly, all of you! There's that strange yacht again!"

I rose from my seat at the piano trembling a little—at last!—I thought—at last! My heart was beating tumultuously, though I could not explain my own emotion to myself. In another moment we were all standing speechless and amazed, gazing at surely the most wonderful sight that had ever been seen by human eyes. There on the dark and lonely waters of Loch Scavaig was poised, rather than anchored, the fairy vessel of my dreams, with all sails spread,—sails that were white as milk and seemingly drenched with a sparkling dewy radiance, for they scintillated like hoar-frost in the sun and glittered against the sombre background of the mountainous shore with an almost blinding splendour. Our whole crew of sailors and servants on the 'Diana' came together in astonished groups, whispering among themselves, all evidently more or less scared by the strange spectacle. Captain Derrick waited for someone to hazard a remark, then, as we remained silent, he addressed Mr. Harland—

"Well, sir, what do you make of it?"

Mr. Harland did not answer. For a man who professed indifference to all events and circumstances he seemed startled for once and a little afraid. Catherine caught me by the arm,—she was shivering nervously.

"Do you think it is a REAL yacht?" she whispered.

I was amused at this question, coming as it did from a woman who denied the supernatural.

"Of course it is!" I answered—"Don't you see people moving about on board?"

For, in the brilliant light shed by those extraordinary sails, the schooner appeared to be fully manned. Several of the crew were busy on her deck and there was nothing of the phantom in their movements.

"Her sails must surely be lit up in that way by electricity"—said Dr. Brayle, who had been watching her attentively—"But how it is done and why, is rather puzzling! I never saw anything quite to resemble it."

"She came into the loch like a flash,"—said Captain Derrick—"I saw her slide in round the point, and then without a sound of any kind, there she was, safe anchored before you could whistle. She behaved in just the same way when we first sighted her off Mull."

I listened to what they were saying, impatiently wondering what would be the end of their surmises and speculations.

"Why not exchange courtesies?" I said, suddenly,—"Here we are—two yachts anchored near each other in a lonely lake,—why should we not know each other? Then all the mysteries you are talking about would be cleared up."

"Quite true!" said Mr. Harland, breaking his silence at last—"But isn't it rather late to pay a call? What time is it?"

"About half-past ten,"—answered Dr. Brayle, glancing at his watch.

"Oh, let us get to bed!" murmured Miss Catherine, pleadingly— "What's the good of making any enquiries to-night?"

"Well, if you don't make them to-night ten to one you won't have the chance to-morrow!"—said Captain Derrick, bluntly—"That yacht will repeat her former manoeuvres and vanish at sunrise."

"As all spectres are traditionally supposed to do!" said Dr. Brayle, lighting a cigarette as he spoke and beginning to smoke it with a careless air—"I vote for catching the ghost before it melts away into the morning."

While this talk went on Mr. Harland stepped back into the saloon and wrote a note which he enclosed in a sealed envelope. With this in his hand he came out to us again.

"Captain, will you get the boat lowered, please?" he said—then, as Captain Derrick hastened to obey this order, he turned to his secretary:—"Mr. Swinton, I want you to take this note to the owner of that yacht, whoever he may be, with my compliments. Don't give it to anyone else but himself."

Mr. Swinton, looking very pale and uncomfortable, took the note gingerly between his fingers.

"Himself—yes!"—he stammered—"And—er—if there should be no one— "

"What do you mean?" and Mr. Harland frowned in his own particularly unpleasant way—"There's sure to be SOMEONE, even if he were the devil! You can say to him that the ladies of our party are very much interested in the beautiful illumination of his yacht, and that we'll be glad to see him on board ours, if he cares to come. Be as polite as you can, and as agreeable as you like."

"It has not occurred to you—I suppose you have not thought—that— that it may be an illusion?" faltered Mr. Swinton, uneasily, glancing at the glistening sails that shamed the silver sheen of the moon—"A sort of mirage in the atmosphere—"

Mr. Harland gave vent to a laugh—the heartiest I had ever heard from him.

"Upon my word, Swinton!" he exclaimed—"I should never have thought you capable of nerves! Come, come!—be off with you! The boat is lowered—all's ready!"

Thus commanded, there was nothing for the reluctant Mr. Swinton but to obey, and I could not help smiling at his evident discomfiture. All his precise and matter-of-fact self-satisfaction was gone in a moment,—he was nothing but a very timorous creature, afraid to examine into what he could not at once understand. No such terrors, however, were displayed by the sailors who undertook to row him over to the yacht. They, as well as their captain, were anxious to discover the mystery, if mystery there was,—and we all, by one instinct, pressed to the gangway as he descended the companion ladder and entered the boat, which glided away immediately with a low and rhythmical plash of oars. We could watch it as it drew nearer and nearer the illuminated vessel, and our excitement grew more and more intense. For once Mr. Harland and his daughter had forgotten all about themselves,—and Catherine's customary miserable expression of face had altogether disappeared in the keenness of her interest for something more immediately thrilling than her own ailments. So far as I was concerned, I could hardly endure the suspense that seemed to weigh on every nerve of my body during the few minutes' interval that elapsed between the departure of the boat and its drawing up alongside the strange yacht. My thoughts were all in a whirl,—I felt as if something unprecedented and almost terrifying was about to happen,—but I could not reason out the cause of my mental agitation.

"There they go!" said Mr. Harland—"They're alongside! See!—those fellows are lowering the companion ladder—there's nothing supernatural about THEM! Swinton's all right—look, he's on board!"

We strained our eyes through the brilliant flare shed by the illuminated sails on the darkness and could see Mr. Swinton talking to a group of sailors. One of them went away, but returned almost immediately, followed by a man clad in white yachting flannels, who, standing near one of the shining sails, caught some of the light on his own figure with undeniably becoming effect. I was the first to perceive him, and as I looked, the impression came upon me that he was no stranger,—I had seen him often before. This sudden consciousness swiftly borne in upon me calmed all the previous tumult of my mind and I was no longer anxious as to the result of our possible acquaintance. Catherine Harland pressed my arm excitedly.

"There he is!" she said—"That must be the owner of the yacht. He's reading father's letter."

He was,—we could see the little sheet of paper turning over in his hands. And while we waited, wondering what would be his answer, the light on the sails of his vessel began to pale and die away,—beam after beam of radiance slipped off as it were like drops of water, and before we could quite realise it there was darkness where all had lately been so bright; and the canvas was hauled down. With the quenching of that intense brilliancy we lost sight of the human figures on deck and could not imagine what was to happen next. The dark shore looked darker than ever,—the outline of the yacht was now truly spectral, like a ship of black cobweb against the moon, and we looked questioningly at each other in silence. Then Mr. Harland spoke in a low tone.

"The boat is coming back,"—he said,—"I hear the oars."

I leaned over the side of our vessel and tried to see through the gloom. How still the water was!—not a ripple disturbed its surface. But there were strange gleams of wandering light in its depths like dropped jewels lost on sands far below. The regular dip of oars sounded nearer and nearer. My heart was beating with painful quickness,—I could not understand the strange feeling that overpowered me. I felt as if my very soul were going out of my body to meet that oncoming boat which was cleaving its way through the darkness. Another brief interval and then we saw it shoot out into a patch of moonlight—we could perceive Mr. Swinton seated in the stern with another figure beside him—that of a man who stood up as he neared our yacht and lifted his cap with an easy gesture of salutation, and then as the boat came alongside, caught at the guide rope and sprang lightly on the first step of the companion ladder.

"Why, he's actually come over to us himself!" ejaculated Mr. Harland,—and he hurried to the gangway just in time to receive the visitor as he stepped on deck.

"Well, Harland, how are you?" said a mellow voice in the cheeriest of accents—"It's strange we should meet like this after so many years!"

VI

RECOGNITION

At these words and at sight of the speaker, Morton Harland started back as if he had been shot.

"Santoris!" he exclaimed—"Not possible! Rafel Santoris! No! You must be his son!"

The stranger laughed.

"My good Harland! Always the sceptic! Miracles are many, but there is one which is beyond all performance. A man cannot be his own offspring! I am that very Santoris who saw you last in Oxford. Come, come!—you ought to know me!"

He stepped more fully into the light which was shed from the open door of the deck saloon, and showed himself to be a man of distinguished appearance, apparently about forty years of age. He was well built, with the straight back and broad shoulders of an athlete,—his face was finely featured and radiant with the glow of health and strength, and as he smiled and laid one hand on Mr. Harland's shoulder he looked the very embodiment of active, powerful manhood. Morton Harland stared at him in amazement and something of terror.

"Rafel Santoris!" he repeated—"You are his living image,—but you cannot be himself—you are too young!"

A gleam of amusement sparkled in the stranger's eyes.

"Don't let us talk of age or youth for the moment"—he said. "Here I am,—your 'eccentric' college acquaintance whom you and several other fellows fought shy of years ago! I assure you I am quite harmless! Will you present me to the ladies?"

There was a brief embarrassed pause. Then Mr. Harland turned to us where we had withdrawn ourselves a little apart and addressed his daughter.

"Catherine,"—he said—"This gentleman tells me he knew me at Oxford, and if he is right I also knew HIM. I spoke of him only the other night at dinner—you remember?—but I did not tell you his name. It is Rafel Santoris—if indeed he IS Santoris!—though my Santoris should be a much older man."

"I extremely regret," said our visitor then, advancing and bowing courteously to Catherine and myself—"that I do not fulfil the required conditions of age! Will you try to forgive me?"

He smiled—and we were a little confused, hardly knowing what to say. Involuntarily I raised my eyes to his, and with one glance saw in those clear blue orbs that so steadfastly met mine a world of memories—memories tender, wistful and pathetic, entangled as in tears and fire. All the inward instincts of my spirit told me that I knew him well—as well as one knows the gold of the sunshine or the colour of the sky,—yet where had I seen him often and often before? While my thoughts puzzled over this question he averted his gaze from mine and went on speaking to Catherine.

"I understand," he said—"that you are interested in the lighting of my yacht?"

"It is most beautiful and wonderful,"—answered Catherine, in her coldest tone of conventional politeness, "And so unusual!"

His eyebrows went up with a slightly quizzical.

"Yes, I suppose it is unusual," he said—"I am always forgetting that what is not quite common seems strange! But really the arrangement is very simple. The yacht is called the 'Dream'—and she is, as her name implies, a 'dream' fulfilled. Her sails are her only motive power. They are charged with electricity, and that is why they shine at night in a way that must seem to outsiders like a special illumination. If you will honour me with a visit to-morrow I will show you how it is managed."

Here Captain Derrick, who had been standing close by, was unable to resist the impulse of his curiosity.

"Excuse me, sir,"—he said, suddenly—"but may I ask how it is you sail without wind?"

"Certainly!—you may ask and be answered!" Santoris replied. "As I have just said, our sails are our only motive power, but we do not need the wind to fill them. By a very simple scientific method, or rather let me say by a scientific application of natural means, we generate a form of electric force from the air and water as we move. This force fills the sails and propels the vessel with amazing swiftness wherever she is steered. Neither calm nor storm affects her progress. When there is a good gale blowing our way, we naturally lessen the draft on our own supplies—but we can make excellent speed even in the teeth of a contrary wind. We escape all the inconveniences of steam and smoke and dirt and noise,—and I daresay in about a couple of hundred years or so my method of sailing the seas will be applied to all ships large and small, with much wonder that it was not thought of long ago."

"Why not apply it yourself?" asked Dr. Brayle, now joining in the conversation for the first time and putting the question with an air of incredulous amusement—"With such a marvellous discovery—if it is yours—you should make your fortune!"

Santoris glanced him over with polite tolerance.

"It is possible I do not need to make it,"—he answered, then turning again to Captain Derrick he said, kindly, "I hope the matter seems clearer to you? We sail without wind, it is true, but not without the power that creates wind."

The captain shook his head perplexedly.

"Well, sir, I can't quite take it in,"—he confessed—"I'd like to know more."

"So you shall! Harland, will you all come over to the yacht to- morrow? There may be some excursion we could do together—and you might remain and dine with me afterwards."

Mr. Harland's face was a study. Doubt and fear struggled for the mastery in his expression and he did not at once answer. Then he seemed to conquer his hesitation and to recover himself.

"Give me a moment with you alone,"—he said, with a gesture of invitation towards the deck saloon.

Our visitor readily complied with this suggestion, and the two men entered the saloon together and closed the door.

Silence followed. Catherine looked at me in questioning bewilderment,—then she called to Mr. Swinton, who had been standing about as though awaiting orders in his usual tiresome and servile way.

"What sort of an interview did you have with that gentleman when you got on board his yacht?" she asked.

"Very pleasant—very pleasant indeed"—he replied—"The vessel is magnificently appointed. I have never seen such luxury. Extraordinary! More than princely! Mr. Santoris himself I found particularly agreeable. When he had read Mr. Harland's note, he said he was glad to find it was from an old college companion, and that he would come over with me to renew the acquaintance. As he has done."

"You were not afraid of him, then?" queried Dr. Brayle, sarcastically.

"Oh dear no! He seems quite well-bred, and I should say he must be very wealthy."

"A most powerful recommendation!" murmured Brayle—"The best in the world! What do YOU think of him?" he asked, turning suddenly to me.

"I have no opinion,"—I answered, quietly.

How could I say otherwise? How could I tell such a man as he was, of one who had entered my life as insistently as a flash of light, illumining all that had hitherto been dark!

At that moment Catherine caught my hand.

"Listen!" she whispered.

A window of the deck saloon was open and we stood near it. Dr. Brayle and Mr. Swinton had moved away to light fresh cigars, and we two women were for the moment alone. We heard Mr. Harland's voice raised to a sort of smothered cry.

"My God! You ARE Santoris!"

"Of course I am!" And the deep answering tones were full of music,— the music of a grave and infinitely tender compassion—"Why did you doubt it? And why call upon God? That is a name which has no meaning for you."

There followed a silence. I looked at Catherine and saw her pale face in the light of the moon, haggard in line and older than her years, and my heart was full of pity for her. She was excited beyond her usual self-I could see that the appearance of the stranger from the yacht had aroused her interest and compelled her admiration. I tried to draw her gently to a farther distance from the saloon, but she would not move.

"We ought not to listen,"—I said—"Catherine, come away!"

She shook her head.

"Hush!" she softly breathed—"I want to hear!"

Just then Mr. Harland spoke again.

"I am sorry!" he said—"I have wronged you and I apologise. But you can hardly wonder at my disbelief, considering your appearance, which is that of a much younger man than your actual years should make you."

The rich voice of Santoris gave answer.

"Did I not tell you and others long ago that for me there is no such thing as time, but only eternity? The soul is always young,—and I live in the Spirit of youth, not in the Matter of age."

Catherine turned her eyes upon me in wide-open amazement.

"He must be mad!" she said.

I made no reply either by word or look. We heard Mr. Harland talking, but in a lower tone, and we could not distinguish what he said. Presently Santoris answered, and his vibrant tones were clear and distinct.

"Why should it seem to you so wonderful?" he said—"You do not think it miraculous when the sculptor, standing before a shapeless block of marble, hews it out to conformity with his inward thought. The marble is mere marble, hard to deal with, difficult to shape,—yet out of its resisting roughness the thinker and worker can mould an Apollo or a Psyche. You find nothing marvellous in this, though the result of its shaping is due to nothing but Thought and Labour. Yet when you see the human body, which is far easier to shape than marble, brought into submission by the same forces of Thought and Labour, you are astonished! Surely it is a simpler matter to control the living cells of one's own fleshly organisation and compel them to do the bidding of the dominating spirit than to chisel the semblance of a god out of a block of stone!"

There was a pause after this. Then followed more inaudible talk on the part of Mr. Harland, and while we yet waited to gather further fragments of the conversation, he suddenly threw open the saloon door and called to us to come in. We at once obeyed the summons, and as we entered he said in a somewhat excited, nervous way:—

"I must apologise before you ladies for the rather doubting manner in which I received my former college friend! He IS Rafel Santoris— I ought to have known that there's only one of his type! But the curious part of it is that he should be nearly as old as I am,—yet somehow he is not!"

I laughed. It would have been hard not to laugh, for the mere idea of comparing the two men, Santoris in such splendid prime and Morton Harland in his bent, lean and wizened condition, as being of the same or nearly the same age was quite ludicrous. Even Catherine smiled—a weak and timorous smile.

"I suppose you have grown old more quickly, father," she said— "Perhaps Mr. Santoris has not lived at such high pressure."

Santoris, standing by the saloon centre table tinder the full blaze of the electric lamp, looked at her with a kindly interest.

"High or low, I live each moment of my days to the full, Miss Harland,"—he said—"I do not drowse it or kill it—I LIVE it! This lady,"—and he turned his eyes towards me—"looks as if she did the same!"

"She does!" said Mr. Harland, quickly, and with emphasis—"That's quite true! You were always a good reader of character, Santoris! I believe I have not introduced you properly to our little friend"— here he presented me by name and I held out my hand. Santoris took it in his own with a light, warm clasp—gently releasing it again as he bowed. "I call her our little friend, because she brings such an atmosphere of joy along with her wherever she goes. We persuaded her to come with us yachting this summer for a very selfish reason— because we are disposed to be dull and she is always bright,—the advantage, you see, is all on our side! Oddly enough, I was talking to her about you the other night—the very night, by the by, that your yacht came behind us off Mull. That was rather a curious coincidence when you come to think of it!"

"Not curious at all,"—said Santoris—"but perfectly natural. When will you realise that there is no such thing as 'coincidence' but only a very exact system of mathematics?"

Mr. Harland gave a slight, incredulous gesture.

"Your theories again," he said—"You hold to them still! But our little friend is likely to agree with you,—when I was speaking of you to her I told her she had somewhat the same ideas as yourself. She is a sort of a 'psychist'—whatever that may mean!"

"Do you not know?" queried Santoris, with a grave smile—"It is easy to guess by merely looking at her!"

My cheeks grew warm and my eyes fell beneath his steadfast gaze. I wondered whether Mr. Harland or Catherine would notice that in his coat he wore a small bunch of the same kind of bright pink bell- heather which was my only 'jewel of adorning' that night. The ice of introductory recognition being broken, we gath- ered round the saloon table and sat down, while the steward brought wine and other refreshments to offer to our guest. Mr. Harland's former uneasiness and embarrassment seemed now at an end, and he gave himself up to the pleasure of renewing association with one who had known him as a young man, and they began talking easily together of their days at college, of the men they had both been acquainted with, some of whom were dead, some settled abroad and some lost to sight in the vistas of uncertain fate. Catherine took very little part in the conversation, but she listened intently—her colourless eyes were for once bright, and she watched the face of Santoris as one might watch an animated picture. Presently Dr. Brayle and Mr. Swinton, who had been pacing the deck together and smoking, paused near the saloon door. Mr. Harland beckoned them.

"Come in, come in!" he said—"Santoris, this is my physician, Dr. Brayle, who has undertaken to look after me during this trip,"— Santoris bowed—"And this is my secretary, Mr. Swinton, whom I sent over to your yacht just now." Again Santoris bowed. His slight, yet perfectly courteous salutation, was in marked contrast with the careless modern nod or jerk of the head by which the other men barely acknowledged their introduction to him. "He was afraid of his life to go to you"—continued Mr. Harland, with a laugh—"He thought you might be an illusion—or even the devil himself, with those fiery sails!" Mr. Swinton looked sheepish; Santoris smiled. "This fair dreamer of dreams"—here he singled me out for notice—"is the only one of us who has not expressed either surprise or fear at the sight of your vessel or the possible knowledge of yourself, though there was one little incident connected with the pretty bunch of bell-heather she is wearing— why!—you wear the same flower yourself!"

There was a moment's silence. Everyone stared. The blood burned in my veins,— I felt my face crimsoning, yet I knew not why I should be embarrassed or at a loss for words. Santoris came to my relief.

"There's nothing remarkable in that, is there?" he queried, lightly- -"Bell-heather is quite common in this part of the world. I shouldn't like to try and count up the number of tourists I've lately seen wearing it!"

"Ah, but you don't know the interest attaching to this particular specimen!" persisted Mr. Harland—"It was given to our little friend by a wild Highland fellow, presumably a native of Mull, the very morning after she had seen your yacht for the first time, and he told her that on the previous night he had brought all of the same kind he could gather to you! Surely you see the connection?"

Santoris shook his head.

"I'm afraid I don't!" he said, smilingly. "Did the 'wild Highland fellow' name me?"

"No—I believe he called you 'the shentleman that owns the yacht.'"

"Oh well!" and Santoris laughed—"There are so many 'shentlemen' that own yachts! He may have got mixed in his customers. In any case, I am glad to have some little thing in common with your friend—if only a bunch of heather!"

"HER bunch behaves very curiously,"—put in Catherine—"It never fades."

Santoris made no comment. It seemed as if he had not heard, or did not wish to hear. He changed the conversation, much to my comfort, and for the rest of the time he stayed with us, rather avoided speaking to me, though once or twice I met his eyes fixed earnestly upon me. The talk drifted in a desultory manner round various ordinary topics, and I, moving a little aside, took a seat near the window where I could watch the moon-rays striking a steel-like glitter on the still waters of Loch Scavaig, and at the same time hear all that was being said without taking any part in it. I did not wish to speak,—the uplifted joy of my soul was too intense for anything but silence. I could not tell why I was so happy,—I only knew by inward instinct that some point in my life had been reached towards which I had striven for a far longer period than I myself was aware of. There was nothing for me now but to wait with faith and patience for the next step forward—a step which I felt would not be taken alone. And I listened with interest while Mr. Harland put his former college friend through a kind of inquisitorial examination as to what he had been doing and where he had been journeying since they last met. Santoris seemed not at all unwilling to be catechised.

"When I escaped from Oxford,"—he said—but here Mr. Harland interposed.

"Escaped!" he exclaimed—"You talk as if you had been kept in prison."

"So I was"—Santoris replied—"Oxford is a prison, to all who want to feed on something more than the dry bones of learning. While there I was like the prodigal son,—exiled from my Father's House. And I 'did eat the husks that the swine did eat.' Many fellows have to do the same. Sometimes—though not often—a man arrives with a constitution unsuited to husks. Mine was—and is—such an one."

"You secured honours with the husks," said Mr. Harland.

Santoris gave a gesture of airy contempt.

"Honours! Such honours! Any fellow unaddicted to drinking, with a fair amount of determined plod could win them. The alleged 'difficulties' in the way are perfectly childish. They scarcely deserve to be called the pothooks and hangers of an education. I always got my work done in two or three hours—the rest of my time at college was pure leisure,—which I employed in other and wiser forms of study than those of the general curriculum—as you know."

"You mean occult mysteries and things of that sort?"

"'Occult' is a word of such new coinage that it is not found in many dictionaries,"—said Santoris, with a mirthful look—"You will not find it, for instance, in the earlier editions of Stormonth's reliable compendium. I do not care for it myself; I prefer to say 'Spiritual science.'"

"You believe in that?" asked Catherine, abruptly.

"Assuredly! How can I do otherwise, seeing that it is the Key to the Soul of Nature?" "That's too deep for me!" said Dr. Brayle, pouring himself out a glass of whisky and mixing it with soda-water—"If it's a riddle I give it up!"

Santoris was silent. There was a moment's pause. Then Catherine leaned forward across the table, looking at him with tired, questioning eyes.

"Could you not explain?" she murmured.

"Easily!" he answered—"Anyone can understand it with a little attention. What I mean is this,—you know that the human body outwardly expresses its inward condition of health, mentality and spirituality—well, in exactly the same way Nature, in her countless varying presentations of beauty and wisdom, expresses the Soul of herself, or the spiritual force which supports her existence. 'Spiritual science' is the knowledge, not of the outward effect so much as of the inward cause which makes the effect manifest. It is a knowledge which can be applied to the individual daily uses of life,—the more it is studied, the more reward it bestows, and the smallest portion of it thoroughly mastered, is bound to lead to some discovery, simple or complex, which lifts the immortal part of a man a step higher on the way it should go."

"You are satisfied with your researches, then?" asked Mr. Harland.

Santoris smiled gravely.

"Do I look like a man that has failed?" he answered.

Mr. Harland studied his handsome face and figure with ill-concealed envy.

"You went abroad from Oxford?" he queried.

"Yes. I went back to the old home in Egypt—the house where I was born and bred. It had been well kept and cared for by the faithful servant to whom my father had entrusted it—as well kept as a Royal Chamber in the Pyramids with the funeral offerings untouched and a perpetual lamp burning. It was the best of all possible places in which to continue my particular line of work without inter-ruption— and I have stayed there most of the time, only coming away, as now, when necessary for a change and a look at the world as the world lives in these days."

"And"—here Mr. Harland hesitated, then went on—"Are you married?"

Santoris lifted his eyes and regarded his former college acquaintance fixedly.

"That question is unnecessary"—he said—"You know I am not."

There was a brief awkward pause. Dr. Brayle looked up with a satirical smile.

"Spiritual science has probably taught you to beware of the fair sex"—he said.

"I do not entirely understand you"—answered Santoris, coldly—"But if you mean that I am not a lover of women in the plural you are right."

"Perhaps of the one woman—the one rare pearl in the deep sea"— hinted Dr. Brayle, unabashed.

"Come, you are getting too personal, Brayle," interrupted Mr. Harland, quickly, and with asperity—"Santoris, your health!"

He raised a glass of wine to his lips—Santoris did the same—and this simple courtesy between the two principals in the conversation had the effect of putting their subordinate in his proper place.

"It seems superfluous to wish health to Mr. Santoris," said Catherine then—"He evidently has it in perfection."

Santoris looked at her with kindly interest.

"Health is a law, Miss Harland"—he said—"It is our own fault if we trespass against it."

"Ah, you say that because you are well and strong," she answered, in a plaintive tone—"But if you were afflicted and suffering you would take a different view of illness."

He smiled, somewhat compassionately.

"I think not,"—he said—"If I were afflicted and suffering, as you say, I should know that by my own neglect, thoughtlessness, carelessness or selfishness I had injured my organisation mentally and physically, and that, therefore, the penalty demanded was just and reasonable."

"Surely you do not maintain that a man is responsible for his own ailments?" said Mr. Harland—"That would be too far-fetched, even for YOU! Why, as a matter of fact a wretched human being is not only cursed with his own poisoned blood but with the poisoned blood of his forefathers, and, according to the latest medical science, the very air and water swarm with germs of death for the unsuspecting victim."

"Or germs of life!" said Santoris, quietly—"According to my knowledge or 'theory,' as you prefer to call it, there are no germs of actual death. There are germs which disintegrate effete forms of matter merely to allow the forces of life to rebuild them again—and these may propagate in the human system if it so happens that the human system is prepared to receive them. Their devastating process is called disease, but they never begin their work till the being they attack has either wasted a vital opportunity or neglected a vital necessity. Far more numerous are the beneficial germs of revivifying and creative power—and if these find place, they are bound to conquer those whose agency is destructive. It all depends on the soil and pasture you offer them. Evil thoughts make evil blood, and in evil blood disease germinates and flourishes. Pure thoughts make pure blood and rebuild the cells of health and vitality. I grant you there is such a thing as inherited disease, but this could be prevented in a great measure by making the marriage of diseased persons a criminal offence,—while much of it could be driven out by proper care in childhood. Unfortunately, the proper care is seldom given."

"What would you call proper care?" asked Catherine.

"Entire absence of self-indulgence, to begin with,"—he answered— "No child should be permitted to have its own way or expect to have it. The first great lesson of life should be renunciation of self."

A faint colour crept into Catherine's faded cheeks. Mr. Harland fidgeted in his chair.

"Unless a man looks after himself, no one else will look after him"- -he said.

"Reasonable care of one's self is UNselfishness," replied Santoris— "But anything in excess of reasonable care is pure vice. A man should work for his livelihood chiefly in order not to become a burden on others. In the same way he should take care of his health so that he may avoid being a troublesome invalid, dependent on others' compassion. To be ill is to acknowledge neglect of existing laws and incapacity of resistance to evil."

"You lay down a very hard and fast rule, Mr. Santoris"—said Dr. Brayle—"Many unfortunate people are ill through no fault of their own."

"Pardon me for my dogmatism when I say such a thing is impossible"— answered Santoris—"If a human being starts his life in health he cannot be ill UNLESS through some fault of his own. It may be a moral or a physical fault, but the trespass against the law has been made. And suppose him to be born with some inherited trouble, he can eliminate even that from his blood if he so determines. Man was not meant to be sickly, but strong—he is not intended to dwell on this earth as a servant but as a master,—and all the elements of strength and individual sovereignty are contained in Nature for his use and advantage if he will but accept them as frankly as they are offered ungrudgingly. I cannot grant you "—and he smiled—"even the smallest amount of voluntary or intended mischief in the Divine plan!"

At that moment Captain Derrick looked in at the saloon door to remind us that the boat was still waiting to take our visitor back to his own yacht. He rose at once, with a briefly courteous apology for having stayed so long, and we all vent with him to see him off. It was arranged that we were to join him on board his vessel next day, and either take a sail with him along the island coast or else do the excursion on foot to Loch Coruisk, which was a point not to be missed. As we walked all together along the moonlit deck a chance moment placed him by my side while the others were moving on ahead. I felt rather than saw his eyes upon me, and looked up swiftly in obedience to his compelling glance. There was a light of eloquent meaning in the expression of his face, but he spoke in perfectly conventional tones:—

"I am glad to have met you at last,"—he said, quietly—"I have known you by name—and in the spirit—a long time."

I did not answer. My heart was beating rapidly with an excitation of nameless joy and fear commingled.

"To-morrow"—he went on—"we shall be able to talk together, I hope,—I feel that there are many things in which we are mutually interested."

Still I could not speak.

"Sometimes it happens"—he continued, in a voice that trembled a little—"that two people who are not immediately conscious of having met before, feel on first introduction to each other as if they were quite old friends. Is it not so?"

I murmured a scarcely audible assent.

He bent his head and looked at me searchingly,—a smile was on his lips and his eyes were full of tenderness.

"Till to-morrow is not long to wait,"—he said—"Not long—after so many years! Good-night!"

A sense of calm and sweet assurance swept over me.

"Good-night!" I answered, with a smile of happy response to his own- -"Till to-morrow!"

We were close to the gangway where the others already stood. In another couple of minutes he had made his adieux to our whole party and was on his way back to his own vessel. The boat in which he sat, rowed strongly by our men, soon disappeared like a black blot on the general darkness of the water, yet we remained for some time watching, as though we could see it even when it was no longer visible.

"A strange fellow!" said Dr. Brayle when we moved away at last, flinging the end of his cigar over the yacht side—"Something of madness and genius combined."

Mr. Harland turned quickly upon him.

"You mistake,"—he answered—"There's no madness, though there is certainly genius. He's of the same mind as he was when I knew him at college. There never was a saner or more brilliant scholar."

"It's curious you should meet him again like this,"—said Catherine- -"But surely, father, he's not as old as you are?"

"He's about three and a half years younger—that's all."

Dr. Brayle laughed.

"I don't believe it for a moment!" he said—"I think he's playing a part. He's probably not the man you knew at Oxford at all."

We were then going to our cabins for the night, and Mr. Harland paused as these words were said and faced us.

"He IS the man!"—he said, emphatically—"I had my doubts of him at first, but I was wrong. As for 'playing a part,' that would be impossible to him. He is absolutely truthful—almost to the verge of cruelty!" A curious expression came into his eyes, as of hidden fear. "In one way I am glad to have met him again— in another I am sorry. For he is a disturber of the comfortable peace of conventions. You"—here he regarded me suddenly, as if he had almost forgotten my presence—"will like him. You have many ideas in common and will be sure to get on well together. As for me, I am his direct opposite,—the two poles are not wider apart than we are in our feelings, sentiments and beliefs." He paused, seeming to be troubled by the passing cloud of some painful thought—then he went on— "There is one thing I should perhaps explain, especially to you, Brayle, to save useless argument. It is, of course, a 'craze'—but craze or not, he is absolutely immovable on one point which he calls the great Fact of Life,—that there is and can be no Death,—that Life is eternal and therefore in all its forms indestructible."

"Does he consider himself immune from the common lot of mortals?" asked Dr. Brayle, with a touch of derision.

"He denies 'the common lot' altogether"—replied Mr. Harland—"For him, each individual life is a perpetual succession of progressive changes, and he holds that a change IS never and CAN never be made till the person concerned has prepared the next 'costume' or mortal presentment of immortal being, according to voluntary choice and liking."

"Then he is mad!" exclaimed Catherine. "He must be mad!"

I smiled.

"Then I am mad too,"—I said—"For I believe as he does. May I say good-night?"

And with that I left them, glad to be alone with myself and my heart's secret rapture.

VII

MEMORIES

Perfect happiness is the soul's acceptance of a sense of joy without question. And this is what I felt through all my being on that never-to-be-forgotten night. Just as a tree may be glad of the soft wind blowing its leaves, or a daisy in the grass may rejoice in the warmth of the sun to which it opens its golden heart without either being able to explain the delicious ecstasy, so I was the recipient of light and exquisite felicity which could have no explanation or analysis. I did not try to think,—it was enough for me simply to BE. I realised, of course, that with the Harlands and their two paid attendants, the materialist Dr. Brayle, and the secretarial machine, Swinton, Rafel Santoris could have nothing in common,—and as I know, by daily experience, that not even the most trifling event happens without a predestined cause for its occurrence and a purpose in its result, I was sure that the reason for his coming into touch with us at all was to be found in connection, through some mysterious intuition, with myself. However, as I say, I did not think about it,—I was content to breathe the invigorating air of peace and serenity in which my spirit seemed to float on wings. I slept like a child who is only tired out with play and pleasure,—I woke like a child to whom the world is all new and brimful of beauty. That it was a sunny day seemed right and natural—clouds and rain could hardly have penetrated the brilliant atmosphere in which I lived and moved. It was an atmosphere of my own creating, of course, and therefore not liable to be disturbed by storms unless I chose. It is possible for every human being to live in the sunshine of the soul whatever may be the material surroundings of the body. The so-called 'practical' person would have said to me:—'Why are you happy?' There is no real cause for this sudden elation. You think you have met someone who is in sympathy with your tastes, ideas and feel-ings,—but you may be quite wrong, and this bright wave of joy into which you are plunging heedlessly may fling you bruised and broken on a desolate shore for the remainder of your life. One would think you had fallen in love at first sight.

To which I should have replied that there is no such thing as falling in love at first sight,—that the very expression—'falling in love'—conveys a false idea, and that what the world generally calls 'love' is not love at all. Moreover, there was noth-ing in my heart or mind with regard to Rafel Santoris save a keen interest and sense of friendship. I was sure that his beliefs were the same as mine, and that he had been working along the same lines which I had endeavoured to follow; and just as two musicians, inspired by a mutual love of their art, may be glad to play their instruments together in time and tune, even so I felt that he and I had met on a plane of thought where we had both for a long time been separately wan-dering.

The 'Dream' yacht, with its white sails spread ready for a cruise, was as beautiful by day in the sunshine under a blue sky as by night with its own electric radiance flashing its outline against the stars, and I was eager to be on board. We were, however, delayed by an 'attack of nerves' on the part of Catherine, who during the morning was seized with a violent fit of hysteria to which she completely gave way, sobbing, laughing and gasping for breath in a manner which showed her to be quite unhinged and swept from self- control. Dr. Brayle took her at once in charge, while Mr. Harland fumed and fretted, pacing up and down in the saloon with an angry face and brooding eyes. He looked at me where I stood waiting, ready dressed for the excursion of the day, and said:

"I'm sorry for all this worry. Catherine gets worse and worse. Her nerves tear her to pieces."

"She allows them to do so,"—I answered—"And Dr. Brayle allows her to give them their way."

He shrugged his shoulders.

"You don't like Brayle,"—he said—"But he's clever, and he does his best."

"To keep his patients,"—I hinted, with a smile.

He turned on his heel and faced me.

"Well now, come!" he said—"Could YOU cure her?"

"I could have cured her in the beginning,"—I replied, "But hardly now. No one can cure her now but herself."

He paced up and down again.

"She won't be able to go with us to visit Santoris," he said—"I'm sure of that."

"Shall we put it off?" I suggested.

His eyebrows went up in surprise at me.

"Why no, certainly not. It will be a change for you and a pleasure of which I would not deprive you. Besides, I want to go myself. But Catherine—"

Dr. Brayle here entered the saloon with his softest step and most professional manner.

"Miss Harland is better now,"—he said—"She will be quite calm in a few minutes. But she must remain quiet. It will not be safe for her to attempt any excursion today."

"Well, that need not prevent the rest of us from going."—said Mr. Harland.

"Oh no, certainly not! In fact, Miss Harland said she hoped you would go, and make her excuses to Mr. Santoris. I shall, of course, be in attendance on her."

"You won't come, then?"—and an unconscious look of relief brightened Mr. Harland's features—"And as Swinton doesn't wish to join us, we shall be only a party of three—Captain Derrick, myself and our little friend here. We may as well be off. Is the boat ready?"

We were informed that Mr. Santoris had sent his own boat and men to fetch us, and that they had been waiting for some few minutes. We at once prepared to go, and while Mr. Harland was getting his overcoat and searching for his field-glasses, Dr. Brayle spoke to me in a low tone—

"The truth of the matter is that Miss Harland has been greatly upset by the visit of Mr. Santoris and by some of the things he said last night. She could not sleep, and was exceedingly troubled in her mind by the most distressing thoughts. I am very glad she has decided not to see him again to-day."

"Do you consider his influence harmful?" I queried, somewhat amused.

"I consider him not quite sane,"—Dr. Brayle answered, coldly—"And highly nervous persons like Miss Harland are best without the society of clever but wholly irresponsible theorists."

The colour burned in my cheeks.

"You include me in that category, of course,"—I said, quietly—"For I said last night that if Mr. Santoris was mad, then I am too, for I hold the same views."

He smiled a superior smile.

"There is no harm in you,"—he answered, condescendingly—"You may think what you like,—you are only a woman. Very clever—very charming—and full of the most delightful fancies,—but weighted (fortunately) with the restrictions of your sex. I mean no offence, I assure you,—but a woman's 'views,' whatever they are, are never accepted by rational beings."

I laughed.

"I see! And rational beings must always be men!" I said—"You are quite certain of that?"

"In the fact that men ordain the world's government and progress, you have your answer,"—he replied.

"Alas, poor world!" I murmured—"Sometimes it rebels against the 'rationalism' of its rulers!"

Just then Mr. Harland called me, and I hastened to join him and Captain Derrick. The boat which was waiting for us was manned by four sailors who wore white jerseys trimmed with scarlet, bearing the name of the yacht to which they belonged—the 'Dream.' These men were dark-skinned and dark-eyed,—we took them at first for Portuguese or Malays, but they turned out to be from Egypt. They saluted us, but did not speak, and as soon as we were seated, pulled swiftly away across the water. Captain Derrick watched their movements with great interest and curiosity.

"Plenty of grit in those chaps,"—he said, aside to Mr. Harland— "Look at their muscular arms! I suppose they don't speak a word of English."

Mr. Harland thereupon tried one of them with a remark about the weather. The man smiled—and the sudden gleam of his white teeth gave a wonderful light and charm to his naturally grave cast of countenance.

"Beautiful day!"—he said,—"Very happy sky!"

This expression 'happy sky' attracted me. It recalled to my mind a phrase I had once read in the translation of an inscription found in an Egyptian sarcophagus—"The peace of the morning befriend thee, and the light of the sunset and the happiness of the sky." The words rang in my ears with an odd familiarity, like the verse of some poem loved and learned by heart in childhood.

In a very few minutes we were alongside the 'Dream' and soon on board, where Rafel Santoris received us with kindly courtesy and warmth of welcome. He expressed polite regret at the absence of Miss Harland—none for that of Dr. Brayle or Mr. Swinton—and then introduced us to his captain, an Italian named Marino Fazio, of whom Santoris said to us, smilingly:—

"He is a scientist as well as a skipper—and he needs to be both in the management of such a vessel as this. He will take Captain Derrick in his charge and explain to him the mystery of our brilliant appearance at night, and also the secret of our sailing without wind."

Fazio saluted, and smiled a cheerful response.

"Are you ready to start now?" he asked, speaking very good English with just the slightest trace of a foreign accent.

"Perfectly!"

Fazio lifted his hand with a sign to the man at the wheel. Another moment and the yacht began to move. Without the slightest noise,— without the grinding of ropes, or rattling of chains, or creaking boards, she swung gracefully round, and began to glide through the water with a swiftness that was almost incredible. The sails filled, though the air was intensely warm and stirless—an air in which any ordinary schooner would have been hopelessly becalmed,—and almost before we knew it we were out of Loch Scavaig and flying as though borne on the wings of some great white bird, all along the wild and picturesque coast of Skye towards Loch Bracadale. One of the most remarkable features about the yacht was the extraordinary lightness with which she skimmed the waves—she seemed to ride on their surface rather than part them with her keel. Everything on board expressed the finest taste as well as the most perfect convenience, and I saw Mr. Plarland gazing about him in utter amazement at the elegant sumptuousness of his surroundings. Santoris showed us all over the vessel, talking to us with the ease of quite an old friend.

"You know the familiar axiom,"—he said—"'Anything worth doing at all is worth doing well.' The 'Dream' was first of all nothing but a dream in my brain till I set to work with Fazio and made it a reality. Owing to our discovery of the way in which to compel the waters to serve us as our motive power, we have no blackening smoke or steam, so that our furniture and fittings are preserved from dinginess and tarnish. It was possible to have the saloon delicately painted, as you see,"—here he opened the door of the apartment mentioned, and we stepped into it as into a fairy palace. It was much loftier than the usual yacht saloon, and on all sides the windows were oval shaped, set in between the most exquisitely paint-ed panels of sea pieces, evidently the work of some great artist. Overhead the ceil-ing was draped with pale turquoise blue silk forming a canopy, which was gath-ered in rich folds on all four sides, having in its centre a crystal lamp in the shape of a star.

"You live like a king"—then said Mr. Harland, a trifle bitterly— "You know how to use your father's fortune."

"My father's fortune was made to be used," answered Santoris, with perfect good-humour—"And I think he is perfectly satisfied with my mode of expending it. But very little of it has been touched. I have made my own fortune."

"Indeed! How?" And Harland looked as he evidently felt, keenly interested.

"Ah, that's asking too much of me!" laughed Santoris. "You may be satisfied, how-ever, that it's not through defrauding my neighbours. It's comparatively easy to be rich if you have coaxed any of Mother Nature's secrets out of her. She is very kind to her children, if they are kind to her,—in fact, she spoils them, for the more they ask of her the more she gives. Besides, every man should make his own money even if he inherits wealth,—it is the only way to feel worthy of a place in this beautiful, ever-working world."

He preceded us out of the saloon and showed us the State-rooms, of which there were five, daintily furnished in white and blue and white and rose.

"These are for my guests when I have any," he said, "Which is very seldom. This for a princess—if ever one should honour me with her presence!"

And he opened a door on his right, through which we peered into a long, lovely room, gleaming with iridescent hues and sparkling with touches of gold and crystal. The bed was draped with cloudy lace through which a shimmer of pale rose-colour made itself visible, and the carpet of dark moss-green formed a perfect setting for the quaintly shaped furniture, which was all of sandal-wood inlaid with ivory. On a small table of carved ivory in the centre of the room lay a bunch of Madonna lilies tied with a finely twisted cord of gold. We murmured our admiration, and Santoris addressed himself directly to me for the first time since we had come on board.

"Will you go in and rest for a while till luncheon?" he said—"I placed the lilies there for your acceptance."

The colour rushed to my cheeks,—I looked up at him in a little wonderment.

"But I am not a princess!"

His eyes smiled down into mine.

"No? Then I must have dreamed you were!"

My heart gave a quick throb,—some memory touched my brain, but what it was I could not tell. Mr. Harland glanced at me and laughed.

"What did I tell you the other day?" he said—"Did I not call you the princess of a fairy tale? I was not far wrong!"

They left me to myself then, and as I stood alone in the beautiful room which had thus been placed at my disposal, a curious feeling came over me that these luxurious surroundings were, after all, not new to my experience. I had been accustomed to them for a great part of my life. Stay!—how foolish of me!—'a great part of my life'?— then what part of it? I briefly reviewed my own career,—a difficult and solitary childhood,—the hard and uphill work which became my lot as soon as I was old enough to work at all,—incessant study, and certainly no surplus of riches. Then where had I known luxury? I sank into a chair, dreamily considering. The floating scent of sandal-wood and the perfume of lilies commingled was like the breath of an odorous garden in the East, familiar to me long ago, and as I sat musing I became conscious of a sudden inrush of power and sense of dominance which lifted me as it were above myself, as though I had, without any warning, been given the full control of a great kingdom and its people. Catching sight of my own reflection in an opposite mirror, I was startled and almost afraid at the expression of my face, the proud light in my eyes, the smile on my lips.

"What am I thinking of!" I said, half aloud—"I am not my true self to-day,— some remnant of a cast-off pride has arisen in me and made me less of a humble student. I must not yield to this overpowering demand on my soul,—it is surely an evil suggestion which asserts itself like the warning pain or fever of an impending disease. Can it be the influence of Santoris? No!—I will never believe it!"

And yet a vague uneasiness beset me, and I rose and paced about restlessly,—then pausing where the lovely Madonna lilies lay on the ivory table, I remembered they had been put there for me. I raised them gently, inhaling their delicious fragrance, and as I did so, saw, lying immediately underneath them, a golden Cross of a mystic shape I knew well,—its upper half set on the face of a seven- pointed Star, also of gold. With joy I took it up and kissed it reverently, and as I compared it with the one I always secretly wore on my own person, I knew that all was well, and that I need have no distrust of Rafel Santoris. No injurious effect on my mind could possibly be exerted by his influence—and I was thrown back on myself for a clue to that singular wave of feeling, so entirely contrary to my own disposition, which had for a moment overwhelmed me. I could not trace its source, but I speedily conquered it. Fastening one of the snowy lilies in my waistband, as a contrast to the bright bit of bell-heather which I cherished even more than if it were a jewel, I presently went up on deck, where I found my host, Mr. Harland, Captain Derrick and Marino Fazio all talking animatedly together.

"The mystery is cleared up,"—said Mr. Harland, addressing me as I approached—"Captain Derrick is satisfied. He has learned how one of the finest schooners he has ever seen can make full speed in any weather without wind."

"Oh no, I haven't learned how to do it,—I'm a long way off that!"— said Derrick, good-humouredly—"But I've seen how it's done. And it's marvellous! If that invention could be applied to all ships—"

"Ah!—but first of all it would be necessary to instruct the shipbuilders!"—put in Fazio—"They would have to learn their trade all over again. Our yacht looks as though she were built on the same lines as all yachts,—but you know—you have seen—she is entirely different!"

Captain Derrick gave a nod of grave emphasis. Santoris meantime had come to my side. Our glances met,—he saw that I had received and understood the message of the lilies, and a light and colour came into his eyes that made them beautiful.

"Men have not yet fully enjoyed their heritage," he said, taking up the conversation—"Our yacht's motive power seems complex, but in reality it is very simple,—and the same force which propels this light vessel would propel the biggest liner afloat. Nature has given us all the materials for every kind of work and progress, physical and mental—but because we do not at once comprehend them we deny their uses. Nothing in the air, earth or water exists which we may not press into our service,—and it is in the study of natural forces that we find our conquest. What hundreds of years it took us to discover the wonders of steam!—how the discoverer was mocked and laughed at!—yet it was not really 'wonderful'—it was always there, waiting to be employed, and wasted by mere lack of human effort. One can say the same of electricity, sometimes called 'miraculous'—it is no miracle, but perfectly common and natural, only we have, until now, failed to apply it to our needs,—and even when wider disclosures of science are being made to us every day, we still bar knowledge by obstinacy, and remain in ignorance rather than learn. A few grains in weight of hydrogen have power enough to raise a million tons to a height of more than three hundred feet,—and if we could only find a way to liberate economically and with discretion the various forces which Spirit and Matter contain, we might change the whole occupation of man and make of him less a labourer than thinker, less mortal than angel! The wildest fairy-tales might come true, and earth be transformed into a paradise! And as for motive power, in a thimbleful of concentrated fuel we might take the largest ship across the widest ocean. I say if we could only find a way! Some think they are finding it—"

"You, for example?"—suggested Mr. Harland.

He laughed.

"I—if you like!—for example! Will you come to luncheon?"

He led the way, and Mr. Harland and I followed. Captain Derrick, who I saw was a little afraid of him, had arranged to take his luncheon with Fazio and the other officers of the crew apart. We were waited upon by dark-skinned men attired in the picturesque costume of the East, who performed their duties with noiseless grace and swiftness. The yacht had for some time slackened speed, and appeared to be merely floating lazily on the surface of the calm water. We were told she could always do this and make almost imperceptible headway, provided there was no impending storm in the air. It seemed as if we were scarcely moving, and the whole atmosphere surrounding us expressed the most delicious tranquillity. The luncheon prepared for us was of the daintiest and most elegant description, and Mr. Harland, who on account of his ill-health seldom had any appetite, enjoyed it with a zest and heartiness I had never seen him display before. He particularly appreciated the wine, a rich, ruby-coloured beverage which was unlike anything I had ever tasted.

"There is nothing remarkable about it,"—said Santoris, I when questioned as to its origin—"It is simply REAL wine,—though you may say that of itself is remarkable, there being none in the market. It is the pure juice of the grape, pre-pared in such a manner as to nourish the blood without inflaming it. It can do you no harm,—in fact, for you, Harland, it is an excellent thing."

"Why for me in particular?" queried Harland, rather sharply.

"Because you need it,"—answered Santoris—"My dear fellow, you are not in the best of health. And you will never get better under your present treatment."

I looked up eagerly.

"That is what I, too, have thought,"—I said—"only I dared not express it!"

Mr. Harland surveyed me with an amused smile.

"Dared not! I know nothing you would not dare!—but with all your boldness, you are full of mere theories,—and theories never made an ill man well yet."

Santoris exchanged a swift glance with me. Then he spoke:—

"Theory without practice is, of course, useless,"—he said—"But surely you can see that this lady has reached a certain plane of thought on which she herself dwells in health and content? And can she not serve you as an object lesson?"

"Not at all,"—replied Mr. Harland, almost testily—"She is a woman whose life has been immersed in study and contemplation, and because she has allowed her-self to forego many of the world's pleasures she can be made happy by a mere nothing—a handful of roses—or the sound of sweet music—"

"Are they 'nothings'?"—interrupted Santoris.

"To business men they are—"

"And business itself? Is it not also from some points of view a 'nothing'?"

"Santoris, if you are going to be 'transcendental' I will have none of you!" said Mr. Harland, with a vexed laugh—"What I wish to say is merely this—that my little friend here, for whom I have a great esteem, let me assure her!—is not really capable of forming an opinion of the condition of a man like myself, nor can she judge of the treatment likely to benefit me. She does not even know the nature of my illness—but I can see that she has taken a dislike to my physician, Brayle—"

"I never 'take dislikes,' Mr. Harland,"—I interrupted, quickly—"I merely trust to a guiding instinct which tells me when a man is sincere or when he is acting a part. That's all."

"Well, you've decided that Brayle is not sincere,"—he replied—"And you hardly think him clever. But if you would consider the point logically—you might enquire what motive could he possibly have for playing the humbug with me?"

Santoris smiled.

"Oh, man of 'business'! YOU can ask that?"

We were at the end of luncheon,—the servants had retired, and Mr. Harland was sipping his coffee and smoking a cigar.

"You can ask that?" he repeated—"You, a millionaire, with one daughter who is your sole heiress, can ask what motive a man like Brayle,—worldly, calculating and without heart—has in keeping you both—both, I say—you and your daughter equally—in his medical clutches?"

Mr. Harland's sharp eyes flashed with a sudden menace.

"If I thought—" he began—then he broke off. Presently he resumed— "You are not aware of the true state of affairs, Santoris. Wizard and scientist as you are, you cannot know everything! I need constant medical attendance—and my disease is incurable—"

"No!"—said Santoris, quietly—"Not incurable."

A sudden hope illumined Harland's worn and haggard face.

"Not incurable! But—my good fellow, you don't even know what it is!"

"I do. I also know how it began, and when,—how it has progressed, and how it will end. I know, too, how it can be checked—cut off in its development, and utterly destroyed,—but the cure would depend on yourself more than on Dr. Brayle or any other physician. At present no good is being done and much harm. For instance, you are in pain now?"

"I am—but how can you tell?"

"By the small, almost imperceptible lines on your face which contract quite unconsciously to yourself. I can stop that dreary suffering at once for you, if you will let me."

"Oh, I will 'let' you, certainly!" and Mr. Harland smiled incredulously,—"But I think you over-estimate your abilities."

"I was never a boaster,"—replied Santoris, cheerfully—"But you shall keep whatever opinion you like of me." And he drew from his pocket a tiny crystal phial set in a sheath of gold. "A touch of this in your glass of wine will make you feel a new man."

We watched him with strained attention as he carefully allowed two small drops of liquid, bright and clear as dew to fall one after the other into Mr. Harland's glass.

"Now,"—he continued—"drink without fear, and say good-bye to all pain for at least forty-eight hours."

With a docility quite unusual to him Mr. Harland obeyed.

"May I go on smoking?" he asked.

"You may."

A minute passed, and Mr. Harland's face expressed a sudden surprise and relief.

"Well! What now?" asked Santoris—"How is the pain?"

"Gone!" he answered—"I can hardly believe it—but I'm bound to admit it!"

"That's right! And it will not come back—not to-day, at any rate, nor to-morrow. Shall we go on deck now?"

We assented. As we left the saloon he said:

"You must see the glow of the sunset over Loch Coruisk. It's always a fine sight and it promises to be specially fine this evening,— there are so many picturesque clouds floating about. We are turning back to Loch Scavaig,—and when we get there we can land and do the rest of the excursion on foot. It's not much of a climb; will you feel equal to it?"

This question he put to me personally.

I smiled.

"Of course! I feel equal to anything! Besides, I've been very lazy on board the 'Diana,' taking no real exercise. A walk will do me good."

Mr. Harland seated himself in one of the long reclining chairs which were placed temptingly under an awning on deck. His eyes were clearer and his face more composed than I had ever seen it.

"Those drops you gave me are magical, Santoris!"—he said—"I wish you'd let me have a supply!"

Santoris stood looking down upon him kindly.

"It would not be safe for you,"—he answered—"The remedy is a sovereign one if used very rarely, and with extreme caution, but in uninstructed hands it is dangerous. Its work is to stimulate certain cells—at the same time (like all things taken in excess) it can destroy them. Moreover, it would not agree with Dr. Brayle's medicines."

"You really and truly think Brayle an impostor?"

"Impostor is a strong word! No!—I will give him credit for believing in himself up to a certain point. But of course he knows that the so-called 'electric' treatment he is giving to your daughter is perfectly worthless, just as he knows that she is not really ill."

"Not really ill!"

Mr. Harland almost bounced up in his chair, while I felt a secret thrill of satisfaction. "Why, she's been a miserable, querulous invalid for years—"

"Since she broke off her engagement to a worthless rascal"—said Santoris, calmly. "You see, I know all about it."

I listened, astonished. How did he know, how could he know, the intimate details of a life like Catherine's which could scarcely be of interest to a man such as he was?

"Your daughter's trouble is written on her face"—he went on— "Warped affections, slain desires, disappointed hopes,—and neither the strength nor the will to turn these troubles to blessings. Therefore they resemble an army of malarious germs which are eating away her moral fibre. Brayle knows that what she needs is the belief that someone has an interest not only in her, but in the particularly morbid view she has taught herself to take of life. He is actively showing that interest. The rest is easy,—and will be easier when—well!—when you are gone."

Mr. Harland was silent, drawing slow whiffs from his cigar. After a long pause, he said—

"You are prejudiced, and I think you are mistaken. You only saw the man for a few minutes last night, and you know nothing of him—"

"Nothing,—except what he is bound to reveal,"—answered Santoris.

"What do you mean?"

"You will not believe me if I tell you,"—and Santoris, drawing a chair close to mine, sat down,—"Yet I am sure this lady, who is your friend and guest, will corroborate what I say,—though, of course, you will not believe HER! In fact, my dear Harland, as you have schooled yourself to believe NOTHING, why urge me to point out a truth you decline to accept? Had you lived in the time of Galileo you would have been one of his torturers!"

"I ask you to explain," said Mr. Harland, with a touch of pique— "Whether I accept your explanation or not is my own affair."

"Quite!" agreed Santoris, with a slight smile—"As I told you long ago at Oxford, a man's life is his own affair entirely. He can do what he likes with it. But he can no more command the RESULT of what he does with it than the sun can conceal its rays. Each individual human being, male and female alike, moves unconsciously in the light of self-revealment, as though all his or her faults and virtues were reflected like the colours in a prism, or were set out in a window for passers-by to gaze upon. Fortunately for the general peace of society, however, most passers-by are not gifted with the sight to see the involuntary display."

"You speak in enigmas," said Harland, impatiently—"And I'm not good at guessing them."

Santoris regarded him fixedly. His eyes were luminous and compassionate.

"The simplest truths are to you 'enigmas,'" he said, regretfully—"A pity it is so! You ask me what I mean when I say a man is 'bound to reveal himself.' The process of self-revealment accompanies self- existence, as much as the fragrance of a rose accompanies its opening petals. You can never detach yourself from your own enveloping aura neither in body nor in soul. Christ taught this when He said:—'Let your light so shine before men that they may see your good works and glorify your Father which is in heaven.' Your 'light'—remember!—that word 'light' is not used here as a figure of speech but as a statement of fact. A positive 'light' surrounds you—it is exhaled and produced by your physical and moral being,— and those among us who have cultivated their inner organs of vision see IT before they see YOU. It can be of the purest radiance,— equally it can be a mere nebulous film,—but whatever the moral and physical condition of the man or woman concerned it is always shown in the aura which each separate individual expresses for himself or herself. In this way Dr. Brayle reveals his nature to me as well as the chief tendency of his thoughts,—in this way YOU reveal yourself and your present state of health,—it is a proved test that cannot go wrong."

Mr. Harland listened with his usual air of cynical tolerance and incredulity.

"I have heard this sort of nonsense before,"—he said—"I have even read in otherwise reliable scientific journals about the 'auras' of people affecting us with antipathies or sympathies for or against them. But it's a merely fanciful suggestion and has no foundation in reality."

"Why did you wish me to explain, then?" asked Santoris—"I can only tell you what I know, and—what I see!"

Harland moved restlessly, holding his cigar between his fingers and looking at it curiously to avoid, as I thought, the steadfast brilliancy of the compelling eyes that were fixed upon him.

"These 'auras,'" he went on, indifferently, "are nothing but suppositions. I grant you that certain discoveries are being made concerning the luminosity of trees and plants which in some states of the atmosphere give out rays of light,—but that human beings do the same I decline to believe."

"Of course!" and Santoris leaned back in his chair easily, as though at once dismissing the subject from his mind—"A man born blind must needs decline to believe in the pleasures of sight."

Harland's wrinkled brow deepened its furrows in a frown.

"Do you mean to tell me,—do you DARE to tell me"—he said—"that you see any 'aura,' as you call it, round my personality?"

"I do, most assuredly,"—answered Santoris—"I see it as distinctly as I see yourself in the midst of it. But there is no actual light in it,—it is mere grey mist,—a mist of miasma."

"Thank you!" and Harland laughed harshly—"You are complimentary!"

"Is it a time for compliments?" asked Santoris, with sudden sternness—"Harland, would you have me tell you ALL?"

Harland's face grew livid. He threw up his hand with a warning gesture.

"No!" he said, almost violently. He clutched the arm of his chair with a nervous grip, and for one instant looked like a hunted creature caught red-handed in some act of crime. Recovering himself quickly, he forced a smile.

"What about our little friend's 'aura'?"-he queried, glancing at me- -"Does she 'express' herself in radiance?"

Santoris did not reply for a moment. Then he turned his eyes towards me almost wistfully.

"She does!"—he answered—"I wish you could see her as I see her!"

There was a moment's silence. My face grew warm, and I was vaguely embarrassed, but I met his gaze fully and frankly.

"And _I_ wish I could see myself as you see me,"—I said, half laughingly—"For I am not in the least aware of my own aura."

"It is not intended that anyone should be visibly aware of it in their own personality,"—he answered—"But I think it is right we should realise the existence of
these radiant or cloudy exhalations which we ourselves weave around ourselves, so
that we may 'walk in the light as children of the light.'"

His voice sank to a grave and tender tone which checked Mr. Harland in something he was evidently about to say, for he bit his lip and was silent.

I rose from my chair and moved away then, looking—from the smooth deck of
the 'Dream' shadowed by her full white sails out to the peaks of the majestic hills
whose picturesque beauties are sung in the wild strains of Ossian, and the projecting crags, deep hollows and lofty pinnacles outlining the coast with its numerous waterfalls, lochs and shadowy creeks. A thin and delicate haze of mist hung
over the land like a pale violet veil through which the sun shot beams of rose and
gold, giving a vaporous unsubstantial effect to the scenery as though it were gliding with us like a cloud pageant on the surface of the calm water. The shores of
Loch Scavaig began to be dimly seen in the distance, and presently Captain
Derrick approached Mr. Harland, spy-glass in hand.

"The 'Diana' must have gone for a cruise,"—he said, in rather a perturbed way—
"As far as I can make out, there's no sign of her where we left her this morning."

Mr. Harland heard this indifferently.

"Perhaps Catherine wished for a sail,"—he answered. "There are plenty on board
to manage the vessel. You're not anxious?"

"Oh, not at all, sir, if you are satisfied,"—Derrick answered.

Mr. Harland stretched himself luxuriously in his chair.

"Personally, I don't mind where the 'Diana' has gone to for the moment,"—he
said, with a laugh—"I'm particularly comfortable where I am. Santoris!"

"Here!" And Santoris, who had stepped aside to give some order to one of his
men, came up at the call.

"What do you say to leaving me on board while you and my little friend go and
see your sunset effect on Loch Coruisk by yourselves?"

Santoris heard this suggestion with an amused look.

"You don't care for sunsets?"

"Oh yes, I do,—in a way. But I've seen so many of them—"

"No two alike"—put in Santoris.

"I daresay not. Still, I don't mind missing a few. Just now I should like a sound sleep rather than a sunset. It's very unsociable, I know,—but—" here he half closed his eyes and seemed inclined to doze off there and then.

Santoris turned to me.

"What do you say? Can you put up with my company for an hour or two and allow me to be your guide to Loch Coruisk? Or would you, too, rather not see the sunset?",

Our eyes met. A thrill of mingled joy and fear ran through me, and again I felt that strange sense of power and dominance which had previously overwhelmed me.

"Indeed, I have set my heart on going to Loch Coruisk"—I answered, lightly—
"And I cannot let you off your promise to take me there! We will leave Mr. Harland to his siesta."

"You're sure you do not mind?"—said Harland, then, opening his eyes drowsily—
"You will be perfectly safe with Santoris."

I smiled. I did not need that assurance. And I talked gaily with Captain Derrick on the subject of the 'Diana' and the course of her possible cruise, while he scanned the waters in search of her,—and I watched with growing impatience our gradual approach to Loch Scavaig, which in the bright afternoon looked scarcely less dreary than at night, especially now that the 'Diana' was no longer there to give some air of human occupation to the wild and barren surroundings. The sun was well inclined towards the western horizon when the 'Dream' reached her former moorings and noiselessly dropped anchor, and about twenty minutes later the electric launch belonging to the vessel was lowered and I entered it with Santoris, a couple of his men managing the boat as it rushed through the dark steel- coloured water to the shore.

VIII

VISIONS

The touch of the earth seemed strange to me after nearly a week spent at sea, and as I sprang from the launch on to the rough rocks, aided by Santoris, I was for a moment faint and giddy. The dark mountain summits seemed to swirl round me,—and the glittering water, shining like steel, had the weird effect of a great mirror in which a fluttering vision of something undefined and undeclared rose and passed like a breath. I recovered myself with an effort and stood still, trying to control the foolish throbbing of my heart, while my companion gave a few orders to his men in a language which I thought I knew, though I could not follow it.

"Are you speaking Gaelic?" I asked him, with a smile.

"No!—only something very like it—Phoenician."

He looked straight at me as he said this, and his eyes, darkly blue and brilliant, expressed a world of suggestion. He went on:—

"All this country was familiar ground to the Phoenician colonists of ages ago. I am sure you know that! The Gaelic tongue is the genuine dialect of the ancient Phoenician Celtic, and when I speak the original language to a Highlander who only knows his native Gaelic he understands me perfectly."

I was silent. We moved away from the shore, walking slowly side by side. Presently I paused, looking back at the launch we had just left.

"Your men are not Highlanders?"

"No—they are from Egypt."

"But surely,"—I said, with some hesitation—"Phoenician is no longer known or spoken?"

"Not by the world of ordinary men,"—he answered—"I know it and speak it,—and so do most of those who serve me. You have heard it before, only you do not quite remember." I looked at him, startled. He smiled, adding gently:—"Nothing dies—not even a language!"

We were not yet out of sight of the men. They had pushed the launch off shore again and were starting it back to the yacht, it being arranged that they should return for us in a couple of hours. We were following a path among slippery stones near a rushing torrent, but as we turned round a sharp bend we lost the view of Loch Scavaig itself and were for the first time truly alone. Huge mountains, crowned with jagged pinnacles, surrounded us on all sides,—here and there tufts of heather clinging to large masses of dark stone blazed rose-purple in the declining sunshine,—the hollow sound of the falling stream made a perpetual crooning music in our ears, and the warm, stirless air seemed breathless, as though hung in suspense above us waiting for the echo of some word or whisper that should betray a life's secret. Such a silence held us that it was almost unbearable,—every nerve in my body seemed like a strained harp- string ready to snap at a touch,—and yet I could not speak. I tried to get the mastery over the rising tide of thought, memory and emotion that surged in my soul like a tempest—swiftly and peremptorily I argued with myself that the extraordinary chaos of my mind was only due to my own imaginings,—nevertheless, despite my struggles, I remained caught as it were in a web that imprisoned every faculty and sense,—a web fine as gossamer, yet unbreakable as iron. In a kind of desperation I raised my eyes, burning with the heat of restrained tears, and saw Santoris watching me with patient, almost appealing tenderness. I felt that he could read my unexpressed trouble, and involuntarily I stretched out my hands to him.

"Tell me!" I half whispered-"What is it I must know? We are strangers—and yet—"

He caught my hands in his own.

"Not strangers!" he said, his voice trembling a little—"You cannot say that! Not strangers—but old friends!"

The strong gentleness of his clasp recalled the warm pressure of the invisible hands that had guided me out of darkness in my dream of a few nights past. I looked up into his face, and every line of it became suddenly, startlingly familiar. The deep-set blue eyes,—the broad brows and intellectual features were all as well known to me as might be the portrait of a beloved one to the lover, and my heart almost stood still with the wonder and terror of the recognition.

"Not strangers,"—he repeated, with quiet emphasis, as though to reassure me— "Only since we last met we have travelled far asunder. Have yet a little patience! You will presently remember me as well as I remember you!"

With the rush of startled recollection I found my voice.

"I remember you now!"—I said, in low, unsteady tones—"I have seen you often—often! But where? Tell me where? Oh, surely you know!"

He still held my hands with the tenderest force,—and seemed, like myself, to find speech difficult. If two deeply attached friends, parted for many years, were all unexpectedly to meet in some solitary place where neither had thought to see a living soul, their emotion could hardly be keener than ours,—and yet—there was an invisible barrier between us—a barrier erected either by him or by myself,— something that held us apart. The sudden and overpowering demand made upon our strength by the swift and subtle attraction which drew us together was held in check by ourselves,—and it was as if we were each separately surrounded by a circle across which neither of us dared to pass. I looked at him in mingled fear and questioning—his eyes were gravely thoughtful and full of light.

"Yes, I know,"—he answered, at last, speaking very softly—while, gently releasing one of my hands, he held the other—"I know,—but we need not speak of that! As I have already said, you will remember all by gradual degrees. We are never per- mitted to entirely forget. But it is quite natural that now—at this immediate hour—we should find it strange—you, perhaps, more than I—that something impels us one to the other,—something that will not be gainsaid,—something that if all the powers of earth and heaven could intervene, which by simplest law they cannot, will take no denial!"

I trembled, not with fear, but with an exquisite delight I dared not pause to analyse. He pressed my hand more closely.

"We had better walk on,"—he continued, averting his gaze from mine for the moment—"If I say more just now I shall say too much—and you will be frightened,—perhaps offended. I have been guilty of so many errors in the past,—you must help me to avoid them in the future. Come!"—and he turned his eyes again upon me with a smile— "Let us see the sunset!"

We moved on for a few moments in absolute silence, he still holding my hand and guiding me up the rough path we followed. The noise of the rushing torrent sounded louder in my ears, sometimes with a clattering insistence as though it sought to match itself against the surging of my own quick blood in an endeavour to drown my thoughts. On we went and still onward,—the path seemed interminable, though it was in reality a very short journey. But there was such a weight of unutterable things pressing on my soul like a pent-up storm craving for outlet, that every step measured itself as almost a mile.

At last we paused; we were in full view of Loch Coruisk and its weird splendour. On all sides arose bare and lofty mountains, broken and furrowed here and there by deep hollows and corries,—supremely grand in their impressive desolation, uplifting their stony peaks around us like the walls and turrets of a gigantic fortress, and rising so abruptly and so impenetrably encompassing the black stretch of water below, that it seemed impossible for a sunbeam to force its shining entrance into such a circle of dense gloom. Yet there was a shower of golden light pouring aslant down one of the highest of the hills, brightening to vivid crimson stray clumps of heather, touching into pale green some patches of moss and lichen, and giving the dazzling flash of silver to the white wings of a sea- gull which soared above our heads uttering wild cries like a creature in pain. Pale blue mists were rising from the surface of the lake, and the fitful gusts of air that rushed over the rocky summits played with these impalpable vapours borne inland from the Atlantic, and tossed them to and fro into fantastic shapes—some like flying forms with long hair streaming behind them—some like armed warriors, hurtling their spears against each other,—and some like veiled ghosts hurrying past as though driven to their land of shadows by shuddering fear. We stood silently hand in hand, watching the uneasy flitting of these cloud phantoms, and waiting for the deepening glow, which, when it should spread upwards from the rays of the sinking sun, would transform the wild, dark scene to one of almost supernatural splendour. Suddenly Santoris spoke:

"Now shall I tell you where we last met?" he asked, very gently— "And may I show you the reasons why we meet again?"

I lifted my eyes to his. My heart beat with suffocating quickness, and thoughts were in my brain that threatened to overwhelm my small remaining stock of self-control and make of me nothing but a creature of tears and passion. I moved my lips in an effort to speak, but no sound came from them.

"Do not be afraid,"—he continued, in the same quiet tone—"It is true that we must be careful now as in the past we were careless,— but perfect comprehension of each other rests with ourselves. May I go on?"

I gave a mute sign of assent. There was a rough craig near us, curiously shaped like a sort of throne and canopy, the canopy being formed by a thickly overhanging mass of rock and heather, and here he made me sit down, placing himself beside me. From this point we commanded a view of the head of the lake and the great mountain which closes and dominates it,—and which now began to be illumined with a strange witch-like glow of orange and purple, while a thin mist moved slowly across it like the folds of a ghostly stage curtain preparing to rise and display the first scene of some great drama.

"Sometimes," he then said, —"it happens, even in the world of cold and artificial convention, that a man and woman are brought together who, to their own immediate consciousness, have had no previous acquaintance with each other, and yet with the lightest touch, the swiftest glance of an eye, a million vibrations are set quivering in them like harp-strings struck by the hand of a master and responding each to each in throbbing harmony and perfect tune. They do not know how it happens—they only feel it is. Then, nothing—I repeat this with emphasis—nothing can keep them apart. Soul rushes to soul,— heart leaps to heart,—and all form and ceremony, custom and usage crumble into dust before the power that overwhelms them. These sudden storms of etheric vibration occur every day among the most ordinary surroundings and with the most unlikely persons, and Society as at present constituted frowns and shakes its head, or jeers at what it cannot understand, calling such impetuosity folly, or worse, while remaining wilfully blind to the fact that in its strangest aspect it is nothing but the assertion of an Eternal Law. Moreover, it is a law that cannot be set aside or broken with impunity. Just as the one point of vibration sympathetically strikes the other in the system of wireless telegraphy, so, despite millions and millions of intervening currents and lines of divergence, the immortal soul-spark strikes its kindred fire across a waste of worlds until they meet in the compelling flash of that God's Message called Love!"

He paused—then went on slowly:—

"No force can turn aside one from the other,—nothing can intervene- -not because it is either romance or reality, but simply because it is a law. You understand?"

I bent my head silently.

"It may be thousands of years before such a meeting is consummated,"—he continued—"For thousands of years are but hours in the eternal countings. Yet in those thousands of years what lives must be lived!—what lessons must be learned!—what sins committed and expiated!—what precious time lost or found!—what happiness missed or wasted!"

His voice thrilled—and again he took my hand and held it gently clasped.

"You must believe in yourself alone,"—he said,—"if any lurking thought suggests a disbelief in me! It is quite natural that you should doubt me a little. You have studied long and deeply—you have worked hard at problems which puzzle the strongest man's brain, and you have succeeded in many things because you have kept what most men manage to lose when grappling with Science,—Faith. You have always studied with an uplifted heart—uplifted towards the things unseen and eternal. But it has been a lonely heart, too,—as lonely as mine!"

A moment's silence followed,—a silence that seemed heavy and dark, like a passing cloud, and instinctively I looked up to see if indeed a brooding storm was not above us. A heaven of splendid colour met my gaze—the whole sky was lighted with a glory of gold and blue. But below this flaming radiance there was a motionless mass of grey vapour, hanging square as it seemed across the face of the lofty mountain at the head of the lake, like a great canvas set ready for an artist's pencil and prepared to receive the creation of his thought. I watched this in a kind of absorbed fascination, conscious that the warm hand holding mine had strengthened its close grasp,— when suddenly something sharp and brilliant, like the glitter of a sword or a forked flash of lightning, passed before my eyes with a dizzying sensation, and the lake, the mountains, the whole landscape, vanished like a fleeting mirage, and in all the visible air only the heavy curtain of mist remained. I made an effort to move—to speak—in vain! I thought some sudden illness must have seized me—yet no!—for the half-swooning feeling that had for a moment unsteadied my nerves had already passed—and I was calm enough. Yet I saw more plainly than I have ever seen anything in visible Nature, a slowly moving, slowly passing panorama of scenes and episodes that presented themselves in marvellous outline and colouring,—pictures that were gradually unrolled and spread out to my view on the grey background of that impalpable mist which like a Shadow hung between myself and impenetrable Mystery, and I realised to the full that an eternal record of every life is written not only in sound, but in light, in colour, in tune, in mathematical proportion and harmony,—and that not a word, not a thought, not an action is forgotten!

A vast forest rose before me. I saw the long shadows of the leafy boughs flung thick upon the sward and the wild tropical vines hanging rope-like from the inter-twisted stems. A golden moon looked warmly in between the giant branches, flooding the darkness of the scene with rippling radiance, and within its light two human beings walked,—a man and woman—their arms round each other,—their faces leaning close together. The man seemed pleading with his companion for some favour which she withheld, and presently she drew herself away from him altogether with a decided movement of haughty rejection. I could not see her face,—but her attire was regal and splendid, and on her head there shone a jew-elled diadem. Her lover stood apart for a moment with bent head—then he threw himself on his knees before her and caught her hand in an evident outburst of pas-sionate entreaty. And while they stood thus together, I saw the phantom-like fig-ure of another woman moving towards them—she came directly into the fore-ground of the picture, her white garments clinging round her, her fair hair flung loosely over her shoulders, and her whole demeanour expressing eagerness and fear. As she approached, the man sprang up from his knees and, with a gesture of fury, drew a dagger from his belt and plunged it into her heart! I saw her reel back from the blow—I saw the red blood well up through the whiteness of her cloth-ing, and as she turned towards her murderer, with a last look of appeal, I recog-nised MY OWN FACE IN HERS!—and in his THE FACE OF SANTORIS! I uttered a cry,—or thought I uttered it—a darkness swept over me—and the vision vanished!

*   *   *
*   *
*

Another vivid flash struck my eyes, and I found myself looking upon the crowd-ed thoroughfares of a great city. Towers and temples, palaces and bridges, pre-sented themselves to my gaze in a network of interminable width and architec-tural splendour, moving and swaying before me like a wave glittering with a thou-sand sparkles uplifted to the light. Presently this unsteadiness of movement resolved itself into form and order, and I became, as it were, one unobserved spec-tator among thousands, of a scene of picturesque magnificence. It seemed that I stood in the enormous audience hall of a great palace, where there were crowds of slaves, attendants and armed men,—on all sides arose huge pillars of stone on which were carved the winged heads of monsters and fabulous gods,—and loom-ing out of the shadows I saw the shapes of four giant Sphinxes which guarded a throne set high above the crowd. A lambent light played quiveringly on the gor-geous picture, growing more and more vivid as I looked, and throbbing with colour and motion,—and I saw that on the throne there sat a woman crowned and veiled,—her right hand held a sceptre blazing with gold and gems. Slaves clad in costumes of the richest workmanship and design abased themselves on either side of her, and I heard the clash of brazen cymbals and war-like music, as the crowd of people surged and swayed, and murmured and shouted, all apparently moved by some special excitement or interest. Suddenly I perceived the object on which the general attention was fixed—the swooning body of a man, heavily bound in chains and lying at the foot of the throne. Beside him stood a tall black slave, clad in vivid scarlet and masked,—this sinister-looking creature held a gleaming dagger uplifted ready to strike,—and as I saw this, a wild yearning arose in me to save the threatened life of the bound and helpless victim. If I could only rush to defend and drag him away from impending peril, I thought!—but no!— I was forced to stand helplessly watching the scene, with every fibre of my brain burning with pent-up anguish. At this moment, the crowned and veiled woman on the throne suddenly rose and stood upright,—with a commanding gesture she stretched out her glittering sceptre—the sign was given! Swiftly the dagger gleamed through the air and struck its deadly blow straight home! I turned away my eyes in shuddering horror,—but was compelled by some invincible power to raise them again,—and the scene before me glowed red as with the hue of blood- -I saw the slain victim,—the tumultuous crowd—and above all, the relentless Queen who, with one movement of her little hand, had swept away a life,—and as I looked upon her loathingly, she threw back her shrouding golden veil. MY OWN FACE LOOKED FULL AT ME from under the jewelled arch of her sparkling diadem—ah, wicked soul!—I wildly cried—pitiless Queen!—then, as they lifted the body of the murdered man, his livid countenance was turned towards me, and I saw again the face of Santoris! Dumb and despairing I sank as it were within myself, chilled with inexplicable misery, and I heard for the first time in this singular pageant of vision a Voice—slow, calm, and thrilling with infi-nite sadness:

"A life for a life!"—it said—"The old eternal law!—a life for a life! There is noth-ing taken which shall not be returned again— nothing lost which shall not be found—a life for a life!"

Then came silence and utter darkness.

* * *
* *
*

Slowly brightening, slowly widening, a pale radiance like the earliest glimmer of dawn stole gently on my eyes when I again raised them. I saw the waving curve of a wide, sluggishly flowing river, and near it a temple of red granite stood surrounded with shadowing foliage and bright clumps of flowers. Huge palms lifted their fronded heads to the sky, and on the edge of the quiet stream there loitered a group of girls and women. One of these stood apart, sad and alone, the others looking at her with something of pity and scorn. Near her was a tall upright column of black basalt, as it seemed, bearing the sculptured head of a god. The features were calm and strong and reposeful, expressive of dignity, wisdom and power. And as I looked, more people gathered together—I heard strains of solemn music pealing from the temple close by—and I saw the solitary woman draw herself farther apart and almost disappear among the shadows. The light grew brighter in the east,—the sun shot a few advancing rays upward,—suddenly the door of the temple was thrown open, and a long procession of priests carrying flaming tapers and attended by boys in white garments and crowned with flowers made their slow and stately way towards the column with the god-like Head upon it and began to circle round it, chanting as they walked, while the flower-crowned boys swung golden censers to and fro, impregnating the air with rich perfume. The people all knelt— and still the priests paced round and round, chanting and murmuring prayers,—till at last the great sun lifted the edge of its glowing disc above the horizon, and its rays springing from the east like golden arrows, struck the brow of the Head set on its basalt pedestal. With the sudden glitter of this morning glory the chanting ceased,—the procession stopped; and one priest, tall and commanding of aspect, stepped forth from the rest, holding up his hands to enjoin silence. And then the Head quivered as with life,—its lips moved—there was a rippling sound like the chord of a harp smitten by the wind,—and a voice, full, sweet and resonant, spoke aloud the words:—

"I face the Sunrise!"

With a shout of joy priests and people responded:

"We face the Sunrise!"

And he who seemed the highest in authority, raising his arms invokingly towards heaven, exclaimed:

"Even so, O Mightiest among the Mighty, let us ever remember that Thy Shadow is but part of Thy Light,—that Sorrow is but the passing humour of Joy—and that Death is but the night which dawns again into Life! We face the Sunrise!"

Then all who were assembled joined in singing a strange half- barbaric song and chorus of triumph, to the strains of which they slowly moved off and disappeared like shapes breathed on a mirror and melting away. Only the tall high priest remained,—and he stood alone, waiting, as it were, for something eagerly expected and desired. And presently the woman who had till now remained hidden among the shadows of the surrounding trees, came swiftly forward. She was very pale—her eyes shone with tears—and again I saw MY OWN FACE IN HERS. The priest turned quickly to greet her, and I distinctly heard every word he spoke as he caught her hands in his own and drew her towards him.

"Everything in this world and the next I will resign," he said—"for love of thee! Honour, dignity and this poor earth's renown I lay at thy feet, thou most beloved of women! What other thing created or imagined can be compared to the joy of thee?—to the sweetness of thy lips, the softness of thy bosom—the love that trembles into confession with thy smile! Imprison me but in thine arms and I will count my very soul well lost for an hour of love with thee! Ah, deny me not!—turn me not away from thee again!—love comes but once in life—such love as ours!—early or late, but once!"

She looked at him with tender passion and pity—a look in which I thankfully saw there was no trace of pride, resentment or affected injury.

"Oh, my beloved!" she answered, and her voice, plaintive and sweet, thrilled on the silence like a sob of pain—"Why wilt thou rush on destruction for so poor a thing as I am? Knowest thou not, and wilt thou not remember that, to a priest of thy great Order, the love of woman is forbidden, and the punishment thereof is death? Already the people view thee with suspicion and me with scorn—forbear, O dearest, bravest soul!—be strong!"

"Strong?" he echoed—"Is it not strong to love?—ay, the very best of strength! For what avails the power of man if he may not bend a woman to his will? Child, wherever love is there can be no death, but only life! Love is as the ever-flowing torrent of eternity in my veins—the pulse of everlasting youth and victory! What are the foolish creeds of man compared with this one Truth of Nature—Love! Is not the Deity Himself the Supreme Lover?—and wouldst thou have me a castaway from His holiest ordinance? Ah no!—come to me, my beloved!—soul of my soul—inmost core of my heart! Come to me in the silence when no one sees and no one hears—come when—"

He broke off, checked by her sudden smile and look of rapture. Some thought had evidently, like a ray of light, cleared her doubts away.

"So be it!" she said—"I give thee all myself from henceforth!—I will come!"

He uttered an exclamation of relief and joy, and drew her closer, till her head rested on his breast and her loosened hair fell in a shower across his arms.

"At last!" he murmured—"At last! Mine—all mine this tender soul, this passionate heart!—mine this exquisite life to do with as I will! O crown of my best manhood!—when wilt thou come to me?"

She answered at once without hesitation.

"To-night!" she said—"To-night, when the moon rises, meet me here in this very place,—this sacred grove where Memnon hears thy vows to him broken, and my vows consecrated to thee!—and as I live I swear I will be all thine! But now—leave me to pray!"

She lifted her head and looked into his adoring eyes,—then kissed him with a strange, grave tenderness as though bidding him farewell, and with a gentle gesture motioned him away. Elated and flushed with joy, he obeyed her sign, and left her, disappearing in the same phantom-like way in which all the other figures in this weird dream- drama had made their exit. She watched him go with a wistful yearning gaze—then in apparent utter desperation she threw herself on her knees before the impassive Head on its rocky pedestal and prayed aloud:

"O hidden and unknown God whom we poor earthly creatures symbolise!- -give me the strength to love unselfishly—the patience to endure uncomplainingly! Thou, Heart of Stone, temper with thy coldest wisdom my poor throbbing heart of flesh! Help me to quell the tempest in my soul, and let me be even as thou art—inflexible, immovable,—save when the sun strikes music from thy dreaming brows and tells thee it is day! Forgive, O great God, forgive the fault of my beloved!—a fault which is not his, but mine, merely because I live and he hath found me fair,—let all be well for him,—but for me let nothing evermore be either well or ill—and teach me—even me—to face the Sunrise!"

Her voice ceased—a mist came before me for a moment—and when this cleared, the same scene was presented to me under the glimmer of a ghostly moon. And she who looked so like myself, lay dead at the foot of the great Statue, her hands clasped on her breast, her eyes closed, her mouth smiling as in sleep, while beside her raved and wept her priestly lover, invoking her by every tender name, clasping her lifeless body in his arms, covering her face with useless passionate kisses, and calling her back with wild grief from the silence into which her soul had fled. And I knew then that she had put all thought of self aside in a sense of devotion

to duty,—she had chosen what she imagined to be the only way out of difficulty,— to save the honour of her lover she had slain herself. But—was it wise? Or
foolish? This thought pressed itself insistently home to my mind. She had given
her life to serve a mistaken creed,—she had bowed to the conventions of a temporary code of human law—yet— surely God was above all strange and unnatural systems built up by man for his own immediate convenience, vanity or advantage, and was not Love the nearest thing to God? And if those two souls were destined lovers, COULD they be divided, even by their own rashness? These questions were curiously urged upon my inward consciousness as I looked again upon
the poor fragile corpse among the reeds and palms of the sluggishly flowing river,
and heard the clamorous despair of the man to whom she might have been joy,
inspiration and victory had not the world been then as it is not now—the man,
who as the light of the moonbeams fell upon him, showed me in his haggard and
miserable features the spectral likeness of Santoris. Was it right, I asked myself,
that the two perfect lines of a mutual love should be swept asunder?—or if it was,
as some might conceive it, right according to certain temporary and conventional views of 'rightness.' was it POSSIBLE to so sever them? Would it not be well
if we all occasionally remembered that there is an eternal law of harmony between
souls as between spheres?—and that if we ourselves bring about a divergence we
also bring about discord? And again,— that if discord results by our inter-med-
dling, it is AGAINST THE LAW, and must by the working of natural forces be
resolved into concord again, whether such resolvance take ten, a hundred, a thousand or ten thousand years? Of what use, then, is the struggle we are for ever making in our narrow and limited daily lives to resist the wise and holy teaching of
Nature? Is it not best to yield to the insistence of the music of life while it sounds
in our ears? For everything must come round to Nature's way in the end—her way
being God's way, and God's way the only way! So I thought, as in half-dreaming
fashion I watched the vision of the dead woman and her despairing lover fade into
the impenetrable shadows of mystery veiling the record of the light beyond.

* * *
* *
*

Presently I became conscious of a deep murmuring sound tike the subdued hum
of many thousands of voices,—and lifting my eyes I saw the wide circular sweep
of a vast arena crowded with people. In the centre, and well to the front of the
uplifted tiers of seats, there was a gorgeous pavilion of gold, draped with gaudy
coloured silk and hung with festoons of roses, wherein sat a heavily-built, brutish-
looking man royally robed and crowned, and wearing jewels In such profusion as
to seem literally clothed in flashing points of light. Beautiful women were gath-

ered round him,—boys with musical instruments crouched at his feet—attendants stood on every hand to minister to his slightest call or signal,—and all eyes were fixed upon him as upon some worshipped god of a nation's idolatry. I felt and knew that I was looking upon the 'shadow-presentment' of the Roman tyrant Nero; and I wondered vaguely how it chanced that he, in all the splendour of his wild and terrible career of wickedness, should be brought into this phantasmagoria of dream in which I and One Other alone seemed to be chiefly concerned. There were strange noises in my ears,—the loud din of trumpets—the softer sound of harps played enchantingly in some far-off distance—the ever- increasing loud buzzing of the voices of the multitude—and then all at once the roar as of angry wild beasts in impatience or pain. The time of this vision seemed to be late afternoon—I thought I could see a line of deep rose colour in a sky where the sun had lately set—the flare of torches glimmered all round the arena and beyond it, striking vivid brilliancy from the jewels on Nero's breast and throwing into strong relief the groups of soldiers and people immediately around him. I perceived now that the centre of the arena, previously empty, had become the one spot on which the looks of the people began to turn—one woman stood there all alone, clad in white, her arms crossed on her breast. So still was she,—so apparently unconscious of her position, that the mob, ever irritated by calmness, grew suddenly furious, and a fierce cry arose:—"Ad leones! Ad leones!" The great Emperor stirred from his indolent, half-reclining position and leaned forward with a sudden look of interest on his lowering features,—and as he did so a man attired in the costume of a gladiator entered the arena from one of its side doors and with a calm step and assured demeanour walked up to the front of the royal dais and there dropped on one knee. Then quickly rising he drew himself erect and waited, his eyes fixed on the woman who stood as immovably as a statue, apparently resigned to some untoward fate. And again the vast crowd shouted "Ad leones! Ad leones!" There came a heavy grating noise of drawn bolts and bars— the sound of falling chains—then a savage animal roar—and two lean and ferocious lions sprang into the arena, lashing their tails, their manes bristling and their eyes aglare. Quick as thought, the gladiator stood in their path—and I swiftly recognised the nature of the 'sport' that had brought the Emperor and all this brave and glittering show of humanity out to watch what to them was merely a 'sensation'— the life of a Christian dashed out by the claws and fangs of wild beasts—a common pastime, all unchecked by either the mercy of man or the intervention of God! I understood as clearly as if the explanation had been volunteered to me in so many words, that the woman who awaited her death so immovably had only one chance of rescue, and that chance was through the gladiator, who, to please the humour of the Emperor, had been brought hither to combat and frighten them off their intended victim,—the reward for him, if he succeeded, being the woman herself. I gazed with aching, straining eyes on the wonderful dream-spec-

tacle, and my heart thrilled as I saw one of the lions stealthily approach the solitary martyr and prepare to spring. Like lightning, the gladiator was upon the fam-
ished brute, fighting it back in a fierce and horrible contest, while the second lion,
pouncing forward and bent on a similar attack, was similarly repulsed. The battle
between man and beasts was furious, prolonged and terrible to witness—and the
excitement became intense. "Ad leones! Ad leones!" was now the universal wild
shout, rising ever louder and louder into an almost frantic clamour. The woman
meanwhile never stirred from her place—she might have been frozen to the
ground where she stood. She appeared to notice neither the lions who were ready
to devour her, nor the gladiator who combated them in her defence—and I studied her strangely impassive figure with keen interest, waiting to see her face,—for
I instinctively felt I should recognise it. Presently, as though in response to my
thought, she turned towards me,—and as in a mirror I saw MY OWN
REFLECTED PERSONALITY again as I had seen it so many times in this chain
of strange episodes with which I was so singularly concerned though still an outside spectator. Between her Shadow-figure and what I felt of my own existing Self
there seemed to be a pale connecting line of light, and all my being thrilled
towards her with a curiously vague anxiety. A swirling mist came before my eyes
suddenly,—and when this cleared I saw that the combat was over—the lions lay
dead and weltering in their blood on the trampled sand of the arena, and the vic-
torious gladiator stood near their prone bodies triumphant, amid the deafening
cheers of the crowd. Wreaths of flowers were tossed to him from the people, who
stood up in their seats all round the great circle to hail him with their acclama-
tions, and the Emperor, lifting his unwieldy body from under his canopy of gold,
stretched out his hand as a sign that the prize which the dauntless combatant had
fought to win was his. He at once obeyed the signal;—but now the woman, hitherto so passive and immovable, stirred. Fixing upon the gladiator a glance of the
deepest reproach and anguish, she raised her arms warningly as though forbidding
him to approach her—and then fell face forward on the ground. He rushed to her
side, and kneeling down sought to lift her;—then suddenly he sprang erect with
a loud cry:—

"Great Emperor! I asked of thee a living love!—and this is dead!"

A ripple of laughter ran through the crowd. The Emperor leaned forward from
his throne and smiled.

"Thank your Christian God for that!" he said—"Our pagan deities are kinder!
They give us love for love!"

The gladiator gave a wild gesture of despair and turned his face upward to the
light—THE FACE OF SANTORIS!

"Dead!—dead!"—he cried—"Of what use then is life? Dark are the beloved eyes!—cold is the generous heart!—the fight has been in vain—my victory mocks me with its triumph! The world is empty!"

Again the laughter of the populace stirred the air.

"Go to, man!"—and the rough voice of Nero sounded harshly above the murmurous din—"The world was never the worse for one woman the less! Wouldst thou also be a Christian? Take heed! Our lions are still hungry! Thy love is dead, 'tis true, but WE have not killed her! She trusted in her God, and He has robbed thee of thy lawful possession. Blame Him, not us! Go hence, with thy laurels bravely won! Nero commends thy prowess!"

He flung a purse of gold at the gladiator's feet—and then I saw the whole scene melt away into a confused mass of light and colour till all was merely a pearl-grey haze floating before my eyes. Yet I was hardly allowed a moment's respite before another scene presented itself like a painting upon the curtain of vapour which hung so persistently in front of me—a scene which struck a closer chord upon my memory than any I had yet beheld.

* * *
* *
*

The cool, spacious interior of a marble-pillared hall or studio slowly disclosed itself to my view—it was open to an enchanting vista of terraced gardens and dark undulating woods, and gay parterres of brilliant blossom were spread in front of it like a wonderfully patterned carpet of intricate and exquisite design. Within it was all the picturesque grace and confusion of an artist's surroundings; and at a great easel, working assiduously, was one who seemed to be the artist himself, his face turned from me towards his canvas. Posed before him, in an attitude of indolent grace, was a woman, arrayed in clinging diaphanous drapery, a few priceless jewels gleaming here and there like stars upon her bosom and arms— her hair, falling in loose waves from a band of pale blue velvet fastened across it, was of a warm brown hue like an autumn leaf with the sun upon it, and I could see that whatever she might be according to the strictest canons of beauty, the man who was painting her portrait considered her more than beautiful. I heard his voice, in the low, murmurous yet perfectly distinct way in which all sounds were conveyed to me in this dream pageant—it was exactly as if persons on the stage were speaking to an audience.

"If we could understand each other,"—he said—"I think all would be well with us in time and eternity!"

There was a pause. The picturesque scene before me seemed to glow and gather intensity as I gazed.

"If you could see what is in my heart,"—he continued—"you would be satisfied that no greater love was ever given to woman than mine for you! Yet I would not say I give it to you—for I have striven against it." He paused—and when he spoke again his words were so distinct that they seemed close to my ears.

"It has been wrung out of my very blood and soul—I can no more resist it than I can resist the force of the air by which I live and breathe. I ought not to love you,—you are a joy forbidden to me— and yet I feel, rightly speaking, that you are already mine—that you belong to me as the other half of myself, and that this has been so from the beginning when God first ordained the mating of souls. I tell you I FEEL this, but cannot explain it,—and I grasp at you as my one hope of joy!—I cannot let you go!"

She was silent, save for a deep sigh that stirred her bosom under its folded lace and made her jewels sparkle like sunbeams on the sea.

"If I lose you now, having known and loved you," he went on—"I lose my art. Not that this would matter—"

Her voice trembled on the air.

"It would matter a great deal"—she said, softly—"to the world!"

"The world!" he echoed—"What need I care for it? Nothing seems of value to me where you are not—I am nerveless, senseless, hopeless without you. My inspiration—such as it is—comes from you—"

She moved restlessly—her face was turned slightly away so that I could not see it.

"My inspiration comes from you,"—he repeated—"The tender look of your eyes fills me with dreams which might—I do not say would— realise themselves in a life's renown—but all this is perhaps nothing to you. What, after all, can I offer you? Nothing but love! And here in Florence you could command more lovers than there are days in the week, did you choose—but people say you are untouchable by love even at its best. Now I—"

Here he stopped abruptly and laid down his brush, looking full at her.

"I," he continued—"love you at neither best nor worst, but simply and entirely with all of myself—all that a man can be in passionate heart, soul and body!"

(How the words rang out! I could have sworn they were spoken close beside me and not by dream-voices in a dream!)

"If you loved me—ah God!—what that would mean! If you dared to brave everything—if you had the courage of love to break down all barriers between yourself and me!—but you will not do this—the sacrifice would be too great—too unusual—"

"You think it would?"

The question was scarcely breathed. A look of sudden amazement lightened his face—then he replied, gently—

"I think it would! Women are impulsive,—generous to a fault—they give what they afterwards regret—who can blame them! You have much to lose by such a sacrifice as I should ask of you—I have all to gain. I must not be selfish. But I love you!—and your love would be to more than the hope of Heaven!"

And now strange echoes of a modern poet's rhyme became mingled in my dream:

> "You have chosen and clung to the chance they sent you—
> Life sweet as perfume and pure as prayer,
> But will it not one day in heaven repent you?
> Will they solace you wholly, the days that were?
> Will you lift up your eyes between sadness and bliss,
> Meet mine and see where the great love is?
> And tremble and turn and be changed?—Content you;
> The gate is strait; I shall not be there.
>
> Yet I know this well; were you once sealed mine,
> Mine in the blood's beat, mine in the breath,
> Mixed into me as honey in wine,
> Not time that sayeth and gainsayeth,
> Nor all strong things had severed us then,
> Not wrath of gods nor wisdom of men,
> Nor all things earthly nor all divine,
> Nor joy nor sorrow, nor life nor death!"

I watched with a deepening thrill of anxiety the scene in the studio, and my thoughts centred themselves upon the woman who sat there so quietly, seeming all unmoved by the knowledge that she held a man's life and future fame in her hands. The artist took up his palette and brushes again and began to work swiftly, his hand trembling a little.

"You have my whole confession now!"—he said—"You know that you are the eyes of the world to me—the glory of the sun and the moon! All my art is in your smile—all my life responds to your touch. Without you I am—can be nothing—Cosmo de Medicis—"

At this name a kind of shadow crept upon the scene, together with a sense of cold.

"Cosmo de Medicis"—he repeated, slowly—"my patron, would scarcely thank me for the avowals I have made to his fair ward!—one whom he intends to honour with his own alliance. I am here by his order to paint the portrait of his future bride!—not to look at her with the eyes of a lover. But the task is too difficult—"

A little sound escaped her, like a smothered cry of pain. He turned towards her.

"Something in your face,"—he said—"a touch of longing in your sweet eyes, has made me risk telling you all, so that you may at least choose your own way of love and life—for there is no real life without love."

Suddenly she rose and confronted him—and once again, as in a magic mirror, I saw MY OWN REFLECTED PERSONALITY. There were tears in her eyes,—yet a smile quivered on her mouth.

"My beloved!"—she said—and then paused, as if afraid.

A look of wonder and rapture came on his face like the light of sunrise, and I RECOGNISED THE NOW FAMILIAR FEATURES OF SANTORIS! Very gently he laid down his palette and brushes and stood waiting in a kind of half expectancy, half doubt.

"My beloved!" she repeated—"Have you not seen?—do you not know? O my genius!—my angel!—am I so hard to read?—so difficult to win?"

Her voice broke in a sob—she made an uncertain step forward, and he sprang to meet her.

"I love you, love you!"—she cried, passionately—"Let the whole world forsake me, if only you remain! I am all yours!—do with me as you will!"

He caught her in his arms—straining her to his heart with all the passion of a long-denied lover's embrace—their lips met—and for a brief space they were lost in that sudden and divine rapture that comes but once in a lifetime,—when like a shivering sense of cold the name again was whispered:

"Cosmo de Medicis!"

A shadow fell across the scene, and a woman, dark and heavy- featured, stood like a blot in the sunlit brightness of the studio,- -a woman very richly attired, who gazed fixedly at the lovers with round, suspicious eyes and a sneering smile. The artist turned and saw her—his face changed from joy to a pale anxiety—yet, holding his love with one arm, he flung defiance at her with uplifted head and fearless demeanour.

"Spy!"—he exclaimed—"Do your worst! Let us have an end of your serpent vigilance and perfidy!—better death than the constant sight of you! What! Have you not watched us long enough to make discovery easy? Do your worst, I say, and quickly!"

The cruel smile deepened on the woman's mouth,—she made no answer, but simply raised her hand. In immediate obedience to the signal, a man, clad in the Florentine dress of the sixteenth century, and wearing a singular collar of jewels, stepped out from behind a curtain, attended by two other men, who, by their dress, were, or seemed to be, of inferior rank. Without a word, these three threw themselves upon the unarmed and defenceless painter with the fury of wild animals pouncing on prey. There was a brief and breathless struggle—three daggers gleamed in air—a shriek rang through the stillness—another instant and the victim lay dead, stabbed to the heart, while she who had just clung to his living body and felt the warmth of his living lips against hers, dropped on her knees beside the corpse with wild waitings of madness and despair.

"Another crime on your soul, Cosmo de Medicis!"—she cried—"Another murder of a nobler life than your own!—may Heaven curse you for it! But you have not parted my love from me—no!—you have but united us for ever! We escape you and your spies—thus!"

And snatching a dagger from the hand of one of the assassins before he could prevent her, she plunged it into her own breast. She fell without a groan, self-slain,—

and I saw, as in a mist of breath on a mirror, the sudden horror on the faces of the
men and the one woman who were left to contemplate the ghastly deed they had
committed. And then—noting as in some old blurred picture the features of the
man who wore the collar of jewels, I felt that I knew him—yet I could not place
him in any corner of my immediate recognition. Gradually this strange scene of
cool white marble vastness with its brilliant vista of flowers and foliage under the
bright Italian sky, and the betrayed lovers lying dead beside each other in the presence of their murderers, passed away like a floating cloud,—and the same slow,
calm Voice I had heard once before now spoke again in sad, stern accents:

"Jealousy is cruel as the grave!—the coals thereof are coals of fire which hath a
most vehement flame! Many waters cannot quench love, neither can the floods
drown it—if a man would give all his substance for love it would be utterly con-
temned!"

*   *   *
*   *
*

I closed my eyes,—or thought I closed them—a vague terror was growing upon
me,—a terror of myself and a still greater terror of the man beside me who held
my hand,—yet something prevented me from turning my head to look at him,
and another still stronger emotion possessed me with a force so overpowering that
I could hardly breathe under the weight and pain of it, but I could give it no
name. I could not think at all—and I had ceased even to wonder at the strangeness and variety of these visions or dream-episodes full of colour and sound which
succeeded each other so swiftly. Therefore it hardly seemed remarkable to me
when I saw the heavy curtain of mist which hung in front of my eyes suddenly
reft asunder in many places and broken into a semblance of the sea.

*   *   *
*   *
*

A wild sea! Gloomily grey and grand in its onsweeping wrath, its huge billows rose
and fell like moving mountains convulsed by an earthquake,—light and shadow
combated against each other in its dark abysmal depths and among its toppling
crests of foam—I could hear the savage hiss and boom of breakers dashing themselves to pieces on some unseen rocky coast far away,—and my heart grew cold
with dread as I beheld a ship in full sail struggling against the heavy onslaught of
the wind on that heaving wilderness of waters, like a mere feather lost from a sea-

gull's wing. Flying along like a hunted creature she staggered and plunged, her bowsprit dipping into deep chasms from which she was tossed shudderingly upward again as in light contempt, and as she came nearer and nearer into my view I could discern some of the human beings on board—the man at the wheel, with keen eyes peering into the gathering gloom of the storm, his hair and face dashed with spray,—the sailors, fighting hard to save the rigging from being torn to pieces and flung into the sea,— then—a sudden huge wave swept her directly in front of me, and I saw the two distinct personalities that had been so constantly presented to me during this strange experience,—THE MAN WITH THE FACE OF SANTORIS—THE WOMAN WITH MY OWN FACE SO TRULY REFLECTED that I might have been looking at myself in a mirror. And just now the resemblance to us both was made more close and striking than it had been in any of the previous visions—that is to say, the likenesses of ourselves were given almost as we now existed. The man held the woman beside him closely clasped with one arm, supporting her and himself, with the other thrown round one of the shaking masts. I saw her look up to him with the light of a great and passionate love in her eyes. And I heard him say:—

"The end of sorrow and the beginning of joy! You are not afraid?"

"Afraid?" And her voice had no tremor—"With you?"

He caught her closer to his heart and kissed her not once but many times in a kind of mingled rapture and despair.

"This is death, my beloved!"—he said.

And her answer pealed out with tender certainty. "No!—not death, but life!—and love!"

A cry went up from the sailors—a cry of heartrending agony,—a mass of enormous billows rolling steadily on together hurled themselves like giant assassins upon the frail and helpless vessel and engulfed it—it disappeared with awful swiftness, like a small blot on the ocean sucked down into the whirl of water— the vast and solemn greyness of the sea spread over it like a pall—it was a nothing, gone into nothingness! I watched one giant wave rise in a crystalline glitter of dark sapphire and curl over the spot where all that human life and human love had disappeared,—and then—there came upon my soul a sudden sense of intense calm. The great sea smoothed itself out before my eyes into fine ripples which dispersed gradually into mist again—and almost I found my voice—almost my lips opened to ask: "What means this vision of the sea?" when a sound of music checked me on the verge of utterance—the music of delicate strings as of a thousand harps in heaven. I listened with every sense caught and entranced—my gaze still fixed half unseeingly upon the heavy grey film which hung before me—that mystic sky-canvas upon which some Divine painter had depicted in life-like form and colour scenes which I, in a sort of dim strangeness, recognised yet could not understand—and as I looked a rainbow, with every hue intensified to such a burning depth of brilliancy that its light was almost intolerably dazzling, sprang in a perfect arch across the cloud! I uttered an involuntary cry of rapture—for it was like no earthly rainbow I had ever seen. Its palpitating radiance seemed to penetrate into the very core and centre of space,—aerially delicate yet deep, each separate colour glowed with the fervent splendour of a heaven undreamed of by mere mortality and too glorious for mortal description. It was the shining repentance of the storm,—the assurance of joy after sorrow- -the passionate love of the soul rising upwards in perfect form and beauty after long imprisonment in ice-bound depths of repression and solitude—it was anything and everything that could be thought or imagined of divinest promise!

My heart beat quickly—tears sprang to my eyes—and almost unconsciously I pressed the kind, strong hand that held mine. It trembled ever so slightly—but I was too absorbed in watching that triumphal arch across the sky to heed the movement. By degrees the lustrous hues began to pale very slowly, and almost imperceptibly they grew fainter and fainter till at last all was misty grey as before, save in one place where there were long rays of light like the falling of silvery rain. And then came strange rapidly passing scenes as of cloud forms constantly shifting and changing, in all of which I discerned the same two personalities so like and yet so unlike ourselves who were the dumb witnesses of every episode,—but everything now passed in absolute silence—there was no mysterious music,—the voices had ceased—all was mute.

Suddenly there came a change over the face of what I thought the sky—the clouds were torn asunder as it were to show a breadth of burning amber and rose, and I beheld the semblance of a great closed Gateway barred across as with gold. Here a figure slowly shaped itself,—the figure of a woman who knelt against the closed barrier with hands clasped and uplifted in pitiful beseeching. So strangely desolate and solitary was her aspect in all that heavenly brilliancy that I could almost have wept for her, shut out as she seemed from some mystic unknown glory. Round her swept the great circle of the heavens—beneath her and above her were the deserts of infinite space—and she, a fragile soul rendered immortal by quenchless fires of love and hope and memory, hovered between the deeps of immeasurable vastness like a fluttering leaf or flake of snow! My heart ached for her—my lips moved unconsciously in prayer:

"O leave her not always exiled and alone!" I murmured, inwardly— "Dear God, have pity! Unbar the gate and let her in! She has waited so long!"

The hand holding mine strengthened its clasp,—and the warm, close pressure sent a thrill through my veins. Almost I would have turned to look at my companion—had I not suddenly seen the closed gateway in the heavens begin to open slowly, allowing a flood of golden radiance to pour out like the steady flowing of a broad stream. The kneeling woman's figure remained plainly discernible, but seemed to be gradually melting into the light which surrounded it. And then— something—I know not what—shook me down from the pinnacle of vision,— hardly aware of my own action, I withdrew my hand from my companion's, and saw—just the solemn grandeur of Loch Coruisk, with a deep amber glow streaming over the summit of the mountains, flung upward by the setting sun! Nothing more!—I heaved an involuntary sigh—and at last, with some little hesitation and dread, looked full at Santoris. His eyes met mine steadfastly—he was very pale. So we faced each other for a moment—then he said, quietly:—

"How quickly the time has passed! This is the best moment of the sunset,—when that glory fades we shall have seen all!"

IX

DOUBTFUL DESTINY

His voice was calm and conventional, yet I thought I detected a thrill of sadness in it which touched me to a kind of inexplicable remorse, and I turned to him quickly, hardly conscious of the words I uttered.

"Must the glory fade?"—I said, almost pleadingly—"Why should it not remain with us?"

He did not reply at once. A shadow of something like sternness clouded his brows, and I began to be afraid—yet afraid of what? Not of him—but of myself, lest I should unwittingly lose all I had gained. But then the question presented itself—What had I gained? Could I explain it, even to myself? There was nothing in any way tangible of which to say—"I possess this," or "I have secured that,"—for, reducing all circumstances to a prosaic level, all that I knew was that I had met in my present companion a man who had a singular, almost compelling attractiveness, and with whose personality I seemed to be familiar; also, that under some power which he might possibly have exerted, I had in an unexpected place and at an unexpected time seen certain visions or 'impressions' which might or might not be the working of my own brain under a temporary magnetic influence. I was fully aware that such things could happen—and yet—I was not by any means sure that they had so happened in this case. And while I was thus hurriedly trying to think out the problem, he replied to my question.

"That depends on ourselves,"—he said—"On you perhaps more than any other."

I looked up at him wonderingly.

"On me?" I echoed.

He smiled a little.

"Why, yes! A woman always decides."

I turned my eyes again towards the sky. Long lines of delicate pale blue and green were now intermingled with the amber light of the after-glow, and the whole scene was one of indescribable grandeur and beauty.

"I wish I could understand,"—I murmured.

"Let me help you,"—he said, gently. "Possibly I can make things clearer for you. You are just now under the spell of your own psychic impressions and memories. You think you have seen strange episodes—these are nothing but pictures stored far away back in the cells of your spiritual brain, which (through the medium of your present material brain) project on your vision not only presentments and reflections of past scenes and events, but which also reproduce the very words and sounds attending those scenes and events. That is all. Loch Coruisk has shown you nothing but itself in varying effects of light and cloud—there is no mystery here but the everlasting mystery of Nature in which you and I play our several parts. What you have seen or heard I do not know—for each individual experience is and always must be different. All that I am fully conscious of is, that our having met and our being here together to-day is, as it were, the mending of a broken chain. But it rests with you—and even with me—to break it once more if we choose."

I was silent, not because I could not but because I dared not speak. All my life seemed suddenly to hang on the point of a hair's-breadth of possibility.

"I think,"—he continued in the same quiet voice—"that just now we may let things take their ordinary course. You and I"—here he paused, and impelled by some secret emotion I lifted my eyes to his. Instinctively, and with a rush of feeling, we stretched out our hands to each other. He clasped mine in his own, and stooping his head kissed them tenderly. "You and I,"—he went on—"have met before in many a phase of life and on many a plane of thought—and I believe we know and realise this. Let us be satisfied so far—and if destiny has anything of happiness or wisdom in store for us let us try to assist its fulfilment and not stand in the way."

I found my voice suddenly.

"But—if others stand in the way?"—I said.

He smiled.

"Surely it will be our own fault if we allow them to assume such a position!" he answered.

I left my hands in his another moment. The fact that he held them gave me a sense of peace and security.

"Sometimes on a long walk through field and forest," I said, softly- -"one may miss the nearest road home. And one is glad to be told which path to follow—"

"Yes,"—he interrupted me—"One is glad to be told!"

His eyes were bent upon me with an enigmatical expression, half commanding, half appealing.

"Then, will you tell me—" I began.

"All that I can!" he said, drawing me a little closer towards him— "All that I may! And you—you must tell me—"

"I! What can I tell you?" and I smiled—"I know nothing!"

"You know one thing which is all things,"—he answered—"But for that I must still wait."

He let go my hands and turned away, shading his eyes from the glare of gold which now spread far and wide over the heavens, turning the sullen waters of Loch Coruisk to a tawny orange against the black purple of the surrounding hills.

"I see our men,"—he then said, in his ordinary tone, "They are looking for us. We must be going."

My heart beat quickly. A longing to speak what I hardly dared to think, was strong upon me. But some inward restraint gripped me as with iron—and my spirit beat itself like a caged bird against its prison bars in vain. I left my rocky throne and heather canopy with slow reluctance, and he saw this.

"You are sorry to come away,"—he said, kindly, and with a smile—"I can quite understand it. It is a beautiful scene."

I stood quite still, looking at him. A host of recollections began to crowd upon me, threatening havoc to my self-control.

"Is it not something more than beautiful?" I asked, and my voice trembled in spite of myself—"To you as well as to me?"

He met my earnest gaze with a sudden deeper light in his own eyes.

"Dear, to me it is the beginning of a new life!"—he said—"But whether it is the same to you I cannot say. I have not the right to think so far. Come!"

A choking sense of tears was in my throat as I moved on by his side. Why could I not speak frankly and tell him that I knew as well as he did that now there was no life anywhere for me where he was not? But—had it come to this? Yes, truly!— it had come to this! Then was it a real love that I felt, or merely a blind obedience to some hypnotic influence? The doubt suggested itself like a whisper from some evil spirit, and I strove not to listen. Presently he took my hand in his as before, and guided me carefully over the slippery boulders and stones, wet with the over-flowing of the mountain torrent and the underlying morass which warned us of its vicinity by the quantity of bog-myrtle growing in profusion everywhere. Almost in silence we reached the shore where the launch was in waiting for us, and in silence we sat together in the stern as the boat cut its swift way through lit-tle waves like molten gold and opal, sparkling with the iridescent reflections of the sun's after-glow.

"I see Mr. Harland's yacht has returned to her moorings,"—he said, after a while, addressing his men, "When did she come back?"

"Immediately after you left, sir,"—was the reply.

I looked and saw the two yachts—the 'Dream' and the 'Diana,' anchored in the widest part of Loch Scavaig—the one with the disfiguring funnels that make even the most magnificent steam yacht unsightly as compared with a sailing vessel,— the other a perfect picture of lightness and grace, resting like a bird with folded wings on the glittering surface of the water. My mind was disturbed and bewil-dered,—I felt that I had journeyed through immense distances of space and cycles of time during that brief excursion to Loch Coruisk,—and as the launch rushed onward and we lost sight of the entrance to what for me had been a veritable

Valley of Vision, it seemed that I had lived through centuries rather than hours. One thing, however, remained positive and real in my experience, and this was the personality of Santoris. With each moment that passed I knew it better—the flash of his blue eyes—his sudden fleeting smile—the turn of his head—the very gesture of his hand,—all these were as familiar to me as the reflection of my own face in a mirror. And now there was no wonderment mingled with the deepening recognition,—I found it quite natural that I should know him well,- -indeed, it was to me evident that I had known him always. What troubled me, however, was a subtle fear that crept insidiously through my veins like a shuddering cold,—a terror lest something to which I could give no name, should separate us or cause us to misunderstand each other. For the psychic lines of attraction between two human beings are finer than the finest gossamer and can be easily broken and scattered even though they may or must be brought together again after long lapses of time. But so many opportunities had already been wasted, I thought, through some recklessness or folly, either on his part or mine. Which of us was to blame? I looked at him half in fear, half in appeal, as he sat in the boat with his head turned a little aside from me,—he seemed grave and preoccupied. A sudden thrill of emotion stirred my heart— tears sprang to my eyes so thickly that for a moment I could scarcely see the waves that glittered and danced on all sides like millions of diamonds. A change had swept over my life,—a change so great that I was hardly able to bear it. It was too swift, too overpowering to be calmly considered, and I was glad when we came alongside the 'Dream' and I saw Mr. Harland on deck, waiting for us at the top of the companion ladder.

"Well!" he called to me—"Was it a good sunset?"

"Glorious!" I answered him—"Did you see nothing of it?"

"No. I slept soundly, and only woke up when Brayle came over to explain that Catherine had taken it into her head to have a short cruise, that he had humoured her accordingly, and that they had just come back to anchorage."

By this time I was standing beside him, and Santoris joined us.

"So your doctor came to look after you,"—he said, with a smile—"I thought he would not trust you out of his sight too long!"

"What do you mean by that?" asked Harland—then his face lightened and he laughed—"Well, I must own you have been a better physician than he for the moment—it is months since I have been so free from pain."

"I'm very glad,"—Santoris answered—"And now would you and your friend like to take the launch back to your own yacht, or will you stay and dine with me?"

Mr. Harland thought a moment.

"I'm afraid we must go"—he said, at last, with obvious reluctance— "Captain Derrick went back with Brayle. You see, Catherine is not strong, and she has not been quite herself—and we must not leave her alone. To-morrow, if you are will-ing, I should like to try a race with our two yachts in open sea—electricity against steam! What do you say?"

"With pleasure!" and Santoris looked amused—"But as I am sure to be the win-ner, you must give me the privilege of entertaining you all to dinner afterwards. Is that settled?" "Certainly!—you are hospitality itself, Santoris!" and Mr. Harland shook him warmly by the hand—"What time shall we start the race?"

"Suppose we say noon?"

"Agreed!"

We then prepared to go. I turned to Santoris and in a quiet voice thanked him for his kindness in escorting me to Loch Coruisk, and for the pleasant afternoon we had passed. The conventional words of common courtesy seemed to myself quite absurd,—however, they had to be uttered, and he accepted them with the usual conventional acknowledgment. When I was just about to descend the companion ladder, he asked me to wait a moment, and going down to the saloon, brought me the bunch of Madonna lilies I had found in that special cabin which, as he had said, was destined 'for a princess.'

"You will take these, I hope?" he said, simply.

I raised my eyes to his as I received the white blossoms from his hand. There was something indefinable and fleeting in his expression, and for a moment it seemed as if we had suddenly become strangers. A sense of loss and pain affected me, such as happens when someone to whom we are deeply attached assumes a cold and distant air for which we can render no explanation. He turned from me as quick-ly as I from him, and I descended the companion ladder followed by Mr. Harland. In a few seconds we had put several boat- lengths between ourselves and the 'Dream,' and a rush of foolish tears to my eyes blurred the figure of Santoris as he lifted his cap to us in courteous adieu. I thought Mr. Harland glanced at me a little inquisitively, but he said nothing—and we were soon on board the 'Diana,' where Catherine, stretched out in a deck chair, watched our arrival with but languid interest. Dr. Brayle was beside her, and looked up as we drew near with a supercilious smile.

"So the electric man has not quite made away with you,"—he said, carelessly—"Miss Harland and I had our doubts as to whether we should ever see you again!"

Mr. Harland's fuzzy eyebrows drew together in a marked frown of displeasure.

"Indeed!" he ejaculated, drily—"Well, you need have had no fears on that score. The 'electric man,' as you call Mr. Santoris, is an excellent host and has no sinister designs on his friends."

"Are you quite sure of that?" and Brayle, with an elaborate show of courtesy, set chairs for his patron and for me near Catherine— "Derrick tells me that the electric appliances on board his yacht are to him of a terrifying character and that he would not risk passing so much as one night on such a vessel!"

Mr. Harland laughed.

"I must talk to Derrick,"—he said—then, approaching his daughter, he asked her kindly if she was better. She replied in the affirmative, but with some little pettishness.

"My nerves are all unstrung,"—she said—"I think that friend of yours is one of those persons who draw all vitality out of everybody else. There are such people, you know, father!—people who, when they are getting old and feeble, go about taking stores of fresh life out of others."

He looked amused.

"You are full of fancies, Catherine,"—he said—"And no logical reasoning will ever argue you out of them. Santoris is all right. For one thing, he gave me great relief from pain to-day."

"Ah! How was that?"—and Brayle looked up sharply with sudden interest.

"I don't know how,"—replied Harland,—"A drop or two of harmless- looking fluid worked wonders for me—and in a few moments I felt almost well. He tells me my illness is not incurable."

A curious expression difficult to define flitted over Brayle's face.

"You had better take care," he said, curtly—"Invalids should never try experiments. I'm surprised that a man in your condition should take any drug from the hand of a stranger."

"Most dangerous!" interpolated Catherine, feebly—"How could you, father?"

"Well, Santoris isn't quite a stranger,"—said Mr. Harland—"After all, I knew him at college—"

"You think you knew him,"—put in Brayle—"He may not be the same man."

"He is the same man,"—answered Mr. Harland, rather testily—"There are no two of his kind in the world."

Brayle lifted his eyebrows with a mildly affected air of surprise.

"I thought you had your doubts—"

"Of course!—I had and have my doubts concerning everybody and everything"—said Mr. Harland, "And I suppose I shall have them to the end of my days. I have sometimes doubted even your good intentions towards me."

A dark flush overspread Brayle's face suddenly, and as suddenly paled. He laughed a little forcedly.

"I hardly think you have any reason to do so," he said.

Mr. Harland did not answer, but turning round, addressed me.

"You enjoyed yourself at Loch Coruisk, didn't you?"

"Indeed I did!" I replied, with emphasis—"It was a lovely scene!— never to be forgotten,"

"You and Mr. Santoris would be sure to get on well together," said Catherine, rather crossly—"'Birds of a feather,' you know!"

I smiled. I was too much taken up with my own thoughts to pay attention to her evident ill-humour. I was aware that Dr. Brayle watched me furtively, and with a suspicious air, and there was a curious feeling of constraint in the atmosphere that made me feel I had somehow displeased my hostess, but the matter seemed to me too trifling to consider, and as soon as the conversation became general I took the opportunity to slip away and get down to my cabin, where I locked the door and gave myself up to the freedom of my own meditations. They were at first bewildered and chaotic—but gradually my mind smoothed itself out like the sea I had looked upon in my vision,—and I began to arrange and connect the various incidents of my strange experience in a more or less coherent form. According to psychic consciousness I knew what they all meant,—but according to merely material and earthly reasoning they were utterly incomprehensible. If I listened to the explanation offered by my inner self, it was this:—That Rafel Santoris and I had known each other for ages,—longer than we were permitted to remember,—that the brain-pictures, or rather soul-pictures, presented to me were only a few selected out of thousands which equally concerned us, and which were stored up among eternal records,—and that these few were only recalled to remind me of circumstances which I might erroneously think were all entirely forgotten. If, on the other hand, I preferred to accept what would be called a reasonable and practical solution of the enigma, I would say:—That, being imaginative and sensitive, I had been easily hypnotised by a stronger will than my own, and that for his amusement, or because he had seen in me the possibility of a 'test case,' Santoris had tried his power upon me and forced me to see whatever he chose to conjure up in order to bewilder and perplex me. But if this were so, what could be his object? If I were indeed an utter stranger to him, why should he take this trouble? I found myself harassed by anxiety and dragged between two opposing influences—one which impelled me to yield myself to the deep sense of exquisite happiness, peace and consolation that swept over my spirit like the touch of a veritable benediction from heaven,—the other which pushed me back against a hard wall of impregnable fact and bade me suspect my dawning joy as though it were a foe.

That night we were a curious party at dinner. Never were five human beings more oddly brought into contact and conversation with each other. We were absolutely opposed at all points; in thought, in feeling and in sentiment, I could not help remembering the wonderful network of shining lines I had seen in that first dream of mine,— lines which were apparently mathematically designed to meet in reciprocal unity. The lines on this occasion between us five human beings were an almost visible tangle. I found my best refuge in silence,—and I listened in vague wonderment to the flow of senseless small talk poured out by Dr. Brayle, apparently for the amusement of Catherine, who on her part seemed suddenly possessed by a spirit of wilfulness and enforced gaiety which moved her to utter a great many foolish things, things which she evidently imagined were clever. There is nothing perhaps more embarrassing than to hear a woman of mature years giving herself away by the childish vapidness of her talk, and exhibiting not only a lack of mental poise, but also utter tactlessness. However, Catherine rattled on, and Dr. Brayle rattled with her,—Mr. Harland threw in occasional monosyllables, but for the most part was evidently caught in a kind of dusty spider's web of thought, and I spoke not at all unless spoken to. Presently I met Catherine's eyes fixed upon me with a sort of round, half-malicious curiosity.

"I think your day's outing has done you good," she said—"You look wonderfully well!"

"I AM well!" I answered her—"I have been well all the time."

"Yes, but you haven't looked as you look to-night," she said—"You have quite a transformed air!"

"Transformed?"—I echoed, smiling—"In what way?"

Mr. Harland turned and surveyed me critically.

"Upon my word, I think Catherine is right!" he said—"There is something different about you, though I cannot explain what it is!"

I felt the colour rising hotly to my face, but I endeavoured to appear unconcerned.

"You look," said Dr. Brayle, with a quick glance from his narrowly set eyes—"as if you had been through a happy experience."

"Perhaps I have!" I answered quietly—"It has certainly been a very happy day!" "What is your opinion of Santoris?" asked Mr. Harland, suddenly—"You've spent a couple of hours alone in his company,—you must have formed some idea."

I replied at once, without taking thought.

"I think him quite an exceptional man," I said—"Good and great- hearted,—and I fancy he must have gone through much difficult experience to make him what he is."

"I entirely disagree with you,"—said Dr. Brayle, quickly—"I've taken his measure, and I think it's a fairly correct one. I believe him to be a very clever and subtle charlatan, who affects a certain profound mysticism in order to give himself undue importance—"

There was a sudden clash. Mr. Harland had brought his clenched fist down upon the table with a force that made the glasses ring.

"I won't have that, Brayle!" he said, sharply—"I tell you I won't have it! Santoris is no charlatan—never was!—he won his honours at Oxford like a man—his conduct all the time I ever knew him was perfectly open and blameless—he did no mean tricks, and pandered to nothing base—and if some of us fellows were frightened of him (as we were) it was because he did everything better than we could do it, and was superior to us all. That's the truth!—and there's no getting over it. Nothing gives small minds a better handle for hatred than superiority—especially when that superiority is never asserted, but only felt."

"You surprise me,"—murmured Brayle, half apologetically—"I thought—"

"Never mind what you thought!" said Mr. Harland, with a sudden ugly irritation of manner that sometimes disfigured him—"Your thoughts are not of the least importance!"

Dr. Brayle flushed angrily and Catherine looked surprised and visibly indignant.

"Father! How can you be so rude!"

"Am I rude?" And Mr. Harland shrugged his shoulders indifferently— "Well! I may be—but I never take a man's hospitality and permit myself to listen to abuse of him afterwards."

"I assure you—" began Dr. Brayle, almost humbly.

"There, there! If I spoke hastily, I apologise. But Santoris is too straightforward a man to be suspected of any dishonesty or chicanery—and certainly no one on board this vessel shall treat his name with anything but respect." Here he turned to me—"Will you come on deck for a little while before bedtime, or would you rather rest?"

I saw that he wished to speak to me, and willingly agreed to accompany him. Dinner being well over, we left the saloon, and were soon pacing the deck together under the light of a brilliant moon. Instinctively we both looked towards the 'Dream' yacht,— there was no illumination about her this evening save the usual lamp hung in the rigging and the tiny gleams of radiance through her port-holes,- -and her graceful masts and spars were like fine black pencillings seen against the bare slope of a mountain made almost silver to the summit by the singularly searching clearness of the moonbeams. My host paused in his walk beside me to light a cigar.

"I'm sure you are convinced that Santoris is honest," he said—"Are you not?"

"In what way should I doubt him?"—I replied, evasively—"I scarcely know him!"

Hardly had I said this when a sudden self-reproach stung me. How dare I say that I scarcely knew one who had been known to me for ages? I leaned against the deck rail looking up at the violet sky, my heart beating quickly. My companion was still busy lighting his cigar, but when this was done to his satisfaction he resumed.

"True! You scarcely know him, but you are quick to form opinions, and your instincts are often, though perhaps not always, correct. At any rate, you have no distrust of him? You like him?"

"Yes,"—I answered, slowly—"I—I like him—very much."

And the violet sky, with its round white moon, seemed to swing in a circle about me as I spoke—knowing that the true answer of my heart was love, not liking!— that love was the magnet drawing me irresistibly, despite my own endeavour, to something I could neither understand nor imagine.

"I'm glad of that," said Mr. Harland—"It would have worried me a little if you had taken a prejudice or felt any antipathy towards him. I can see that Brayle hates him and has imbued Catherine with something of his own dislike."

I was silent.

"He is, of course, an extraordinary man," went on Mr. Harland—"and he is bound to offend many and to please few. He is not likely to escape the usual fate of unusual characters. But I think—indeed I may say I am sure—his integrity is beyond question. He has curious opinions about love and marriage—almost as curious as the fixed ideas he holds concerning life and death."

Something cold seemed to send a shiver through my blood—was it some stray fragment of memory from the past that stirred me to a sense of pain? I forced myself to speak.

"What are those opinions?" I asked, and looking up in the moonlight to my companion's face I saw that it wore a puzzled expression— "Hardly conventional, I suppose?"

"Conventional! Convention and Santoris are farther apart than the poles! No— he doesn't fit into any accepted social code at all. He looks upon marriage itself as a tacit acknowledgment of inconstancy in love, and declares that if the passion existed in its truest form between man and woman any sort of formal or legal tie would be needless,—as love, if it be love, does not and cannot change. But it is no use discussing such a matter with him. The love that he believes in can only exist, if then, once in a thousand years! Men and women marry for physical attraction, convenience, necessity or respectability,—and the legal bond is necessary both for their sakes and the worldly welfare of the children born to them; but love which is physical and transcendental together,—love that is to last through an imagined eternity of progress and fruition, this is a mere dream—a chimera!—and he feasts his brain upon it as though it were a nourishing fact. However, one must have patience with him—he is not like the rest of us."

"No!" I murmured—and then stood silently beside him watching the moonbeams ripple on the waters in wavy links of brightness.

"When you married," I said, at last—"did you not marry for love?"

He puffed at his cigar thoughtfully.

"Well, I hardly know," he replied, after a long pause,—"Looking back upon everything, I rather doubt it! I married as most men marry—on impulse. I saw a pretty face—and it seemed advisable that I should marry—but I cannot say I was moved by any great or absorbing passion for the woman I chose. She was charming and amiable in our courting days—as a wife she became peevish and querulous,—apt to sulk, too,—and she devoted herself almost entirely to the most commonplace routine of life;—however, I had nothing to justly complain of. We lived five years together before her child Catherine was born,—and then she died. I cannot say that either her life or her death left any deep mark upon me—not if I am honest. I don't think I understand love—certainly not the love which Rafel Santoris looks upon as the secret key of the Universe."

Instinctively my eyes turned towards the 'Dream' at anchor. She looked like a phantom vessel in the moonlight. Again the faint shiver of cold ran through my veins like a sense of spiritual terror. If I should lose now what I had lost before! This was my chief thought,—my hidden shuddering fear. Did the whole responsibility rest with me, I wondered? Mr. Harland laid his hand kindly on my arm.

"You look like a wan spirit in the moonbeams," he said—"So pale and wistful! You are tired, and I am selfish in keeping you up here to talk to me. Go down to your cabin. I can see you are full of mystical dreams, and I am afraid Santoris has rather helped you to indulge in them. He is of the same nature as you are—inclined to believe that this life as we live it is only one phase of many that are past and of many yet to come. I wish I could accept that faith!"

"I wish you could!" I said—"You surely would be happier."

"Should I?" He gave a quick sigh. "I have my doubts! If I could be young and strong and lie through many lives always possessed of that same youth and strength, then there would be something in it—but to be old and ailing, no! The Faust legend is an eternal truth—Life is only worth living as long as we enjoy it."

"Your friend Santoris enjoys it!" I said.

"Ah! There you touch me! He does enjoy it, and why? Because he is young! Though nearly as old in years as I am, he is actually young! That's the mystery of him! Santoris is positively young—young in heart, young in thought, ambition, feeling and sentiment, and yet— "

He broke off for a moment, then resumed.

"I don't know how he has managed it, but he told me long ago that it was a man's own fault if he allowed himself to grow old. I laughed at him then, but he has certainly carried his theories into fact. He used to declare that it was either yourself or your friends that made you old. 'You will find,' he said, 'as you go on in years, that your family relations, or your professing dear friends, are those that will chiefly insist on your inviting and accepting the burden of age. They will remind you that twenty years ago you did so and so,—or that they have known you over thirty years—or they will tell you that considering your age you look well, or a thousand and one things of that kind, as if it were a fault or even a crime to be alive for a certain span of time,—whereas if you simply shook off such unnecessary attentions and went your own way, taking freely of the constant output of life and energy supplied to you by Nature, you would outwit all these croakers of feebleness and decay and renew your vital forces to the end. But to do this you must have a constant aim in life and a ruling passion.' As I told you, I laughed at him and at what I called his 'folly,' but now—well, now—it's a case of 'let those laugh who win.'"

"And you think he has won?" I asked.

"Most assuredly—I cannot deny it. But the secret of his victory is beyond me."

"I should think it is beyond most people," I replied—"For if we could all keep ourselves young and strong we would take every means in our power to attain such happiness—"

"Would we, though?" And his brows knitted perplexedly—"If we knew, would we take the necessary trouble? We will hardly obey a physician's orders for our good even when we are really ill—would we in health follow any code of life in order to keep well?"

I laughed.

"Perhaps not!" I said—"I expect it will always be the same thing— 'Many are called, but few are chosen.' Goodnight!"

I held out my hand. He took it in his own and kept it a moment.

"It's curious we should have met Santoris so soon after my telling you about him," he said—"It's one of those coincidences which one cannot explain. You are very like him in some of your ideas—you two ought to be very great friends."

"Ought we?"—and I smiled—"Perhaps we shall be! Again, Good-night!"

"Good-night!" And I left him to his meditations and went down to my cabin, only stopping for a moment to say good-night to Catherine and Dr. Brayle, who were playing bridge with Mr. Swinton and Captain Derrick in the saloon. Once in my room, I was thankful to be alone. Every extraneous thing seemed an intrusion or an impertinence,—the thoughts that filled my brain were all absorbing, and went so far beyond the immediate radius of time and space that I could hardly follow their flight. I smiled as I imagined what ordinary people would think of the experience through which I had passed and was passing. 'Foolish fancies!' 'Neurotic folly!' and other epithets of the kind would be heaped upon me if they knew—they, the excellent folk whose sole objects in life are so ephemeral as to be the things of the hour, the day, or the month merely, and who if they ever pause to consider eternal possibilities at all, do so reluctantly perhaps in church on Sundays, comfortably dismissing them for the more solid prospect of dinner. And of Love? What view of the divine passion do they take as a rule? Let the millions of mistaken marriages answer! Let the savage lusts and treacheries and cruelties of merely brutish and unspiritualised humanity bear witness? And how few shall be found who have even the beginnings of the nature of true love—'the love of soul for soul, angel for angel, god for god!'—the love that accepts this world and its events as one phase only of divine and immortal existence—a phase of trial and proving in which the greater number fail to pass even a first examination! As for myself, I felt and knew that _I_ had failed hopelessly and utterly in the past—and I stood now as it were on the edge of new circumstances—in fear, yet not without hope, and praying that whatsoever should chance to me I might not fail again!

X

STRANGE ASSOCIATIONS

The next day the race agreed upon was run in the calmest of calm weather. There was not the faintest breath of wind,—the sea was still as a pond and almost oily in its smooth, motionless shining— and it was evident at first that our captain entertained no doubt whatever as to the 'Diana,' with her powerful engines, being easily able to beat the aerial-looking 'Dream' schooner, which at noon-day, with all sails spread, came gliding up beside us till she lay point to point at equal distance and at nearly equal measurement with our more cumbersome vessel. Mr. Harland was keenly excited; Dr. Brayle was ready to lay any amount of wagers as to the impossibility of a sailing vessel, even granted she was moved by electricity, out- racing one of steam in such a dead calm. As the two vessels lay on the still waters, the 'Diana' fussily getting up steam, and the 'Dream' with sails full out as if in a stiff breeze, despite the fact that there was no wind, we discussed the situation eagerly—or rather I should say my host and his people discussed it, for I had nothing to say, knowing that the victory was sure to be with Santoris. We were in very lonely waters,—there was room and to spare for plenty of racing, and when all was ready and Santoris saluted us from the deck, lifting his cap and waving it in response to a similar greeting from Mr. Harland and our skipper, the signal to start was given. We moved off together, and for at least half an hour or more the 'Dream' floated along in a kind of lazy indolence, keeping up with us easily, her canvas filled, and her keel cutting the water as if swept by a favouring gale. The result of the race was soon a foregone conclusion,—for presently, when well out on the mirror-like calm of the sea, the 'Dream' showed her secret powers in earnest, and flew like a bird with a silent swiftness that was almost incredible. Our yacht put on all steam in the effort to keep up with her,—in vain! On, on, with light grace and celerity her white sails carried her like the wings of a sea-gull, and almost before we could realise it she vanished altogether from our sight! I saw a waste of water spread around us emptily like a wide circle of crystal reflecting the sky, and a sense of desolation fell upon me in the mere fact that we were temporarily left alone. We steamed on and on in the direction of the vanished 'Dream,'—our movements suggesting those of some clumsy four-footed animal panting its way after a bird, but unable to come up with her.

"Wonderful!" said Mr. Harland, at last, drawing a long breath,—"I would never have believed it possible!"

"Nor I!" agreed Captain Derrick—"I certainly thought she would never have managed it in such a dead calm. For though I have seen some of her mechanism I cannot entirely understand it."

Dr. Brayle was silent. It was evident that he was annoyed—though why he should be so was not apparent. I myself was full of secret anxiety—for the 'Dream' yacht's sudden and swift disappearance had filled me with a wretched sense of loneliness beyond all expression. Suppose she should not return! I had no clue to her whereabouts—and with the loss of Santoris I knew I should lose all that was worth having in my life. While these miserable thoughts were yet chasing each other through my brain I suddenly caught a far glimpse of white sails on the horizon.

"She's coming back!" I cried, enraptured, and heedless of what I said—"Oh, thank God! She's coming back!"

They all looked at me in amazement.

"Why, what's the matter with you?" asked Mr. Harland, smiling. "You surely didn't think she was in any danger?"

My cheeks grew warm.

"I didn't know—I could not imagine—" I faltered, and turning away I met Dr. Brayle's eyes fixed upon me with a gleam of malice in them.

"I'm sure," he said, suavely, "you are greatly interested in Mr. Santoris! Perhaps you have met each other before?"

"Never!" I answered, hurriedly,—and then checked myself, startled and confused. He kept his narrow brown eyes heedfully upon me and smiled slightly.

"Really! I should have thought otherwise!"

I did not trouble myself to reply. The white sails of the 'Dream' were coming nearer and nearer over the smooth width of the sunlit water, and as she approached my heart grew warm with gratitude. Life was again a thing of joy!—the world was no longer empty! That ship looked to me like a beautiful winged spirit coming towards me with radiant assurances of hope and consolation, and I lost all fear, all sadness, all foreboding, as she gradually swept up alongside in the easy triumph she had won. Our crew assembled to welcome her, and cheered lustily. Santoris, standing on her deck, lightly acknowledged the salutes which gave him the victory, and presently both our vessels were once more at their former places of anchorage. When all the excitement was over, I went down to my cabin to rest for a while before dressing for the dinner on board the 'Dream' to which we were all invited,—and while I lay on my sofa reading, Catherine Harland knocked at my door and asked to come in, I admitted her at once, and she flung herself into an armchair with a gesture of impatience.

"I'm so tired of all this yachting!" she said, peevishly. "It isn't amusing to me!"

"I'm very sorry!" I answered;—"If you feel like that, why not give it up at once?"

"Oh, it's father's whim!" she said-"And if he makes up his mind there's no moving him. One thing, however, I'm determined to do—and that is—" Here she stopped, looking at me curiously.

I returned her gaze questioningly.

"And that is—what?"

"To get as far away as ever we can from that terrible 'Dream' yacht and its owner!"—she replied—"That man is a devil!"

I laughed. I could not help laughing. The estimate she had formed of one so vastly her superior as Santoris struck me as more amusing than blamable. I am often accustomed to hear the hasty and narrow verdict of small-minded and unintelligent persons pronounced on men and women of high attainment and great mental ability; therefore, that she should show herself as not above the level of the common majority did not offend so much as it entertained me. However, my laughter made her suddenly angry.

"Why do you laugh?" she demanded. "You look quite pagan in that lace rest-gown—I suppose you call it a restgown!—with all your hair tumbling loose about you! And that laugh of yours is a pagan laugh!"

I was so surprised at her odd way of speaking that for a moment I could find no words. She looked at me with a kind of hard disfavour in her eyes.

"That's the reason,"—she went on—"why you find life agreeable. Pagans always did. They revelled in sunshine and open air, and found all sorts of excuses for their own faults, provided they got some pleasure out of them. That's quite your temperament! And they laughed at serious things—just as you do!"

The mirror showed me my own reflection, and I saw myself still smiling.

"Do I laugh at serious things?" I said. "Dear Miss Harland, I am not aware of it! But I cannot take Mr. Santoris as a 'devil' seriously!"

"He is!" And she nodded her head emphatically—"And all those queer beliefs he holds—and you hold them too!—are devilish! If you belonged to the Church of Rome, you would not be allowed to indulge in such wicked theories for a moment."

"Ah! The Church of Rome fortunately cannot control thought!"—I said—"Not even the thoughts of its own children! And some of the beliefs of the Church of Rome are more blasphemous and barbarous than all the paganism of the ancient world! Tell me, what are my 'wicked theories'?"

"Oh, I don't know!" she replied, vaguely and inconsequently—"You believe there's no death—and you think we all make our own illnesses and misfortunes,—and I've heard you say that the idea of Eternal Punishment is absurd—so in a way you are as bad as father, who declares there's nothing in the Universe but gas and atoms—no God and no anything. You really are quite as much of an atheist as he is! Dr. Brayle says so."

I had been standing in front of her while she thus talked, but now I resumed my former reclining attitude on the sofa and looked at her with a touch of disdain.

"Dr. Brayle says so!"—I repeated—"Dr. Brayle's opinion is the least worth having in the world! Now, if you really believe in devils, there's one for you!"

"How can you say so?" she exclaimed, hotly—"What right have you—"

"How can he call ME an atheist?" I demanded-"What right has HE to judge me?"

The flush died off her face, and a sudden fear filled her eyes.

"Don't look at me like that!" she said, almost in a whisper—"It reminds me of an awful dream I had the other night!"—She paused.— "Shall I tell it to you?"

I nodded indifferently, yet watched her curiously the while. Something in her hard, plain face had become suddenly and unpleasantly familiar.

"I dreamed that I was in a painter's studio watching two murdered people die— a man and a woman. The man was like Santoris—the woman resembled you! They had been stabbed,—and the woman was clinging to the man's body. Dr. Brayle stood beside me also watching—but the scene was strange to me, and the clothes we wore were all of some ancient time. I said to Dr. Brayle: 'We have killed them!' and he replied: 'Yes! They are better dead than living!' It was a horrible dream!—it seemed so real! I have been frightened of you and of that man Santoris ever since!"

I could not speak for a moment. A recollection swept over me to which I dared not give utterance,—it seemed too improbable.

"I've had nerves," she went on, shivering a little—"and that's why I say I'm tired of this yachting trip. It's becoming a nightmare to me!"

I lay back on the sofa looking at her with a kind of pity.

"Then why not end it?" I said—"Or why not let me go away? It is I who have dis-pleased you somehow, and I assure you I'm very sorry! You and Mr. Harland have both been most kind to me—I've been your guest for nearly a fortnight,—that's quite sufficient holiday for me—put me ashore anywhere you like and I'll go home and get myself out of your way. Will that be any comfort to you?"

"I don't know that it will," she said, with a short, querulous sigh- -"Things have happened so strangely." She paused, looking at me— "Yes—you have the face of that woman I saw in my dream!—and you have always reminded me of—"

I waited eagerly. She seemed afraid to go on.

"Well!" I said, as quietly as I could—"Do please finish what you were saying!"

"It goes back to the time when I first saw you," she continued, now speaking quickly as though anxious to get it over—"You will perhaps hardly remember the occasion. It was at that great art and society "crush" in London where there was such a crowd that hundreds of people never got farther than the staircase. You were pointed out to me as a "psychist"—and while I was still listening to what was being said about you, my father came up with you on his arm and introduced us. When I saw you I felt that your features were somehow familiar,—though I could not tell where I had met you before,—and I became very anxious to see more of you. In fact, you had a perfect fascination for me! You have the same fascination now,—only it is a fascination that terrifies me!"

I was silent.

"The other night," she went on—"when Mr. Santoris first came on board I had a singular impression that he was or had been an enemy of mine,—though where or how I could not say. It was this that frightened me, and made me too ill and nervous to go with you on that excursion to Loch Coruisk. And I want to get away from him! I never had such impressions before—and even now,—looking at you,—I feel there's something in you which is quite "uncanny,"—it troubles me! Oh!—I'm sure you mean me no harm—you are bright and amiable and adaptable and all that—but—I'm afraid of you!"

"Poor Catherine!" I said, very gently—"These are merely nervous ideas! There is nothing to fear from me—no, nothing!" For here she suddenly leaned forward and took my hand, looking earnestly in my face—"How can you imagine such a thing possible?"

"Are you sure?" she half whispered—"When I called you "pagan" just now I had a sort of dim recollection of a fair woman like you,—a woman I seemed to know who was really a pagan! Yet I don't know how I knew her, or where I met her—a woman who, for some reason or other, was hateful to me because I was jealous of her! These curious fancies have haunted my mind only since that man Santoris came on board,—and I told Dr. Brayle exactly what I felt."

"And what did he say?" I asked.

"He said that it was all the work of Santoris, who was an evident professor of psychical imposture—"

I sprang up.

"Let him say that to ME!" I exclaimed—"Let him dare to say it! and I will prove who is the impostor to his face!"

She retreated from me with wide-open eyes of alarm.

"Why do you look at me like that?" she said. "We didn't really kill you—except—in a dream!"

A sudden silence fell between us; something cold and shadowy and impalpable seemed to possess the very air. If by some supernatural agency we had been momentarily deprived of life and motion, while a vast dark cloud, heavy with rain, had made its slow way betwixt us, the sense of chill and depression could hardly have been greater.

Presently Catherine spoke again, with a little forced laugh.

"What silly things I say!" she murmured—"You can see for yourself my nerves are in a bad state!—I am altogether unstrung!"

I stood for a moment looking at her, and considering the perplexity in which we both seemed involved.

"If you would rather not dine with Mr. Santoris this evening," I said, at last,—"and if you think his presence has a bad effect on you, let us make some excuse not to go. I will willingly stay with you, if you wish me to do so."

She gave me a surprised glance.

"You are very unselfish," she said—"and I wish I were not so fanciful. It's most kind of you to offer to stay with me and to give up an evening's pleasure—for I suppose it IS a pleasure? You like Mr. Santoris?"

The colour rushed to my face in a warm glow.

"Yes," I answered, turning slightly away from her—"I like him very much."

"And he likes YOU better than he likes any of us," she said—"In fact, I believe if it had not been for you, we should never have met him in this strange way—"

"Why, how can you make that out?" I asked, smiling. "I never heard of him till your father spoke of him,—and never saw him till—"

"Till when?"—she demanded, quickly.

"Till the other night," I answered, hesitatingly.

She searched my face with questioning eyes.

"I thought you were going to say that you, like myself, had some idea or recollection of having met him before," she said. "However, I shall not ask you to sacrifice your pleasure for me,—in fact, I have made up my mind to go to this dinner, though Dr. Brayle doesn't wish it."

"Oh! Dr. Brayle doesn't wish it!" I echoed—"And why?"

"Well, he thinks it will not be good for me—and—and he hates the very sight of Santoris!"

I said nothing. She rose to leave my cabin.

"Please don't think too hardly of me!" she said, pleadingly,—"I've told you frankly just how I feel,—and you can imagine how glad I shall be when this yachting trip comes to an end."

She went away then, and I stood for some minutes lost in thought. I dared not pursue the train of memories with which she had connected herself in my mind. My chief idea now was to find some convenient method of immediately concluding my stay with the Harlands and leaving their yacht at some easy point of departure for home. And I resolved I would speak to Santoris on this subject and trust to him for a means whereby we should not lose sight of each other, for I felt that this was imperative. And my spirit rose up within me full of joy and pride in its instinctive consciousness that I was as necessary to him as he was to me.

It was a warm, almost sultry evening, and I was able to discard my serge yachting dress for one of soft white Indian silk, a cooler and more presentable costume for a dinner-party on board a yacht which was furnished with such luxury as was the 'Dream.' My little sprig of bell-heather still looked bright and fresh in the glass where I always kept it—but to-night when I took it in my hand it suddenly crumbled into a pinch of fine grey dust. This sudden destruction of what had seemed well-nigh indestructible startled me for a moment till I began to think that after all the little bunch of blossom had done its work,—its message had been given— its errand completed. All the Madonna lilies Santoris had given me were as fresh as if newly gathered,—and I chose one of these with its companion bud as my only ornament. When I joined my host and his party in the saloon he looked at me with inquisitive scrutiny.

"I cannot quite make you out," he said—"You look several years younger than you did when you came on board at Rothesay! Is it the sea air, the sunshine, or— Santoris?"

"Santoris!" I repeated, and laughed. "How can it be Santoris?"

"Well, he makes HIMSELF young," Mr. Harland answered—"And perhaps he may make others young too. There's no telling the extent of his powers!"

"Quite the conjurer!" observed Dr. Brayle, drily—"Faust should have consulted him instead of Mephistopheles!"

"'Faust' is a wonderful legend, but absurd in the fact that the old philosopher sold his soul to the Devil, merely for the love of woman,"—said Mr. Harland. "The joy, the sensation and the passion of love were to him supreme temptation and the only satisfaction on earth."

Dr. Brayle's eyes gleamed.

"But, after all, is this not a truth?" he asked—"Is there anything that so completely dominates the life of a man as the love of a woman? It is very seldom the right woman—but it is always a woman of some kind. Everything that has ever been done in the world, either good or evil, can be traced back to the influence of women on men—sometimes it is their wives who sway their actions, but it is far more often their mistresses. Kings and emperors are as prone to the universal weakness as commoners,—we have only to read history to be assured of the fact. What more could Faust desire than love?"

"Well, to me love is a mistake," said Mr. Harland, throwing on his overcoat carelessly—"I agree with Byron's dictum 'Who loves, raves!' Of course it should be an ideal passion—but it never is. Come, are we all ready?"

We were—and we at once left the yacht in our own launch. Our party consisted of Mr. Harland, his daughter, myself, Dr. Brayle and Mr. Swinton, and with such indifferent companions I imagined it would be difficult, if not impossible, to get even a moment with Santoris alone, to tell him of my intention to leave my host and hostess as soon as might be possible. However, I determined to make some effort in this direction, if I could find even the briefest opportunity.

We made our little trip across the water from the 'Diana' to the 'Dream' in the light of a magnificent sunset. Loch Scavaig was a blaze of burning colour,—and the skies above us were flushed with deep rose divided by lines of palest blue and warm gold. Santoris was waiting on the deck to receive us, attended by his captain and one or two of the principals of the crew, but what attracted and charmed our eyes at the moment was a beautiful dark youth of some twelve or thirteen years of age, clad in Eastern dress, who held a basket full of crimson and white rose petals, which, with a graceful gesture, he silently emptied at our feet as we stepped on board. I happened to be the first one to ascend the companion ladder, so that it looked as if this fragrant heap of delicate leaves had been thrown down for me to tread upon, but even if it had been so intended it appeared as though designed for the whole party. Santoris welcomed us with the kindly courtesy which always distinguished his manner, and he himself escorted Miss Harland down to one of the cabins, there to take off the numerous unnecessary wraps and shawls with which she invariably clothed herself on the warmest day,—I followed them as they went, and he turned to me with a smile, saying:—

"You know your room? The same you had yesterday afternoon."

I obeyed his gesture, and entered the exquisitely designed and furnished apartment which he had said was for a 'princess,' and closing the door I sat down for a few minutes to think quietly. It was evident that things were coming to some sort of crisis in my life,—and shaping to some destiny which I must either accept or avoid. Decisive action would rest, as I saw, entirely with myself. To avoid all difficulty, I had only to hold my peace and go my own way—refuse to know more of this singular man who seemed to be so mysteriously connected with my life, and return home to the usual safe, if dull, routine of my ordinary round of work and effort. On the other hand, to accept the dawning joy that seemed showering upon me like a light from Heaven, was to blindly move on into the Unknown,— to trust unquestioningly to the secret spiritual promptings of my own nature and to give myself up wholly and ungrudgingly to a love which suggested all things yet promised nothing! Full of the most conflicting thoughts, I paced the room up and down slowly—the tall mirror reflected my face and figure and showed me the startlingly faithful presentment of the woman I had seen in my strange series of visions,—the woman who centuries ago had fought against convention and custom, only to be foolishly conquered by them in a thousand ways,—the woman who had slain love, only that it should rise again and confront her with deathless eyes of eternal remembrance—the woman who, drowned at last for love's sake in a sea of wrath and trembling, knelt outside the barred gate of Heaven praying to enter in! And in my mind I heard again the words spoken by that sweet and solemn Voice which had addressed me in the first of my dreams:

"One rose from all the roses in Heaven! One—fadeless and immortal— only one, but sufficient for all! One love from all the million loves of men and women— one, but enough for Eternity! How long the rose has awaited its flowering—how long the love has awaited its fulfilment—only the recording angels know! Such roses bloom but once in the wilderness of space and time; such love comes but once in a Universe of worlds!"

And then I remembered the parting command: "Rise and go hence! Keep the gift God sends thee!—take that which is thine!—meet that which hath sought thee sorrowing for many centuries! Turn not aside again, neither by thine own will nor by the will of others, lest old errors prevail. Pass from vision into waking!—from night to day!—from seeming death to life!—from loneliness to love!—and keep within thy heart the message of a Dream!"

Dared I trust to these suggestions which the worldly-wise would call mere imagination? A profound philosopher of these latter days has defined Imagination as 'an advanced perception of truth,' and avers that the discoveries of the future can always be predicted by the poet and the seer, whose receptive brains are the first to catch the premonitions of those finer issues of thought which emanate from the Divine intelligence. However this may be, my own experience of life had taught me that what ordinary persons pin their faith upon as real, is often unreal,—while such promptings of the soul as are almost incapable of expression lead to the highest realities of existence. And I decided at last to let matters take their own course, though I was absolutely resolved to get away from the Harlands within the next two or three days. I meant to ask Mr. Harland to land me at Portree, where I could take the steamer for Glasgow;—any excuse would serve for a hurried departure—and I felt now that departure was necessary.

A soft sound of musical bells reached my ears at this moment announcing dinner,—and leaving the 'princess's' apartment, I met Santoris at the entrance to the saloon. There was no one else there for the moment but himself, and as I came towards him he took my hands in his own and raised them to his lips.

"You are not yet resolved!" he said, in a low tone, smiling—"Take plenty of time!"

I lifted my eyes to his, and all doubt seemed swept away in the light of our mutual glances—I smiled in response to his look,—and we loosened our hands quickly as Mr. Harland with his doctor and secretary came down from the deck, Catherine joining us from the cabin where she had disburdened herself of her invalid wrappings. She was rather more elegantly attired than usual—she wore a curious purple-coloured gown with threads of gold interwoven in the stuff, and a

collar of lace turned back at the throat gave her the aspect of an old Italian picture—a sort of 'Portrait of a lady,—Artist unknown.' Not a pleasant portrait, perhaps—but characteristic of a certain dull and self-centred type of woman. We
were soon seated at table—a table richly, yet daintily, appointed, and adorned
with the costliest flowers and fruits. The men who waited upon us were all
Easterns, dark-eyed and dark-skinned, and wore the Eastern dress,— all their
movements were swift yet graceful and dignified—they made no noise in the
business of serving,—not a dish clattered, not a glass clashed. They were perfect
servants, taking care to avoid the common but reprehensible method of offering
dishes to persons conversing, thus interrupting the flow of talk at inopportune
moments. And what talk it was!—all sorts of subjects, social and impersonal,
came up for discussion, and Santoris handled them with such skill that he made
us forget that there was anything remarkable or unusual about himself or his surroundings, though, as a matter of fact, no more princely banquet could ever have
been served in the most luxurious of palaces. Half-way through the meal, when
the conversation came for a moment to a pause, the most exquisite music
charmed our ears—beginning softly and far away, it swelled out to rich and glorious harmonies like a full orchestra playing under the sea. We looked at each
other and then at our host in charmed enquiry.

"Electricity again!" he said—"So simply managed that it is not worth talking
about! Unfortunately, it is mechanical music, and this can never be like the music
evolved from brain and fingers; however, it fills in gaps of silence when conventional minds are at a strain for something to say—something quite 'safe' and
unlikely to provoke discussion!"

His keen blue eyes flashed with a sudden gleam of scorn in them. I looked at him
half questioningly, and the scorn melted into a smile.

"It isn't good form to start any subject which might lead to argument," he went
on—"The modern brain must not be exercised too strenuously,—it is not strong
enough to stand much effort. What do you say, Harland?"

"I agree," answered Mr. Harland. "As a rule people who dine as well as we are din-
ing to-night have no room left for mentality—they become all digestion!"

Dr. Brayle laughed.

"Nothing like a good dinner if one has an appetite for it. I think it quite possible
that Faust would have left his Margaret for a full meal!"

"I'm sure he would!" chimed in Mr. Swinton—"Any man would!"

Santoris looked down the table with a curious air of half-amused inspection. His eyes, clear and searching in their swift glance, took in the whole group of us—Mr. Harland enjoying succulent asparagus; Dr. Brayle drinking champagne; Mr. Swinton helping himself out of some dish of good things offered to him by one of the servants; Catherine playing in a sort of demure, old-maidish way with knife and fork as if she were eating against her will—and finally they rested on me, to whom the dinner was just a pretty pageant of luxury in which I scarcely took any part.

"Well, whatever Faust would or would not do," he said, half laughingly—"it's certain that food is never at a discount. Women frequently are."

"Women," said Mr. Harland, poising a stem of asparagus in the air, "are so constituted as to invariably make havoc either of themselves or of the men they profess to love. Wives neglect their husbands, and husbands naturally desert their wives. Devoted lovers quarrel and part over the merest trifles. The whole thing is a mistake."

"What whole thing?" asked Santoris, smiling.

"The relations between man and woman," Harland answered. "In my opinion we should conduct ourselves like the birds and animals, whose relationships are neither binding nor lasting, but are just sufficient to preserve the type. That's all that is really needed. What is called love is mere sentiment."

"Do you endorse that verdict, Miss Harland?" Santoris asked, suddenly.

Catherine looked up, startled—her yellow skin flushed a pale red.

"I don't know," she answered—"I scarcely heard—""

"Your father doesn't believe in love," he said—"Do you?"

"I hope it exists," she murmured—"But nowadays people are so VERY practical—"

"Oh, believe me, they are no more practical now than they ever were!" averred Santoris, laughing. "There's as much romance in the modern world as in the ancient;—the human heart has the same passions, but they are more deeply suppressed and therefore more dangerous. And love holds the same eternal sway—so does jealousy."

Dr. Brayle looked up.

"Jealousy is an uncivilised thing," he said—"It is a kind of primitive passion from which no well-ordered mind should suffer."

Santoris smiled.

"Primitive passions are as forceful as they ever were," he answered. "No culture can do away with them. Jealousy, like love, is one of the motive powers of progress. It is a great evil—but a necessary one—as necessary as war. Without strife of some sort the world would become like a stagnant pool breeding nothing but weeds and the slimy creatures pertaining to foulness. Even in love, the most divine of passions, there should be a wave of uncertainty and a sense of unsolved mystery to give it everlastingness."

"Everlastingness?" queried Mr. Harland—"Or simply life lastingness?"

"Everlastingness!" repeated Santoris. "Love that lacks eternal stability is not love at all, but simply an affectionate understanding and agreeable companionship in this world only. For the other world or worlds—"

"Ah! You are going too far," interrupted Mr. Harland—"You know I cannot follow you! And with all due deference to the fair sex I very much doubt if any one of them would care for a love that was destined to last for ever."

"No MAN would," interrupted Brayle, sarcastically.

Santoris gave him a quick glance.

"No man is asked to care!" he said—"Nor woman either. SOULS are not only asked, but COMMANDED, to care! This, however, is beyond you!"

"And beyond most people," answered Brayle—"Such ideas are purely imaginary and transcendental."

"Granted!" And Santoris gave him a quick, straight glance—"But what do you mean by 'imaginary' and 'transcendental'? Imagination is the faculty of conceiving in the brain ideas which may with time spring to the full fruition of realisation. Every item of our present-day civilisation has been 'imagined' before taking practical shape. 'Transcendental' means BEYOND the ordinary happenings of life and life's bodily routine—and this 'beyond' expresses itself so often that there are few lives lived for a single day without some touch of its inexplicable marvel. It is on such lines as these that human beings drift away from happiness,—they will only believe what they can see, while all the time their actual lives depend on what they do NOT see!"

There was a moment's silence. The charm of his voice was potent—and still more so the fascination of his manner and bearing, and Mr. Harland looked at him in something of wonder and appeal.

"You are a strange fellow, Santoris!" he said, at last, "And you always were! Even now I can hardly believe that you are really the very Santoris that struck such terror into the hearts of some of us undergrads at Oxford! I say I can hardly believe it, though I know you ARE the man. But I wish you would tell me—"

"All about myself?" And Santoris smiled—"I will, with pleasure!—if the story does not bore you. There is no mystery about it—no 'black magic,' or 'occultism' of any kind. I have done nothing since I left college but adapt myself to the forces of Nature, AND TO USE THEM WHEN NECESSARY. The same way of life is open to all—and the same results are bound to follow."

"Results? Such as—?" queried Brayle.

"Health, youth and power!" answered Santoris, with an involuntary slight clenching of the firm, well-shaped hand that rested lightly on the table,—"Command of oneself!—command of body, command of spirit, and so on through an ever ascending scale! Every man with the breath of God in him is a master, not a slave!"

My heart beat quickly as he spoke; something rose up in me like a response to a call, and I wondered—Did he assume to master ME? No! I would not yield to that! If yielding were necessary, it must be my own free will that gave in, not his compelling influence! As this thought ran through my brain I met his eyes,—he smiled a little, and I saw he had guessed my mind. The warm blood rushed to my cheeks in a fervent glow, nevertheless the defiance of my soul was strong— as strong as the love which had begun to dominate me. And I listened eagerly as he went on.

"I began at Oxford by playing the slave part," he said—"a slave to conventions and fossil-methods of instruction. One can really learn more from studying the actual formation of rocks than from those worthy Dons whom nothing will move out of their customary ruts of routine. Even at that early time I felt that, given a man of health and good physical condition, with sound brain, sound lungs and firm nerves, it was not apparent why he, evidently born to rule, should put himself into the leading strings of Oxford or any other forcing- bed of intellectual effort. That it would be better if such an one took HIMSELF in hand and tried to find out HIS OWN meaning, both in relation to the finite and infinite gradations of Spirit and Matter. And I resolved to enter upon the task—without allowing myself to fear failure or to hope for success. My aim was to discover Myself and my meaning, if such a thing were possible. No atom, however infinitesimal, is without origin, history, place and use in the Universe—and I, a conglomerated mass of atoms called Man, resolved to search out the possibilities, finite and infinite, of my own entity. With this aim I began—with this aim I continued."

"Your task is not finished, then?" put in Dr. Brayle, with a smilingly incredulous air.

"It will never be finished," answered Santoris—"An eternal thing has no end."

There was a moment's silence.

"Well,—go on, Santoris!" said Mr. Harland, with a touch of impatience,—"And tell us especially what we all of us are chiefly anxious to know—how it is that you are young when according to the time of the world you should be old?"

Santoris smiled again.

"Ah! That is a purely personal touch of inquisitiveness!" he answered—"It is quite human and natural, of course, but not always wise. In every great lesson of life or scientific discovery people ask first of all 'How can _I_ benefit by it?' or 'How will it affect ME?' And while asking the question they yet will not trouble to get an answer OUT OF THEMSELVES,—but they turn to others for the solution of the mystery. To keep young is not at all difficult; when certain simple processes of Nature are mastered the difficulty is to grow old!"

We all sat silent, waiting in mute expectancy. The servants had left us, and only the fruits and dainties of dessert remained to tempt us in baskets and dishes of exquisitely coloured Venetian glass, contrasting with the graceful clusters of lovely roses and lilies which added their soft charm to the decorative effect of the table, and Santoris passed the wine, a choice Chateau-Yquem, round to us all before beginning to speak again. And when he did speak, it was in a singularly quiet, musical voice which exercised a kind of spell upon my ears—I had heard that voice before—ah!—how often! How often through the course of my life had I listened to it wonderingly in dreams of which the waking morning brought no explanation! How it had stolen upon me like an echo from far away, when alone in the pauses of work and thought I had longed for some comprehension and sympathy! And I had reproached myself for my own fancies and imaginings, deeming them wholly foolish and irresponsible! And now! Now its gentle and familiar tone went straight to the centre of my spiritual consciousness, and forced me to realise that for the Soul there is no escape from its immortal remembrance!

XI

ONE WAY OF LOVE

"When I left Oxford," he said—"as I told you before, I left what I conceived to be slavery—that is, a submissively ordered routine of learning in which there occurred nothing new—nothing hopeful— nothing really serviceable. I mastered all there was to master, and carried away 'honours' which I deemed hardly worth winning. It was supposed then—most people would suppose it—that as I found myself the possessor of an income of between five and six thousand a year, I would naturally 'live my life,' as the phrase goes, and enter upon what is called a social career. Now to my mind a social career simply means social sham—and to live my life had always a broader application for me than for the majority of men. So, having ascertained all I could concerning myself and my affairs from my father's London solicitors, and learning exactly how I was situated with regard to finances and what is called the 'practical' side of life, I left England for Egypt, the land where I was born. I had an object in view,—and that object was not only to see my own old home, but to find out the whereabouts of a certain great sage and mystic philosopher long known in the East by the name of Heliobas." I started, and the blood rushed to my cheeks in a burning flame.

"I think YOU knew him," he went on, addressing me directly, with a straight glance—"You met him some years back, did you not?"

I bent my head in silent assent,—and saw the eyes of my host and hostess turned upon me in questioning scrutiny.

"In a certain circle of students and mystics he was renowned," continued Santoris,—"and I resolved to see what he could make of me—what he would advise, and how I should set to work to discover what I had resolved to find. However, at the end of a long and tedious journey, I met with disappointment— Heliobas had removed to another sphere of action—"

"He was dead, you mean," interposed Mr. Harland.

"Not at all," answered Santoris, calmly. "There is no death. To put it quite simply, he had reached the top of his class in this particular school of life and learning and, therefore, was ready and willing to pass on into the higher grade. He, however, left a successor capable of maintaining the theories he inculcated,—a man named Aselzion, who elected to live in an almost inaccessible spot among mountains with a few followers and disciples. Him I found after considerable difficulty—and we came to understand each other so well that I stayed with him some time studying all that he deemed needful before I started on my own voyage of discovery. His methods of instruction were arduous and painful—in fact, I may say I went through a veritable ordeal of fire—"

He broke off, and for a moment seemed absorbed in recollections.

"You are speaking, I suppose, of some rule of life, some kind of novitiate to which you had to submit yourself," said Mr. Harland— "Or was it merely a course of study?"

"In one sense it was a sort of novitiate or probation," answered Santoris, slowly, with the far-away, musing look still in his eyes— "In another it was, as you put it, 'merely' a course of study. Merely! It was a course of study in which every nerve, every muscle, every sinew was tested to its utmost strength—and in which a combat between the spiritual and material was fiercely fought till the one could master the other so absolutely as to hold it in perfect subjection. Well! I came out of the trial fairly well—strong enough at any rate to stand alone—as I have done ever since."

"And to what did your severe ordeal lead?" asked Dr. Brayle, who by this time appeared interested, though still wearing his incredulous, half-sneering air—"To anything which you could not have gained just as easily without it?"

Santoris looked straight at him. His keen eyes glowed as though some bright fire of the soul had leaped into them.

"In the first place," he answered—"it led me to power! Power,—not only over myself but over all things small and great that surround or concern my being. I think you will admit that if a man takes up any line of business, it is necessary for him to understand all its technical methods and practical details. My business was and IS Life!—the one thing that humanity never studies, and therefore fails to master."

Mr. Harland looked up.

"Life is mysterious and inexplicable," he said—"We cannot tell why we live. No one can fathom that mystery. We are Here through no conscious desire of our own,—and again we are NOT here just as we have learned to accommodate ourselves to the fact of being Anywhere!"

"True!" answered Santoris—"But to understand the 'why' of life we must first of all realise that its origin Is Love. Love creates life because it MUST; even agnostics, when pushed to the wall in argument grant that some mysterious and mighty Force is at the back of creation,—a Force which is both intelligent and beneficent. The trite saying 'God is Love' is true enough, but it is quite as true to say 'Love is God.' The commencement of universes, solar systems and worlds is the desire of Love to express Itself. No more and no less than this. From desire springs action,—from action life. It only remains for each living unit to bring itself into harmonious union with this one fundamental law of the whole cosmos,—the expression and action of Love which is based, as naturally it must be, on a dual entity."

"What do you mean by that?" asked Dr. Brayle.

"As a physician, and I presume as a scientist, you ought scarcely to ask," replied Santoris, with a slight smile. "For you surely know there is no single thing in the Universe. The very microbes of disease or health go in pairs. Light and darkness,—the up and the down,—the right and the left,—the storm and the calm,—the male and the female,—all things are dual; and the sorrows of humanity are for the most part the result of ill-assorted numbers,—figures brought together that will not count up properly—wrong halves of the puzzle that will never fit into place. The mischief runs through all civilization,—wrong halves of races brought together which do not and never can assimilate,—and in an individual personal sense wrong halves of spirit and matter are often forced together which are bound by law to separate in time with some attendant disaster. The error is caused by the obstinate miscomprehension of man himself as to the nature and extent of his own powers and faculties. He forgets that he is not 'as the beasts that perish,' but that he has the breath of God in him,—that he holds within himself the seed of immortality which is perpetually re-creative. He is bound by all the laws of the Universe to give that immortal life its dual entity and attendant power, without which he cannot attain his highest ends. It may take him thousands of years—cycles of time,—but it has to be done. Materially speaking, he may perhaps consider that he has secured his dual entity by a pleasing or fortunate marriage—but if he is not spiritually mated, his marriage is useless,—ay! worse than useless, as it only interposes fresh obstacles between himself and his intended progress."

"Marriage can hardly be called a useless institution," said Dr. Brayle, with an uplifting of his sinister brows; "It helps to populate the world."

"It does," answered Santoris, calmly—"But if the pairs that are joined in marriage have no spiritual bond between them and nothing beyond the attraction of the mere body—they people the world with more or less incapable, unthinking and foolish creatures like themselves. And supposing these to be born in tens of millions, like ants or flies, they will not carry on the real purpose of man's existence to anything more than that stoppage and recoil which is called Death, but which in reality is only a turning back of the wheels of time when the right road has been lost and it becomes imperative to begin the journey all over again."

We sat silent; no one had any comment to offer.

"We are arriving at that same old turning-point once more," he continued—"The Western civilisation of two thousand years, assisted (and sometimes impeded) by the teachings of Christianity, is nearing its end. Out of the vast wreckage of nations, now imminent, only a few individuals can be saved,—and the storm is so close at hand that one can almost hear the mutterings of the thunder! But why should I or you or anyone else think about it? We have our own concerns to attend to—and we attend to these so well that we forget all the most vital necessities that should make them of any importance! However—in this day—nothing matters! Shall I go on with my own story, or have you heard enough?"

"Not half enough!" said Catherine Harland, quite suddenly—she had scarcely spoken before, but she now leaned forward, looking eagerly interested—"You speak of power over yourself,—do you possess the same power over others?"

"Not unless they come into my own circle of action," he answered. "It would not be worth my while to exert any influence on persons who are, and ever must be, indifferent to me. I can, of course, defend myself against enemies—and that without lifting a hand."

Everyone, save myself, looked at him inquisitively,—but he did not explain his meaning. He went on very quietly with his own personal narrative.

"As I have told you," he said—"I came out of my studies with Aselzion success-fully enough to feel justified in going on with my work alone. I took up my res-idence in Egypt in my father's old home- -a pretty place enough with wide pleas-ure grounds planted thickly with palm trees and richly filled with flowers,—and here I undertook the mastery and comprehension of the most difficult subject ever propounded for learning—the most evasive, complex, yet exact piece of mathematics ever set out for solving—Myself! Myself was my puzzle! How to unite myself with Nature so thoroughly as to insinuate myself into her secrets,— possess all she could offer me,- -and yet detach myself from Self so completely as to be ready to sacrifice all I had gained at a moment's notice should that moment come."

"You are paradoxical," said Mr. Harland, irritably. "What's the use of gaining any-thing if it is to be lost at a moment's bidding?" "It is the only way to hold and keep whatever there is to win," answered Santoris, calmly—"And the paradox is no greater than that of 'He that loveth his life shall lose it.' The only 'moment' of supreme self-surrender is Love—when that comes everything else must go. Love alone can compass life, perfect it, complete it and carry it on to eternal happiness. But please bear in mind that I am speaking of real Love,—not mere physical attraction. The two things are as different as light from darkness."

"Is your curious conception or ideal of love the reason, why you have never mar-ried?" asked Brayle, abruptly.

"Precisely!" replied Santoris. "It is most unquestionably and emphatically the rea-son why I have never married."

There was a pause. I saw Catherine glancing at him with a strange furtiveness in which there was something of fear.

"You have never met your ideal, I suppose?" she asked, with a faint smile.

"Oh yes, I've met her!" he answered—"Ages ago! On many occasions I have met her;—sometimes she has estranged herself from me,— sometimes she has been torn from me by others—and still more often I have, through my own folly and obstinacy, separated myself from her—but our mutual mistakes do no more than delay the inevitable union at last."—Here he spoke slowly and with marked meaning—"For it IS an inevitable union!—as inevitable as that of two electrons which, after spinning in space for certain periods of time, rush together at last and remain so indissolubly united that nothing can ever separate them."

"And then?" queried Dr. Brayle, with an ironical air.

"Then? Why, everything is possible then! Beauty, perfection, wisdom, progress, creativeness, and a world—even worlds—of splendid thought and splendid ideals, bound to lead to still more splendid realisation! It is not difficult to imagine two brains, two minds moving so absolutely in unison that like a grand chord of music they strike harmony through hitherto dumb life-episodes—but think of two immortal souls full of a love as deathless as themselves, conjoined in highest effort and superb attainment!—the love of angel for angel, of god for god! You think this ideal imaginative,— transcendental—impossible!—yet I swear to you it is the most REAL possibility in this fleeting mirage of a world!"

His voice thrilled with a warmth of feeling and conviction, and as I heard him speak I trembled inwardly with a sudden remorse—a quick sense of inferiority and shame. Why could I not let myself go? Why did I not give the fluttering spirit within me room to expand its wings? Something opposing,—something inimical to my peace and happiness held me back—and presently I began to wonder whether I should attribute it to the influence of those with whom I was temporarily associated. I was almost confirmed in this impression when Mr. Harland's voice, harsh and caustic as it could be when he was irritated or worsted in an argument, broke the momentary silence.

"You are more impossible now than you ever were at Oxford, Santoris!" he said—"You out-transcend all transcendentalism! You know, or you ought to know by this time, that there is no such thing as an immortal soul—and if you believe otherwise you have brought yourself voluntarily into that state of blind credulity. All science teaches us that we are the mere spawn of the planet on which we live,—we are here to make the best of it for ourselves and for others who come after us—and there's an end. What is called Love is the mere physical attraction between the two sexes—no more,—and it soon palls. All that we gain we quickly cease to care for—it is the way of humanity."

"What a poor creation humanity is, then!" said Santoris, with a smile—"How astonishing that it should exist at all for no higher aims than those of the ant or the mouse! My dear Harland, if your beliefs were really sound we should be bound in common duty and charity to stop the population of the world altogether—for the whole business is useless. Useless and even cruel, for it is nothing but a crime to allow people to be born for no other end than extinction! However, keep your creeds! I thank Heaven they are not mine!"

Mr. Harland gave a slight movement of impatience. I could see that he was disturbed in his mind.

"Let's talk of something I can follow," he said—"the personal and material side of things. Your perennial condition of health, for example. Your apparent youth—"

"Oh, is it only 'apparent'?" laughed Santoris, gaily—"Well, to those who never knew me in my boyhood's days and are therefore never hurling me back to their 'thirty years or more ago' of friendship, etc., my youth seems very actual! You see their non-ability to count up the time I have spent on earth obliges them to accept me at my own valuation! There's really nothing to explain in the matter. Everyone can keep young if he understands himself and Nature. If I were to tell you the literal truth of the process, you would not believe me,—and even if you did you would not have the patience to carry it out! But what does it matter after all? If we only live for the express purpose of dying, the sooner we get the business over and done with the better—youth itself has no charms under such circumstances. All the purposes of life, however lofty and nobly planned, are bound to end in nothingness,—and it is hardly worth while taking the trouble to breathe the murderous air!"

He spoke with a kind of passion—his eyes were luminous—his face transfigured with an almost superhuman glow, and we all looked at him in something of amazement.

Mr. Harland fidgeted uneasily in his chair.

"You go too far!" he said—"Life is agreeable as long as it lasts—"

"Have you found it so?" Santoris interrupted him. "Has it not, even in your pursuit and attainment of wealth, brought you more pain than pleasure? Number up all the possibilities of life, from the existence of the labourer in his hut to that of the king on his throne, they are none of them worth striving for or keeping if death is the ultimate end. Ambition is merest folly,—wealth a temporary possession of perishable goods which must pass to others,—fame a brief noise of one's name in mouths that will soon be dumb,—and love, sex-attraction only. What a treacherous and criminal act, then, is this Creation of Universes!—what mad folly!—what sheer, blind, reasonless wickedness!"

There was a silence. His eyes flashed from one to the other of us.

"Can you deny it?" he demanded. "Can you find any sane, logical reason for the continuance of life which is to end in utter extinction, or for the creation of worlds doomed to eternal destruction?"

No one spoke.

"You have no answer ready," he said—and smiled—"Naturally! For an answer is impossible! And here you have the key to what you consider my mystery—the mystery of keeping young instead of growing old—the secret of living instead of dying! It is simply the conscious PRACTICAL realisation that there is no Death, but only Change. That is the first part of the process. Change, or transmutation and transformation of the atoms and elements of which we are composed, is going on for ever without a second's cessation,—it began when we were born and before we were born—and the art of LIVING YOUNG consists simply in using one's soul and will-power to guide this process of change towards the ends we desire, instead of leaving it to blind chance and to the association with inimical influences, which interfere with our best actions. For example—I—a man in sound health and condition—realise that with every moment SOME change is working in me towards SOME end. It rests entirely with myself as to whether the change shall be towards continuance of health or towards admission of disease— towards continuance of youth or towards the encouragement of age,—towards life as it presents itself to me now, or towards some other phase of life as I perceive it in the future. I can advance or retard myself as I please—the proper management of Myself being my business. If I should suffer pain or illness I am very sure it will be chiefly through my own fault—if I invite decay and decrepitude, it will be because I allow these forces to encroach upon my well-being—in fact, briefly—I AM what I WILL to be!—and all the laws that brought me into existence support me in this attitude of mind, body and spirit!"

"If we could all become what we WOULD be," said Dr. Brayle, "we should attain the millennium!"

"Are you sure of that?" queried Santoris. "Would it not rather depend on the particular choice each one of us might make? You, for example, might wish to be something that would hardly tend to your happiness,—and your wish being obtained you might become what (if you had only realised it) you would give worlds not to be! Some men desire to be thieves—even murderers—and become so—but the end of their desires is not perhaps what they imagined!"

"Can you read people's thoughts?" asked Catherine, suddenly.

Santoris looked amused. He replied by a counter question.

"Would you be sorry if I could?"

She flushed a little. I smiled, knowing what was in her mind.

"It would be a most unpleasant accomplishment—that of reading the thoughts of others," said Mr. Harland; "I would rather not cultivate it." "But Mr. Santoris almost implies that he possesses it," said Dr. Brayle, with a touch of irritation in his manner; "And, after all, 'thought-reading' is a kind of society amusement nowadays. There is nothing very difficult in it."

"Nothing, indeed!" agreed Santoris, lightly; "And being as easy as it is, why do you not show us at once that antique piece of jewellery you have in your pocket! You brought it with you this evening to show to me and ask my opinion of its value, did you not?"

Brayle's eyes opened in utter amazement. If ever a man was taken completely by surprise, he was.

"How did you know?" he began, stammeringly, while Mr. Harland, equally aston-ished, stared at him through his round spectacles as though challenging some defiance.

Santoris laughed.

"Thought-reading is only a society amusement, as you have just observed," he said—"And I have been amusing myself with it for the last few minutes. Come!—let us see your treasure!"

Dr. Brayle was thoroughly embarrassed,—but he tried to cover his confusion by an awkward laugh.

"Well, you have made a very clever hit!" he said—"Quite a random shot, of course—which by mere coincidence went to its mark! It's quite true I have brought with me a curious piece of jewel-work which I always carry about wher-ever I go—and something moved me to- night to ask your opinion of its value, as well as to place its period. It is old Italian; but even experts are not agreed as to its exact date."

He put his hand in his breast pocket and drew out a small silk bag from which he took with great care a collar of jewels, designed in a kind of chain-work which made it perfectly flexible. He laid it out on the table,—and I bit my lip hard to suppress an involuntary exclamation. For I had seen the thing before—and for the immediate moment could not realise where, till a sudden flash of light through the cells of my brain reminded me of that scene of love and death in the vision of the artist's studio when the name 'Cosmo de Medicis' had been whispered like an evil omen. The murderer in that dream- picture had worn a collar of jewels precisely similar to the one I now saw; but I could only keep silence and listen with every nerve strained to utmost attention while Santoris took the ornament in his hand and looked at it with an intent earnestness in which there was almost a touch of compassion.

"A beautiful piece of workmanship," he said, at last, slowly, while Mr. Harland, Catherine, and Swinton the secretary all drew up closer to him at the table and leaned eagerly forward—"And I should say"— here he raised his eyes and looked full at the dark, brooding, sinister face of Brayle—"I should say that it belonged to the Medici period. It must have been part of the dress of a nobleman of that time—the design seems to me to be Florentine. Perhaps if these jewels could speak they might tell a strange story!—they are unhappy stones!"

"Unhappy!" exclaimed Catherine—"You mean unlucky?"

"No!—there is no such thing as luck," answered Santoris, quietly, turning the collar over and over in his hands—"Not for either jewels or men! But there IS unhappiness,—and unhappiness simply means life being put to wrong uses. I call these gems 'unhappy' because they have been wrongfully used. A precious stone is a living thing—it absorbs influences as the earth absorbs light, and these jewels have absorbed some sense of evil that renders them less beautiful than they might be. These diamonds and rubies, these emeralds and sapphires, have not the full lustre of their own true nature,—they are in the condition of pining flowers. It will take centuries before they resume their natural brilliancy. There is some tragedy hidden among them."

Dr. Brayle looked amused.

"Well, I can give you no history of them," he said—"A friend of mine bought the collar from an old Jew curiosity dealer in a back street of Florence and sent it to me to wear with a Florentine dress at a fancy dress ball. Curiously enough I chose to represent one of the Medicis, some artist having told me my features resembled their type of countenance. That's the chronicle, so far as I am concerned. I rather liked it on account of its antiquity. I could have sold it many times over, but I have no desire to part with it."

"Naturally!"—and Santoris passed on the collar to everyone to examine—"You feel a sense of proprietorship in it."

Catherine Harland had the trinket in her hand, and a curious vague look of terror came over her face as she presently passed it back to its owner. But she made no remark and it was Mr. Harland who resumed the conversation.

"That's an odd idea of yours about unhappy jewels," he said— "Perhaps the misfortune attending the possessors of the famous blue Hope diamond could be traced to some early tragedy connected with it."

"Unquestionably!" replied Santoris. "Now look at this!"—and he drew from his watch pocket a small fine gold chain to which was attached a moonstone of singular size and beauty, set in a circle of diamonds—"Here is a sort of talismanic jewel—it has never known any disastrous influences, nor has it been disturbed by malevolent surroundings. It is a perfectly happy, unsullied gem! As you see, the lustre is perfect—as clear as that of a summer moon in heaven. Yet it is a very old jewel and has seen more than a thousand years of life."

We all examined the beautiful ornament, and as I held it in my hand a moment it seemed to emit tiny sparks of luminance like a flash of moonlight on rippling waves.

"Women should take care that their jewels are made happy," he continued, looking at me with a slight smile, "That is, if they want them to shine. Nothing that lives is at its best unless it is in a condition of happiness—a condition which after all is quite easy to attain."

"Easy! I should have thought nothing was so difficult!" said Mr. Harland.

"Nothing certainly is so difficult in the ordinary way of life men choose to live," answered Santoris—"For the most part they run after the shadow and forsake the light. Even in work and the creative action of thought each ordinary man imagines that his especial work being all-important, it is necessary for him to sacrifice everything to it. And he does,—if he is filled with worldly ambition and selfish concentration; and he produces something—anything—which frequently proves to be ephemeral as gossamer dust. It is only when work is the outcome of a great love and keen sympathy for others that it lasts and keeps its influence. Now we have talked enough about all these theories, which are not interesting to anyone who is not prepared to accept them—shall we go up on deck?"

We all rose at once, Santoris holding out a box of cigars to the men to help themselves. Catherine and I preceded them up the saloon stairs to the deck, which was now like a sheet of silver in the light shed by one of the loveliest moons of the year. The water around was sparkling with phosphorescence and the dark mountains looked higher and more imposing than ever, rising as they seemed to do sheer up from the white splendour of the sea. I leaned over the deck rail, gazing down into the deep liquid mirror of stars below, and my heart was heavy and full of a sense of bitterness and tears. Catherine had dropped languidly into a chair and was leaning back in it with a strange, far-away expression on her tired face. Suddenly she spoke with an almost mournful gentleness.

"Do you like his theories?"

I turned towards her enquiringly.

"I mean, do you like the idea of there being no death and that we only change from one life to another and so on for ever?" she continued. "To me it is appalling! Sometimes I think death the kindest thing that can happen—especially for women."

I was in the mood to agree with her. I went up to her and knelt down by her side.

"Yes!" I said, and I felt the tremor of tears in my voice—"Yes, for women death often seems very kind! When there is no love and no hope of love,—when the world is growing grey and the shadows are deepening towards night,—when the ones we most dearly love misjudge and mistrust us and their hearts are closed against our tenderness, then death seems the greatest god of all!—one before whom we may well kneel and offer up our prayers! Who could, who WOULD live for ever quite alone in an eternity without love? Oh, how much kinder, how much sweeter would be utter extinction—"

My voice broke; and Catherine, moved by some sudden womanly impulse, put her arm round me.

"Why, you are crying!" she said, softly. "What is it? You, who are always so bright and happy!"

I quickly controlled the weakness of my tears.

"Yes, it is foolish!" I said—"But I feel to-night as if I had wasted a good part of my life in useless research,—in looking for what has been, after all, quite close to my hand,—only that I failed to see it!—and that I must go back upon the road I thought I had passed—"

Here I paused. I saw she could not understand me.

"Catherine," I went on, abruptly—"Will you let me leave you in a day or two? I have been quite a fortnight with you on board the 'Diana,' and I think I have had enough holiday. I should like"—and I looked up at her from where I knelt—"I should like to part from you while we remain good friends—and I have an idea that perhaps we shall not agree so well if we learn to know more of each other."

She bent her eyes upon me with a half-frightened expression.

"How strange you should think that!" she murmured—"I have felt the same— and yet I really like you very much—I always liked you—I wish you would believe it!"

I smiled.

"Dear Catherine," I said—"it is no use shutting our eyes to the fact that while there is something which attracts us to each other, there is also something which repels. We cannot argue about it or analyse it. Such mysterious things DO occur,—and they are beyond our searching out—"

"But," she interrupted, quickly—"we were not so troubled by these mysterious things till we met this man Santoris—"

She broke off, and I rose to my feet, as just then Santoris approached, accompanied by Mr. Harland and the others.

"I have suggested giving you a sail by moonlight before you leave," he said. "It will be an old experience for you under new conditions. Sailing by moonlight in an ordinary sense is an ordinary thing,—but sailing by moonlight with the moonlight as part of our motive power has perhaps a touch of originality."

As he spoke he made a sign to one of his men who came up to receive his orders, which were given in too low a tone for us to hear. Easy deck chairs were placed for all the party, and we were soon seated in a group together, somewhat silently at first, our attention being entirely riveted on the wonderful, almost noiseless way in which the sails of the 'Dream' were unfurled. There was no wind,—the night was warm and intensely still—the sea absolutely calm. Like broad white wings, the canvas gradually spread out under the deft, quick hands of the sailors employed in handling it,—the anchor was drawn up in the same swift and silent manner—then there came an instant's pause. Mr. Harland drew his cigar from his mouth and looked up amazed, as we all did, at the mysterious way in which the sails filled out, pulling the cordage tightly into bands of iron strength,—and none of us could restrain an involuntary cry of wonder and admiration as their whiteness began to glitter with the radiance of hoar-frost, the strange luminance deepening in intensity till it seemed as if the whole stretch of canvas from end to end of the magnificent schooner was a mass of fine jewel-work sparkling under the moon.

"Well! However much I disagree with your theories of life, Santoris," said Mr. Harland,—"I will give you full credit for this extraordinary yacht of yours! It's the most wonderful thing I ever saw, and you are a wonderful fellow to have carried out such an unique application of science. You ought to impart your secret to the world."

Santoris laughed lightly.

"And the world would take a hundred years or more to discuss it, consider it, deny it, and finally accept it," he said—"No! One grows tired of asking the world to be either wise or happy. It prefers its own way—just as I prefer mine. It will discover the method of sailing without wind, and it will learn how to make every sort of mechanical progress without steam in time—but not in our day,—and I, personally, cannot afford to wait while it is slowly learning its ABC like a big child under protest. You see we're going now!"

We were 'going' indeed,—it would have been more correct to say we were flying. Over the still water our vessel glided like a moving beautiful shape of white fire, swiftly and steadily, with no sound save the little hissing murmur of the water cleft under her keel. And then like a sudden whisper from fairyland came the ripple of harp-strings, running upward in phrases of exquisite melody, and a boy's voice, clear, soft and full, began to sing, with a pure enunciation which enabled us to hear every word:

Sailing, sailing! Whither?
What path of the flashing sea
Seems best for you and me?
 No matter the way,
 By night or day,
So long as we sail together!

Sailing, sailing! Whither?
Into the rosy grace
Of the sun's deep setting-place?
 We need not know
 How far we go,
So long as we sail together!

Sailing, sailing! Whither?
To the glittering rainbow strand
Of Love's enchanted land?
 We ask not where
 In earth or air,
So long as we sail together!

Sailing, sailing! Whither?
On to the life divine,—
Your soul made one with mine!
 In Heaven or Hell
 All must be well,
So long as we sail together!

The song finished with a passionate chord which, played as it was with swift intensity, seemed to awaken a response from the sea,—at any rate a strange shivering echo trembled upward as it were from the water and floated into the spacious silence of the night. My heart beat with uncomfortable quickness and my eyes grew hot with the weight of suppressed tears;—why could I not escape from the cruel, restraining force that held my real self prisoner as with manacles of steel? I could not even speak; and while the others were clapping their hands in delighted applause at the beauty of both voice and song, I sat silent.

"He sings well!" said Santoris—"He is the Eastern lad you saw when you came on deck this morning. I brought him from Egypt. He will give us another song presently. Shall we walk a little?"

We rose and paced the deck slowly, gradually dividing in couples, Catherine and Dr. Brayle—Mr. Harland and his secretary,—Santoris and myself. We two paused together at the stern of the vessel looking towards the bowsprit, which seemed to pierce the distance of sea and sky like a flying arrow.

"You wish to speak to me alone," said Santoris, then—"Do you not? Though I know what you want to say!"

I glanced at him with a touch of defiance.

"Then I need not speak," I answered.

"No, you need not speak, unless you give utterance to what is in your true soul," he said—"I would rather you did not play at conventions with me."

For the moment I felt almost angry.

"I do not play at conventions," I murmured.

"Oh, do you not? Is that quite candid?"

I raised my eyes and met his,—he was smiling. Some of the oppression in my soul suddenly gave way, and I spoke hurriedly in a low tone.

"Surely you know how difficult it is for me?" I said. "Things have happened so strangely,—and we are surrounded here by influences that compel conventionality. I cannot speak to you as frankly as I would under other circumstances. It is easy for YOU to be yourself;- -you have gained the mastery over all lesser forces than your own. But with me it is different—perhaps when I am away I shall be able to think more calmly—"

"You are going away?" he asked, gently.

"Yes. It is better so."

He remained silent. I went on, quickly.

"I am going away because I feel inadequate and unable to cope with my present surroundings. I have had some experience of the same influences before—I know I have—"

"I also!" he interrupted.

"Well, you must realise this better than I," and I looked at him now with greater courage—"and if you have, you know they have led to trouble. I want you to help me."

"I? To help you?" he said. "How can I help you when you leave me?"

There was something infinitely sad in his voice,—and the old fear came over me like a chill—'lest I should lose what I had gained!'

"If I leave you," I said, tremblingly—"I do so because I am not worthy to be with you! Oh, can you not see this in me?" For as I spoke he took my hand in his and held it with a kindly clasp—"I am so self-willed, so proud, so unworthy! There are a thousand things I would say to you, but I dare not—not here, or now!"

"No one will approach us," he said, still holding my hand—"I am keeping the others, unconsciously to themselves, at a distance till you have finished speaking. Tell me some of these thousand things!"

I looked up at him and saw the deep lustre of his eyes filled with a great tenderness. He drew me a little closer to his side.

"Tell me," he persisted, softly—"Is there very much that we do not, if we are true to each other, know already?"

"YOU know more than I do!" I answered—"And I want to be equal with you! I do! I cannot be content to feel that I am groping in the dark weakly and blindly while you are in the light, strong and self- contained! You can help me—and you WILL help me! You will tell me where I should go and study as you did with Aselzion!"

He started back, amazed.

"With Aselzion! Dear, forgive me! You are a woman! It is impossible that you should suffer so great an ordeal,—so severe a strain! And why should you attempt it? If you would let me, I would be sufficient for you." "But I will not let you!" I said, quickly, roused to a kind of defiant energy—"I wish to go to the very source of your instruction, and then I shall see where I stand with regard to you! If I stay here now—"

"It will be the same old story over again!" he said—"Love—and mistrust! Then drifting apart in the same weary way! Is it not possible to avoid the errors of the past?"

"No!" I said, resolutely—"For me it is not possible! I cannot yield to my own inward promptings. They offer me too much happiness! I doubt the joy,—I fear the glory!"

My voice trembled—the very clasp of his hand unnerved me.

"I will tell you," he said, after a brief pause, "what you feel. You are perfectly conscious that between you and myself there is a tie which no power, earthly or heavenly, can break,—but you are living in a matter-of-fact world with matter-of-fact persons, and the influence they exert is to make you incredulous of the very truths which are an essential part of your spiritual existence. I understand all this. I understand also why you wish to go to the House of Aselzion, and you shall go—"

I uttered an exclamation of relief and pleasure. His eyes grew dark with earnest gravity as he looked at me.

"You are pleased at what you cannot realise," he said, slowly—"If you go to the House of Aselzion—and I see you are determined—it will be a matter of such vital import that it can only mean one of two things,—your entire happiness or your entire misery. I cannot contemplate with absolute calmness the risk you run,—and yet it is better that you should follow the dictates of your own soul than be as you are now—irresolute,—uncertain of yourself and ready to lose all you have gained!"

'To lose all I have gained.' The old insidious terror! I met his searching gaze imploringly.

"I must not lose anything!" I said, and my voice sank lower,—"I cannot bear—to lose YOU!"

His hand closed on mine with a tighter grasp.

"Yet you doubt!" he said, softly.

"I must KNOW!" I said, resolutely.

He lifted his head with a proud gesture that was curiously familiar to me.

"So the old spirit is not dead in you, my queen," he said, smiling. "The old indomitable will!—the desire to probe to the very centre of things! Yet love defies analysis,—and is the only thing that binds the Universe together. A fact beyond all proving—a truth which cannot be expounded by any given rule or line but which is the most emphatic force of life! My queen, it is a force that must either bend or break you!"

I made no reply. He still held my hand, and we looked out together on the shining expanse of the sea where there was no vessel visible and where our schooner alone flew over the watery, moonlit surface like a winged flame.

"In your working life," he continued, gently, "you have done much. You have thought clearly, and you have not been frightened away from any eternal fact by the difficulties of research. But in your living life you have missed more than you will care to know. You have been content to remain a passive recipient of influences—you have not thoroughly learned how to combine and use them. You have overcome altogether what are generally the chief obstacles in the way of a woman's higher progress,—her inherent childishness—her delight in imagining herself wronged or neglected,—her absurd way of attaching weighty importance to the merest trifles—her want of balance, and the foolish resentment she feels at being told any of her faults,— this is all past in you, and you stand free of the shackles of sheer stupidity which makes so many women impossible to deal with from a man's standpoint, and which renders it almost necessary for men to estimate them at a low intellectual standard. For even in the supreme passion of love, millions of women are only capable of understanding its merely physical side, while the union of soul with soul is never consummated:

> Where is that love supreme
> In which souls meet? Where is it satisfied?
> En-isled on heaving sands
> Of lone desire, spirit to spirit cries,
> While float across the skies
> Bright phantoms of fair lands,
> Where fancies fade not and where dreams abide."

His voice dropped to the softest musical cadence, and I looked up. He answered my look.

"Dear one!" he said, "You shall go to the House of Aselzion, and with you will be the future!"

He let go my hand very gently—I felt a sudden sense of utter loneliness.

"You do not—you will not misjudge me?" I said.

"I! Dear, I have made so many errors of judgment in the past and I have lost you so many times, that I shall do nothing now which might lose you again!"

He smiled, and for one moment I was impelled to throw hesitation to the winds and say all that I knew in my inmost self ought to be said,—but my rebellious will held me back, and I remained silent,— while he turned away and rejoined the rest of the party, with whom he was soon chatting in such a cheery, easy fashion that they appeared to forget that there was anything remarkable about him or about his wonderful vessel, which had now turned on her course and was carrying us back to Loch Scavaig at a speed which matched the fleetest wind. When she arrived at her former anchorage just opposite the 'Diana,' we saw that all the crew of Mr. Harland's yacht were on deck watching our movements, which must have been well worth watching considering what an amazing spectacle the 'Dream' made of herself and her glittering sails against the dark loch and mountains,—so brilliant indeed as almost to eclipse the very moon. But the light began to pale as soon as we dropped anchor, and very soon faded out completely, whereupon the sailors hauled down canvas, uttering musical cries as they pulled and braced it together. This work done, they retired, and a couple of servants waited upon our party, bringing wine and fruit as a parting refreshment before we said good-night,—and once again the sweet voice of the Egyptian boy singer smote upon our ears, with a prelude of harp-strings:

Good-night,—farewell! If it should chance that nevermore we meet, Remember that the hours we spent together here were sweet!

Good-night,—farewell! If henceforth different ways of life we wend, Remember that I sought to walk beside you to the end!

Good-night,—farewell! When present things are merged into the past, Remember that I love you and shall love you to the last!

My heart beat with a quick and sudden agony of pain—was it, could it be true that I was of my own accord going to sever myself from one whom I knew,— whom I felt—to be all in all to me?

"Good-night!" said a low voice close to my ear.

I started. I had lost myself in a wilderness of thought and memory. Santoris stood beside me.

"Your friends are going," he said,—"and I too shall be gone to- morrow!"

A wave of desolation overcame me.

"Ah, no!" I exclaimed—"Surely you will not go—"

"I must," he answered, quietly,—"Are not YOU going? It has been a joy to meet you, if only for a little while—a pause in the journey,—an attempt at an under-standing!—though you have decided that we must part again."

I clasped my hands together in a kind of desperation.

"What can I do?" I murmured—"If I yielded now to my own impulses—"

"Ah! If you did"—he said, wistfully—"But you will not; and perhaps, after all, it is better so. It is no doubt intended that you should be absolutely certain of your-self this time. And I will not stand in the way. Good-night,—and farewell!"

I looked at him with a smile, though the tears were in my eyes.

"I will not say farewell!" I answered.

He raised my hands lightly to his lips.

"That is kind of you!" he said—"and to-morrow you shall hear from me about Aselzion and the best way for you to see him. He is spending the summer in Europe, which is fortunate for you, as you will not have to make so far a journey."

We broke off our conversation here as the others joined us,—and in a very little while we had left the 'Dream' and were returning to our own yacht. To the last, as the motor launch rushed with us through the water, I kept my eyes fixed on the reposeful figure of Santoris, who with folded arms on the deck rail of his ves-sel, watched our departure. Should I never see him again, I wondered? What was the strange impulse that had more or less moved my spirit to a kind of opposition against his, and made me so determined to seek out for myself the things that he assumed to have mastered? I could not tell. I only knew that from the moment he had begun to relate the personal narrative of his own studies and experiences, I had resolved to go through the same training whatever it was, and learn what he had learned, if such a thing were possible. I did not think I should succeed so well,—but some new knowledge I felt I should surely gain. The extraordinary attraction he exercised over me was growing too strong to resist, yet I was deter-mined not to yield to it because I doubted both its cause and its effect. Love, I knew, could not, as he had said, be analysed—but the love I had always dreamed of was not the love with which the majority of mankind are content—the mere physical delight which ends in satiety. It was something not only for time, but for eternity. Away from Santoris I found it quite easy to give myself up to the dream of joy which shone before me like the mirage of a promised land,— but in his company I felt as though something held me back and warned me to beware of too quickly snatching at a purely personal happiness.

We reached the 'Diana' in a very few minutes—we had made the little journey almost in silence, for my companions were, or appeared to be, as much lost in thought as I was. As we descended to our cabins Mr. Harland drew me back and detained me alone for a moment.

"Santoris is going away to-morrow," he said—"He will probably have set those wonderful sails of his and flown before daybreak. I'm sorry!"

"So am I," I answered—"But, after all—you would hardly want him to stay, would you? His theories of life are very curious and upsetting, and you all think him a sort of charlatan playing with the mysteries of earth and heaven! If he is able to read thoughts, he cannot be altogether flattered at the opinion held of him by Dr. Brayle, for example!"

Mr. Harland's brows knitted perplexedly.

"He says he could cure me of my illness," he went on,—"and Brayle declares that a cure is impossible."

"You prefer to believe Brayle, of course?" I queried.

"Brayle is a physician of note," he replied,—"A man who has taken his degree in medicine and knows what he is talking about. Santoris is merely a mystic."

I smiled a little sadly.

"I see!" And I held out my hand to say good-night. "He is a century before his time, and maybe it is better to die than forestall a century."

Mr. Harland laughed as he pressed my hand cordially.

"Enigmatical, as usual!" he said—"You and Santoris ought to be congenial spirits!"

"Perhaps we are!" I answered, carelessly, as I left him;—"Stranger things than that have happened!"

XII

A LOVE-LETTER

To those who are ignorant of, or indifferent to, the psychic forces working behind all humanity and creating the causes which evolve into effect, it cannot but seem strange,—even eccentric and abnormal,—that any one person, or any two persons for that matter, should take the trouble to try and ascertain the immediate intention and ultimate object of their lives. The daily routine of ordinary working, feeding and sleeping existence, varied by little social conventions and obligations which form a kind of break to the persistent monotony of the regular treadmill round, should be, they think, sufficient for any sane, well-balanced, self-respecting creature,—and if a man or woman elects to stand out of the common ruck and say: "I refuse to live in a chaos of uncertainties—I will endeavour to know why my particular atom of self is considered a necessary, if infinitesimal, part of the Universe,"—such an one is looked upon with either distrust or derision. In matters of love especially, where the most ill-assorted halves persist in fitting themselves together as if they could ever make a perfect whole, a woman is considered foolish if she gives her affections where it is 'not expedient'—and a man is looked upon as having 'ruined his career' if he allows a great passion to dominate him, instead of a calm, well-weighed, respectable sort of sentiment which has its fitting end in an equally calm, well-weighed, respectable marriage. These are the laws and observances of social order, excellent in many respects, but frequently responsible for a great bulk of the misery attendant upon many forms of human relationship. It is not, however, possible to the ordinary mind to realise that somewhere and somehow, every two component parts of a whole MUST come together, sooner or later, and that herein may be found the key to most of the great love tragedies of the world. The wrong halves mated,—the right halves finding each other out and rushing together recklessly and inopportunely because of the resistless Law which draws them together,—this is the explanation of many a life's disaster and despair, as well as of many a life's splendid attainment and victory. And the trouble or the triumph, whichever it be, will never be lessened till human beings learn that in love, which is the greatest and most divine Force on earth or in heaven, the Soul, not the body, must first be considered, and that no one can fulfil the higher possibilities of his or her nature, till each individual unit is conjoined with that only other portion of itself which is as one with it in thought and in the intuitive comprehension of its higher needs.

I knew all this well enough, and had known it for years, and it was hardly necessary for me to dwell upon it, as I sat alone in my cabin that night, too restless to sleep, and, almost too uneasy even to think. What had happened to me was simply that I had by a curious chance or series of chances been brought into connection again with the individual Soul of a man whom I had known and loved ages ago. To the psychist, such a circumstance does not seem as strange as it is to the great majority of people who realise no greater force than Matter, and who have no comprehension of Spirit, and no wish to comprehend it, though even the dullest of these often find themselves brought into contact with persons whom they feel they have met and known before, and are unable to understand why they receive such an impression. In my case I had not only to consider the one particular identity which seemed so closely connected with my own—but also the other individuals with whom I had become more or less reluctantly associated,— Catherine Harland and Dr. Brayle especially. Mr. Harland had, unconsciously to himself, been merely the link to bring the broken bits of a chain together—his secretary, Mr. Swinton, occupied the place of the always necessary nonentity in a group of intellectually or psychically connected beings,—and I was perfectly sure, without having any actual reason for my conviction, that if I remained much longer in Catherine Harland's company, her chance liking for me would turn into the old hatred with which she had hated me in a bygone time,—a hatred fostered by Dr. Brayle, who, plainly scheming to marry her and secure her fortune, considered me in the way (as I was) of the influence he desired to exercise over her and her father. Therefore it seemed necessary I should remove myself,—moreover, I was resolved that all the years I had spent in trying to find the way to some of Nature's secrets should not be wasted—I would learn, I too, what Rafel Santoris had learned in the House of Aselzion—and then we might perhaps stand on equal ground, sure of ourselves and of each other! So ran my thoughts in the solitude and stillness of the night—a solitude and stillness so profound that the gentle push of the water against the sides of the yacht, almost noiseless as it was, sounded rough and intrusive. My port-hole was open, and I could see the sinking moon showing through it like a white face in sorrow. Just then I heard a low splash as of oars. I started up and went to the sofa, where, by kneeling on the cushions. I could look through the porthole. There, gliding just beneath me, was a small boat, and my heart gave a sudden leap of joy as I recognised the man who rowed it as Santoris. He smiled as I looked down,—then, standing up in the boat, guided himself alongside, till his head was nearly on a level with the port-hole. He put one hand on its edge.

"Not asleep yet!" he said, softly—"What have you been thinking of? The moon and the sea?—or any other mystery as deep and incomprehensible?"

I stretched out my hand and laid it on his with an involuntary caressing touch.

"I could not leave you without another last word,"—he said—"And I have brought you a letter"—he gave me a sealed envelope as he spoke—"which will tell you how to find Aselzion. I myself will write to him also and prepare him for your arrival. When you do see him you will understand how difficult is the task you wish to undertake,—and, if you should fail, the failure will be a greater sadness to yourself than to me—for I could make things easier for you—"

"I do not want things made easy for me,"—I answered quickly—"I want to do all that you have done—I want to prove myself worthy at least—"

I broke off,—and looked down into his eyes. He smiled.

"Well!" he said—"Are you beginning to remember the happiness we have so often thrown away for a trifle?"

I was silent, though I folded my hand closer over his. The soft white sleepy radiance of the moon on the scarcely moving water around us made everything look dream-like and unreal, and I was hardly conscious of my own existence for the moment, so completely did it seem absorbed by some other influence stronger than any power I had ever known.

"Here are we two,"—he continued, softly—"alone with the night and each other, close to the verge of a perfect understanding—and yet— determined NOT to understand! How often that happens! Every moment, every hour, all over the world, there are souls like ours, barred severally within their own shut gardens, refusing to open the doors! They talk over the walls, through the chinks and crannies, and peep through the keyholes—but they will not open the doors. How fortunate am I to-night to find even a port-hole open!"

He turned up his face, full of light and laughter, to mine, and I thought then, how easy it would be to fling away all my doubts and scruples, give up the idea of making any more search for what perhaps I should never find, and take the joy which seemed proffered and the love which my heart knew was its own to claim! Yet something still pulled me back, and not only pulled me back, but on and away— something which inwardly told me I had much to learn before I dared accept a happiness I had not deserved. Nevertheless some of my thoughts found sudden speech.

"Rafel—" I began, and then paused, amazed at my own boldness in thus addressing him. He drew closer to me, the boat he stood in swaying under him.

"Go on!" he said, with a little tremor in his voice—"My name never sounded so sweetly in my own ears! What is it you would have me do?"

"Nothing!" I answered, half afraid of myself as I spoke—"Nothing— but this. Just to think that I am not merely wilful or rebellious in parting from you for a little while—for if it is true—"

"If what is true?" he interposed, gently.

"If it is true that we are friends not for a time but for eternity"- -I said, in steadier tones—"then it can only be for a little while that we shall be separated. And then afterwards I shall be quite sure—"

"Yes—quite sure of what you are sure of now!" he said—"As sure as any immortal creature can be of an immortal truth! Do you know how long we have been separated already?"

I shook my head, smiling a little.

"Well, I will not tell you!" he answered—"It might frighten you! But by all the powers of earth and heaven, we shall not traverse such distances apart again—not if I can prevent it!"

"And can you?" I asked, half wistfully.

"I can! And I will! For I am stronger than you—and the strongest wins! Your eyes look startled—there are glimpses of the moon in them, and they are soft eyes— not angry ones. I have seen them full of anger,—an anger that stabbed me to the heart!—but that was in the days gone by, when I was weaker than you. This time the position has changed—and _I_ am master!"

"Not yet!" I said, resolutely, withdrawing my hand from his—"I yield to nothing—not even to happiness—till I KNOW!"

A slight shadow darkened the attractiveness of his features.

"That is what the world says of God—'I will not yield till I know!' But it is as plastic clay in His hands, all the time, and it never knows!"

I was silent—and there was a pause in which no sound was heard but the movement of the water under the little boat in which he stood. Then—

"Good-night!" he said.

"Good-night!" I answered, and moved by a swift impulse, I stooped and kissed the firm hand that rested so near me, gripping the edge of the port-hole. He looked up with a sudden light in his eyes.

"Is that a sign of grace and consolation?" he asked, smiling—"Well! I am content! And I have waited so long that I can wait yet a little longer."

So speaking, he let go his hold from alongside the yacht, and in another minute had seated himself in the boat and was rowing away across the moonlit water. I watched him as every stroke of the oars widened the distance between us, half hoping that he might look back, wave his hand, or even return again—but no!— his boat soon vanished like a small black speck on the sea, and I knew myself to be left alone. Restraining with difficulty the tears that rose to my eyes, I shut the port-hole and drew its little curtain across it— then I sat down to read the letter he had left with me. It ran as follows:

Beloved,—

I call you by this name as I have always called you through many cycles of time,— it should sound upon your ears as familiarly as a note of music struck in response to another similar note in far distance. You are not satisfied with the proofs given you by your own inner consciousness, which testify to the unalterable fact that you and I are, and must be, as one,—that we have played with fate against each other, and sometimes striven to escape from each other, all in vain;—it is not enough for you to know (as you do know) that the moment our eyes met our spirits rushed together in a sudden ecstasy which, had we dared to yield to it, would have outleaped convention and made of us no more than two flames in one fire! If you are honest with yourself as I am honest with myself, you will admit that this is so,—that the emotion which overwhelmed us was reasonless, formless and wholly beyond all analysis, yet more insistent than any other force having claim on our lives. But it is not sufficient for you to realise this,—or to trace through every step of the journey you have made, the gradual leading of your soul to mine,—from that last night you passed in your own home, when every fibre of your being grew warm with the prescience of coming joy, to this present moment, even through dreams of infinite benediction in which I shared—no!—it is not sufficient for you!— you must 'know'—you must learn—you must probe into deeper mysteries, and study and suffer to the last! Well, if it must be so, it must,— and I shall rely on the eternal fitness of things to save you from your own possible rashness and bring you back to me,—for without you now I can do nothing more. I have done much—and much remains to be done—but if I am to attain, you must crown the attainment—if my ambition is to find completion, you alone can be its completeness. If you have the strength and the courage to face the ordeal through which Aselzion sends those who seek to follow his teaching, you will indeed have justified your claim to be considered higher than merest woman,—though you have risen above that level already. The lives of women generally, and of men too, are so small and sordid and self-centred, thanks to their obstinate refusal to see anything better or wider than their own immediate outlook, that it is hardly worth while considering them in the light of that deeper knowledge which teaches of the REAL life behind the seeming one. In the ordinary way of existence men and women meet and mate with very little more intelligence or thought about it than the lower animals; and the results of such meeting and mating are seen in the degenerate and dying nations of to-day. Moreover, they are content to be born for no other visible reason than to die—and no matter how often they may be told there is no such thing as death, they receive the assertion with as much indignant incredulity as the priesthood of Rome received Galileo's assurance that the earth moves round the sun. But we—you and I—who know that life, being ALL Life, CANNOT die,—ought to be wiser in our present space of time than to doubt each other's infinite capability for love and the perfect world of beauty which love creates. _I_ do not doubt—my doubting days are past, and the whips of sorrow have lashed me into shape as well as into strength, but YOU hesitate,—because you have been rendered weak by much misunderstanding. However, it has partially comforted me to place the position fully before you, and having done this I feel that you must be free to go your own way. I do not say 'I love you!'—such a phrase from me would be merest folly, knowing that you must be mine, whether now or at the end of many more centuries. Your soul is deathless as mine is—it is eternally young, as mine is,—and the force that gives us life and love is divine and indestructible, so that for us there can be no end to the happiness which is ours to claim when we will. For the rest I leave you to decide—you will go to the House of Aselzion and perhaps you will remain there some time,—at any rate when you depart from thence you will have learned much, and you will know what is best for yourself and for me.

My beloved, I commend you to God with all my adoring soul and am

Your lover, Rafel Santoris

A folded paper fell out of this letter,—it contained full instructions as to the way I should go on the journey I intended to make to the mysterious House of Aselzion—and I was glad to find that I should not have to travel as far as I had at first imagined. I began at once to make my plans for leaving the Harlands as soon as possible, and before going to bed I wrote to my friend Francesca, who I knew would certainly expect me to visit her in Inverness-shire as soon as my cruise in the Harlands' yacht was over, and briefly stated that business of an important nature called me abroad for two or three weeks, but that I fully anticipated being at home in England again before the end of October. As it was now just verging on the end of August, I thought I was allowing myself a fairly wide margin for absence. When I had folded and sealed my letter ready for posting, an irresistible sense of sleep came over me, and I yielded to it gratefully. I found myself too overcome by it even to think,— and I laid my head down upon the pillows with a peaceful consciousness that all was well,—that all would be well—and that in trying to make sure of the intentions of Fate towards me both in life and love, I could not be considered as altogether foolish. Of course, judged by the majority of people, I know I am already counted as worse than foolish for the impressions and experiences I here undertake to narrate, but that kind of judgment does not affect me, seeing that their own daily and hourly folly is so visibly pronounced and has such unsatisfactory and frequently disastrous results, that mine—if it indeed be folly to choose lasting and eternal things rather than ephemeral and temporal ones,—cannot but seem light in comparison. Love, as the world generally conceives of it, is hardly worth having—for if we become devoted to persons who must in time be severed from us by death or other causes, we have merely wasted the wealth of our affections. Only as a perfect, eternal, binding force is love of any value,—and unless one can be sure in one's own self that there is the strength and truth and courage to make it thus perfect, eternal and binding, it is better to have nothing to do with what after all is the divinest of divine passions,—the passion of creativeness, from which springs all thought, all endeavour, all accomplishment.

When I woke the next morning I did not need to be told that the 'Dream' had set her wonderful sails and flown. A sense of utter desolation was in the air, and my own loneliness was impressed upon me with overwhelming bitterness and force. It was a calm, brilliant morning, and when I went up on deck the magnificent scenery of Loch Scavaig was, to my thinking, lessened in effect by the excessive glare of the sun. The water was smooth as oil, and where the 'Dream' had been anchored, showing her beautiful lines and tapering spars against the background of the mountains, there was now a dreary vacancy. The whole scene looked intolerably dull and lifeless, and I was impatient to be away from it. I said as much at breakfast, a meal at which Catherine Harland never appeared, and where I was accustomed to take the head of the table, at Mr. Harland's request, to dispense the tea and coffee. Dr. Brayle seemed malignly amused at my remark.

"The interest of the place has evidently vanished with Mr. Santoris, so far as you are concerned!" he said—"He is certainly a remarkable man, and owns a remarkable yacht—but beyond that I am not sure that his room is not better than his company."

"I daresay you feel it so,"—said Mr. Harland, who had for some moments been unusually taciturn and preoccupied—"Your theories are diametrically opposed to his, and, for that matter, so are mine. But I confess I should like to have tested his medical skill—he assured me positively that he could cure me of my illness in three months."

"Why do you not let him try?" suggested Brayle, with an air of forced lightness—"He will be a man of miracles if he can cure what the whole medical profession knows to be incurable. But I'm quite willing to retire in his favour, if you wish it."

Mr. Harland's bristling eyebrows met over his nose in a saturnine frown.

"Well, are you willing?" he said—"I rather doubt it! And if you are, I'm not. I've no faith in mysticism or psychism of any kind. It bores me to think about it. And nothing has puzzled me at all concerning Santoris except his extraordinarily youthful appearance. That is a problem to me,—and I should like to solve it."

"He looks about thirty-eight or forty,"—said Brayle, "And I should say that is his age." "That his age!" Mr. Harland gave a short, derisive laugh—"Why, he's over sixty if he's a day! That's the mystery of it. There is not a touch of 'years' about him. Instead of growing old, he grows young."

Brayle looked up quizzically at his patron.

"I've already hinted," he said, "that he may not be the Santoris you knew at Oxford. He may be a relative, cleverly masquerading as the original man—"

"That won't stand a moment's argument," interposed Mr. Harland—"And I'll tell you how I know it won't. We had a quarrel once, and I slashed his arm with a clasp-knife pretty heavily." Here a sudden quiver of something,—shame or remorse perhaps—came over his hard face and changed its expression for a moment. "It was all my fault— I had a devilish temper, and he was calm—his calmness irritated me;—moreover, I was drunk. Santoris knew I was drunk,—and he wanted to get me home to my rooms and to bed before I made too great a disgrace of myself—then—THAT happened. I remember the blood pouring from his arm—it frightened me and sobered me. Well, when he came on board here the other night he showed me the scar of the very wound I had inflicted. So I know he's the same man."

We all sat silent.

"He was always studying the 'occult'"—went on Mr. Harland—"And I was scarcely surprised that he should 'think out' that antique piece of jewellery from your pocket last night. He actually told me it belonged to you ages ago, when you were quite another and more important person!"

Dr. Brayle laughed loudly, almost boisterously.

"What a fictionist the man must be!" he exclaimed. "Why doesn't he write a novel? Mr. Swinton, I wish you would take a few notes for me of what Mr. Santoris said about that collar of jewels,—I should like to keep the record."

Mr. Swinton smiled an obliging assent.

"I certainly will,"—he said. "I was fortunately present when Mr. Santoris expressed his curious ideas about the jewels to Mr. Harland."

"Oh, well, if you are going to record it,"—said Mr. Harland, half laughingly—"you had better be careful to put it all down. The collar—according to Santoris—belonged to Dr. Brayle when his personality was that of an Italian nobleman residing in Florence about the year 1537—he wore it on one unfortunate occasion when he murdered a man, and the jewels have not had much of a career since that period. Now they have come back into his possession—"

"Father, who told you all this?"

The voice was sharp and thin, and we turned round amazed to see Catherine standing in the doorway of the saloon, white and trembling, with wild eyes looking as though they saw ghosts. Dr. Brayle hastened to her.

"Miss Harland, pray go back to your cabin—you are not strong enough—"

"What's the matter, Catherine?" asked her father—"I'm only repeating some of the nonsense Santoris told me about that collar of jewels—"

"It's not nonsense!" cried Catherine. "It's all true! I remember it all—we planned the murder together—he and I!"—and she pointed to Dr. Brayle—" I told him how the lovers used to meet in secret,—the poor hunted things!—how he—that great artist he patronised—came to her room from the garden entrance at night, and how they talked for hours behind the rose-trees in the avenue—and she— she!—I hated her because I thought you loved her—YOU!" and again she turned to Dr. Brayle, clutching at his arm—"Yes—I thought you loved her!—but she— she loved HIM!—and—" here she paused, shuddering violently, and seemed to lose herself in chaotic ideas— "And so the yacht has gone, and there is peace!— and perhaps we shall forget again!—we were allowed to forget for a little while, but it has all come back to haunt and terrify us—"

And with these words, which broke off in a kind of inarticulate cry, she sank downward in a swoon, Dr. Brayle managing to save her from falling quite to the ground.

Everything was at once in confusion, and while the servants were busy hurrying to and fro for cold water, smelling salts and other reviving cordials, and Catherine was being laid on the sofa and attended to by Dr. Brayle, I slipped away and went up on deck, feeling myself quite overpowered and bewildered by the suddenness and strangeness of the episodes in which I had become involved. In a minute or two Mr. Harland followed me, looking troubled and perplexed.

"What does all this mean?" he said—"I am quite at a loss to understand Catherine's condition. She is hysterical, of course,—but what has caused it? What mad idea has she got into her head about a murder?"

I looked away from him across the sunlit expanse of sea.

"I really cannot tell you," I said, at last—"I am quite as much in the dark as you are. I think she is overwrought, and that she has perhaps taken some of the things Mr. Santoris said too much to heart. Then"—here I hesitated—"she said the other day that she was tired of this yachting trip—in fact, I think it is simply a case of nerves."

"She must have very odd nerves if they persuade her to believe that she and Brayle committed a murder together ages ago"—said Mr. Harland, irritably;—"I never heard of such nonsense in all my life!"

I was silent.

"I have told Captain Derrick to weigh anchor and get out of this,"— he continued, brusquely. "We shall make for Portree at once. There is something witch-like and uncanny about the place"—and he looked round as he spoke at the splendour of the mountains, shining with almost crystalline clearness in the glory of the morning sun—"I feel as if it were haunted!"

"By what?" I asked.

"By memories," he answered—"And not altogether pleasant ones!"

I looked at him, and a moment's thought decided me that the opportunity had come for me to broach the subject of my intended departure, and I did so. I said that I felt I had allowed myself sufficient holiday, and that it would be necessary for me to take the ordinary steamer from Portree the morning after our arrival there in order to reach Glasgow as soon as possible. Mr. Harland surveyed me inquisitively.

"Why do you want to go by the steamer?" he asked—"Why not go with us back to Rothesay, for example?"

"I would rather lose no time,"—I said—then I added impulsively:— "Dear Mr. Harland, Catherine will be much better when I am gone—I know she will! You will be able to prolong the yachting trip which will benefit your health,—and I should be really most unhappy if you curtailed it on my account—"

He interrupted me.

"Why do you say that Catherine will be better when you are gone?" he demanded—"It was her own most particular wish that you should accompany us."

"She did not know what moved her to such a desire," I said,—then, seeing his look of astonishment, I smiled; "I am not a congenial spirit to her, nor to any of you, really! but she has been most kind, and so have you—and I thank you ever so much for all you have done for me—you have done much more than you know!—only I feel it is better to go now—now, before—"

"Before what?" he asked.

"Well, before we all hate each other!" I said, playfully—"It is quite on the cards that we shall come to that! Dr. Brayle thinks my presence quite as harmful to Catherine as that of Mr. Santoris;—I am full of 'theories' which he considers prejudicial,—and so, perhaps, they ARE—to HIM!"

Mr. Harland drew closer to me where I stood leaning against the deck rail and spoke in a lower tone.

"Tell me," he said,—"and be perfectly frank about it—what is it you see in Brayle that rouses such a spirit of antagonism in you?"

"If I give you a straight answer, such as I feel to be the truth in myself, will you be offended?" I asked.

He shook his head.

"No"—he answered—"I shall not be offended. I simply want to know what you think, and I shall remember what you say and see if it proves correct."

"Well, in the first place," I said—"I see nothing in Dr. Brayle but what can be seen in hundreds of worldly-minded men such as he. But he is not a true physician, for he makes no real effort to cure you of your illness, while Catherine has no illness at all that demands a cure. He merely humours the weakness of her nerves, a weakness she has created by dwelling morbidly on her own self and her own particular miseries,—and all his future plans with regard to her and to you are settled. They are quite clear and reasonable. You will die,—in fact, it is, in his opinion, necessary for you to die,—it would be very troublesome and inconvenient to him if, by some chance, you were cured, and continued to live. When you are gone he will marry Catherine, your only child and heiress, and he will have no further personal anxieties. I dislike this self-seeking attitude on his part, and my only wonder is that you do not perceive it. For the rest, my antagonism to Dr. Brayle is instinctive and has its origin far back—perhaps in a bygone existence!"

He listened to my words with attentive patience.

"Well, I shall study the man more carefully,"—he said, after a pause;—"You may be right. At present I think you are wrong. As for any cure for me, I know there is none. I have consulted medical works on the subject and am perfectly convinced that Brayle is doing his best. He can do no more. And now one word to yourself;"—here he laid a hand kindly on mine—"I have noticed—I could not help noticing that you were greatly taken by Santoris—and I should almost have fancied him rather fascinated by you had I not known him to be absolutely indifferent to womenkind. But let me tell you he is not a safe friend or guide for anyone. His theories are extravagant and impossible—his idea that there is no death, for example, when death stares us in the face every day, is perfectly absurd—and he is likely to lead you into much perplexity, the more so as you are too much of a believer in occult things already. I wish I could persuade you to listen to me seriously on one or two points—"

I smiled. "I am listening!" I said.

"Well, child, you listen perhaps, but you are not convinced. Realise, if you can, that these fantastic chimeras of a past and future life exist only in the heated imagination of the abnormal idealist. There is nothing beyond our actual sight and immediate living consciousness;—we know we are born and that we die—but why, we cannot tell and never shall be able to tell. We must try and manage the 'In-Between,'—the gap dividing birth and death,—as best we can, and that's all. I wish you would settle down to these facts reasonably—you would be far better balanced in mind and action—"

"If I thought as you do,"—I interrupted him—"I would jump from this vessel into the sea and let the waters close over me! There would be neither use nor sense in living for an 'In-Between' leading merely to nothingness."

He passed his hand across his brows perplexedly.

"It certainly seems useless,"—he admitted—"but there it is. It is better to accept it than run amok among inexplicable infinities."

We were interrupted here by the sailors busying themselves in preparations for getting the yacht under way, and our conversation being thus broken off abruptly was not again resumed. By eleven o'clock we were steaming out of Loch Scavaig, and as I looked back on the sombre mountain-peaks that stood sentinelwise round the deeply hidden magnificence of Loch Coruisk, I wondered if my visionary experience there had been only the work of my own excited imagination, or whether it really had foundation in fact? The letter from Santoris lay against my heart as actual testimony that he at least was real—that I had met and known him, and that so far as anything could be believed he had declared himself my 'lover'! But was ever love so expressed?—and had it ever before such a far-off beginning?

I soon ceased to perplex myself with futile speculations on the subject, however, and as the last peaks of the Scavaig hills vanished in pale blue distance I felt as if I had been brought suddenly back from a fairyland to a curiously dull and commonplace world. Everyone on board the 'Diana' seemed occupied with the veriest trifles,—Catherine remained too ill to appear all day, and Dr. Brayle was in almost constant attendance upon her. A vague sense of discomfort pervaded the whole atmosphere of the yacht,—she was a floating palace filled with every imaginable luxury, yet now she seemed a mere tawdry upholsterer's triumph compared with the exquisite grace and taste of the 'Dream'—and I was eager to be away from her. I busied myself during the day in packing my things ready for departure with the eagerness of a child leaving school for the holidays, and I was delighted when we arrived at Portree and anchored there that evening. It was after dinner, at about nine o'clock, that Catherine sent for me, hearing I had determined to go next morning. I found her in her bed, looking very white and feeble, with a scared look in her eyes which became intensified the moment she saw me.

"You are really going away?" she said, faintly—"I hope we have not offended you?"

I went up to her, took her poor thin hand and kissed it.

"No indeed!"—I answered—"Why should I be offended?"

"Father is vexed you are going,"—she went on—"He says it is all my silly nonsense and hysterical fancies—do you think it is?"

"I prefer not to say what I think,"—I replied, gently. "Dear Catherine, there are some things in life which cannot be explained, and it is better not to try and explain them. But believe me, I can never thank you enough for this yachting trip—you have done more for me than you will ever know!—and so far from being 'offended' I am grateful!—grateful beyond all words!"

She held my hands, looking at me wistfully.

"You will go away,"—she said, in a low tone—"and we shall perhaps never meet again. I don't think it likely we shall. People often try to meet again and never do—

haven't you noticed that? It seems fated that they shall only know each other for a little while just to serve some purpose, and then part altogether. Besides, you live in a different world from ours. You believe in things that I can't even understand— You think there is a God—and you think each human being has a soul—"

"Are you not taught the same in your churches?" I interrupted.

She looked startled.

"Oh yes!—but then one never thinks seriously about it! You know that if we DID think seriously about it we could never live as we do. One goes to church for con- vention's sake—because it's respectable; but suppose you were to say to a clergy- man that if your soul is 'immortal' it follows in reason that it must always have existed and always will exist, he would declare you to be 'unorthodox.' That's where all the puzzle and contradiction comes in—so that I don't believe in the soul at all."

"Are you sure you do not?" I enquired, meaningly.

She was silent. Then she suddenly broke out.

"Well, I don't want to believe in it! I don't want to think about it! I'd rather not! It's terrible! If a soul has never died and never will die, its burden of memories must be awful!—horrible!—no hell could be worse!"

"But suppose they are beautiful and happy memories?" I suggested.

She shuddered.

"They couldn't be! We all fail somewhere."

This was true enough, and I offered no comment.

"I feel,"—she went on, hesitatingly—"that you are leaving us for some undiscov- ered country—and that you will reach some plane of thought and action to which we shall never rise. I don't think I am sorry for this. I am not one of those who want to rise. I should be perfectly content to live a few years in a moderate state of happiness and then drop into oblivion—and I think most people are like me."

"Very unambitious!" I said, smiling.

"Yes—I daresay it is—but one gets tired of it all. Tired of things and people—at least I do. Now that man Santoris—"

Despite myself, I felt the warm blood flushing my cheeks.

"Yes? What of him?" I queried, lightly. "Well, I can understand that HE has always been alive!" and she turned her eyes upon me with an expression of positive dread— "Immensely, actively, perpetually alive! He seems to hold some mastery over the very air! I am afraid of him—terribly afraid! It is a relief to me to know that he and his strange yacht have gone!"

"But, Catherine,"—I ventured to say—"the yacht was not really 'strange,'—it was only moved by a different application of electricity from that which the world at present knows. You would not call it 'strange' if the discovery made by Mr. Santoris were generally adopted?"

She sighed.

"Perhaps not! But just now it seems a sort of devil's magic to me. Anyhow, I'm glad he's gone. You're sorry, I suppose?"

"In a way I am,"—I answered, quietly—"I thought him very kind and charming and courteous—no one could be a better host or a pleasanter companion. And I certainly saw nothing 'devilish' about him. As for that collar of jewels, there are plenty of so-called 'thought-readers' who could have found out its existence and said as much of it as he did—"

She uttered a low cry.

"Don't speak of it!" she said—"For Heaven's sake, don't speak of it!"

She buried her face in her pillow, and I waited silently for her to recover. When she turned again towards me, she said—

"I am not well yet,—I cannot bear too much. I only want you to know before you go away that I have no unkind feeling towards you,— things seem pushing me that way, but I have not really!—and you surely will believe me—"

"Surely!" I said, earnestly—"Dear Catherine, do not worry yourself! These impressions of yours will pass."

"I hope so!" she said—"I shall try to forget! And you—you will meet Mr. Santoris again, do you think?" I hesitated.

"I do not know."

"You seem to have some attraction for each other," she went on—"And I suppose your beliefs are alike. To me they are dreadful beliefs!— worse than barbarism!"

I looked at her with all the compassion I truly felt.

"Why? Because we believe that God is all love and tenderness and justice?—because we cannot think He would have created life only to end in death?—because we are sure that He allows nothing to be wasted, not even a thought?—and nothing to go unrecompensed, either in good or in evil? Surely these are not barbarous beliefs?"

A curious look came over her face.

"If I believed in anything,"—she said—"I would rather be orthodox, and believe in the doctrine of original sin and the Atonement."

"Then you would start with the idea that the supreme and all-wise Creator could not make a perfect work!" I said—"And that He was obliged to invent a scheme to redeem His own failure! Catherine, if you speak of barbarism, this is the most barbarous belief of all!"

She stared at me, amazed.

"You would be put out of any church in Christendom for such a speech as that!" she said.

"Possibly!" I answered, quietly—"But I should not and could not be put out of God's Universe—nor, I am certain, would He reject my soul's eternal love and adoration!"

A silence fell between us. Then I heard her sobbing. I put my arm round her, and she laid her head on my shoulder.

"I wish I could feel as you do,"—she whispered—"You must be very happy! The world is all beautiful in your eyes—and of course with your ideas it will continue to be beautiful—and even death will only come to you as another transition into life. But you must not think anybody will ever understand you or believe you or follow you- -people will only look upon you as mad, or the dupe of your own foolish imagination!"

I smiled as I smoothed her pillow for her and laid her gently back upon it.

"I can stand that!" I said—"If somebody who is lost in the dark jeers at me for finding the light, I shall not mind!"

We did not speak much after that—and when I said good-night to her I also said good-bye, as I knew I should have to leave the yacht early in the morning.

I spent the rest of the time at my disposal in talking to Mr. Harland, keeping our conversation always on the level of ordinary topics. He seemed genuinely sorry that I had determined to go, and if he could have persuaded me to stay on board a few days longer I am sure he would have been pleased.

"I shall see you off in the morning,"—he said—"And believe me I shall miss you very much. We don't agree on certain subjects—but I like you all the same."

"That's something!" I said, cheerfully—"It would never do if we were all of the same opinion!"

"Will you meet Santoris again, do you think?"

This was the same question Catherine had put to me, and I answered it in the same manner.

"I really don't know!"

"Would you LIKE to meet him again?" he urged.

I hesitated, smiling a little.

"Yes, I think so!"

"It is curious," he pursued—"that I should have been the means of bringing you together. Your theories of life and death are so alike that you must have thoughts in common. Many years have passed since I knew Santoris—in fact, I had completely lost sight of him, though I had never forgotten his powerful personality—and it seemt rather odd to me that he should suddenly turn up again while you were with me—"

"Mere coincidence,"—I said, lightly—"and common enough, after all. Like attracts like, you know."

"That may be. There is certainly something in the law of attraction between human beings which we do not understand,"—he answered, musingly—"Perhaps if we did—"

He broke off and relapsed into silence.

That night, just before going to bed, I was met by Dr. Brayle in the corridor leading to my cabin. I was about to pass him with a brief good-night, but he stopped me.

"So you are really going to-morrow!" he said, with a furtive narrowing of his eyelids as he looked at me—"Well! Perhaps it is best! You are a very disturbing magnet."

I smiled.

"Am I? In what way?"

"I cannot tell you without seeming to give the lie to reason,"—he answered, brusquely. "I believe to a certain extent in magnetism—in fact, I have myself tested its power in purely nervous patients,— but I have never accepted the idea that persons can silently and almost without conscious effort, influence others for either malign or beneficial purposes. In your presence, however, the thing is forced upon me as though it were a truth, while I know it to be a fallacy."

"Isn't it too late to talk about such things to-night?" I asked, wishing to cut short the conversation.

"Perhaps it is—but I shall probably never have the chance to say what I wish to say,"—he replied,—and he leaned against the stairway just where the light in the saloon sent forth a bright ray upon his face, showing it to be dark with a certain frowning perplexity—"You have studied many things in your own impulsive feminine fashion, and you are beyond all the stupidity of the would- be agreeable female who thinks a prettily feigned ignorance becoming, so that I can speak frankly. I can now tell you that from the first day I saw you I felt I had known you before—and you filled me with a curious emotion of mingled liking and repulsion. One night when you were sitting with us on deck—it was before we met that fellow Santoris—I watched you with singular interest— every turn of your head, every look of your eyes seemed familiar— and for a moment I—I almost loved you! Oh, you need not mind my saying this!"—and he laughed a little at my involuntary exclamation—"it was nothing—it was only a passing mood,—for in another few seconds I hated you as keenly! There you have it. I do not know why I should have been visited by these singular experiences—but I own they exist—that is why I am rather glad you are going."

"I am glad, too,"—I said—and I held out my hand in parting—"I should not like to stay where my presence caused a moment's uneasiness or discomfort."

"That's not putting it quite fairly,"—he answered, taking my offered hand and holding it loosely in his own—"But you are an avowed psychist, and in this way you are a little 'uncanny.' I should not like to offend you—"

"You could not if you tried," I said, quickly.

"That means I am too insignificant in your mind to cause offence,"— he observed—"I daresay I am. I live on the material plane and am content to remain there. You are essaying very high flights and ascending among difficulties of thought and action which are entirely beyond the useful and necessary routine of life,—and in the end these things may prove too much for you." Here he dropped my hand. "You bring with you a certain atmosphere which is too rarefied for ordinary mortals—it has the same effect as the air of a very high mountain on a weak heart—it is too strong—one loses breath, and the power to think coherently. You produce this result on Miss Harland, and also to some extent on me—even slightly on Mr. Harland,—and poor Swinton alone does not fall under the spell, having no actual brain to impress. You need someone who is accustomed to live in the same atmosphere as yourself to match you in your impressions and opinions. We are on a different range of thought and feeling and experience—and you must find us almost beyond endurance—"

"As you find me!" I interposed, smiling.

"I will not say that—no! For there seems to have been a time when we were all on the same plane—"

He paused, and there was a moment's tense silence. The little silvery chime of a clock in the saloon struck twelve.

"Good-night, Dr. Brayle!" I said.

He lifted his brooding eyes and looked at me.

"Good-night! If I have annoyed you by my scepticism in certain matters, you must make allowances for temperament and pardon me. I should be sorry if you bore me any ill-will—"

What a curious note of appeal there was in his voice! All at once it seemed to me that he was asking me to forgive him for that long-ago murder which I had seen reflected in a vision!—and my blood grew suddenly heated with an involuntary wave of deep resentment.

"Dr. Brayle," I said,—"pray do not trouble yourself to think any more about me. Our ways will always be apart, and we shall probably never see each other again. It really does not matter to you in the least what my feeling may be with regard to you,—it can have no influence on either your present or your future. Friendships cannot be commanded."

"You will not say," he interrupted me—"that you have no dislike of me?"

I hesitated—then spoke frankly.

"I will not,"—I answered—"because I cannot!"

For one instant our eyes met—then came SOMETHING between us that suggested an absolute and irretrievable loss—"Not yet!" he murmured—"Not yet!" and with a forced smile, he bowed and allowed me to pass to my cabin. I was glad to be there—glad to be alone— and overwhelmed as I was by the consciousness that the memories of my soul had been too strong for me to resist, I was thankful that I had had the courage to express my invincible opposition to one who had, as I seemed instinctively to realise, been guilty of an unrepented crime.

That night I slept dreamlessly, and the next morning before seven o'clock I had left the luxurious 'Diana' for the ordinary passenger steamer plying from Portree to Glasgow. Mr. Harland kept his promise of seeing me off, and expressed his opinion that I was very foolish to travel with a crowd of tourists and other folk, when I might have had the comfort and quiet of his yacht all the way; but he could not move me from my resolve, though in a certain sense I was sorry to say good-bye to him.

"You must write to us as soon as you get home,"—he said, at parting—"A letter will find us this week at Gairloch—I shall cruise about a bit longer."

I made no reply for the moment. He had no idea that I was not going home at all, nor did I intend to tell him. "You shall hear from me as soon as possible,"— I said at last, evasively—" I shall be very busy for a time—"

He laughed.

"Oh, I know! You are always busy! Will you ever get tired, I wonder?"

I smiled. "I hope not!"

With that we shook hands and parted, and within the next twenty minutes the steamer had started, bearing me far away from the Isle of Skye, that beautiful, weird and mystic region full of strange legends and memories, which to me had proved a veritable wonderland. I watched the 'Diana' at anchor in the bay of Portree till I could see her no more,—and it was getting on towards noon when I suddenly noticed the people on board the steamer making a rush to one side of the deck to look at something that was evidently both startling and attractive. I followed the crowd,—and my heart gave a quick throb of delight when I saw poised on the sparkling waters the fairylike 'Dream'!—her sails white as the wings of a swan, and her cordage gleaming like woven gold in the brilliant sunshine. She was a thing of perfect beauty as she seemed to glide on the very edge of the horizon like a vision between sky and sea. And as I pressed forward among the thronging passengers to look at her, she dipped her flag in salutation—a salutation I knew was meant for me alone. When the flag ran up again to its former position, murmurs of admiration came from several people around me—

"The finest schooner afloat!"—I heard one man remark—"They say she goes by electricity as well as sailing power."

"She's often seen about here," said another—"She belongs to a foreigner—some prince or other named Santoris."

And I watched and waited,—with unconscious tears in my eyes, till the exquisite fairy vessel disappeared suddenly as though it had become absorbed and melted into the sun; then all at once I thought of the words spoken by the wild Highland 'Jamie' who had given me the token of the bell-heather—"One way in and another way out! One road to the West, and the other to the East, and round about to the meeting-place!"

The meeting-place! Where would it be? I could only think and wonder, hope and pray, as the waves spread their silver foaming distance between me and the vanished 'Dream.'

XIII

THE HOUSE OF ASELZION

It is not necessary to enter into particular details of the journey I now entered upon and completed during the ensuing week. My destination was a remote and mountainous corner of the Biscayan coast, situated a little more than three days' distance from Paris. I went alone, knowing that this was imperative, and arrived without any untoward adventure, scarcely fatigued though I had travelled by night as well as by day. It was only at the end of my journey that I found myself confronted by any difficulty, and then I had to realise that though the 'Chateau d'Aselzion,' as it was called, was perfectly well known to the inhabitants of the surrounding district, no one seemed inclined to show me the nearest way there or even to let me have the accommodation of a vehicle to take me up the steep ascent which led to it. The Chateau itself could be seen from all parts of the village, especially from the seashore, over which it hung like a toppling crown of the fortress-like rock on which it was erected.

"It is a monastery,"—said a man of whom I asked the way, speaking in a curious kind of guttural patois, half French and half Spanish— "No woman goes there."

I explained that I was entrusted with an important message.

He shook his head.

"Not for any money would I take you," he declared. "I should be afraid for myself."

Nothing could move him from his resolve, so I made up my mind to leave my small luggage at the inn and walk up the steep road which I could see winding like a width of white ribbon towards the goal of my desires. A group of idle peasants watched me curiously as I spoke to the landlady and asked her to take care of my few belongings till I either sent for them or returned to fetch them, to which arrangement she readily consented. She was a buxom, pleasant little Frenchwoman, and inclined to be friendly.

"I assure you, Mademoiselle, you will return immediately!" she said, with a bright smile—"The Chateau d'Aselzion is a place where no woman is ever seen—and a lady alone!—ah, mon Dieu!—impossible! There are terrible things done there, so they say—it is a house of mystery! In the daytime it looks as it does now—dark, as though it were a prison!—but sometimes at night one sees it lit up as though it were on fire—every window full of something that shines like the sun! It is a Brotherhood that lives there,—not of the Church—ah no! Heaven forbid!—but they are rich and powerful men—and it is said they study some strange science— our traders serve them only at the outer gates and never go beyond. And in the midnight one hears the organ playing in their chapel, and there is a sound of singing on the very waves of the sea! I beg of you, Mademoiselle, think well of what you do before you go to such a place!—for they will send you away—I am sure they will send you away!"

I smiled and thanked her for her well-meant warning.

"I have a message to give to the Master of the Brotherhood," I said- -"If I am not allowed to deliver it and the gate is shut in my face, I can only come back again. But I must do my best to gain an entrance if possible."

And with these words I turned away and commenced my solitary walk. I had arrived in the early afternoon and the sun was still high in the heavens,—the heat was intense and the air was absolutely still. As I climbed higher and higher, the murmuring noises of human life in the little village I had left behind me grew less and less and presently sank altogether out of hearing, and I became gradually aware of the great and solemn solitude that everywhere encompassed me. No stray sheep browsed on the burnt brown grass of the rocky height I was slowly ascending—no bird soared through the dazzling deep blue of the vacant sky. The only sound I could hear was the soft, rhythmic plash of small waves on the beach below, and an indefinite deeper murmur of the sea breaking through a cave in the far distance. There was something very grand in the silence and loneliness of the scene,—and something very pitiful too, so I thought, about my own self, toiling up the rocky path in mingled hope and fear towards that grim pile of dark stone towers and high forbidding walls, where it was just possible I might meet with but a discouraging reception. Yet with the letter from him who signed himself 'Your lover' lying against my heart, I felt I had a talisman to open doors even more closely barred. Nevertheless, my courage gave way a little when I at last stood before the heavy iron gates set in a lofty archway of stone through which I could see nothing but cavernous blackness. The road I had followed ended in a broad circular sweep opposite this archway, and a few tall pines twisted and gnarled in bough and stem, as though the full force of many storm winds had battered and bent them out of their natural shapes, were the only relief to the barrenness of the ground. An iron chain with a massive ring at the end suggested itself as the possible means of pulling a bell or otherwise attracting attention; but for some minutes I had not the boldness to handle it.

I stood gazing at the frowning portal with a sense of utter loneliness and desolation,—the quick, resistless impulse that had fired me to make the journey and which, as it were, had driven me along by its own impetus, suddenly died away into a dreary consciousness of inadequateness and folly on my own part,—and I began to reproach myself for yielding so utterly to the casual influence of one who, after all, must in a reasonable way be considered a stranger. For what was Rafel Santoris to me? Merely an old college friend of the man who for a fortnight had been my host, and with whom he chanced to renew acquaintanceship during a yachting tour. Anything more simple and utterly commonplace never occurred,— yet, here was I full of strange impressions and visions, which were possibly only the result of clever hypnotism, practised on me because the hypnotist had possibly discovered in my temperament some suitable 'subject' matter for an essay of his skill. And I had so readily succumbed to his influence as to make a journey of hundreds of miles to a place I had never heard of before on the chance of seeing a man of whom I knew nothing!—except—that, according to what Rafel Santoris had said of him, he was the follower of a great psychic Teacher whom once I had known.

Such doubtful and darkening thoughts as these, chasing one another rapidly through my brain, made me severely accuse myself of rash and unpardonable folly in all I had done or was doing,—and I was almost on the point of turning away and retracing my steps, when a sudden ray of light, not of the sun, struck itself sharply as it were before my eyes and hurt them with its blinding glitter. It was like a whip of fire lashing my hesitating mind, and it startled me into instant action. Without pausing further to think what I was about, I went straight up to the entrance of the Chateau and pulled at the iron chain. The gates swung open at once and swiftly, without sound- -and I stepped into the dark passage within—

whereupon they as noiselessly closed again behind me. There was no going back now,— and nerving myself to resolution, I walked quickly on through what was evidently a long corridor with a lofty arched roof of massive stone; it was dark and cool and refreshing after the great heat outside, and I saw a faint light at the end towards which I made my way. The light widened as I drew near, and an exclamation of relief and pleasure escaped me as I suddenly found myself in a picturesque quadrangle, divided into fair green lawns and parterres of flowers. Straight opposite me as I approached, a richly carved double oaken door stood wide open, enabling me to look into a vast circular domed hall, in the centre of which a fountain sent up tall silver columns of spray which fell again with a tinkling musical splash into a sunken pool bordered with white marble, where delicate pale blue water-lilies floated on the surface of the water. Enchanted by this glimpse of loveliness, I went straight on and entered without seeking the right of admission,— and then stood looking about me in wonder and admiration. If this was the House of Aselzion, where such difficult lessons had to be learned and such trying ordeals had to be faced, it certainly did not seem like a house of penance and mortification but rather of luxury. Exquisite white marble statues were set around the hall in various niches between banked-up masses of roses and other blossoms— many of them perfect copies of the classic models, and all expressing either strength and resolution, or beauty and repose. And most wonderful of all was the light, that poured in from the high dome—I could have said with truth that it was like that 'light which never was on sea or land.' It was not the light of the sun, but something more softened and more intense, and was totally indescribable.

Fascinated by the restful charm of my surroundings, I seated myself on a marble bench near the fountain and watched the sparkle of the water as it rose in rainbow radiance and fell again into the darker shadows of the pool,—and I had for a moment lost myself in a kind of waking dream,—so that I started with a shock of something like terror when I suddenly perceived a figure approaching me,— that of a man, clothed in white garments fashioned somewhat after the monastic type, yet hardly to be called a monk's dress, though he wore a sort of hood or cowl pulled partially over his face. My heart almost stopped beating and I could scarcely breathe for nervous fear as he came towards me with an absolutely noiseless tread,—he appeared to be young, and his eyes, dark and luminous, looked at me kindly and, as I fancied, with a touch of pity.

"You are seeking the Master?" he enquired, in a gentle voice—"He has instructed me to receive you, and when you have rested for an hour, to take you to his presence."

I had risen as he spoke, and his quiet manner helped me to recover myself a little.

"I am not tired,"—I answered—"I could go to him at once—"

He smiled.

"That is not possible!" he said—"He is not ready. If you will come to the apartment allotted to you I am sure you will be glad of some repose. May I ask you to follow me?"

He was perfectly courteous in demeanour, and yet there was a certain impressive authority about him which silently impelled obedience. I had nothing further to demand or to suggest, and I followed him at once. He preceded me out of the domed hall into a long stone passage, where every sign of luxury, beauty or comfort disappeared in cold vastness, and where at every few steps large white boards with the word 'Silence!' printed upon them in prominent black letters confronted the eyes. The way we had to go seemed long and dreary and dungeon-like, but presently we turned towards an opening where the sun shone through, and my guide ascended a steep flight of stone stairs, at the top of which was a massive door of oak, heavily clamped with iron. Taking a key from his girdle, he unlocked this door, and throwing it open, signed to me to pass in. I did so, and found myself in a plain stone-walled room with a vaulted roof, and one very large, lofty, uncurtained window which looked out upon the sea and sheer down the perpendicular face of the rock on which the Chateau d'Aselzion was built. The furniture consisted of one small camp bedstead, a table, and two easy chairs, a piece of rough matting on the floor near the bed, and a hanging cupboard for clothes. A well-fitted bathroom adjoined this apartment, but beyond this there was nothing of modern comfort and certainly no touch of luxury. I moved instinctively to the window to look out at the sea,- -and then turned to thank my guide for his escort, but he had gone. Thrilled with a sudden alarm, I ran to the door—it was locked! I was a prisoner! I stood breathless and amazed;—then a wave of mingled indignation and terror swept over me. How dared these people restrain my liberty? I looked everywhere round the room for a bell or some means of communication by which I could let them know my mind—but there was nothing to help me. I went to the window again, and finding it was like a French casement, merely latched in the centre, I quickly unfastened and threw it open. The scent of the sea rushed at me with a delicious freshness, reminding me of Loch Scavaig and the 'Dream'—and I leaned out, looking longingly over the wide expanse of glittering water just now broken into little crests of foam by a rising breeze. Then I saw that my room was a kind of turret chamber, projecting itself sheer over a great wall of rock which evidently had its base in the bed of the ocean. There was no escape for me that way, even if I had sought it. I drew back from the window and paced round and round my room like a trapped animal— angry with myself for having ventured into such a place, and forgetting entirely my previous determination to go through all that might happen to me with patience and unflinching nerve.

Presently I sat down on my narrow camp bed and tried to calm myself. After all, what was the use of my anger or excitement? I had come to the House of Aselzion of my own wish and will,—and so far I had endured nothing difficult. Apparently Aselzion was willing to receive me in his own good time—and I had only to wait the course of events. Gradually my blood cooled, and in a few minutes I found myself smiling at my own absurdly useless indignation. True, I was locked up in my own room like a naughty child, but did it matter so very much? I assured myself it did not matter at all,—and as I accustomed my mind to this conviction I became perfectly composed and quite at home in my strange surroundings. I took off my hat and cloak and put them by—then I went into the bathroom and refreshed my face with delicious splashes of cold water. The bathroom possessed a full-length mirror fitted into the wall, a fact which rather amused me, as I felt it must have been there always and could not have been put up specially for me, so that it would seem these mystic 'Brothers' were not without some personal vanity. I surveyed myself in it with surprise as I took down my hair and twisted it up again more tidily, for I had expected to look fagged and tired, whereas my face presented a smiling freshness which was unexpected and astonishing to myself. The plain black dress I wore was dusty with travel—and I shook it as free as I could from railway grimness, feeling that it was scarcely the attire I should have chosen for an audience of Aselzion.

"However,"—I said to myself—"if he has me locked up like this, and gives me no chance of sending for my luggage at the inn, I can only submit and make the best of it."

And returning from the bathroom to the bedroom, I again looked out of my lofty window across the sea. As I did so, leaning a little over the ledge, something soft and velvety touched my hand;—it was a red rose clambering up the turret just within my reach. Its opening petals lifted themselves towards me like sweet lips turned up for kisses, and I was for a moment startled, for I could have sworn that no rose of any kind was there when I first looked out. 'One rose from all the roses in Heaven!' Where had I heard those words? And what did they signify? Then— I remembered! Carefully and with extreme tenderness, I bent over that beautiful, appealing flower:

"I will not gather you!"—I whispered, following the drift of my own dreaming fancy—"If you are a message—and I think you are I—stay there as long as you can and talk to me! I shall understand!"

And so for a while we made silent friends with each other till I might have said with the poet—'The soul of the rose went into my blood.' At any rate something keen, fine and subtle stole over my senses, moving me to an intense delight in merely being alive. I forgot that I was in a strange place among strange men,—I forgot that I was to all intents and purposes a prisoner—I forgot everything except that I lived, and that life was ecstasy!

I had no very exact idea of the time,—my watch had stopped. But the afternoon light was deepening, and long lines of soft amber and crimson in the sky were beginning to spread a radiant path for the descent of the sun. While I still remained at the window I suddenly heard the rise and swell of deep organ music, solemn and sonorous; it was as though the waves of the sea had set themselves to song. Some instinct then told me there was someone in the room,—and I turned round quickly to find my former guide in the white garments standing silently behind me, waiting. I had intended to complain at once of the way in which I had been imprisoned as though I were a criminal—but at sight of his grave, composed figure I lost all my hardihood and could say nothing. I merely stood still, attendant on his pleasure. His dark eyes, gleaming from under his white cowl, looked at me with a searching enquiry as though he expected me to speak, but as I continued to keep silence, he smiled.

"You are very patient!" he said, quietly—"And that is well! The Master awaits you."

A tremor ran through me, and my heart began to beat violently. I was to have my wilful desires granted, then! I was actually to see and speak with the man to whom Rafel Santoris owed his prolonged youth and power, and under whose training he had passed through an ordeal which had taught him some of the deepest mysteries of life! The result of my own wishes seemed now so terrifying to me that I could not have uttered a word had I tried, I followed my escort in absolute silence;—once in my nervous agitation I slipped on the stone staircase and nearly fell,—he at once caught me by the hand and supported me, and the kindness and gentle strength of his touch renewed my courage. His wonderful eyes looked steadily into mine.

"Do not be afraid!" he said, in a low tone—"There is really nothing to fear!"

We passed the domed hall and its sparkling fountain, and in two or three minutes came to a deep archway veiled by a portiere of some rich stuff woven in russet brown and gold,—this curtain my guide threw back noiselessly, showing a closed door. Here he came to a standstill and waited—I waited with him, trying to be calm, though my mind was in a perfect tumult of expectation mingled with doubt and dread,—that closed door seemed to me to conceal some marvellous secret with which my whole future life and destiny were likely to be involved. Suddenly it opened,—I saw a beautiful octagonal room, richly furnished, with the walls lined, so it appeared, from floor to ceiling with books,—one or two great stands and vases of flowers made flashes of colour among the shadows, and a quick upward glance showed me that the ceiling was painted in fresco, then my guide signed to me to enter.

"The Master will be with you in a moment,"—he said—"Please sit down"—here he gave me an encouraging smile—"You are a little nervous—try and compose yourself! You need not be at all anxious or frightened!"

I tried to smile in response, but I felt far more ready to weep. I was possessed by a sudden hopeless and helpless depression which I could not overcome. My guide went away at once, and the door closed after him in the same mysteriously silent fashion in which it had opened. I was left to myself,—and I sat down on one of the numerous deep easy chairs which were placed about the room, trying hard to force myself into at least the semblance of quietude. But, after all, what was the use of even assuming composure when the man I had come to meet probably had the power to gauge the whole gamut of a human being's emotion at a moment's notice? Instinctively I pressed my hand against my heart and felt the letter my 'lover' had given me—surely that was no dream?

I drew a long breath like a sigh, and turned my eyes towards the window, which was set in a sort of double arch of stone, and which showed me a garden stretching far away from the edges of soft lawns and flower borders into a picturesque vista of woodland and hill. A warmth of rosy light illumined the fair scene, indicating that the glory of the sunset had begun. Impulsively I rose to go and look out—then stopped—checked and held back by a swift compelling awe— I was no longer alone. I was confronted by the tall commanding figure of a man wearing the same white garments as those of my guide,—a man whose singular beauty and dignity of aspect would have enforced admiration from even the most callous and unobservant—and I knew that I was truly at last in the presence of Aselzion. Overpowered by this certainty, I could not speak—I could only look and wonder as he drew near me. His cowl was thrown back, fully displaying his fine intellectual head—his eyes, deep blue and full of light, studied my face with a keen scrutiny which I could FEEL as though it were a searching ray burning into every nook and cranny of my heart and soul. The blood rushed to my cheeks in a warm wave— then suddenly rallying my forces I returned him glance for glance. Thus we moved, each on our own lines of spiritual attraction, closer together; till presently a slight smile brightened the gravity of his handsome features, and he extended both hands to me.

"You are welcome!" he said, in a voice that expressed the most perfect music of human speech—"Rash and undisciplined as you are, you are welcome!"

Timidly I laid my hands in his, grateful for the warm, strong clasp he gave them,—then, all at once, hardly knowing how it happened, I sank on my knees as before some saint or king, silently seeking his blessing. There was a moment's deep stillness,—and he laid his hands on my bowed head.

"Poor child!" he said, gently—"You have adventured far for love and life!—it will be hard if you should fail! May all the powers of God and Nature help you!"

This said, he raised me with an infinitely courteous kindness, and placed a chair for me near a massive table-desk on which there were many papers—some neatly tied up and labelled,—others lying about in apparent confusion—and when we were both seated he began conversation in the simplest and easiest fashion.

"You know, of course, that I have been prepared for your arrival here,"—he said—"by one of my students, Rafel Santoris. He has been seeking you for a long time, but now he has found you he is hardly better off—for you are a rebellious child and unwilling to recognise him—is it not so?"

I felt a little more courageous now, and answered him at once.

"I am not unwilling to recognise any true thing," I said—"But I do not wish to be deceived—or to deceive myself."

He smiled.

"Do you not? How do you know that you have not been deceiving yourself ever since your gradual evolvement from subconscious into conscious life? Nature has not deceived you—Nature always takes herself seriously—but you—have you not tried in various moods or phases of existence, to do something cleverer than Nature?—to more or less outwit her as it were? Come, come!—don't look so puzzled about it!—you have only done what all so-called 'reasonable' human beings do, and think themselves justified in doing. But now, in your present state,—which is an advancement, and not a retrogression,— you have begun to gain a little wider knowledge, with a little deeper humility—and I am inclined to have great patience with you!"

I raised my eyes and was reassured by his kindly glance.

"Now, to begin with,"—he went on—"you should know at once that we do not receive women here. It is against our rule and Order. We are not prepared for them,—we do not want them. They are never more than HALF souls!"

My heart gave an indignant bound,—but I held my peace. He looked straight at me, while with one hand he put together a few stray papers on his desk.

"Well, why do you not give me the obvious answer?" he queried—"Why do you not say that if women are half souls, men are the same,—and that the two halves must conjoin to make one? Foolish child!—you need not burn with suppressed offence at what sounds a slighting description of your sex—it is not meant as such. You ARE half souls,—and the chief trouble with you is that you seldom have the sense to see it, or to make any endeavour to form the perfect and indivisible union,—a sacred task which is left in your hands. Nature is for ever working to bring the right halves together,—man is for ever striving to scatter them apart—and though it all comes right at the last, as it must, there is no need for delay involving either months or centuries. You women were meant to be the angels of salvation, but instead of this you are the ruin of your own 'ideals.'"

I could offer no contradiction to this, for I felt it to be true.

"As I have just said," he went on—"this is no place for women. The mere idea that you should imagine yourself, capable of submitting to the ordeal of a student here is, on the face of it, incredible. Only for Rafel's sake have I consented to see you and explain to you how impossible it is that you should remain—"

I interrupted him.

"I MUST remain!" I said, firmly. "Do with me whatever you like—put me in a cell and keep me a prisoner,—give me any hardship to endure and I will endure it—but do not turn me away without teaching me something of your peace and power—the peace and power which Rafel possesses, and which I too must possess if I would help him and be all in all to him—"

Here I paused, overcome by my own emotion. Aselzion looked full at me.

"That is your desire?—to help him and to be all in all to him?" he said—"Why did you not realise this ages ago? And even now you have wavered in the allegiance you owe to him—you have doubted him, though all your inward instincts tell you that he is your soul's true mate, and that your own heart beats towards him like a bird in a cage beating against the bars towards liberty!"

I was silent. My fate seemed in a balance,—but I left it to Aselzion, who, if his power meant anything, could read my thoughts better than I could express them. He rose from his desk and paced slowly up and down, absorbed in meditation. Presently he stopped abruptly in front of me.

"If you stay here," he said—"you must understand what it means. It means that you must dwell as one apart in your own room, entirely alone except when summoned to receive instruction—your meals will be served there—and you will feel like a criminal undergoing punishment rather than enlightenment—and you may speak to no one unless spoken to first. Moreover"—he interrupted himself and beckoned me to follow him into another room adjoining the one we were in. Here, leading me to a window, he showed me a very different view from the sun-lit landscape and garden I had lately looked upon,- -a dismal square of rank grass in which stood a number of black crosses.

"These do not mark deaths,"—he said—"but failures! Failures—not in a worldly sense—but failures in making of life the eternal and creative thing it is—eternal HERE and now,—as long as we shall choose! Do you seek to be one of them?"

"No,"—I answered, quietly—"I shall not fail!"

He gave a slight, impatient sigh.

"So they all said—they whose records are here"—and he pointed to the crosses with an impressive gesture—"Some of the men who have thus left their mark with us, are at this moment among the world's most brilliant and successful personalities—wealthy, and in great social request,—and only they themselves know where the canker lies—only they are aware of their own futility,—and they live, knowing that their life must lead into other lives, and dreading that inevitable Change which is bound by law to bring them into whatever position they have chiefly sought!"

His voice was grave and compassionate, and a faint tremor of fear ran through me.

"These were—and are—MEN!"—he continued—"And you—a woman—would boldly attempt the adventures in which they failed! Think for a moment how weak and ignorant and all unprepared you are! When you first began your psychic studies with a Teacher whom we both loved and honoured—one whom you knew by the name of Heliobas—you had scarcely lived at all in the world;—since then you have worked hard and done much, but in your close application to the conquest of difficulties you have missed many things by the way. I give you credit for patience and faith—these have accomplished much for you- -and now you are at a crucial point in your career when your Will, like the rudder of a ship, trembles in your hand, and you are plunging into unknown further deeps where there may be storm and darkness. There is danger ahead for any doubting, proud, or rebellious soul,—it is but fair to warn you!"

"I am not afraid!" I said, in a low tone—"I can but die!"

"Child, that is just what you cannot do! Grasp that fact firmly at once and for ever! You cannot die,—there is no such thing as death! If you could die and have done with all duties, cares, perplexities and struggles altogether, the eternal problem would be greatly simplified. But the idea of death is only one of a million human delusions. Death is an impossibility in the scheme of Life—what is called by that name is merely a shifting and re-investiture of imperishable atoms. The endless varying forms of this shifting and re-investiture of atoms is the secret we and our students have set ourselves to master—and some of us have mastered it sufficiently to control both the matter and spirit whereof we are made. But the way of learning is not an easy way—Rafel Santoris himself could have told you that he was all but overcome in the trial—for I spare no one!—and if you persist in your rash intention I cannot spare you simply because of your sex."

"I do not ask to be spared,"—I said, gently—"I have already told you I will endure anything."

A slight smile crossed his face.

"So you will, I believe!" he answered—"In the old days I can well understand your enduring martyrdom! I can see you facing lions in the Roman arena,"—as he thus spoke I started, and the warm blood rushed to my cheeks—"rather than not carry out your own fixed resolve, whether such resolve was right or wrong! I can see you preparing to drown yourself in the waters of the Nile rather than break through man's stupid superstition and convention! Why do you look so amazed? Am I touching on some old memory? Come, let us leave these black embers of coward mortality and return to the more cheerful room."

We re-entered the library together, and he seated himself again at his desk, turning towards me with an air of settled and impressive authority.

"What you want to learn,—and what every beginner in the study of psychic law generally wants to learn first of all, is how to obtain purely personal satisfaction and advantage,"—he said—"You want to know three things—the secret of life— the secret of youth—the secret of love! Thousands of philosophers and students have entered upon the same research, and one perhaps out of the thousand has succeeded where all the rest have failed. The story of Faust is perpetually a thing of interest, because it treats of these secrets, which according to the legend are only discoverable through the aid of the devil. WE know that there is no devil, and that everything is divinely ordained by a Divine Intelligence, so that in the deepest researches which we are permitted to make there is nothing to fear— but Ourselves! Failure is always brought about by the students, not by the study in which they are engaged,—the reason of this being that when they know a little, they think they know all,—with the result that they become intellectually arro- gant, an attitude that instantly nullifies all previous attainment. The secret of life is a comparatively easy matter to understand—the secret of youth a little more difficult—the secret of love the most difficult of all, because out of love is gener- ated both the perpetuity of life and of youth. Now your object in coming here is, down at the root of it, absolutely personal—I will not say selfish, because that sounds hard—and I will give you credit for the true womanly feeling you have, that being conscious in your own soul of Rafel Santoris as your superior and mas- ter as well as your lover, you wish to be worthy of him, if only in the steadfastness and heroism of your character. I will grant you all that. I will also grant that it is perfectly natural, and therefore right, that you should wish to retain youth and beauty and health for his sake,—and I would even urge that this desire should be SOLELY for his sake! But just now you are not quite sure whether it is for his sake,—you wish to hold, for YOURSELF, the secret of life and the power of life's continuance—the secret of youth and the power of youth's continuance,—and you most certainly wish to have for yourself, as well as for Rafel, the secret of love and the power of love's continuance. None of these secrets can be disclosed to worldlings— by which term I mean those who allow themselves to be moved from their determination, and distracted by a thousand ephemeral matters. I do not say you are such an one,—but you, like all who live in the world, have your friends and acquaintances—people who are ready to laugh at you and make mock of your highest aims—people whose delight would be to block the way to your progress—and the question with me is—Are you strong enough to ensure the mental strain which will be put upon you by ignorant and vulgar opposition and even positive derision? You may be,—you are self-willed enough, though not always rightly so—for example, you want to gain knowledge apart from and inde- pendently of Rafel Santoris, yet you are an incomplete identity without him! The women of your day all follow this vicious policy—the desire to be independent and apart from men—which is the suicide of their nobler selves. None of them are complete creatures without their stronger halves—they are like deformed birds with only one wing,—and a straight flight is impossible to them."

He ceased, and I looked up.

"Whether I agree with you or not hardly matters,"—I said—"I admit all my faults and am ready to amend them. But I want to learn from you all that I may—all that you think I am capable of learning—and I promise absolute obedience—"

A slight smile lightened his eyes.

"And humility?"

I bent my head.

"And humility!"

"You are resolved, then?"

"I am resolved!"

He paused a moment, then appeared to make up his mind.

"So be it!" he said—"But on your own head be your own mischance, if any mischance should happen! I take no responsibility. Of your own will you have come here—of your own will you elect to stay here, where there is no one of your own sex with whom you can communicate- -and of your own will you must accept all the consequences. Is that agreed?"

His steel-blue eyes flashed with an almost supernatural brilliancy as he put the question, and I was conscious of a sense of fear. But I conquered this and answered simply:

"It is agreed!"

He gave me a keen glance that swept me as it were from head to foot- -then turning from me abruptly, struck a handle on his desk which set a loud bell clanging in some outer corridor. My former guide entered almost immediately, and Aselzion addressed him:

"Honorius,"—he said—"show this lady to her room, She will follow the course
of a probationer and student"—as he spoke, Honorius gave me a look of undis-
guised amazement and pity—"The moment she desires to leave, every facility for
her departure is to be granted to her. As long as she remains under instruction the
rule for her, as you know, is solitude and silence."

I looked at him, and thought how swiftly his face had changed. It was no longer
softened by the grave benevolence and kindness that had sustained my courage,—
a stern shadow darkened it, and his eyes were averted. I saw I was expected to
leave the room, but I hesitated.

"You will let me thank you,"—I murmured, holding out my hands timidly—
almost pleadingly.

He turned to me slowly and took my hands in his own.

"Poor child, you have nothing to thank me for!"—he said. "Bear in mind, as one
of your first lessons in the difficult way you are going, that you have nothing to
thank anyone for, and nothing to blame anyone for in the shaping of your destiny but—Yourself! Go!— and may you conquer your enemy!"

"My enemy?" I repeated, wonderingly.

"Yes—again Yourself! The only power any man or woman has ever had, or ever
will have, to contend with!"

He dropped my hands, and I suppose I must have expressed some mute appeal in
my upward glance at him, for the faintest shadow of a smile came on his lips.

"God be with you!" he said, softly, and then with a gentle gesture signed to me to
leave him. I at once obeyed, and followed the guide Honorius, who led me back
to my own room, where, without speaking a word, he closed and locked the door
upon me as before. To my surprise, I found my luggage which I had left at the
inn placed ready for me—and on a small dresser set in a niche of the wall which
I had not noticed before, there was a plate of fruit and dry bread, with a glass of
cold water. On going to look at this little refection, which was simply yet daintily set out, I saw that the dresser was really a small lift, evidently connected with
the domestic offices of the house, and I concluded that this would be the means
by which all my meals would be served. I did not waste much time in thinking
about it, however,—I was only too glad to be allowed to remain in the House of
Aselzion on any terras, and the fact that I was imprisoned under lock and key did

not now trouble me. I unpacked my few things, among which were three or four favourite books,—then I sat down to my frugal repast, for which hunger provided a keen appetite. When I had finished, I took a chair to the open window and sat there, looking out on the sea. I saw my friendly little rose leaning its crimson head against the wall just below me with quite a confidential air, and it gave me a sense of companionship, otherwise the solitude was profound. The sky was darkening into night, though one or two glowing bars of deep crimson still lingered as memories of the departed sun—and a pearly radiance to the eastward showed a suggestion of the coming moon. I felt the sense of deep environing silence closing me in like a wall- -and looking back over my shoulder from the window to the interior of my room it seemed full of drifting shadows, dark and impalpable. I remembered I had no candle or any other sort of light—and this gave me a passing uneasiness, but only for a moment. I could go to bed, I thought, when I was tired of watching the sea. At any rate, I would wait for the moonrise,—the scene I looked upon was divinely peaceful and beautiful,—one that a painter or poet would have revelled in—and I was content. I was not conscious of any fear,— but I did feel myself being impressed as it were and gradually overcome by the deepening stillness and great loneliness of my surroundings. 'The rule for her is solitude and silence.' So had said Aselzion. And evidently the rule was being enforced.

XIV

CROSS AND STAR

The moon rose slowly between two bars of dark cloud which gradually whitened into silver beneath her shining presence, and a scintillating pathway of diamond-like reflections began to spread itself across the sea. I remained at the window, feeling an odd disinclination to turn away into the darkness of my room. And I began to think that perhaps it was rather hard that I should be left all by myself locked up in this way;—surely I might have been allowed a light of some sort! Then I at once reproached myself for allowing the merest suggestion of a complaint to enter my mind, for, after all, I was an uninvited guest in the House of Aselzion—I was not wanted—and I remembered the order that had been issued concerning me: 'The moment she desires to leave, every facility for departure is to be granted to her.' I was much more afraid of this 'facility for departure' than I was of my present solitude, and I determined to look upon the whole adventure in the best and most cheerful light. If it was best I should be alone, then loneliness was good—if it was necessary I should be in darkness, then darkness was also agreeable to me.

Scarcely had I thus made up my mind to these conditions when my room was suddenly illumined by a soft yet effulgent radiance-and I started up in amazement, wondering where it came from. I could see no lamps or electric burners,—it was as if the walls glowed with some surface luminance. When my first surprise had passed, I was charmed and delighted with the warm and comforting brightness around me,—it rather reminded me of the electric brilliancy on the sails of the 'Dream.' I moved away from the window, leaving it open, as the night was very close and warm, and sat down at the table to read a little, but after a few minutes laid the book aside to listen to a strange whispering music that floated towards me, apparently from the sea, and thrilled me to the soul. No eloquent description could give any idea of the enthralling sweetness of the harmonies that were more BREATHED upon the air than sounded—and I became absorbed in following the rhythm of the delicious cadences as they rose and fell. Then by degrees my thoughts wandered away to Rafel Santoris,— where was he now?—in what peaceful expanse of shining waters had his fairy vessel cast anchor? I pictured him in my brain till I could almost see his face,—the broad brow,—the fearless, tender eyes and smile—and I could fancy that I heard the deep, soft accents of his voice, always so gentle when he spoke to me—me, who had half resented his influence! And a quick wave of long pent-up tenderness rose in my heart—my whole soul ran out, as it were, to greet him with outstretched arms—I knew in my own consciousness that he was more than all the world to me, and I said aloud:—"My beloved, I love you! I love you!" to the silence, almost as if I thought it could convey the words to him whom most I desired to hear them.

Then I felt how foolish and futile it was to talk to the empty air when I might have confessed myself to the real lover of my life face to face, had I been less sceptical,—less proud! Was not my very journey to the House of Aselzion a testimony of my own doubting attitude?—for I had come, as I now admitted to myself, first to make sure that Aselzion really existed—and secondly, to prove to my own satisfaction that he was truly able to impart the mystical secrets which Rafel seemed to know. I wearied myself out at last with thinking to no purpose, and closing the window I undressed and went to bed. As I lay down, the light in my room was suddenly extinguished, and all was darkness again except for the moon, which sent a clear white ray straight through the lattice, there being no curtain to shut it out. For some time I remained awake on my hard little couch, looking at this ray, and steadily refusing to allow any sense of fear or loneliness to gain the mastery over me—the music which had so enchanted me ceased—and everything was perfectly still. And by and by my eyes closed—my tired limbs relaxed,—and I fell into a sound and dreamless sleep.

When I awoke it was full morning, and the sunshine poured into my room like a shower of gold. I sprang up, full of delight that the night had passed so peacefully and that nothing strange or terrifying had occurred, though I do not know why I should have expected this. Everything seemed wonderfully fresh and beautiful in the brightness of the new day, and the very plainness of my room had a fascination greater than any amount of luxury. The only unusual thing I noticed was that the soft cold water with which my bath was supplied sparkled as though it were effervescent,—once or twice it seemed to ripple with a diamond-like foam, and it was never actually still. I watched its glittering movement for some minutes before bathing—then, feeling certain it was charged with some kind of electricity, I plunged into it without hesitation and enjoyed to the utmost the delicious sense of invigoration it gave me. When my toilet was completed and I had attired myself in a simple morning gown of white linen, as being more suitable to the warmth of the weather than the black one I had travelled in, I went to throw open my window and let in all the freshness of the sea-air, and was surprised to see a small low door open in the side of the turret, through which I discovered a winding stair leading downward. Yielding to the impulse of the moment, I descended it, and at the end found myself in an exquisite little rock garden abutting on the seashore. I could actually open a gate, and walk to the very edge of the sea. I was no longer a prisoner, then!—I could run away if I chose!

I looked about me—and smiled as I saw the impossibility of any escape. The little garden belonged exclusively to the turret, and on each side of it impassable rocks towered up almost to the height of the Chateau d'Aselzion itself, while the bit of shore on which I stood was equally hemmed in by huge boulders against which the waves had dashed for centuries without making much visible impression. Yet it was delightful to feel I was allowed some liberty and open air, and I stayed for some minutes watching the sea and revelling in the warmth of the southern sun. Then I retraced my steps slowly, looking everywhere about me as I went, to see if there was anyone near. Not a soul was in sight.

I returned to my room to find my bed made as neatly as though it had never been slept upon,—and my breakfast, consisting of a cup of milk and some wheaten biscuits, set out upon the table. I was quite ready for the meal, and enjoyed it. When I had finished, I took my empty cup and plate and put them on the dresser in the niche, whereupon the dresser was instantly lowered, and very soon disappeared. Then I began to wonder how I should employ myself. It was no use writing letters, though I had my own travelling desk ready for this purpose,—I did not wish my friends or acquaintances to know where I was—and even if I had written to any of them it was hardly likely that my correspondence would ever reach them. For I felt sure the mystic Brotherhood of Aselzion would not allow me to communicate with the outside world so long as I remained with them. I sat meditating,—and I began to consider that several days passed thus aimlessly would be difficult to bear. I could not keep correct count of time, my watch having stopped, and there was no clock or chime of any sort in the place that I could hear. The stillness around me would have been oppressive but for the soft dash of little waves breaking on the beach below my window. All at once, to my great joy, the door of my room opened, and the personage called Honorius entered. He bent his head slightly by way of salutation, and then said briefly,—

"You are commanded to follow me."

I rose obediently, and stood ready. He looked at me intently and with curiosity, as though he sought to read my mind. Remembering that Aselzion had said I was not to speak unless spoken to, I only returned his look steadfastly, and with a smile.

"You are not unhappy, or afraid, or restless,"—he said, slowly— "That is well! You are making a good beginning. And now, whatever you see or hear, keep silence! If you desire to speak, speak now— but after we leave this room not a word must escape your lips—not a single exclamation,—your business is to listen, learn and obey!"

He waited—giving me the opportunity to say something in reply—but I preferred to hold my peace. He then handed me a folded length of soft white material, opaque, yet fine and silky as gossamer.

"Cover yourself with this veil,"—he said—"and do not raise it till you return here."

I unfolded it and threw it quickly over me—it was as delicate as a filmy cloud and draped me from head to foot, effectually concealing me from the eyes of others though I myself could see through it perfectly. Honorius then signed to me to follow, and I did so, my heart beating quickly with excitement and expectation.

We went through many passages with intricate turnings that seemed to have no outlet,—it was like threading one's way through a maze— till at last I found myself shut within a small cell-like place with an opening in front of me through which I gazed upon a strange and picturesque scene. I saw the interior of a small but perfectly beautiful Gothic chapel, exquisitely designed, and lit by numerous windows of stained glass, through which the sunlight filtered in streams of radiant colour, patterning with gold, crimson and blue, the white marble flooring below. Between every tapering column that supported the finely carved roof, were two rows of benches, one above the other, and here sat an array of motionless white figures,- -men in the garb of their mysterious Order, their faces almost concealed by their drooping cowls. There was no altar in this chapel,—but at its eastern end where the altar might have been, was a dark purple curtain against which blazed in brilliant luminance a Cross and Seven-pointed Star. The rays of light shed by this uplifted Symbol of an unwritten Creed were so vivid as to be almost blinding, and nearly eclipsed the summer glory of the sun itself. Awed by the strange and silent solemnity of my surroundings, I was glad to be hidden under the folds of my enshrouding white veil, though I realised that I was in a sort of secret recess made purposely for the use of those who were summoned to see all that went on in the chapel without being seen. I waited, full of eager anticipation,—and presently the low vibrating sound of the organ trembled on the air, gradually increasing in volume and power till a magnificent rush of music poured from it like a sudden storm breaking through clouds. I drew a long breath of pure ecstasy,—I could have knelt and wept tears of gratitude for the mere sense of hearing! Such music was divine!—the very idea of mortality was swallowed up in it and destroyed, and the imprisoned soul mounted up to the highest life on wings of light, rejoicing!

When it ceased, as it did all too soon, there followed a profound silence,—so profound that I could hear the quick beating of my own heart as if I were the only living thing in the place. I turned my eyes towards the dazzling Cross and Star with its ever darting rays of fiery brilliancy, and the effect of its perpetual sparkle of lambent fire was as if an electric current were giving off messages which no mortal skill would ever be able to decipher or put into words, but which found their way to one's deepest inward consciousness. All at once there was a slight movement among the rows of white-garmented, white-cowled figures hitherto sitting so motionless,—and with one accord they rose to their feet as a figure, tall, stately and imposing, came walking slowly across the chapel and stood directly in front of the flaming Symbol, holding both hands outstretched as though invoking a blessing. It was the Master, Aselzion,—Aselzion invested with such dignity and splendour as I had never thought possible to man. He might have posed for some god or hero,—his aspect was one of absolute power and calm self- poise,— other men might entertain doubts of themselves at the intention of their lives, but this one in his mere bearing expressed sureness, strength and authority. He wore his cowl thrown back, and from where I sat in my secluded corner I could see his features distinctly, and could watch the flash of his fine steadfast eyes as he turned them upon his followers. Keeping his hands extended, he said, in a firm, clear voice:

"To the Creator of all things visible and invisible let us offer up our gratitude and praise, and so begin this day!"

And a responsive murmur of voices answered him:

> "We praise Thee, O Divine Power of Love and Life eternal!
> We praise Thee for all we are!
> We praise Thee for all we have been!
> We praise Thee for all we hope to be!—Amen."

There followed a moment's tense silence. Then the assembled brethren sat down in their places, and Aselzion spoke in measured, distinct accents, with the easy and assured manner of a practised orator.

"Friends and Brethren!

"We are gathered here together to consider in this moment of time the things we have done in the past, and the things we are preparing to do in the future. We know that from the Past, stretching back into infinity, we have ourselves made the Present,—and according to Divine law we also know that from this Present, stretching forward into infinity, we shall ourselves evolve all that is yet To Come. There is no power, no deity, no chance, no 'fortuitous concurrence of atoms' in what is simply a figure of the Universal Mathematics. Nothing can be 'forgiven' under the eternal law of Compensation,— nothing need be 'prayed for,' since everything is designed to accomplish each individual spirit's ultimate good. You are here to learn not only the secret of life, but something of how to live that life; and I, in my capacity, am only striving to teach what Nature has been showing you for thousands of centuries, though you have not cared to master her lessons. The science of to-day is but Nature's first primer—a spelling-book as it were, with the alphabet set out in pictures. You are told by sagacious professors,—who after all are no more than children in their newly studied wisdom,—that human life was evolved in the first instance from protoplasm—as they THINK,—but they lack the ability to tell you how the protoplasm was itself evolved—and WHY; where the material came from that went to the making of millions of solar systems and trillions of living organisms concerning whose existence we have no knowledge or perception. Some of them deny a God,—but most of them are driven to confess that there must be an Intelligence, supreme and omnipotent, behind the visible Universe. Order cannot come out of Chaos without a directing Mind; and Order would be quickly submerged into Chaos again were not the directing Mind of a nature to sustain its method and condition.

"We start, therefore, with this Governing Intelligence or directing Mind, which must, like the brain of man, be dual, combining the male and female attributes, since we see that it expresses itself throughout all creation in dual form and type. Intelligence, Mind, or Spirit, whichever we may elect to call it, is inherently active and must find an outlet for its powers,—and the very fact of this necessity produces Desire to perpetuate Itself in varied ways: this again is the first attribute of Love. Hence Love is the foundation of worlds, and the source of all living organisms,—the dual atoms, or ions of spirit and matter yielding to Attraction, Union and Reproduction. If we master this fact reasonably and thoroughly, we shall be nearer the comprehension of life."

He paused a moment,—then advanced a step or two and went on, the flaming Symbol behind him seeming literally to envelop him in its beams,

"What we have to learn first of all is, how these laws affect us as individual human beings and as separate personalities. It is necessary to avoid all obscurity of language in setting forth the simple principles which should guide and preserve each human existence, and my explanation shall be as brief and plain as I can make it. Granted that there is a Divine Mind or Governing Intelligence behind the infinitude of vital and productive atoms which in their union and reproduction build up the wonders of the Universe, we see and admit that one of the chief results of the working of this Divine Mind is Man. He is, so we have been told— 'the image of God.' This expression may be taken as a poetic line in the Scriptures, meaning no more than poetic imagery,—but it is nevertheless a truth. Man is a kind of Universe in himself—he too is a conglomeration of atoms—atoms that are active, reproductive, and desirous of perpetual creativeness. Behind them, as in the nature of the Divine, there is the Governing Intelligence, the Mind, the Spirit,— dual in type, double-sexed in action. Without the Mind to control it, the constitution of Man is chaos,—just as the Universe itself would be without the Creator's governance. What we have chiefly to remember is, that just as the Spirit behind visible Nature is Divine and eternal, so is the Spirit behind each one of our individual selves also Divine and eternal. It HAS BEEN always,— it WILL BE always, and we move as distinct personalities through successive phases of life, each one under the influence of his or her own controlling Soul, to higher and ever higher perception and attainment. The great majority of the world's inhabitants live with less consciousness of this Spirit than flies or worms—they build up religions in which they prate of God and immortality as children prattle, without the smallest effort to understand either,—and at the Change which they call death, they pass out of this life without having taken the trouble to discover, acknowledge or use the greatest gift God has bestowed upon them. But we,—we who are here to realise the existence of the all-powerful Force which gives us complete mastery over the things of space and time and matter—we, who know that over that individual moving universe of atoms called Man, It can hold absolute control,—we can prove for ourselves that the whole earth is subject to the dominance of the immortal Soul,— ay!—and the very elements of air, fire and water!—for these are but the ministers and servants to Its sovereign authority!"

He paused again—and after a minute or two of silence, went on—

"This beautiful earth, this over-arching sky, the exquisite things of Nature's form and loveliness, are all given to Man, not only for his material needs, but for his spiritual growth and evolvement. From the light of the sun he may draw fresh warmth and colour for his blood—from the air new supplies of life—from the very trees and herbs and flowers he may renew his strength,—and there is nothing created that is not intended to add in some measure to his pleasure and well-being. For if the foundation of the Universe be Love, as it is, then Love desires to see its creatures happy. Misery has no place in the Divine scheme of things—it is the result of Man's own opposition to Natural Law. In Natural Law, all things work calmly, slowly and steadfastly together for good—Nature silently obeys God's ordinance. Man, on the contrary, questions, argues, denies, rebels,—with the result that he scatters his force and fails in his highest effort. It is in his own power to renew his own youth—his own vitality,—yet we see him sink of his own accord into feebleness and decrepitude, giving himself up, as it were, to be devoured by the disintegrating influences which he could easily repel. For, as the directing Spirit of God governs the infinitude of atoms and star-dust which go to make up universes, so the mind of a Man should govern the atoms and star-dust of which he himself is composed—guiding their actions and renewing them at pleasure,— forming them into suns and systems of thought and creative power, and wasting no particle of his eternal life forces. He can be what he elects to be,— a god,—or merely one of a mass of units in embryo, drifting away from one phase of existence to another in unintelligent indifference, and so compelling himself to pass centuries of aimless movement before entering upon any marked or decisive path of individual and separate action. The greater number prefer to be nothings in this way, though they cannot escape the universal grinding mill,—they must be used for some purpose in the end, be they never so reluctant. Therefore, we, who study the latent powers of man, judge it wiser to meet and accept our destiny rather than fall back in the race and allow destiny to overtake US and whip us into place with rods of sharp experience. If there is anyone here present who now desires to speak,—to ask a question,—or deny a statement, let him come forward boldly and say what he has to say without fear."

As he thus spoke, I, looking from my little hidden recess, saw a movement among the seated brethren; one of them rose and descending from his place, walked slowly towards Aselzion till he was within a few paces of him—then he paused, and threw back his cowl, showing a worn handsome face on which some great sorrow seemed to be marked too strongly to be ever erased.

"I do not wish to live!"—he said—"I came here to study life, but not to learn how to keep it. I would lose it gladly for the merest trifle! For life is to me a bitter thing—a hideous and inexplicable torment! Why should you, O Aselzion, teach us how to live long? Why not rather teach us how to die soon?"

Aselzion's eyes were bent upon him with a grave and tender compassion.

"What accusation do you bring against life?" he asked—"How has life wronged you?"

"How has life wronged me?" and the unhappy man threw up his hands with a gesture of desperation—"You, who profess to read thought and gauge the soul, can you ask? How has life wronged me? By sheer injustice! From my first breath—for I never asked to be born!—from my early days when all my youthful dreams and aspirations were checked, smothered and killed by loving parents!—loving parents, forsooth!—whose idea of 'love' was money! Every great ambition frustrated—every higher hope slain!—and in my own love—that love of woman which is man's chief curse—even she was false and worthless as a spurious coin—caring nothing whether my life was saved or ruined—it was ruined, of course!—but what matter?—who need care! Only the weariness of it all!—the day after day burden of time!—the longing to lie down and hide beneath the comfortable grass in peace,—where no false friend, no treacherous love, no 'kind' acquaintances, glad to see me suffer, can ever point their mocking hands or round their cruel eyes at me again! Aselzion, if the God you serve is half as wicked as the men He made, then Heaven itself is Hell!"

He spoke deliberately, yet with passion. Aselzion silently regarded him. The fiery Cross and Star blazed with strange colours like millions of jewels, and the deep stillness in the chapel was for many minutes unbroken. All at once, as though impelled by some irresistible force, he sank on his knees.

"Aselzion! As you are strong, have patience with the weak! As you see the Divine, pity those who are blind! As you stand firm, stretch a hand to those whose feet are on the shifting quicksands, and if death and oblivion are among the gifts of your bestowal, withhold them not from me, for I would rather die than live!"

There was a pause. Then Aselzion's voice, calm, clear and very gentle, vibrated on the silence.

"There is no death!" he said—"You cannot die! There is no oblivion,—you may not forget! There is but one way of life—to live it!"

Another moment's stillness—then again the steady, resolute voice went on.

"You accuse life of injustice,—it is you who are unjust to life! Life gave you those dreams and aspirations you speak of,—it was in your power to realise them! I say it was in your power, had you chosen! No parents, no friends, not God Himself, can stop you from doing what you WILL to do! Who frustrated any great ambition of yours but yourself? Who can slay a hope but him in whose soul it was born? And that love of woman?—was she your true mate?—or only a thing of eyes and hair and vanity? Did your passion touch her body only, or did it reach her Soul? Did you seek to know whether that Soul had ever wakened within her, or were you too well satisfied with her surface beauty to care? In all these things blame Yourself, not life!—for life gives you earth and heaven, time and eternity for the attainment of joy—joy, in which, but for Yourself, there would never be a trace of sorrow!"

The kneeling penitent—for such he now appeared to be—covered his face with his hands.

"I cannot give you death,"—continued Aselzion-"You can take what is called by that name for yourself if you choose—you can by your own action, sudden or premeditated, destroy this present form and composition of yourself for just so long as it takes the forces of Nature to build you up again—an incredibly brief moment of time! But you gain nothing—you neither lose your consciousness nor your memory! Ponder this well before you pull down your present dwelling- house!—for ingratitude breeds narrowness, and your next habitation might be smaller and less fitted for peace and quiet breathing!"

With these words, gently spoken, he raised the penitent from his knees, and signed to him to return to his place. He did so obediently, without another word, pulling his cowl closely about him so that none of his fellow-brethren might see his features. Another man then stepped forward and addressed Aselzion.

"Master"—he said, "would it not be better to die than to grow old? If, as you teach us, there is no real death, should there be any real decay? What pleasure is there in life when the strength fails and the pulses slacken—when the warm blood grows chill and stagnant, and when even those we have loved consider we have lived too long? I who speak now am old, though I am not conscious of age— but others are conscious for me,—their looks, their words, imply that I am in their way—that I am slowly dying like a lopped tree and that the process is too tedious for their impatience. And yet—I could be young!—my powers of work have increased rather than lessened—I enjoy life more than those that have youth on their side—but I know I carry the burden of seventy years upon me, and I say that surely it is better to die than live even so long!"

Aselzion, standing in the full light of the glittering Cross and Star, looked upon him with a smile.

"I also carry the burden—if burden you must call it—of seventy years!" he said—
"But years are nothing to me—they should be nothing to you. Who asked you to
count them or to consider them? In the world of wild Nature, time is measured
by seasons only—the bird does not know how old it is—the rose-tree does not
count its birthdays! You, whom I know to be a brave man and patient student,
have lived the usual life of men in the world—you are wedded to a Woman who
has never cared to understand the deeper side of your nature, and who is now far
older than you, though in actual years younger,—you have children who look
upon you as their banker merely and who, while feigning affection, really wait for
your death with eagerness in order to possess your fortune. You might as well have
never had those children!—I know all this as you yourself know it— I also know
that through the word-impressions and influence of so- called 'friends' who wish
to persuade you of your age, the disintegrating process has begun,—but this can
be arrested. You yourself can arrest it!—the dream of Faust is no fallacy!—only
that the renewal of youth is not the work of magic evil, but of natural good. If
you would be young, leave the world as you have known it and begin it anew,—
leave wife, children, friends, all that hang like fungi upon an oak, rotting its trunk
and sapping its strength without imparting any new form of vitality. Live again—
love again!"

"I!"—and he who was thus spoken to threw back his cowl, showing a face wan
and deeply wrinkled, yet striking in its fine intellectuality of feature—"I!—with
these white hairs! You jest with me, Aselzion!"

"I never jest!"—replied Aselzion—"I leave jesting to the fools who prate of life
without comprehending its first beginnings. I do not jest with you—put me to
the proof! Obey my rules here but for six months and you shall pass out of these
walls with every force in your body and spirit renewed in youth and vitality! But
Yourself must work the miracle,—which, after all, is no miracle! Yourself must
build Yourself!—as everyone is bound to do who would make the fullest living
out of life. If you hesitate,—if you draw back,—if you turn with one foolish regret
or morbid thought to your past mistakes in life which ARE past—to her, your
wife, a wife in name but never in soul,—to your children, born of animal instinct
but not of spiritual deep love,—to those your 'friends' who count up your years
as though they were crimes,—you check the work of re- invigoration, and you
stultify the forces of renewal. You must choose—and the choice must be voluntary and deliberate,—for no man becomes aged and effete without his own intention and inclination to that end,—and equally, no man retains or renews his
youth without a similar intention and inclination. Take two days to consider—
and then tell me your mind."

The man he thus addressed hesitated as though he had something more to say—
then with a deep obeisance went back to his place. Aselzion waited till he was seated—and after the brief interval spoke again- -

"If all of you here present are content with your rule of life in this place, and with
the studies you are undertaking, and none of you wish to leave, I ask for the usual
sign."

All the brethren rose, and raised their arms above their heads— dropping them
slowly again after a second's pause.

"Enough!" and Aselzion now moved towards the Cross and Star, fronting it fully.
As he did so, I saw to my astonishment and something of terror that the rays pro-
ceeding from the centre of the Symbol flamed out to an extraordinary length, surrounding his whole figure and filling the chapel with a lurid brilliancy as though
it were suddenly on fire. Straight into the centre of the glowing flames he steadily advanced—then, at a certain point, turned again and faced his followers. But
what an aspect now was his! The light about him seemed to be part of his very
body and garments—he was transfigured into the semblance of something god-
like and angelic— and I was overcome with fear and awe as I looked upon him.
Lifting one hand, he made the sign of the cross,—whereat the white-robed
brethren descended from their places, and walking one by one in line, came up to
him where he stood. He spoke—and his voice rang out like a silver clarion—

"O Divine Light!" he exclaimed—"We are a part of Thee, and into Thee we desire
to become absorbed! From Thee we know we may obtain an immortality of life
upon this gracious earth! O Nature, beloved Mother, whose bosom burns with
hidden fires of strength, we are thy children, born of thee in spirit as in matter,—
in us thou hast distilled thy rains and dews, thy snows and frosts, thy sunlight and
thy storm!—in us thou hast embodied thy prolific beauty, thy productiveness, thy
power and thy advancement towards good—and more than all thou hast
endowed us with the divine passion of Love which kindles the fire whereof thou
art created and whereby we are sustained! Take us, O Light! Keep us, O Nature!—
and Thou, O God, Supreme Spirit of Love, whose thought is Flame, and whose
desire is Creation, be Thou our guide, supporter and instructor through all worlds
without end! Amen!" Once more the glorious music of the organ surged through
the chapel like a storm,—and I, trembling in every limb, knelt, covering my
veiled face closely with my hands, overcome by the splendour of the sound and
the strangeness of the scene. Gradually, very gradually, the music died away—a
deep silence followed—and when I lifted my head, the chapel was empty!

Aselzion and his disciples had vanished, noiselessly, as though they had never been present. Only the Cross and Star still remained glittering against its dark purple background—darting out long tremulous rays, some of which were pale violet, others crimson, others of the delicate hues of the pink topaz.

I looked round,—then behind me,—and to my surprise saw that the door of my little recess had been unlocked and left open. Acting on an impulse too strong to resist, I stole softly out, and stepping on tiptoe, scarcely daring to breathe, I found my way through a low archway into the body of the chapel, and stood there all alone, my heart beating loudly with positive terror. Yet there was nothing to fear. No one was near me that I could see, but I felt as if there were thousands of eyes watching me from the roof, from behind the columns, and from the stained-glass windows that shed their light on the marble pavement. And the glowing radiance of the Cross and Star in all that stillness was almost terrible!—the long bright rays were like tongues of fire mutely expressing unutterable things! Fascinated, I drew nearer and nearer—then paused abruptly, checked by a kind of vibration under me, as though the ground rocked— presently, however, I gained fresh courage to go on, and by degrees was drawn into a perfect vortex of light which rushed upon me like great waves on all sides so forcibly that I had hardly any knowledge of my own movements. Like a creature in a dream I moved,—my very hands looked transparent and spirit-like as I stretched them out towards that marvellous Symbol!—and when my eyes glanced for a moment at the folds of my covering veil I saw that its white silkiness shone with a pale amethystine hue. On—on I went,—a desperate idea possessing me to go as far as I could into that strange starry centre of living luminance—the very boldness of the thought appalled me even while I encouraged it—but step by step I went on resolutely till I suddenly felt myself caught as it were in a wheel of fire! Round and round me it whirled,—darting points of radiance as sharp as spears which seemed to enter my body and stab it through and through—I struggled for breath and tried to draw back,—impossible! I was tangled up in a net of endless light- vibrations which, though they gave forth no heat, yet quivered through my whole being with searching intensity as though bent on probing to the very centre of my soul! I could not utter a sound,—I stood there dumb, immovable, and shrouded in million-coloured flame, too stunned with the shock to realise my own identity. Then all at once something dark and cool floated over me like the shadow of a passing cloud—I looked up and strove to utter a cry,—a word of appeal!—and then fell to the ground, lost in complete unconsciousness.

XV

A FIRST LESSON

I do not know how long I lay there lost to sight and sense, but when I came to myself, I was in a quiet, shadowy place, like a kind of little hermitage, with a window opening out upon the sea. I was lying on a couch, with the veil I had worn still covering me, and as I opened my eyes and looked about me I saw that it was night, and that the moon was tracing a silver network of beams across the waves. There was a delicious fragrance on the air—it came from a group of roses set in a tall crystal vase close to where I lay. Then, as I gradually regained full knowledge of my own existence, I perceived a table in the room with a lamp burning upon it, and at the table sat no less a personage than Aselzion himself, reading. I was so amazed at the sight of him that for the moment I lay inert, afraid to move—for I was almost sure I had incurred his displeasure—till suddenly, with the feeling of a child seeking pardon for an offence, I sprang up and ran to him, throwing myself on my knees at his feet.

"Aselzion, forgive me!" I murmured—"I have done wrong—I had no right to go so far—"

He turned his eyes upon me, smiling, and took me gently by the hands.

"Who denies your right to go far if you have the strength and courage?"—he said—"Dear child, I have nothing to forgive! You are the maker of your own destiny! But you have been bold!—though you are a mere woman you have dared to do what few men attempt. This is the power of love within you—that perfect love which casteth out fear! You risked a danger which has not harmed you—you have come out of it unscathed,—so may it be with every ordeal through which you may yet be tried as by fire!"

He raised me from where I knelt,—but I still held his hands.

"I could not help it!" I said—"Your command for me was 'silence and solitude'—and in that silence and solitude I remained while I watched you all,—and I heard everything that was said—this was your wish and order. And when you all went away, the silence and solitude would have been the same but for that Cross and Star! THEY seemed to speak!—to call me—to draw me to them—and I went—hardly knowing why, yet feeling that I MUST go!—and then—"

Aselzion pressed my hands gently.

"Then the Light claimed its own,"—he said—"and courage had its reward! The door of your recess in the chapel was opened by my instructions,—I wished to see what you would do. You have no conception as yet of what you HAVE done!—but that does not matter. You have passed one test successfully—for had you remained passive in your place till someone came to remove you, I should have known you for a creature of weak will and transitory impulses. But you are stronger than I thought—so to-night I have come to give you your first lesson."

"My first lesson!" I repeated the words after him wonderingly as he let go my hands and put me gently into a chair which I had not perceived but which stood in the shadow cast by the lamp almost immediately opposite to him.

"Yes!—your first lesson!" he answered, smiling gravely—"The first lesson in what you have come here to learn,—the perpetuation of your life on earth for just so long as you desire it—the secret which gives to Rafel Santoris his youth and strength and power, as well as his governance over certain elemental forces. But first take this"—and he poured out from a quaintly shaped flask a full glass of deep red-coloured wine—"This is no magic potion—it is simply a form of nourishment which will be safer for you than solid food,— and I know you have eaten nothing all day since your light breakfast. Drink it all—every drop!"

I obeyed—it seemed tasteless and strengthless, like pure water.

"Now"—he continued—"I will put before you a very simple illustration of the truth which underlies all Nature. If you were taken into a vast plain, and there saw two opposing armies, the one actuated by a passion for destruction, the other moved only by a desire for good, you would naturally wish the latter force to win, would you not?"

I answered "Yes" at once, without hesitation.

"But suppose"—he went on—"that BOTH armies were actuated by good, and that the object of the destroying force was only to break down what was effete and mischievous, in order to build it up again in stronger and nobler forms, while the aim of the other was to strictly preserve and maintain the advantages it possessed, which side would then have your sympathy?"

I tried to think, but could not instantly determine.

"Here is your point of hesitation,"—he said—"and here the usual limit of human comprehension. Both forces are good,—but as a rule we can only side with one. We name that one Life,—the other Death. We think Life alone stands for what is living, and that Death is a kind of cessation of Life instead of being one of Life's most active forms. The Universe is entirely composed of these two fighting forces—we call them good and evil—but there is no evil-there is only a destruction of what MIGHT be harmful if allowed to exist. To put it clearly, the million millions of atoms and electrons which compose the everlasting elements of Spirit and Matter are dual—that is to say, of two kinds—those which preserve their state of equilibrium, and those whose work is to disintegrate, in order to build up again. As with the Universe, so with the composition of a human being. In you, as in myself, there exist these two forces—and our souls are, so to speak, placed on guard between them. The one set of atoms is prepared to maintain the equilibrium of health and life, but if through the neglect and unwatchfulness of the sentinel Soul any of them are allowed to become disused and effete, the other set, whose business it is to disintegrate whatever is faulty and useless for the purpose of renewing it in better form, begins to work—and this disintegrating process is our conception of decay and death. Yet, as a matter of fact, such process cannot even BEGIN without our consent and collusion. Life can be retained in our possession for an indefinite period on this earth,—but it can only be done through our own actions—our own wish and will."

I looked at him questioningly.

"One may wish and will many things,"—I said—"But the result is not always successful."

"Is that your experience?" he asked, bending his keen eyes full upon me—"You know, if you are true to yourself, that no power can resist the insistence of a strong

Will brought steadily to bear on any intention. If the effort fails, it is only because the Will has hesitated. What have you made of some of your past lives—you and your lover both—through hesitation at a supreme moment!"

I looked at him appealingly.

"If we made mistakes, could we altogether help it?" I asked—"Does it not seem that we tried for the best?"

He smiled slightly.

"No, it does not seem so to me,"—he replied—"The mainspring of your various previous existences,—the law of attraction drawing you together was, and is, Love. This you fought against as though it were a crime, and in many cases you obeyed the temporary conventionalities of man rather than the unchanging ordinance of God. And now—divided as you have been—lost as you have been in endless whirlpools of infinitude, you are brought together again— and though your lover has ceased to question, you have not ceased to doubt!"

"I do not doubt!" I exclaimed, suddenly, and with passion—"I love him with all my soul!—I will never lose him again!"

Aselzion looked at me questioningly.

"How do you know you have not lost him already?" he said.

At this a sudden wave of despair swept over me—a chill sense of emptiness and desolation. Could it be possible that my own rashness and selfishness had again separated me from my beloved?—for so I now called him in my heart—had I by some foolish, distrustful thought estranged him once more from my soul? The rising tears choked me—I rose from my seat, hardly knowing what I did, and went to the window for air—Aselzion followed me and laid his hand gently on my shoulder.

"It is not so difficult to win love as to keep it!"—he said— "Misunderstanding, and want of quick sympathy, end in heart-break and separation. And this is far worse than what mortals call death."

The burning tears fell slowly from my eyes—every word seemed to pierce my heart—I looked yearningly out on the sea, rippling under the moon. I thought of the day, barely a week ago, when Rafel stood beside me, his hand clasping mine,—such a little division of time seemed to have elapsed since we were together, and yet how long! At last I spoke—

"I would rather die, if death were possible, than lose his love"—I said—"And where there is no love, surely there must be death?"

Aselzion sighed.

"Poor child! Now you understand why the lonely Soul hurls itself wildly from one phase of existence to another till it finds its true mate!"—he answered—"You say truly that where there is no love there is no real life. It is merely a semi-conscious existence. But you have no cause to grieve—not now,—not if you are firm and faithful. Rafel Santoris is safe and well—and his soul is so much with you—you are so constantly in his thoughts, that it is as if he were himself here—see!"

And he placed his two hands for a moment over my eyes and then removed them. I uttered a cry of ecstasy—for there before me on the moonlit water I saw the 'Dream'!—her sails glittering with light, and her aerial shape clearly defined against the sky! Oh, how I longed to fly across the strip of water which alone seemed to divide us!—and once more to stand on the deck beside him whom I now loved more than my very hopes of heaven! But I knew it was only a vision conjured up before me by the magic of Aselzion,—a magic used gently for my sake, to help and comfort me in a moment of sadness and heart's longing. And I watched, knowing that the picture must fade,- -as it slowly did,—vanishing like a rainbow in a swirl of cloud.

"It is indeed a 'Dream'!" I said, smiling faintly, as I turned again to Aselzion—"I pray that love itself may never be so fleeting!"

"If love is fleeting, it is not love!"—he answered—"As ephemeral passion called by that name is the ordinary sort of attraction existing between ordinary men and women,—men, who see no farther than the gratification of a desire, and women, who see no higher than the yielding to that desire. Men who love in the highest and most faithful meaning of the term, are much rarer than women,—women are very near the divine in love when it is first awakened in them— if afterwards they sink to a lower level, it is generally the men who have dragged them down. Unless a man is bent on the highest, he is apt to settle on the lowest—whereas a woman generally soars to the highest ideals at first in the blind instinct of a Soul seeking its mate—how often she is hurled back from the empyrean only the angels know! Not to all is given power to master and control the life-forces—and it is this I would have you understand before I leave you to-night. I can teach you the way to hold your life safely above all disintegrating elements—but the learning of the lesson rests with yourself."

He sat down, and I resumed my place in the chair opposite to him, prepared to hear him with the closest attention. There were a few things on the table which I had not previously noticed, and one of these was a circular object covered with a cloth. He removed this covering, and showed me a crystal globe which appeared to be full of some strange volatile fluid, clear in itself, but intersected with endless floating brilliant dots and lines.

"Look well at this"—he said—"for here you have a very simple manifestation of a great truth. These dots and lines which you observe perpetually in motion are an epitome of what is going on in the composition of every human being. Some of them, as you see, go in different directions, yet meet and mingle with each other at various points of convergence—then again become separated. They are the building-up and the disintegrating forces of the whole cosmos— and—mark this well!—they are all, when unimprisoned, directed by a governing will-power. You, in your present state of existence, are simply an organised Form, composed of these atoms, and your will- power, which is part of the Divine creative influence, is set within you to govern them. If you govern them properly, the building-up and revivifying atoms within you obey your command, and with increasing strength gradually control and subdue their disintegrating opponents,— opponents which after all are only their servants, ready to disencumber them from all that is worthless and useless at the first sign of disablement. There is nothing more simple than this law, which has only to be followed in order to preserve both life and youth. It 5s all contained in an effort of the WILL, to which everything in Nature responds, just as a well-steered ship obeys the compass. Remember this well!—I say, EVERYTHING IN NATURE! This crystal globe holds momentarily imprisoned atoms which cannot just now be directed because they are shut in, away from all Will to govern them—but if I left them as they are for a few more hours their force would shatter the crystal, and they would escape to resume their appointed way. They are only shown to you as an object lesson, to prove that such things ARE—they are facts, not dreams. You, like this crystal globe, are full of imprisoned atoms—atoms of Spirit and Matter which work together to make you what you are—but you have also the governing Will which is meant to control them and move them either to support, sustain and revivify you, or else to weaken, break down and finally disperse and disintegrate you, preparatory to your assumption of another form and phase of existence. Now, do you begin to understand?"

"I think I do,"—I answered—"But is it possible always to make this effort of the Will?"

"There is no moment in which you do not, consciously or subconsciously, 'will' something"—he answered—"And the amount of power you use up in 'willing' perfectly trifling and ephemeral things, could almost lift a planet! But let us take simple actions— such as raising a hand. You think this movement instinctive or mechanical—but it is only because you WILL to raise it that you can do it. If you willed NOT to raise it, it could not raise itself OF itself. This tremendous force,— this divine gift of will-power, is hardly exercised at all by the majority of men and women—hence their manner of drifting here and there—their pliable yielding to this or that opinion—the easy sway obtained over the million by a few leaders and reformers—the infectious follies which possess whole communities at a time—the caprices of fashion—the moods of society—all these are due to scattered will-power, which if concentrated would indeed 'replenish the earth and subdue it.' But we cannot teach the world, and therefore we must be content to teach and train a few individuals only. And when you ask if it is possible always to make the necessary effort of will, I answer yes,—of course it is possible. The secret of it all is to resolve upon a firm attitude and maintain it. If you encourage thoughts of fear, hesitation, disease, trouble, decay, incompetency, failure and feebleness, you at once give an impetus to the disintegrating forces within you to begin their work—and you gradually become ill, timorous, and diseased in mind and body. If, on the contrary, your thoughts are centred on health, vitality, youth, joy, love and creativeness, you encourage all the revivifying elements of your system to build up new nerve tissue and fresh brain cells, as well as to make new blood. No scientist has ever really discovered any logical cause why human beings should die—they are apparently intended to live for an indefinite period. It is they them-selves who kill themselves,—even so-called 'accidents' are usually the result of their own carelessness, recklessness or inattention to warning circumstance. I am trying to put all this as simply as I can to you,—there are hundreds of books which you might study, in which the very manner of expression is so abstruse and involved that even the most cultured intelligence can scarcely grasp it,—but what I have told you is perfectly easy of comprehension,—the only difficulty lies in its practical application. To-night, therefore, and for the remainder of the time you are here, you will enter upon certain tests and trials of your will-force—and the result of these will prove whether you are strong enough to be successful in your quest of life and youth and love. If you are capable of maintaining the true atti-tude,—if you can find and keep the real centre-poise of the Divine Image within you, all will be well. And remember, that if you once learn how to govern and control the atomic forces within yourself, you will equally govern and control all atomic forces which come within your atmosphere. This gives you what would be called by the ignorant 'miraculous' power, though it is no miracle. It is nothing more than the attitude of Spirit controlling Matter. You will find yourself not only able to govern your own forces but also to draw upon Nature for fresh supplies—the air, the sunshine, the trees, the flowers, will give you all they have to give on demand—and nothing shall be refused to you. 'Ask, and ye shall receive—seek, and ye shall find—knock, and it shall be opened unto you.' Naturally the law is, that what you receive you must give out again in an ungrudging outflow of love and generosity and beneficence and sympathy, not only towards mankind but to everything that lives—for as you are told—'Give, and it shall be given unto you; good measure, pressed down and shaken together and running over, shall men give into your bosom. For with the same measure that ye mete withal, it shall be measured to you again.' These sayings of our greatest Master are heard so often that they are considered by many people almost trite and commonplace,—but they hold a truth from which we cannot escape. Even such a little matter as a kind word is paid back to the one who uttered it with a double interest of kindness, while a cruel or coarse one carries its own punishment. Those who take without giving are generally unsuccessful in their lives and aims—while those who give without taking appear to be miraculously served by both fame and fortune,—this being merely the enactment of the spiritual law."

"I do not want fame or fortune,"—I said—"Love is enough for me!"

Aselzion smiled.

"Enough for you indeed! My child, it is enough for all! If you have love, you have entered into the secret mind of God! Love inspires all nobleness, all endurance, all courage,—and I think you have some of its attributes, for you have been bold in your first independent essay—and it is this very boldness that has brought me here to speak to you to-night. You have, of your own accord, and without preparation, passed what we students and mystics call 'the first circle of fire,' and you are therefore ready for the rest of your trial. So I will now take you back to your own room and leave you there, for you must face your ordeal alone."

My heart sank a little, but I said nothing, and watched him as he took up the crystal globe, full of the darting lines and points of light gleaming like imprisoned fire, and held it for a moment between his two hands. Then he set it down again, and covered it as it had been covered before. The next moment he had extinguished the lamp, and we stood together in the pale brilliancy of the moonlight which now spread itself in a broad path of silver across the sea. The tide was coming in, and I heard the solemn sound of rising waves breaking rhythmically upon the shore. In silence Aselzion took me by the hand and led me through a low doorway out of the little hermitage into the open air, where we stood within a few feet of the sea. The moonbeams bathed us in a shower of pearly radiance, and I turned instinctively to look at my companion. His face appeared transfigured into something of supernatural beauty, and for one second the remembrance of how he had said in the chapel that he carried the burden of seventy years upon him flashed across me with a shock of surprise. Seventy years! He appeared to be in the very prime and splendour of life, and the mere idea of age as connected with him was absurd and incongruous. And while I gazed upon him, wondering and fascinated, he lifted one hand as though in solemn invocation to the stars that gleamed in their countless millions overhead, and his voice, deep and musical, rang out softly yet clearly on the silence:—

"O Supreme Guide of all the worlds created, accept this Soul which seeks to be consecrated unto Thee! Help her to attain to all that shall be for her wisdom and betterment, and make her one with that Nature whereof she is born. Thou, silent and peaceful Night, invest her with thy deep tranquillity!—thou, bright Moon, penetrate her spirit with the shining in of holy dreams!—give her of thy strength and depth, O Sea!—and may she draw from the treasures of the air all health, all beauty, all life, all sweetness, so that her existence may be a joy to the world, and her love a benediction! Amen!"

My whole being thrilled with a sense of keen rapture as he thus prayed for me,—I could have knelt to him in reverence but that I instinctively knew he would not wish this act of homage. I felt that it was best to keep silence, and I obeyed his guiding touch as, still holding my hand, he led me into a vaulted stone passage and up a long winding stair at the head of which he paused, and taking a key from his girdle, unlocked a small door.

"There is your room, my child,"—he said, with a grave kindliness which moved me strangely—"Farewell! The future is with yourself alone."

I clung to his hand for an instant.

"Shall I not see you again?" I asked, with a little tremor in my voice.

"Yes—you will see me again if you pass your ordeal successfully"— he answered—"Not if you fail."

"What will happen if I fail?"

"Nothing but the most ordinary circumstance,"—he answered—"You will leave this place in perfect safety and return to your home and your usual avocations,—you will live as most women live, perhaps on a slightly higher grade of thought and action—and in time you will come to look upon your visit to the House of Aselzion as the merest wilful escapade of folly! The world and its conventions will hold you—"

"Never!" I exclaimed, passionately—"Aselzion, I will not fail!"

He looked earnestly in my face—then laid his hands on my head in a mute bless-ing, and signed to me to pass into my turret room. I obeyed. He closed the door upon me instantly—I heard the key turn in the lock—and then—just the faint echo of his retreating footsteps down the winding stair. My room was illumined by a very faint light, the source of which I knew not. Everything was as I had left it before I had been summoned to the mysterious Chapel of the Cross and Star,— and I looked about me, tranquillised by the peace and simplicity of my sur-roundings. I did not feel disposed to sleep, and I resolved to write down from memory all that Aselzion had told me while it was fresh in my mind. The white veil I had been given still clung about me,—I now took it off and carefully fold-ed it ready for further use if needed. Sitting down at the little table, I took out pen, ink and paper,—but somehow I could not fix my attention on what I intended to do. The silence around me was more intense than ever, and though my window was open I could not even hear the murmur of the sea. I listened— hardly drawing breath—there was not a sound. The extraordinary silence deep-ened—and with it came a sense of cold; I seemed to be removed into a place apart, where no human touch, no human voice could reach me,—and I felt as I had never felt in all my life before, that I was indeed utterly alone.

XVI

SHADOW AND SOUND

The stillness deepened. It seemed to myself that I could hear the quickened beating of every pulse in my body. A curious vague terror began to possess me,—I fought against its insidious influence, and bending my head down over the paper I had set out before me, I prepared to write. After a few minutes I managed to gain some control over my nerves, and started to put down clearly and in sequence the things Aselzion had told me, though I knew there was little danger of my ever forgetting them. And then—a sudden sensation came over me which forced me to realise that something or someone was in the room, looking steadfastly at me.

With an effort, I raised my head, and saw nothing at first—then, by degrees, I became aware that a Shadow, dark and impenetrable, stood between me and the open window. At first it seemed simply a formless mass of black vapour,—but very gradually it assumed the outline of a Shape which did not seem human. I laid down my pen,—and, with my heart thumping hammer-strokes of fear, looked at this strange Darkness gathered as it were in one place and blocking out the silver gleam of the moon. As I looked, all the light in my room was suddenly extinguished. A cry rose involuntarily to my lips—and physical fright began to gain the mastery over me. For with the increasing gloom the mysterious Shadow grew more and more defined—a blackness standing out as it were against another blackness,—the pale glint of the moonbeams only illumining it faintly as a cloud may be edged with a suggestion of light. It was not motionless,—it stirred now and then as though about to lift itself to some supernatural stature and bend above me or swoop down upon me like an embodied storm,—and as I still gazed upon it fearingly, every nerve strained to an almost unsupportable tension, I could have sworn that two eyes, large and luminous, were fixed with a searching, piti-less intensity on mine. It is impossible to describe what I felt,—a sense of sick, swooning horror overcame me,—my head swam giddily, and I could not now utter a sound.

Trembling violently, I rose to my feet in a kind of mechanical impulse, deter-mined to turn away from the dreadful contemplation of this formless Phantom, when suddenly, as if by a lightning flash of conviction, the thought came to me that it was not by coward avoidance that I could expect to overcome either my own fears or the nameless danger which apparently threatened me. I closed my eyes and retreated, as it were, within myself to find that centre-poise of my own spirit which I knew must remain an invincible force despite all attack, being in itself immortal,—and I mentally barricaded my soul with thoughts of armed resistance. Then, opening my eyes again, I saw that the Shadow loomed blacker and vaster—while the luminance around it was more defined, and was not the radiance of the moon, but some other light that was ghostly and terrifying. But I had now regained a little courage,—and slight as it was I held to it as my last hope, and gradually steadied myself upon it like a drowning creature clinging to a plank for rescue. Presently I found myself able to ask questions of my inner con-sciousness. What, after all, could this Phantom—if Phantom it were—do to work me harm? Could it kill me with sheer terror? Surely in that case the terror would be my own fault, for why should I be afraid? The thing called Death being no more than a Living Change did it matter so much when or how the change was effected?

"Who is responsible,"—I said to myself—"for the sense of fear? Who is it that so mistrusts the Divine order of the Universe as to doubt the ultimate intention of goodness in things which appear evil? Is it not I alone who am the instigator of my own dread?—and can this dark, dumb Spectre do more to me than is ordained for my blessing in the end?"

With these thoughts I grew bold—my nervous trembling ceased. I now chose deliberately to consider, and WILLED to determine, that this mysterious Shadow, darker still as it grew, was something of a friend in disguise. I lifted my head half defiantly, half hopefully in the gloom, and the strange fact that the only light I saw came from the weirdly gleaming edge of radiance round the Phantom itself did not frighten me from the attitude I had resolved upon. The more I settled myself into that attitude the firmer it became—and the stronger grew my courage. I gently moved aside the table on which I had been writing, and stood up. Once on my feet I felt still bolder and surer of myself, and though the Shadow opposite to me looked darker and more threatening than before, I began to move steadily towards it. I made an effort to speak to it, and at last found my voice.

"Whatever you are," I said aloud, "you cannot exist at all without God's will! God ordains nothing that is not for good, therefore you cannot be here with any evil purpose! If I am afraid of you, my fear is my own weakness. I will not look at you as a thing that can or would do me harm, and therefore I am coming to you to find out your meaning! You shall prove to me what you are made of, to the very depth and heart of your darkness!—you shall unveil to me all that you hide behind your terrifying aspect,—because I KNOW that whatever your intention towards me may be, you cannot hurt my Soul!"

As I spoke I drew nearer and nearer—and the luminous edge round the Phantom grew lighter and lighter, till—suddenly a flash of brilliant colour like a rainbow glittered full on my eyes so sharply that I fell back, half blinded by its splendour. Then—as I looked— I dropped to my knees in speechless awe—for the Shadow had changed to a dazzling Shape of winged radiance,—a figure and face so glorious that I could only gaze and gaze, with all my soul entranced in wonder! I heard delicious music around me, but I could not listen—all my soul was in my eyes. The Vision grew in stature and in splendour, and I stretched out my hands to it in prayerful appeal, conscious that I was in the shining Presence of some inhabitant of higher and more heavenly spheres than ours. The beautiful head, crowned with a diadem of flowers like white stars, bent towards me—the luminous eyes smiled into mine, and a voice sweeter than all sweet singing spoke to me in accents of thrilling tenderness.

"Thou hast done well!" it said—"Even so always approach Darkness without fear! Then shalt thou find the Light! Meet Sorrow with a trusting heart—so shalt thou discover an angel in disguise! God thinks no evil of thee—desires no wrong towards thee—has no punishment in store for thee—give Thyself into His Hand, and be at peace!"

Slowly,—like the colours of the sunset melting away into the grey of twilight, the Vision faded,—and when I recovered from the dazzled bewilderment into which I had been thrown, I found myself again in complete solitude and darkness— darkness unrelieved save by the dim light of the setting moon. I was for a long time unable to think of anything but the strange experience through which I had just passed—and I wondered what would have happened if instead of boldly advancing and confronting the dark Phantom which had so terrified me I had striven to escape from it? I believed, and I think I was right in my belief, that I should have found every door open, and every facility offered for a cowardly retreat had I chosen to make it. And then—everything would have been at an end!—I should have probably had to leave the House of Aselzion—and perhaps I too should have been marked with a black cross as a failure! Inwardly I rejoiced that so far I had not given way, and presently yielding to a drowsiness that began to steal over me, I undressed and went to bed, perfectly tranquil in mind and happy.

I must have slept several hours when I was awakened suddenly by the sound of voices conversing quite close to me—in fact, they seemed to be on the other side of the wall against which my bed was placed. They were men's voices, and one or two were curiously harsh and irritable in tone. There was plenty of light in my room—for the night had passed, and as far as I could tell it seemed to be early morning. The voices went on, and I found myself compelled to listen.

"Aselzion is the cleverest humbug of his time,"—said one—"He is never so happy as when he can play the little god and dupe his worshippers!" A laugh followed this sentence.

"He's a marvel in his way,"—said another—"He must be a kind of descendant of some ancient Egyptian conjurer who had the trick of playing with fire. There is nothing in the line of so-called miracle he cannot do,—and of course those who are ignorant of his methods, and who are credulous themselves—"

"Like the woman here,"—interposed the first voice.

"Yes—like the woman here—little fool!"—and there was more laughter—"Fancying herself in love with Rafel Santoris!"

I sat up in bed, straining my ears now for every word. My cheeks were burning—my heart beating—I hardly knew what to think. There was a silence for two or three minutes—minutes that seemed like ages in my longing to hear more.

"Santoris always managed to amuse himself!"—said a thin, sharp voice with a mocking ring in its tone—"There was always some woman or other in love with him. Some woman he could take in easily, of course!"

"Not difficult to find!"—rejoined the first voice that had spoken, "Most women are blind where their affections are concerned."

"Or their vanity!"

Another silence. I rose from my bed, shivering with a sense of sudden cold, and threw on my dressing-gown. Going to the window, I looked out on the fair expanse of the calm sea, silver-grey in the early dawn. How still and peaceful it looked!—what a contrast to the storm of doubt and terror that was beginning to rage within my own heart! Hush! The voices began again.

"Well, it's all over now, and his theory of perpetuating life at pleasure has come to an untimely end. Where did the yacht go down?"

"Off Armadale, in Skye."

For a moment I could not realise what had been said and tried to repeat both question and answer—'Where did the yacht go down?' 'Off Armadale, in Skye.'

What did it mean?—The yacht? Gone down? What yacht? They were talking of Santoris—of Rafel, my beloved!—MY lover, lost through ages of time and space, and found again only to be once more separated from me through my own fault—my own fault!—that was the horror of it—a horror I could not contemplate without an almost maddening anguish. I ran to the wall through which I had heard the voices talking and pressed my ear against it, murmuring to myself— "Oh no!—it is not possible!—not possible! God would not be so cruel!" For many minutes I heard nothing—and I was rapidly losing patience and self-control, when at last I heard the conversation resumed,—"He should never have risked his life in such a vessel"— said one of the voices in a somewhat gentler tone—"It was a wonderfully clever contrivance, but the danger of all that electricity was obvious. In a storm it would have no chance."

"That has been thoroughly proved,"—answered another voice—"Just half a gale of wind with a dash of thunder and lightning, and down it went, with every soul on board."

"Santoris might have saved himself. He was a fine swimmer."

"Was he?"

Another silence. I thought my head would have burst with its aching agony of suspense,—my eyes were burning like hot coals with a weight of unshed tears. I felt that I could have battered down the wall between me and those torturing voices in my feverish desire to know the worst—the worst at all costs! If Rafel were dead—but no!- -he could not die! He could not actually perish—but he could be parted from me as he had been parted before—and I—I should be alone again—alone as I had been all my life! And in my foolish pride I had voluntarily severed myself from him!—was this my punishment? More talking began, and I listened, like a criminal listening to a cruel sentence.

"Aselzion will tell her, of course. Rather a difficult business!—as he will have to admit that his teachings are not infallible. And on the whole there was something very taking about Santoris—I'm sorry he's gone. But he would only have fooled the woman had he lived."

"Oh! That, naturally! But that hardly matters. She would only have had herself to blame for falling into the trap."

I drew myself away from the wall, trembling and sick with dread. Mechanically I dressed myself, and stared out at the gold of the sun which was now pouring its radiance full on the sea. The beauty of the scene moved me not at all—nothing mattered. All that my consciousness could take in was that, according to what I had heard, Rafel was dead,—drowned in the sea over which his fairy vessel the 'Dream' had sailed so lightly—and that all he had said of our knowledge of each other in former lives, and of the love which had drawn us together, was mere 'fooling'! I leaned out of the window, and my eyes rested on the little crimson rose that still blossomed against the wall in fragrant confidence. And then I spoke aloud, hardly conscious of my own words—

"It is wicked"—I said—"wicked of God to allow us to imagine beautiful things that have no existence! It is cruel to ordain us to love, if love must end in disappointment and treachery! It would be better to teach us at once that life is intended to be hard and plain and without tenderness or truth, than to lead our souls into a fool's paradise!"

Then—all at once—I remembered the dark Phantom of the night and its transformation into the Vision of an Angel. I had struggled against the terror of its first spectral appearance, and had conquered my fears,—why was I now shaken from my self-control? What was the cause? Voices, merely! Voices behind a wall that spoke of death and falsehood,—voices belonging to persons I did not know and could not see—like the voices of the world which delight in uttering scandals and cruelties and which never praise so much as they condemn. Voices merely! Ah!—but they spoke of the death of him whom I loved!—must I not listen? They spoke of his treachery and 'fooling.' Should I not hear?

And yet—who were those persons, if persons they were, who talked of him with such easy callousness? I had met no one in the House of Aselzion save Aselzion himself and his servant or secretary Honorius,—who then could there be except those two to know the reasons that had brought me hither? I began to question myself and to doubt the accuracy of the terrible news I had inadvertently over-heard. If any evil had chanced to Rafel Santoris, would Aselzion have told me he was 'safe and well' when he had conjured up for my comfort the picture of the 'Dream' yacht on the moonlit sea only a few hours ago? Yet with my bravest effort I could not recover myself sufficiently to be quite at peace,—and in my restless condition of mind I looked towards the turret door opening to the stairway which led to the little garden below and the seashore—but it was fast shut, and I remem-bered Aselzion had locked it. But, to my complete surprise, another door stood open,—a door that had seemed part of the wall—and a small room was disclosed beyond it,—a kind of little shrine, hung with pale purple silk, and looking as though it were intended to hold something infinitely precious. I entered it hesi-tatingly, not sure whether I was doing right or wrong, and yet impelled by some-thing more than curiosity. As I stepped across the threshold I heard the voices behind the wall again—they sounded louder and more threatening, and I paused,—half afraid, yet longing to know all that might yet be said, though such knowledge might mean nothing but misery and despair to me.

"All women are fools!"—and this trite observation was made by someone speak-ing in harsh and bitter accents—"It is not love that really moves them so much as the self-satisfaction of BEING LOVED. No woman could be faithful for long to a dead man—she would lack the expected response to her superabundant senti-mentality, and she would tire of waiting to meet him in Paradise—if she believed in such a possibility, which in nine cases out of ten she would not."

"With Aselzion there are no dead men"—said another of the unseen speakers—"They have merely passed into another living state. And according to his theories, lovers cannot be separated, even by what is called death, for long."

"Poor comfort!" and with the words I heard a laugh of scornful mockery—"The women who have loved Rafel Santoris would hardly thank you for it!"

I shuddered a little, as with cold. 'The women who have loved Rafel Santoris!' This phrase seemed to darken the very recollection of the handsome face and form of the man I had, almost unconsciously to myself, begun to idealise—some-thing coarse and common suggested itself in association with him, and my heart sank within me, deprived of hope. Voices, merely!—yet how they tortured me! If I could only know the truth, I thought!—if Aselzion would only come and tell

me the worst at once! In a kind of stupor of unnameable grief I stood in the little purple-hung shrine so suddenly opened to me, and began to dreamily consider the unkindness and harshness of those voices!—Ah! so like the voices of the
world! Voices that sneer and mock and condemn!—voices that would rather utter
a falsehood than any word that should help and comfort—voices that take a cruel
pleasure in saying just the one thing that will wound and crush an aspiring spirit!—voices that cannot tune themselves to speak of love without grudging bitterness and scorn—voices—ah God!—if only all the harsh and calumniating voices
of humanity were stilled, what a heaven this earth would be!

And yet—why should we listen to them? What have they really to do with us? Is
the Soul to be moved from its centre by casual opinion? What is it to me that this
person or that person approves or disapproves my actions? Why should I be disturbed by rumours, or frightened by ill report?

Absorbed in these thoughts, I hardly realised the almost religious peace of my surroundings,—and it was only when the voices ceased for a few minutes that I saw
what was contained in this small room I had half unwittingly entered,—an exquisite little table, apparently made of crystal which shone like a diamond—and on
the table, an open book. A chair was placed in position for the evident purpose
of reading—and as I approached, at first indifferently and then with awakening
interest, I saw that the open book showed an inscription on its fly-leaf—"To a
faithful student.—From Aselzion." Was _I_ 'a faithful student'? I asked myself the
question doubtingly. There was no 'faithfulness' in fears and depressions! Here
was I, shaken in part from self-control from the mere hearing of voices behind a
wall! I, who had said that "God ordains nothing that is not for good"—was suddenly ready to believe that He had ordained the death of the lover to whom His
laws had guided me! I, to whom had been vouchsafed the beatific vision of an
Angel—an Angel who had said— "God thinks no evil of thee—desires no wrong
towards thee—has no punishment in store for thee—give thyself into His Hand,
and be at peace!" was already flinching and turning away from the Faith that
should keep me strong! A sense of shame stole over me—and almost timidly I
approached the table on which the open book lay, and sat down in the chair so
invitingly placed. I had scarcely done this when the voices began again, in rather
louder and angrier tones.

"She imagines she can learn the secret of life! A woman, too! The brazen arrogance
of such an attempt!"

"No, no! It is not the secret of life she wants to discover so much as the secret of
perpetual youth! That, to a woman, is everything! To be always young and always
fair! What feminine thing would not 'adventure for such merchandise'!"

A loud laugh followed this observation.

"Santoris was well on his way to the goal"—said a voice that was suave and calm of accent—"Certainly no one would have guessed his real age."

"He had all the ardour and passion of youth"—said another voice— "The fire of love ran as warmly in his veins as though he were a Romeo! None of the coldness and reluctance of age affected him where the fair sex was concerned!"

More laughter followed. I sat rigidly in the chair by the crystal table, listening to every word.

The woman here is the latest victim of his hypnotic suggestions, isn't she?"

"Yes. One may say his LAST victim—he will victimise no more."

"I suppose if Aselzion told her the truth she would go at once?"

"Of course! Why should she remain? It is only a dream of love that has brought her here—when she knows the dream is over, there will be nothing left."

True! Nothing left! The whole world a desert, and Heaven itself without hope! I pressed my hands to my eyes to try and cool their burning ache—was it possible that what these voices said could be true? They had ceased speaking, and there was a blessed silence. As a kind of desperate resource, I took out the letter Rafel Santoris had written to me, and read its every word with an eager passion of yearning—especially the one passage that ran thus—"We—you and I— who know that Life, being ALL Life, CANNOT die,—ought to be wiser in our present space of time than to doubt each other's infinite capability for love and the perfect world of beauty which love creates."

'Wiser than to doubt'! Ah, I was not wise enough! I was full of doubts and imagined evils—and why? Because of voices behind a wall! Surely a foolish cause for sorrow! I tried to extricate my mind from the darkness of despondency into which it had fallen, and to distract my attention from my own unhappy thoughts I glanced at the book which lay open before me. As I looked, its title, printed in letters of gold, flashed on my eyes like a gleam of the sun—'The Secret of Life.' A sudden keen expectancy stirred in me—I folded Rafel's letter and slipped it back into its resting-place near my heart—then I drew my chair close up to the table, and bending over the book began to read. All was now perfectly still around me—the voices had ceased. Gradually I became aware that what I was reading was intended for my instruction, and that the book itself was a gift to me from Aselzion if I proved a 'faithful student.' A thrill of hope and gratitude began to relieve the cold weight upon my heart,— and I suddenly resolved that I would not listen to any more voices, even if they spoke again.

"Rafel Santoris is not dead!"—I said aloud and resolutely—"He could not so sever himself from me now! He is not treacherous—he is true! He is not 'fooling' me— he is relying upon me to believe in him. And I WILL believe in him!—my love and faith shall not be shaken by mere rumour! I will give him no cause to think me weak or cowardly,—I will trust him to the end!"

And with these words spoken to the air, I went on reading quietly in a stillness made suddenly fragrant with the scent of unseen flowers.

XVII

THE MAGIC BOOK

It is not possible here to transcribe more than a few extracts from the book on which my attention now became completely riveted. The passages selected are chosen simply because they may by chance be useful to those few—those very few—who desire to make of their lives something more than a mere buy and sell business, and also because they can hardly be called difficult to understand. When Paracelsus wrote 'The Secret of Long Life' he did so in a fashion sufficiently abstruse and complex to scare away all but the most diligent and persevering of students, this no doubt being his intention. But the instructions given in the volume placed, as I imagined, for my perusal, were simple and in accordance with many of the facts discovered by modern science, and as I read on and on I began to see light through the darkness, and to gain a perception of the way in which I might become an adept in what the world deems 'miracle,' but which after all is nothing but the scientific application of common sense. To begin with, I will quote the following,—headed

LIFE AND ITS ADJUSTMENT

"Life is the Divine impetus of Love. The Force behind the Universe is Love—and from that Love is bred Desire and Creation. Even as the human lover passionately craves possession of his beloved, so that from their mutual tenderness the children of Love are born, the Divine Spirit, immortally creative and desirous of perfect beauty, possesses space with eternal energy, producing millions of solar systems, each one of which has a different organisation and a separate individuality.

Man, the creature of our small planet, the Earth, is but a single result of the resist-less output of Divine fecundity,—nevertheless Man is the 'image of God' in that he is endowed with reason, will and intelligence beyond that of the purely animal creation, and that he is given an immortal Soul, formed for love and for the eter-nal things which love creates. He can himself be Divine, in the Desire and Perpetuation of Life. Considered in a strictly material sense, he is simply an embodied force composed of atoms held together in a certain organised form,—but within this organised form is contained a spiritual Being capable of guiding and controlling its earthly vehicle and adjusting it to surroundings and circum-stances. In his dual nature Man has the power of holding his life-cells under his own command—he can renew them or destroy them at pleasure. He generally elects to destroy them through selfishness and obstinacy,—the two chief disinte-grating elements of his mortal composition. Hence the result which he calls 'death'—but which is merely the necessary transposition of his existence (which he has himself brought about) into a more useful phase. If he were to learn once for all that he can prolong his life on this earth in youth and health for an indef-inite period, in which days and years are not counted, but only psychic 'episodes' or seasons, he could pass from one joy to another, from one triumph to another, as easily as breathing the air. It is judged good for a man's body that he should stand upright, and that he should move his limbs with grace and ease, perform-ing physical exercises for the improvement and strengthening of his muscles,—and he is not considered a fool for any feats of physical valour or ability which he may accomplish. Why then should he not train his Soul to stand as upright as his body, so that it may take full possession of all the powers which natural and spir-itual energy can provide?

"Reader and Student!—you for whom these words are written, learn and remem-ber that the secret strength and renewal of life is Adjustment—the adjustment of the atoms whereof the body is composed to the commands of the Soul. Be the god of your own universe! Control your own solar system that it may warm and revivify you with an ever recurring spring! Make Love the summer of your life, and let it create within you the passion of noble desire, the fervour of joy, the fire of idealism and faith! Know yourself as part of the Divine Spirit of all things, and be divine in your own creative existence. The whole Universe is open to the searchings of your Soul if Love be the torch to light your way!"

Having read thus far, I paused—the little room in which I sat appeared darker—or was it my fancy? I listened for the voices which had so confused and worried me—but there was no sound. I turned the pages of the book before me, and found the following:

THE ACTION OF THOUGHT

"Thought is an actual motive Force, more powerful than any other motive force in the world. It is not the mere pulsation in a particular set of brain cells, destined to pass away into nothingness when the pulsation has ceased. Thought is the voice of the Soul. Just as the human voice is transmitted through distance on the telephone wires, so is the Soul's voice carried through the radiant fibres connected with the nerves to the brain. The brain receives it, but cannot keep it—for it again is transmitted by its own electric power to other brains,—and you can no more keep a thought to yourself than you can hold a monopoly in the sunshine. Everywhere in all worlds, throughout the whole cosmos, Souls are speaking through the material medium of the brain,—souls that may not inhabit this world at all, but that may be as far away from us as the last star visible to the strongest telescope. The harmonies that suggest themselves to the musician here to-day may have fallen from Sirius or Jupiter, striking on his earthly brain with a spiritual sweetness from worlds unknown,—the poet writes what he scarcely realises, obeying the inspiration of his dreams,-and we are all, at our best, but mediums for conveying thought, first receiving it from other spheres to ourselves, and then transmitting it from ourselves to others. Shakespeare, the chief poet and prophet of the world, has written: 'There is nothing good or bad but thinking makes it so,'—thus giving out a profound truth,—one of the most profound truths of the Psychic Creed. For what we THINK, we are; and our thoughts resolve themselves into our actions.

"In the renewal of life and the preservation of youth, Thought is the chief factor. If we THINK we are old—we age rapidly. If, on the contrary, we THINK we are young, we preserve our vitality indefinitely. The action of thought influences the living particles of which our bodies are composed, so that we positively age them or rejuvenate them by the attitude we assume. The thinking attitude of the human Soul should be one of gratitude, love and joy. There is no room in Spiritual Nature for fear, depression, sickness or death. God intends His creation to be happy, and by bringing the Soul and Body both into tune with happiness we obey His laws and fulfil His desire. Therefore, to live long, encourage thoughts of happiness! Avoid all persons who talk of disease, misery and decay—for these things are the crimes of man, and are offences against God's primal design of beauty. Drink in deep draughts of sunshine and fresh air,- -inhale the perfume of flowers and trees,—keep far away from cities and from crowds—seek no wealth that is not earned by hand or brain- -and above all things remember that the Children of Light may walk in the Light without fear of darkness!"

Something in this latter sentence made me stop, and look again around me—and again I felt sure that the room was growing darker, and not only darker but smaller. The purple silk hangings which draped the walls were almost within my touch, and I knew they had not been so close to me when I first sat down to read. A nervous tremor ran through me, but I resolved I would not be the dupe of my own fancy, and I set myself once more resolutely to the study of the volume before me. The next paragraph which attracted me was headed

ON THE COMMAND OF LIFE'S FORCES

and began thus:

"To live long you must have perfect control of the forces that engender life. The atoms of which your body is composed are in perpetual movement,—your Spiritual Self must guide them in the way they should go, otherwise they resemble an army without organisation or equipment, easily put to rout by a first assault. If you have them under your spiritual orders you are practically immune from all disease. Disease can never enter your system save through some unguarded corner. You may meet with accident—through the fault of others or through your own wilfulness,—if through your own wilfulness, you have only yourself to blame—if through the fault of others, you may know that it was a destined and pre-ordained removal of yourself from a sphere for which you are judged to be unfitted. Barring such accident, your life need know no end, even on this earth. Your Spirit, called the Soul, is a Creature of Light—and it can supply revivifying rays to every atom and cell in your body without stint or cessation. It is an exhaustless supply of 'radium' from which the forces of your life may draw perpetual sustenance. Man uses every exterior means of self-preservation, but forgets the interior power he possesses, which was bestowed upon him that he might 'replenish the earth and subdue it.' To 'replenish' the earth is to give out love ungrudgingly to all Nature,—to 'subdue' the earth, is first, to master the atoms of which the human organisation is composed, and hold them completely under control, so that by means of this mastery, all other atomic movements and forces upon this planet and its encircling atmosphere may be equally controlled. Much is talked of the 'light rays' which pierce solid matter as though it were nothing but clear air—yet this discovery is but the beginning of wonders. There are rays which divine metals, even as the hazel wand divines the presence of water,—and the treasures of the earth, the gold, the silver, the jewels and precious things that are hidden beneath its surface and in the depth of the sea can be seen in their darkest recesses by the penetrating flash of a Ray as yet unknown to any but adepts in the Psychic Creed. No true adept is ever poor,—poverty cannot exist where perfect control of the life forces is maintained. Gladness, peace and plenty must naturally attend the Soul that is in tune with Nature and life is always perpetuated from the joy of life.

"Stand, therefore, O patient Student, erect and firm!—let the radiating force of the Soul possess every nerve and blood-vessel of the body, and learn to command all things pertaining to good with that strength which compels obedience! Not idly did the Supreme Master speak when He told His disciples that if their faith were but as a grain of mustard seed they could command a mountain to be cast into the sea, and it would obey. Remember that the Spirit within your bodily house of clay is Divine, and of God!—and that with God all things are possible!"

I raised my head from its bent position over the book, and drew a long breath—something oppressed me with a sense of suffocation, and looking up I saw that I was being steadily closed in, as by a contracting cage. The little room, draped with its soft purple hangings, was now too small for me to move about, I was pinned to my chair, and the ceiling was apparently descending upon me. With a shock of horrified memory I recalled the old torture of the 'living tomb' practised by the Spanish Inquisition, when the wretched victim was compelled to watch the walls of his prison slowly narrowing round him inch by inch till he was crushed to death. How could I be sure that no such cruelties were used among the mysterious members of a mysterious Brotherhood, whose avowed object of study was the searching out of the secret of life? I made an effort to rise, and found I could stand upright—and there straight opposite to me was the entrance to my own room from which I had wandered into this small inner chamber. It seemed easy enough to get there, and yet—I found myself hindered by an invisible barrier. I stood, with my heart beating nervously—wondering what was my threatening danger. Almost involuntarily my eyes still perused the printed page of the book before me, and I read the following sentences in a kind of waking dream:—

"To the Soul that will not study the needs of its immortal nature, life itself becomes a narrow cell. All God's creation waits upon it to supply what it shall demand,—yet it starves in the midst of plenty. Fear, suspicion, distrust, anger, envy and callousness paralyse its being and destroy its action,—love, courage, patience, sweetness, generosity and sympathy are actual life-forces to it and to the body it inhabits. All the influences of the social world work AGAINST it—all the influences of the natural world work WITH it. There is nothing of pure Nature that will not obey its behest, and this should be enough for its happy existence. Sorrow and despair result from the misguidance of the Will—there is no other cause in earth or heaven for any pain or trouble."

Misguidance of the Will! I spoke the words aloud—then went on reading—

"What is Heaven? A state of perfect happiness. What is Happiness? The immortal union of two Souls in one, creatures of God's eternal light, partaking each other's thoughts, bestowing upon each other the renewal of joy, and creating loveliness in form and action by their mutual sympathy and tenderness. Age cannot touch them—death has no meaning for them,—life is their air and space and movement— life palpitates through them and warms them with colour and glory as the sunshine warms and reddens the petals of the rose—they grow beyond mortality and are immune from all disaster—they are a world in themselves, involuntarily creating other worlds as they pass from one phase to another of production and fruition. For there is no good work accomplished without love,—no great triumph achieved without love,—no fame, no victory gained without love! The lovers of God are the beloved of God!—their passion is divine, knowing no weariness, no satiety, no end! For God is the Supreme Lover and there is nothing higher than Love!"

Here, on a sudden impulse, I took up the book, closed it and held it clasped in my two hands. As I did this, a great darkness overwhelmed me—a sound like thunder crashed on my ears, and I felt the whole room reeling into chaos. The floor sank, and I sank with it, down to a great depth so swiftly that I had no time to think what had happened till the sensation of falling stopped abruptly, and I found myself in a narrow green lane, completely shadowed by the wide boughs of over-arching trees. Hardly could I realise my surroundings when I saw Rafel!—Rafel Santoris himself walking towards me—but— not alone! The eager impulse to run to him was checked—I stood quiet, and cold to the heart. A woman was with him—a woman young and very beautiful—his arm was round her, and his eyes looked with unwearied tenderness at her face. I heard his voice—caressing, and infinitely gentle.

"Beloved!" he said—"I call you by this name as I have always called you through many cycles of time! Is it not strange that even the eager spirit, craving for its pre-ordained mate, is subject to error? I thought I had found her whom I should love a little while before I met you—but this was a momentary blindness!—YOU are the one I have sought for many centuries!—YOU are the one and only beloved!—promise never to leave me again!" She answered—and I heard her murmur, soft as a sigh—"I promise!" Still walking together like lovers, they came on—I knew they must pass me,—and I stood in their way that Rafel Santoris at least might see me—might know that I had adventured into the House of Aselzion for his sake, and that so far I had not failed! If he were false, then surely the failure would be his! With a sickening heart I watched him approach,—his blue eyes rested on me carelessly with a cold smile—his fair companion glanced at me as at a stranger—and they moved on and passed out of sight. I could not have spoken, had I tried—I was stricken dumb and feeble. This was the end, then? I had made my journey to no purpose,—he had already found another 'subject' for his influence!

Stunned and bewildered with the confusion of thought in my brain, I tried to walk a few paces, and found the ground soft as velvet, while a cool breeze blowing through the trees refreshed my aching forehead and eyes. I still held the book—'The Secret of Life'—and in a dull, aimless way thought how useless it was! What does Life matter if Love be untrue? The sun was shining somewhere above me, for I saw glinting reflections of it through the close boughs, and there were birds singing. But both beauty of sight and beauty of sound were lost to me—I had no real consciousness left save that the lover who professed to love me with an eternal love loved me no more! So the world was desolate, and heaven itself a blank!—death, and death alone seemed dear and desirable! I walked slowly and with difficulty—my limbs were languid, and I had lost all courage. If I could have found my way to Aselzion I would have told him—"This is enough! No more do I need the secret of youth or life, since love has left me."

Presently I began to think more coherently. A little while back I had heard voices behind a wall saying that Rafel Santoris was dead,- -drowned in his own yacht 'off Armadale, in Skye.' If that was true how came he here? I questioned myself in vain,—till presently I gathered up sufficient force to remember that love—REAL love—knows no change. Did I believe in my lover's love, or did I doubt it? That was a point for my own consideration! But, had I not the testimony of my own eyes? Was I not myself the witness of his altered mind?

Here, seeing a rustic seat under one of the shadiest trees, I sat down, and my mind gradually steadied itself. Why, I inwardly asked, had I been so suddenly and forcibly brought into this place for no apparent reason save to look upon Rafel Santoris in the company of another woman whom it seemed that he now preferred to me? Ought that to make any difference in my love for him? "In love, if love be love, if love be ours, Faith and unfaith can ne'er be equal powers, Unfaith in aught is want of faith in all." If the happiness of the one I loved was obtained through other means than mine, ought I to grudge it? And yet!—my heart was full of a sick heaviness,—it seemed to me that I had lately been the possessor of an inestimable joy which had been ruthlessly snatched from me. Still meditating in solitary sadness, I sat in the soft gloom wondering at the strange chance that had brought me into such a place, and, curiously enough, never thinking that the whole adventure might be the result of a pre-ordained design.

Presently, hearing slow footsteps approaching, I looked up and saw an aged man walking towards me, accompanied by a woman of gentle and matronly appearance who supported him on her arm. The looks of both these personages were kindly, and inspired confidence at a glance,— and I watched them coming with a kind of hope that perhaps they might explain my present dilemma. I was particularly attracted by the venerable and benevolent aspect of the man—and as he drew near, seeing that he evidently intended to speak to me, I rose from my seat, and made a step or two forward to meet him. He inclined his head courteously, and smiled upon me with a grave and compassionate air.

"I am very glad,"—he said, in a friendly tone—"that we have not come too late. We feared—did we not?" here he looked to his companion for confirmation of his words—"that you might have been hopelessly ensnared and victimised before we could come to the rescue."

"Alas, yes!" said the woman, in accents of deep pity; "And that would have been terrible indeed!"

I stared at them both, utterly bewildered. They spoke of rescue,— rescue from what? 'Hopelessly ensnared and victimised.' What did they mean? Since I had seen Rafel Santoris with another woman he called 'beloved'—I had felt almost incapable of speech—but now I found my voice suddenly.

"I do not understand you"—I said, as clearly and firmly as I could- -"I am here by my own desire, and I am not being ensnared or victimised. Why should I need rescue?"

The old man shook his head compassionately.

"Poor child!" he said—"Are you not a prisoner in the House of Aselzion?"

"With my own consent,"—I answered.

He lifted his hands in a kind of appealing astonishment, and the woman smiled sadly.

"Not so!"—she told me—"You are under a very serious delusion. You are here by the wicked will of Rafel Santoris—a man who would sacrifice any life remorselessly in the support of his own mad theories! You are under his influence, you poor creature!—so easily trapped, too!—you think you are following your own way and carrying out your own wishes, but you are really the slave of Santoris and have been so ever since you met him. You are a mere instrument on which he can play any tune." And she turned to the old man beside her with an appealing gesture—"Is it not so?"

He bent his head in the affirmative.

For a moment my brain was in a whirl. Could it be possible that what they said was true? Their looks were sincere,—they could have no object but kindness in warning me of intended mischief. I tried to conceal the torturing anxiety that possessed me, and asked quietly—

"If you have good reason to think all this, what would you advise me to do? If I am in danger how shall I escape from it?"

The woman looked curiously at me, and her eyes glittered with sudden interest. Her venerable companion replied to my question—

"Escape is quite easy here and now. You have only to follow us and we will take you out of this wood and escort you to a place of safety. Then you can return to your own home and forget—"

"Forget what?" I interrupted him.

"All this foolishness"—he answered, with a gentle seriousness— "This idea of eternal life and love which the artful conjurer Rafel Santoris has instilled into your too sensitive and credulous imagination—these fantastic beliefs in the immortality and individuality of the soul,—and you will accept old age and death with the sane resignation of ordinary mortals. Such love as he professes to believe in does not exist,—such life can never be,— and the secret of his youth—"

"Ah!" I exclaimed eagerly—"Tell me of that! And of Aselzion's splendid prime when he should be old and feeble? Tell me of that also!"

For the first time during this interview, my two companions looked confused. I saw this, and I gained confidence from their evident embarrassment.

"Why," I pursued—"should you come to me with warnings against those whom God or Destiny has brought into my life? You may perhaps say that you yourselves have been sent by God—but does Deity contradict Itself? I am not conscious of having suffered any evil through Rafel Santoris or through Aselzion—I am pained and perplexed and tortured by what I hear and see—but my hearing and sight are capable of being deceived—why should I think of evil things which are not proved?"

The woman surveyed me with sudden scorn.

"So you will stay here, the dupe of your own sentiments and dreams!"—she said, contemptuously—"You, a woman, will remain among a community of men who are known impostors, and sacrifice your name and reputation to a mere chimera!"

Her look and manner had completely changed, and I was at once on my guard.

"My name and reputation are my own to protect,"—I answered, coldly- -"Whatever I do I shall be ready to answer for to anyone having the right to ask."

The old man now advanced and laid his hand on my arm. His eyes sparkled angrily.

"You must be saved from yourself"—he said, sharply, "You must come with us whether you will or no! We have seen too many victims of Aselzion's art already— we are resolved to save you from the peril which threatens you."

And he made an effort to draw me closer to him—but my spirit was up and I held back with all my force.

"No, I will not go with you!" I exclaimed, hotly—"God alone shall remove me from harm if any harm is really meant towards me. I do not believe one word you have said against Rafel Santoris or against Aselzion—I love the one, and I trust the other!—let me go my own way in peace!"

Hardly had I spoken these words when both the old man and woman threw themselves upon me and seizing me by force, endeavoured to drag me away with them. I resisted with all my strength, still holding tightly the book of the 'Secret of Life' in one hand. But their united efforts were beginning to overpower me, and feeling myself growing weaker and weaker I cried aloud in desperation:

"Rafel! Rafel!"

In an instant I stood free. My captors loosed their hold of me, and I rushed away, not knowing whither—only running, running, running, afraid of pursuit—till I suddenly found myself alone on the borders of a dark stretch of water spreading away in cold blackness to an unseen horizon.

XVIII

DREAMS WITHIN A DREAM

I stopped abruptly, brought perforce to a standstill. There was nothing but the black water heaving in front of me with a slow and dizzying motion and faintly illumined by a dim, pearly light like that of a waning moon. I looked behind me, fearing my persecutors were following, and saw that a thick mist filled the air and space to the obliteration of everything that might otherwise have been visible. I had thought it was day, and that the sun was shining, but now it appeared to be night. Utterly fatigued in body and mind, I sank down wearily on the ground, close to the edge of the strange dark flood which I could scarcely see. The quiet and deep obscurity had a lulling effect on my senses—and I thought languidly how good it would be if I might be allowed to rest where I was for an indefinite time.

"I can understand"—I said to myself—"why many people long for death and pray for it as a great blessing! They have lost love—and without love, life is valueless. To live on and on through cycles of time in worlds that are empty of all sweetness,—companionless and deprived of hope and comfort—this would be hell!—not heaven!"

"Hell—not heaven!" said a voice near me.

I started and looked up—a shadowy figure stood beside me—that of a woman in dark trailing garments, whose face shone with a pale beauty in the dim light surrounding us both.

"So you have found your way here at last!" she said, gently—"Here, where all things end, and nothing begins!"

I rose to my feet and confronted her.

"Where all things end!" I repeated—"Surely where life exists there is no end?"

She gave me a fleeting smile.

"Life is a dream,"—she said—"And the things of life are dreams within the dream! There are no realities. You imagine truths which are deceptions."

I looked at her in wonder and bewilderment. She was beautiful—and the calm sadness of her eyes expressed compassion and tenderness.

"Then—is Creation a lie?" I asked.

She made no immediate answer, but pointed with one hand towards the dark water. I looked, and uttered a cry of ecstasy—there, shining in the heaving blackness like a vision from fairyland, was the 'Dream'—glittering from stem to stern with light that sparkled like millions of diamonds!

"Your Dream of Love!" said the woman beside me—"Behold it for the last time!"

With straining eyes and beating heart I watched—and saw the shining vessel begin to sink slowly into the deep watery blackness—down, down still lower, till only her masts were visible—then something defiant and forceful sprang up within me,—I would master this torture, I thought—I would not yield to the agony that threatened to drive me to utter despair.

"This is a phantom of sorrow!"—I said—"It has no meaning! The love that is in my heart is my own!—it is my life, my soul, my inmost being!—it is eternal as God Himself, and to Him I commend it!"

I spoke these words aloud, holding the book of the 'Secret of Life' clasped to my breast—and raised my eyes trustfully to the dense darkness which should have been the sky. Then I felt the woman's hand on mine. Her touch was warm and gentle.

"Come!" she said, softly.

And I saw a small boat slip out on the gloomy water, guided towards me by One whose face was hidden in a fold of black. My companion drew me with her and signed to me to enter. Something in myself, as well as in her looks, impelled me to obey, and as she stepped into the boat I followed. We were borne along in silence for what seemed to me a long time, till suddenly I began to hear strange sounds of wailing, and shuddering cries of appeal, and our darkness was lightened by the drifting to and fro of pale forms that were luminous and human in shape though scarcely of human resemblance.

"What are these?" I whispered.

My companion took my hand and held it.

"Listen!" she answered.

And gradually, out of a clamour of weeping and complaint, I heard voices which uttered distinct things.

"I am the Phantom of Wealth"—said one—"For me men and nations have rushed on destruction,—for me they have sacrificed happiness and missed the way to God! For me innocence has been betrayed and honour murdered. I am but a Shadow, but the world follows me as if I were Light—I am but the gold dust of earth, and men take me for the glory of Heaven!"

"I am the Phantom of Fame"—said another—"I come with music and sweet promises—I float before the eyes of man, seeming to him an Angel!—I speak of triumph and power!—and for me brave hearts have broken, and bright spirits have been doomed to despair! I am but a Shadow—but the world believes me Substance—I am but a breath and a colour, but men take me for a fixed Star!"

"I am the Phantom of Pride!"—said a third voice—"For me humanity scales the height of ambition—for my sake king's and queens occupy uneasy thrones, and surround themselves with pomp and panoply—for me men lie and cheat and wrong their neighbours—for me the homes that should be happy are laid waste—for me false laws are made and evil conquers good I am but a Shadow—and the world takes me for the Sun!—I am but a passing flash of light, and men take me for the perfect Day!"

Other voices joined in and echoed wildly around me—and I rose up in the boat, loosing my hold from the clasp of the woman who was with me.

"You are phantoms all!" I cried, half unconscious of my own words— "I want God's angels! Where is Love?"

The voices ceased—the strange flitting figures that wailed round me faded away into mist, and disappeared—and a light, deep and golden and wonderful, began to shine through the gloom. My companion spoke.

"We have been looking at dreams,"—she said—"You ask for the only Real!"

I smiled. A sudden inrush of strength and authority possessed me.

"You bade me look my last upon my dream of Love!" I said—"But you knew that was impossible, for Love is no dream!"

The golden radiance widened into a perfect splendour, and our boat now glided over a shining sea. As in a vision I saw the figure that steered and guided it, change from darkness to brightness—the black fold fell from its face—Angel eyes looked at me—Angel lips smiled!—and then—I found myself suddenly alone on the shore of a little bay, blue as a sapphire in the reflection of the blue sky above it. The black stretch of water which had seemed so dreary and impassable had disappeared, and to my astonishment I recognised the very shore near the rock garden which was immediately under my turret room. I looked everywhere for the woman who had been in the boat with me—for the boat itself and its guide—but there was no trace of them. Where and how far I had wandered I could not imagine- -but presently, regaining nerve and courage, I began to fancy that perhaps my strange experience had been preordained and planned as some test of my faith and fortitude. Had I failed? Surely not! For I had not doubted the truth of God or the power of Love! There was only one thing which puzzled me,—the memory of those voices behind a wall—the voices which had spoken of Rafel's death and treachery. I could not quite rid myself of the anxiety they had awakened in my mind though I tried hard not to yield to the temptation of fear and suspicion. I knew and felt that after all it is the voices of the world which work most harm to love—and that neither poverty nor sorrow can cut the threads of affection between lovers so swiftly as falsehood and calumny. And yet I allowed myself to be moved by vague uneasiness on this account, and could not entirely regain perfect composure.

The door of the winding stair leading to my room in the turret stood open—and I availed myself of this tacit permission to return thither. I found everything as I had left it, except that when I sought for the mysterious little room hung with purple silk, where I had begun to read the book called 'The Secret of Life,' a book which through all my strange adventure I still had managed to keep with me, I could not find it. The walls around me were solid; there was no sign of an opening anywhere.

I sat down by the window to think. There before my eyes was the sea, calm, and in the full radiance of a brilliant sun. No mysterious or magic art suggested itself in the visible scene of a smiling summer day. Had I been long absent from this room, I wondered? I could not tell. Time seemed to be annihilated. And so far as I myself was concerned I desired nothing in this world or the next save just to know if Rafel Santoris still lived—and—yes!—one other assurance— to feel that I still possessed the treasure of his love. All the past, present and future hung on this possibility,—there was nothing more to hope for or to attain. For if I had lost Love, then God Himself could give me no comfort, since the essential link with Divine things was broken.

Gradually a great and soothing quietude stole over me and the cloud of depression that had hung over my mind began to clear. I thought of my recent experience with the man and woman who had sought to 'rescue' me, as they said, and how when in sheer desperation I had called "Rafel! Rafel!" they had suddenly disappeared and left me free. Surely this was a sufficient proof that I was not forgotten by him who had professed to love me?—and that his aid might still be depended upon? Why should I doubt him?

I had placed my book, 'The Secret of Life,' on the table when I re- entered my room—but now I took it up again, and the pages fell open at the following passage:—

"When once you possess the inestimable treasure of love, remember that every effort will be made to snatch it from you. There is nothing the world envies so much as a happy soul! Those who have been your dearest friends will turn against you because you have a joy in which they do not share,—they will unite with your foes to drag you down from your height of Paradise. The powers of the coarse and commonplace will be arrayed against you—shafts of disdain and ridicule will be hurled at your tenderest feelings,—venomous lies and cruel calumnies will be circulated around you,—all to try and draw you from the circle of light into darkness and chaos. If you would stand firm, you must stand within the whirlwind; if you would maintain the centre-poise of your Soul, you must preserve the balance of movement,—the radiant and deathless atoms whereof your Body and Spirit are composed must be under steady control and complete organisation like a well disciplined army, otherwise the disintegrating forces set up by the malign influences of others around you will not only attack your happiness, but your health, break down your strength and murder your peace. Love is the only glory of Life,—the Heart and Pulse of all things,—a possession denied to earth's greatest conquerors—a talisman which opens all the secrets of Nature—a Divinity whose power is limitless, and whose benediction bestows all beauty, all sweetness, all joy!

Bear this in mind, and never forget how such a gift is grudged to those who have it by those who have it not!"

Reading thus far, a light began to break in upon me. Had not all the weird and inexplicable experience of the past hours (or days) tended to shake me from Love and destroy my allegiance to the ideal I cherished? And—had I yielded to the temptation? Had I failed? I dared not estimate either failure or success!

Leaving my place at the window, I saw that the little 'lift' or dresser in the wall had come up noiselessly with its usual daintily prepared refection of fruit and bread and deliciously cool spring water. I had felt neither hunger nor thirst during my strange wanderings in unknown places, but now I was quite ready for a meal, and enjoyed it with all the zest of an unspoilt appetite. When I had finished, I returned to my precious book, and placing it on the table, I propped up my head between my two hands and set myself resolutely to study. And I write down here the passages I read, exactly as I found them, for those who care to practise the lessons they teach.

FREE-WILL

"The exercise of the Will is practically limitless. It is left unfettered so that we may be free to make our own choice of life and evolve our own destiny. It can command all things save Love, for Love is of God and God is not subject to authority. Love must be born IN the Soul and OF the Soul. It must be a dual flame,— that is to say, it must find its counterpart in another Soul which is its ordained mate, before it can fulfil its highest needs. Then, like two wings moved by the same soaring impulse, it assists the Will and carries it to the highest heaven. Through its force life is generated and preserved—without it, life escapes to other phases to find its love again. Nothing is perfect, nothing is lasting without the light and fire of this dual flame. It cannot be WILLED either to kindle or to burn; it must be born of itself and IN itself, and shed its glory on the souls of its own choice. All else is subject to order and command. Love alone is free."

POWER

"Power over all things and all men is obtained by organisation—that is to say, 'setting one's house in order.' The 'house' implied is the body in which the Soul has temporary dwelling; every corner of it must be 'in order,'—every atom working healthfully in its place without any suggestion of confusion. Then, whatever is desired shall be attained. Nothing in the Universe can resist the force of a steadfastly fixed resolve; what the Spirit truly seeks must, by eternal law, be given to it, and what the body needs for the fulfilment of the Spirit's commands will be bestowed. From the sunlight and the air and the hidden things of space strength shall be daily and hourly renewed; everything in Nature shall aid in bringing to the resolved Soul that which it demands. There is nothing within the circle of Creation that can resist its influence. Success, wealth, triumph upon triumph come to every human being who daily 'sets his house in order'—whom nothing can move from his fixed intent,—whom no malice can shake, no derision drive from his determined goal,—whom no temptation can drag from his appointed course, and who is proof against spite and calumny. For men's minds are for the most part like the shifting sands of the sea, and he alone rules who evolves Order from Chaos."

ETERNAL LIFE

"Life is eternal because it cannot die. Everything that lives MUST live for ever. Everything that lives has ALWAYS lived. What is called death, is by law impossible. Life is perpetually changing into various forms,—and every change it makes we call 'death' because to us it seems a cessation of life, whereas it is simply renewed activity. Every soul imprisoned to-day in human form has lived in human form before,—the very rose that flowers on its stem has flowered in this world before. Each individual Spirit preserves its individuality and, to a certain extent, its memory. It is permitted to remember a few out of the million incidents and episodes with which its psychic brain is stored, but ONLY a few during its period of evolvement. When it reaches the utmost height of spiritual capacity, and is strong enough to know and see and understand, then it will remember all from the beginning. Nothing can ever be forgotten, inasmuch as forgetfulness implies waste, and there is no waste in the scheme of the Universe. Every thought is kept for use,—every word, every sigh and tear is recorded. Life itself, in our limited view of it, can be continued indefinitely on this earth, if we use the means given to us to preserve and renew it. It was easy to preserve and prolong it in the early days of the world's prime, for our planet was then nearer to the sun. In the present day it is returning to a position in the heavens which encourages and sustains life—and men live longer without knowing why, never thinking that it is the result of the immediate situation of the planet with regard to the sun. The Earth is not where it was in the days of Christ; it has been rushing through space these two thousand years, and yet mankind forgets that its place in the heavens is different from that which it formerly occupied, and that with this difference the laws of climate, custom and living are changed. It is not Man who alters his surroundings—it is Nature, whose order cannot be disobeyed. Man thinks that the growth of science and what he calls his 'progress' is the result of his own cleverness alone; on the contrary, it is the result of a change in his atmospheric ether which not only helps scientific explanation and discovery, but which tends to give him greater power over the elements, as well as to prolong his life and intellectual capability. There is no such thing as 'standing still' in the Universe. Every atom, every organism is doing something, or going somewhere, and there is no stop. Rest itself is merely a form of Progress towards Beauty and Perfection, and there is no flaw anywhere in the majestic splendour of God's scheme for the ultimate happiness of His entire Creation."

ARROGANT ASCETICISM

"The ascetic is a blasphemer of God and of the work for which God alone is responsible. By withdrawing himself from the world of men he withdraws himself from human sympathy. By chastising the body and its natural emotions and desires, he chastises that which God has made as a temple for his soul to dwell in. By denying the pleasures of this world, he denies all the good which God has prepared and provided for him, and he wrongs the fair happiness of Nature and the order in which the Universe is planned. The so-called 'religious' person who retires into a monastery, there to pray and fast and bemoan the ills of the flesh, is an unnatural creature and displeasing to his Maker. For God looked upon everything He had made and found it 'good.' Good—not bad, as the arrogant ascetic would assume. Joy, not sorrow, should be the keynote of life—the world is not a 'vale of tears' but a flower-filled garden, basking in the perpetual sunshine of the smile of God. What is called 'sin' is the work of Man—God has no part in it. 'By pride the angels fell.' By pride Man delays his eternal delight. When he presumes to be wiser than his Creator,—when he endeavours to upset the organisation of Nature, and invents a kind of natural and moral code of his own, then comes disaster. The rule of a pure and happy life is to take all that God sends with thankfulness in moderation—the fruits of the earth, the joys of the senses, the love of one's fellow- creatures, the delights of the intellect, the raptures of the soul; and to find no fault with that which is and must ever be faultless. We hear of wise men and philosophers sorrowing over 'the pain and suffering of the world'—but the pain and suffering are wrought by Man alone, and Man's cruelty to his fellows. From Man's culpable carelessness and neglect of the laws of health has come every disease, as from Man's egotism, unbelief and selfishness have sprung all the crimes in the calendar." I paused here, for it seemed to me that it was getting dark,—at any rate I could not see to read very clearly. I looked at the window, but very little light came through it,—a sudden obscurity, like a heavy cloud, darkened all visible things. I quickly made up my mind that I would not yield to any more fanciful terrors, or leave the room, even if I saw another outlet that night. With this determination I undressed quickly and went to bed. As I laid my head on the pillow I felt a kind of coldness in the air which made me shiver a little—an 'uncanny' sensation to which I would not yield. I saw the darkness thickening round me, and closed my eyes, resolving to rest—and so succeeded in ordering all my faculties to this end that within a very few minutes I was soundly asleep.

XIX

THE UNKNOWN DEEP

My slumber was so profound and dreamless that I have no idea how long it lasted, but when finally I awoke it was with a sense of the most vivid and appalling terror. Every nerve in my body seemed paralysed—I could not move or cry out,— invisible bands stronger than iron held me a prisoner on my bed—and I could only stare upwards in horror as a victim bound to the rack might stare at the pitiless faces of his torturers. A Figure, tall, massive and clothed in black, stood beside me—I could not see its face—but I felt its eyes gazing down upon me with a remorseless, cold inquisitiveness—a silent, searching enquiry which answered itself without words. If every thought in my brain and every emotion of my soul could have been cut out of me with a dissecting knife and laid bare to outward inspection, those terrible eyes, probing deep into the very innermost recesses of my being, would have done the work.

The beating of my heart sounded loud and insistent in my own ears,— I lay still, trying to gain control over my trembling spirit,—and it was almost with an awful sense of relief that I saw the figure move at last from its rigid attitude and beckon me—beckon slowly and commandingly with one outstretched arm from which the black, dank draperies hung like drifting cloud. Mechanically obeying the signal, I strove to rise from my bed—and found that I could do so,- -I sat up shiveringly, looking at the terrifying Form that towered above me, enclosing me as it were in its own shadow—and then, managing to stand on my feet, though unsteadily, I mutely prepared to follow where it should lead. It moved on—and I went after it, compelled by some overpowering instinct against which I dared not rebel. Once the vague, half-formed thought flitted through my brain- -"This is Death that summons me away,"—till with the thought came the remembrance that according to the schooling I was receiving, there is no such thing as 'Death,' but only the imaginary phantom we call by that name.

Slowly, sedately, and with an indescribable majesty of movement, the dark Figure glided on before me, and I, a trembling little creature, followed it, I knew not whither. There was no obstacle in our course,—doors, walls and windows seemed to melt asunder into nothingness as we passed—and there was no stop to our onward progress till suddenly I saw before me a steep and narrow spiral stairway of stone winding up into the very centre of a rocky pinnacle, which in its turn lifted its topmost peak into the darkness of a night sky sprinkled with millions of stars. The sombre Figure paused: and again I felt the search-light of its invisible eyes burning through me. Then, as though satisfied with its brief survey, it began to ascend the spiral stair.

I followed step by step,—the way was long and difficult—the sharp turns dizzying to the senses, and there seemed no end to the upward winding. Sometimes I stumbled and nearly fell—sometimes I groped on hands and knees, always seeing before me the black-draped Form that moved on with such apparently little care as to whether or no I fared ill or well in my obedience to its summons.

And now, as I climbed, all sorts of strange memories began to creep into the crannies of my brain and perplex me with trouble and uncertainty. Chiefly did my mind dwell on cruelties—the cruelties practised by human beings to one another,—moral cruelties especially, they being so much worse than any physical torture. I thought of the world's wicked misjudgments passed on those who are greater in spirit than itself,—how, even when we endeavour to do good to others, our kindest actions are often represented as merely so many forms of self-interest and self-seeking,—how our supposed 'best' friends often wrong us and listen credulously to enviously invented tales against us,—how even in Love—ah!-Love!—that most etherial yet most powerful of passions!—a rough word, an unmerited slight, may separate for a lifetime those whose love would otherwise have been perfect. And still I climbed, and still I thought, and still the dark Phantom-Figure beckoned me on and on.

And then I began to consider that in climbing to some unknown, unseen height in deep darkness I was, after all, doing a wiser thing than living in the world with the ways of the world,—ways that are for the most part purely hypocritical, and are practised merely to overreach and out-do one's fellow-men and women—ways of fashion, ways of society, ways of government which are merely temporary, while Nature, the invincible and eternal, moves on her appointed course with the same inborn intuition, namely, to destroy that which is evil and preserve only that which is good. And Man, the sole maker of evil, the only opposer of Divine Order, fools himself into the belief that his evil shall prosper and his falsehood be accepted as truth, if he can only sham a sufficient show of religious faith to deceive himself and others on the ascending plane of History. He who has invented Sin has likewise invented a God to pardon it, for there is no sin in the natural Universe. The Divine Law cannot pardon, for it is inviolate and bears no trespass without punishment.

So I mused in my inward self, and still I climbed, keeping my eyes fixed on the Figure that led me on, and which now, having reached the end of the spiral stair, was slowly mounting to the highest peak of the rocky pinnacle which lifted itself to the stars. An icy wind began to blow,—my feet were bare, and I was thinly clad in my night-gear with only the addition of a white woollen wrap I had hastily flung round me for warmth when I left my bed to follow my spectral leader—and I shivered through and through with the bitter cold. Yet I went on resolutely,— indeed, having started on this perilous adventure, there was no returning, for when I looked back on the way I had come, the spiral stair had completely vanished, and there was nothing but black and empty space!

This discovery so terrified me that for the moment I lost breath, and I came to a halt in the very act of ascending. Then I saw the Figure in front of me turn round with a threatening movement, and I felt that with one second more of hesitation I should lose my footing altogether and slip away into some vast abysmal depth of unimaginable doom. Making a strong effort, I caught back my escaping self-control, and forced my shuddering limbs to obey my will and resume their work-and so, slowly, inch by inch, I resumed my climb, sick with giddiness and fear and chilled to the very heart. Presently I heard a rumbling roar like the sound of great billows rushing into hollow caverns which echoed their breaking in thuds of booming thunder. Looking up, I saw the Figure I had followed standing still; and I fancied that the sombre draperies in which it was enveloped showed an outline of glimmering light. Fired by a sudden hope, I set myself to tread the difficult path anew, and presently I too stood still, beside my mysterious Leader. Above me was a heaven of stars;—below an unfathomable deep of darkness where nothing was visible;—but from this nothingness arose a mighty turbulence as of an angry sea. I remained where I found myself, afraid to move;—one false step might, I felt, hurl me into a destruction which though it would not be actual death would certainly be something like chaos. Almost I felt inclined to catch at the cloudy garments of the solemn Figure at my side for safety and protection, and while this desire was yet upon me it turned its veiled head towards me and spoke in a low, deep tone that was infinitely gentle.

"So far!—and yet not far enough!" it said—"To what end wilt thou adventure for the sake of Love?"

"To no End whatsoever,"—I answered with sudden boldness—"But to everlasting Continuance!"

Again I thought I saw a faint glowing light within its sombre draperies.

"What wouldst thou do for Love?" its voice again enquired—"Wouldst thou bear all things and believe all things? Canst thou listen to falsehood bearing witness against truth, and yet love on? Wilt thou endure all suffering, all misunderstanding, all coldness and cruelty, and yet keep thy soul bright as a burning lamp with the flame of faith and endeavour? Wouldst thou scale the heavens and plunge to the uttermost hell for the sake of him thou lovest, knowing that thy love must make him one with thee at the God- appointed hour?"

I looked up at the Figure, vainly striving to see its face.

"All these things I would do!" I answered—"All that is in the power of my soul to endure mortally or immortally, I will bear for Love's sake!"

Again the light flashed through its black garments. When it next spoke, its voice rang out harshly in ominous warning.

"Thy lover is dead!" it proclaimed—"He has passed from this sphere to another, and ye shall not meet again for many cycles of time! DOST THOU BELIEVE IT?"

A cold agony gripped my breast, but I would not yield to it, and answered resolutely—

"No! I do not believe it! He could not die without my knowing and feeling the parting of his soul from mine!"

There was a pause, in which only the thunder of that invisible sea far down below us was audible. Then the voice went on,

"Thy lover is false!" it said—"His love for thee was a passing mood—already he regrets—already he wearies in thought of thee and loves thee no more! DOST THOU BELIEVE IT?"

I took no time for thought, but answered at once without hesitation- -

"No! For if he does not love me his Spirit lies!—and no Spirit CAN lie!"

Another pause. Then the voice put this question—

"Dost thou truly believe in God, thy Creator, the Maker of heaven and earth?"

Lifting my eyes half in hope, half in appeal to the starry deep sky above me, I replied fervently—

"I do believe in Him with all my soul!"

A silence followed which seemed long and weighted with suspense. Then the voice spoke once more—

"Dost thou believe in Love, the generator of Life and the moving Cause and Mind of all created things?"

And again I replied—

"With all my soul!"

The Figure now bent slightly towards me, and the light within its darkness became more denned and brilliant. Presently an arm and hand, white and radiant—a shape as of living flame—was slowly outstretched from the enfolding black draperies. It pointed steadily to the abyss below me.

"If thy love is so great"—said the voice—"If thy faith is so strong—if thy trust in God is sure and perfect—descend thither!"

I heard—but could not credit my own hearing. I gazed at the shrouded and veiled speaker—at the commanding arm that signed my mortal body to destruction. For a moment I was lost in wild terror and wilder doubt. Was this fearful suggestion a temptation or a test? Should it be obeyed? I strove to find the centre-poise of my own self—to gather all my forces together,—to make myself sure of my own will and responsible for my own deeds,—and then—then I paused. All that was purely mortal in me shuddered on the brink of the Unknown. One look upward to the soft gloom of the purple sky and its myriad stars—one horrified glance downward at the dark depth where I heard the roaring of the sea! I clasped my hands in a kind of prayerful desperation, and looked once more at the solemn Shadow beside me.

"If thy love is so great!" it repeated, in slow and impressive tones—"If thy faith is so strong! If thy trust in God is so sure and perfect!"

There came a moment of tense stillness—a moment in which my life seemed detached from myself so that I held it like a palpitating separate creature in my hands, Suddenly the recollection of the last vision of all those I had seen among the dark mountains of Coruisk came back to me vividly—that of the woman who had knelt outside a barred gate in Heaven, waiting to enter in—"O leave her not always exiled and alone!" I had prayed then—"Dear God, have pity! Unbar the gate and let her in! She has waited so long!"

A sob broke unconsciously from my lips—my eyes filled with burning tears that blinded me. Imploringly I turned towards the relentless Figure beside me once more—its hand still pointed downwards—and again I seemed to hear the words—

"If thy love is so great! If thy faith is so strong! If thy trust in God is so sure and perfect!"

And then I suddenly found my own Soul's centre,—the very basis of my own actual being—and standing firmly upon that plane of imperishable force, I came to a quick resolve.

"Nothing can destroy me!" I said within myself—"Nothing can slay the immortal part of me, and nothing can separate my soul from the soul of my beloved! In all earth, in all heaven, there is no cause for fear!"

Hesitating no longer, I closed my eyes,—then extending my clasped hands I threw myself forward and plunged into the darkness!—down, down, interminably down! A light followed me like a meteoric shaft of luminance piercing the blackness—I retained sufficient consciousness to wonder at its brilliancy, and for a time I was borne along in my descent as though on wings. Down, still down!—and I saw ocean at my feet!—a heaving mass of angry waters flecked with a wool-like fleece of foam!

"The Change that is called Death, but which is Life!"

This was the only clear thought that flashed like lightning through my brain as I sank swiftly towards the engulfing desert of the sea!- -then everything swirled into darkness and silence!

* * *
* *
*

A delicate warm glow like the filtering of sunbeams through shaded silk and crystal—a fragrance of roses—a delicious sound of harp- like music—to these things I was gradually awakened by a gentle pressure on my brows. I looked up—and my whole heart relieved itself in a long deep sigh of ecstasy!—it was Aselzion himself who bent over me,—Aselzion whose grave blue eyes watched me with earnest and anxious solicitude. I smiled up at him in response to his wordless questioning as to how I felt, and would have risen but that he imperatively signed to me to lie still.

"Rest!" he said,—and his voice was very low and tender. "Rest, poor child! You have done more than well!"

Another sigh of pure happiness escaped me,—I stretched out my arms lazily like one aroused from a long and refreshing slumber. My sensations were now perfectly exquisite; a fresh and radiant life seemed pouring itself through my veins, and I was content to remain a perfectly passive recipient of such an inflow of health and joy. The room I found myself in was new to me—it seemed made up of lovely colourings and a profusion of sweet flowers—I lay enshrined as it were in the centre of a little temple of beauty. I had no desire to move or to speak,—every trouble, every difficulty had passed from my mind, and I watched Aselzion dreamily as he brought a chair to the side of my couch and sat down—then, taking my hand in his, felt my pulse with an air of close attention.

I smiled again.

"Does it still beat?" I asked, finding my voice suddenly—"Surely the great sea has drowned it!"

Still holding my hand, he looked full into my eyes.

"'Many waters cannot quench love'!" he quoted softly. "Dear child, you have proved that truth. Be satisfied!"

Raising myself on my pillows, I studied his grave face with an earnest scrutiny.

"Tell me,"—I half whispered—"Have I failed?"

He pressed my hand encouragingly.

"No! You have almost conquered!"

Almost! Only 'almost'! I sank back again on the couch, wondering and waiting. He remained beside me quite silent. After a little the tension of suspense became unbearable and I spoke again—

"How did I escape?" I asked—"Who saved me when I fell?"

He smiled gravely.

"There was nothing to escape from"—he answered—"And no one saved you since you were not in danger."

"Not in danger!" I echoed, amazed.

"No! Only from yourself!"

I gazed at him, utterly bewildered. He gave me a kind and reassuring glance.

"Have patience!" he said, gently—"All shall be explained to you in good time! Meanwhile this apartment is yours for the rest of your stay here, which will not now be long—I have had all your things removed from the Probation room in the tower, so that you will no more be troubled by its scenic transformations!" Here he smiled again. "I will leave you now to recover from the terrors through which you have passed so bravely;—rest and refresh yourself thoroughly, for you have nothing more to fear. When you are quite ready touch this"—and he pointed to a bell—"I shall hear its summons and will come to you at once."

Before I could say a word to detain him, he had retired, and I was left alone.

I rose from my couch,—and the first impression I had was that of a singular ease and lightness—a sense of physical strength and well- being that was delightful beyond expression. The loveliness and peace of the room in which I was enchant- ed me,—everything my eyes rested upon suggested beauty. The windows were shaded with rose silk hangings—and when I drew these aside I looked out on a marble loggia or balcony overhung with climbing roses,—this, in its turn, opened on an exquisite glimpse of garden and blue sea. There was no clock anywhere to tell me the time of day, but the sun was shining, and I imagined it must be afternoon. Adjoining this luxurious apartment was an equally luxurious bathroom, furnished with every conceivable elegance,—the bath itself was of marble, and the water bubbled up from its centre like a natural spring, sparkling as it came. I found all my clothes, books and other belongings arranged with care where I could most easily get at them, and to my joy the book 'The Secret of Life,' which I thought I had lost on my last perilous adventure, lay on a small table by itself like a treasure set apart.

I bathed and dressed quickly, allowing myself no time to think upon any strange or perplexing point in my adventures, but giving myself entirely up to the joy of the new and ecstatic life which thrilled through me. A mirror in the room showed me my own face, happy and radiant,—my own eyes bright and smiling,—no care seemed to have left a trace on my features, and I was fully conscious of a perfect strength and health that made the mere act of breathing a pleasure. In a very short time I was ready to receive Aselzion, and I touched the bell he had indicated as a signal. Then I sat down by the window and looked out on the fair prospect before me. How glorious was the world, I thought!—how full of perfect beauty! That heavenly blue of sky and sea melting into one—the tender hues of the clambering roses against the green of the surrounding foliage—the lovely light that filtered through the air like powdered gold!—were not all these things to be thankful for? and can there be any real unhappiness so long as our Souls are in tune with the complete harmony of Creation?

Hearing a step behind me, I rose—and with a glad smile stretched out my hands to Aselzion, who had just then entered. He took them in his own and pressed them lightly—then drawing a chair opposite to mine, he sat down. His face expressed a certain gravity, and his voice when he began to speak was low and gentle.

"I have much to tell you"—he said—"but I will make it as brief as I can. You came here to pass a certain psychic ordeal—and you have passed it successfully—all but the last phase. Of that we will speak presently. For the moment you are under the impression that you have been through certain episodes of a more or less perplexing and painful nature. So you have—but not in the way you think. Nothing whatever has happened to you, save in your own mind—your adventures have been purely mental—and were the result of several brains working on yours and compelling you to see and to hear what they chose. There!—do not look so startled!"—for I had risen with an involuntary exclamation—"I will explain everything quite clearly, and you will soon understand."

He paused—and I sat down again by the window, wondering and waiting.

"In this world," he went on, slowly—"it is not climate, or natural surroundings that affect man so much as the influences brought to bear upon him by his fellow-men. Human beings really live surrounded by the waves of thought flung off by their own brains and the brains of those around them,—and this is the reason why, if they are not strong enough to find a centre-poise, they are influenced by ways and moods of thought which would never be their own by choice and free-will. If a mind, or let us say a Soul, can resist the impressions brought to bear upon it by other forces than itself—if it can stand alone, clear of obstacle, in the light of the Divine Image, then it has gained a mastership over all things. But the attainment of such a position is difficult enough to be generally impossible. Influences work around us everywhere,—men and women with great aims in life are swept away from their intentions by the indifference or discouragement of their friends—brave deeds are hindered from accomplishment by the suggestion of fears which do not really exist—and the daily scattering and waste of psychic force and powerful mentality by disturbing or opposing brain-waves, is sufficient to make the world a perfect paradise were it used to that end."

He waited a moment—then bent his eyes earnestly upon me as he resumed—

"You do not need to be told by me that you have lived on this earth before, and that you have many times been gently yet forcibly drawn into connection with the other predestined half of yourself,—that Soul of love which blindly seeking, you have often rejected when found—not of yourself have you rejected it—but simply because of the influences around you to which you have yielded. Now in this further phase of your existence you have been given another chance— another opportunity. It is quite possible that had you not come to me you would have lost your happiness again, and it was this knowledge which made me receive you, against all the rules of our Order, when I saw that you were fairly resolved. Your ordeal would have been longer had you not made the first bold advance yourself on the occasion of your entrance into our chapel. The light of the Cross and Star drew you, and your Soul obeyed the attraction of its native element. Had you opposed its intention by doubts and fears, I should have had more trouble with you than I should have cared to undertake. But you made the first step yourself with a rare courage- -the rest was comparatively easy."

He paused again and again went on.

"I have already said that you are under the impression of having gone through certain adventures or episodes, which have more or less distressed and perplexed you. These things have had NO EXISTENCE except in your mind! When I took you up to your room in the turret, I placed you under my influence and under the influence of four other brains acting in conjunction with myself. We took entire possession of your mentality, and made it as far as possible like a blank slate, on which we wrote what we chose. The test was to see whether your Soul, which is the actual You, could withstand and overcome our suggestions. At first hearing, this sounds as if we had played a trick upon you for our own entertainment—but it is not so,—it is merely an application of the most powerful lesson in life— namely, THE RESISTANCE AND CONQUEST OF THE INFLUENCES OF OTHERS, which are the most disturbing and weakening forces we have to con- tend with."

I began to see clearly what he meant me to understand, and I hung upon his words with eager attention.

"You have only to look about you in the world," he continued—"to realise the truth of what I say. Every day you may meet some soul whose powers of accom- plishment might be superb if it were not for the restricting influences to which it allows itself to succumb. How often do you not come upon a man or woman of brilliant genius, who is nevertheless rendered incompetent by opposing influ- ences, and who therefore lives the life of a bird in a cage! Take the thousands of men wrongly mated, whose very wives and children drag them down and kill every spark of ambition and accomplishment within them! Take the thousands of women persuaded or forced into unions with men whose low estimate of woman's intellect coarsens and degrades her to a level from which it is almost impossible to rise! This is the curse of 'influences'—the magnetic currents of other brains which set our own awry, and make half the trouble and mischief in the world. Not one soul in a hundred thousand has force or courage to resist them! The man accustomed to live with a wife who without doing any other harm, simply kills his genius by the mere fact of her daily contact, moods, and methods, makes no effort to shake himself free from the apathy her influence causes, but simply sinks passively into inaction. The woman, bound to a man who insists on considering her lower than himself, and often pulled this way and that by the selfish desires or aims of her children or other family belongings, becomes a mere domestic drudge or machine, with no higher aims than are contained in the general order- ing of household business. Love,—the miraculous touchstone which turns every- thing to gold,—is driven out of the circle of Life with the result that Life itself grows weary of its present phase, and makes haste to seek another more congen- ial. Hence proceeds what we call age and death."

I was about to interrupt by an eager question—but he silenced me by a gesture.

"Your position," he went on—"from a psychic standard,—which is the only nec-essary, because the only lasting attitude,—is that of being brought into connec-tion with the other half of your spiritual and immortal Ego,—which means the possession of perfect love, and with it perfect life. And because this is so great a gift, and so entirely Divine, influences are bound to offer opposition in order that the Soul may make its choice VOLUNTARILY. Therefore, when I, and the other brains acting with me, placed you under our power, we impressed you with all that most readily shakes the feminine mind— doubt, jealousy, suspicion, and all the wretched terrors these wretched emotions engender. We suggested the death of Rafel Santoris as well as his treachery,—you heard, as you thought, voices behind a wall—but there were no voices—only the suggestion of voices in your mind. You saw strange phantoms and shadows,—they had no existence except in so far as we made them exist and present themselves to your mental vision. You wandered away into unknown places, so you imagined,—but as a matter of fact you NEVER LEFT YOUR ROOM!"

"Never left my room!" I echoed—"Oh, that cannot be!"

"It can be, because it is!" he answered me, smiling gravely—"The only thing in your experience that was REAL was the finding of the book 'The Secret of Life'— in the purple-draped shrine. Here it is"- -and he took it up from the table on which it lay—"and if you had turned it over a little more, you would have found this"—and he read aloud—

"'All action is the material result of Thought. Suffering is the result of THINK-ING INTO PAIN—disease the result of THINKING INTO WEAKNESS. Every emotion is the result of wrong or right THINKING, with one exception— Love. Love is not an Emotion but a Principle, and as the generator of Life per-vades all things, and is all things. Thought, working WITHIN this Principle, cre-ates the things of beauty and lastingness,—Thought, working OUTSIDE this Principle, equally creates the things of terror, doubt, confusion, and destruction. There is no other Secret of Life—no other Elixir of Youth—no other Immortality!'"

He pronounced the last words with gentle and impressive emphasis, and a great sweetness and calm filled my mind as I listened.

"I—or I should say we—for four of my Brethren were deeply interested in you on account of the courage you had shown—we took you up to the utmost height of endurance in the way of mental terror—and, to our great joy, found your Soul strong enough to baffle and conquer the ultimate suggestion of Death itself. You held firmly to the truth that there is NO death, and with that spiritual certainty risked all for Love. Now we have released you from our spells!"—and his eyes were full of kindness as he looked at me— "and I want to know if you thoroughly realise the importance of the lesson we have taught?"

I met his enquiring glance fully and steadily.

"I think I do,"—I said—"You mean that I must stand alone?"

"Alone, yet not alone!"—he answered, and his fine face was transfigured into light with its intense feeling and power—"Alone with Love!—which is to say alone with God, and therefore surrounded by all god-like, lasting and revivifying things. You will go back from this place to the world of conventions,—and you will meet a million influences to turn you from your chosen way. Opinion, criticism, ridicule, calumny and downright misunderstanding—these will come out against you like armed foes, bristling at every point with weapons of offence. If you tell them of your quest of life and youth and love, and of your experience here, they will cover you with their mockery and derision—if you were to breathe a word of the love between you and Rafel Santoris, a thousand efforts would be instantly made to separate you, one from the other, and snatch away the happiness you have won. How will you endure these trials?—what will be your method of action?"

I thought a moment.

"The same that I have tried to practise here"—I answered—"I shall believe nothing of ill report—but only of good."

He bent his eyes upon me searchingly.

"Remember," he said—"what force there is in a storm of opinion! The fiercest gale that ever blew down strong trees and made havoc of men's dwellings is a mere whisper compared with the fury of human minds set to destroy one heaven-aspiring soul! Think of the petty grudge borne by the loveless against Love!—the spite of the restless and unhappy against those who have won peace! All this you will have to bear,—for the world is envious—and even a friend breaks down in the strength of friendship when thwarted or rendered jealous by a greater and more resistless power!" I sighed a little.

"I have few friends,"—I said—"Certainly none that have ever thought it worth while to know my inner and truest self. Most of them are glad to be my friends if

I go THEIR way—but if I choose a way of my own their 'friendship' becomes mere quarrel. But I talk of choosing a way! How can I choose—yet? You say my ordeal is not over?"

"It will be over to-night,"—he answered—"And I have every hope that you will pass through it unflinchingly. You have not heard from Santoris?"

The question gave me a little thrill of surprise.

"Heard from him?—No"—I replied—"He never suggested writing to me."

Aselzion smiled.

"He is too closely in touch with you to need other correspondence,"- -he said— "But be satisfied that he is safe and well. No misadventure has befallen him."

"Thank God!" I murmured. "And—if—"

"If he loves you no more,"—went on Aselzion—"If he has made an 'error of selection' as the scientists would say, and is not even now sure of his predestined helper and inspirer whose love will lift him to the highest attainment—what then?"

"What then? Why, I must submit!" I answered, slowly—"I can wait, even for another thousand years!"

There was a silence, during which I felt Aselzion's eyes upon me. Then he spoke again in a lighter tone.

"Let us for the moment talk of what the world calls 'miracle'"—he said—"I believe you are just now conscious of perfect health, and of a certain joy in the mere fact of life. Is it not so?"

Smiling, I bent my head in acquiescence.

"Understand then"—he continued—"that while you control the life- forces of which you are made, by the power of an all-commanding spirit, this perfect health, this certain joy will continue. And more than this—everything in Nature will serve you to this end. You have but to ask your servants and they will obey. Ask of the sun its warmth and radiance,—it will answer with a quick bestowal— ask of the storm and wind and rain their powers of passion,—they will give you their all,—ask of the rose its fragrance and colour, and the very essence of it shall steal into your blood,—there is nothing you shall seek that you will not find. Try your own powers now!"— and with the word he got up and opened the window a little wider, then signed to me to step out on the balcony—"Here are roses climbing up on their appointed way—bend them to-wards you by a single effort of the will!"

I gazed at him in complete surprise and bewilderment. His answering looks were imperative.

"By a single effort of the will!" he repeated.

I obeyed him. Raising my eyes to the roses where they clambered upwards round the loggia, I inwardly commanded them to turn towards me. The effect was instantaneous. As though blown by a light breeze they all bent down with their burden of bright blossom—some of the flowers touching my hands.

"That would be called 'miraculous' by the ignorant," said Aselzion— "And it is nothing more than the physical force of the magnetic light-rays within you, which, being focused in a single effort, draw the roses down pliantly to your will. No more miracle is there in this than that of the common magnet which has been vainly trying to teach us lessons about ourselves these many years. Now, relax your will!"

Again I obeyed, and the roses moved gently away and upward to their former branching height.

"This is an object lesson for you,"—said Aselzion, smiling then— "You must understand that you are now in a position to draw everything to you as easily as you drew those roses! You can draw the germs of health and life to mix and mingle with your blood—or— you can equally draw the germs of disease and disintegration. The ACTION is with you. From the sun you can draw fresh fuel for your brain and nerves—from the air the sustenance you demand—from beautiful things their beauty, from wise things their learning, from powerful things their force—NOTHING can resist the radiating energy you possess if you only remember HOW to employ it. In every action it must be focused on the given point—it must not be disturbed or scattered. The more often it is used the more powerful it becomes— the more all-conquering. But never forget that it must work WITHIN the Creative Principle of Love—not outside it."

I sat absorbed and half afraid.

"And to-night—?" I said, softly.

He rose from his chair and stood up to his full superb stature, looking down upon me with a certain mingling of kindness and pity.

"To-night,"—he replied—"we shall send for you! You will confront the Brethren, as one who has passed the same mental test through which they are passing! And you will face the last fear! I do not think you will go back upon yourself—I hope not—I strongly desire you to keep your courage to the end!"

I ventured to touch his hand.

"And afterwards?" I queried.

He smiled.

"Afterwards—Life and its secrets are all with you and Love!"

XX

INTO THE LIGHT

When I was left alone once more I gave myself up to the enchanting sense of perfect happiness that now seemed to possess my whole being. The world of glorious Nature showed me an aspect of brilliancy and beauty that could no more be shadowed by fear or foreboding—it was a mirror in which I saw reflected the perfect Mind of the Divine. Nothing existed to terrify or daunt the advancing Soul which had become cognisant of its own capabilities, and which, by the very laws governing it, is preordained to rise to the utmost height of supernal power. I had dimly guessed this truth- -but I had never surely known it till now. Now, I recognised that everything is and must be subservient to this interior force which exists to 'replenish the earth and subdue it'—and that nothing can hinder the accomplishment of its resolved Will. As I sat by the window thinking and dreaming, I began to wonder what would be the nature of that 'last fear' of which Aselzion had spoken? Why should the word 'fear' be mentioned, when there was no cause for fear of any kind? Fear can only arise from a sense of cowardice,—and cowardice is the offspring of weakness. From this argument it followed that my strength was not yet thoroughly tested to Aselzion's satisfaction,—that he still thought it possible that some latent weakness in my spirit might display itself on further trial. And I resolved that if such was his idea, he should be proved wrong. Nothing, I vowed, should move me now—not all the world arrayed in arms against me should hinder my advance towards the completion of myself in the love of my Beloved!

I have already said that there was no visible chronicle of time in the House of Aselzion, save such as was evidenced by the broadening or waning light of day. Just now I knew it was late afternoon, as the window where I sat faced the west, and the sun was sinking in a blaze of glory immediately opposite to me. Bars of gold and purple and pale blue formed a kind of cloud gateway across the heavens, and behind this the splendid orb shone in a halo of deep rose. Watching the royal pageantry of colour on all sides, I allowed myself to go forth as it were in spirit to meet and absorb it,—inwardly I set my whole being in tune with the great wave of light which opened itself over the sea and land, and as I did so found every nerve in my body thrilled with responsive ecstasy, even as harpstrings may be thrilled into sound by the sweep of the wind. I rose and went out, through the loggia into the garden—feeling more like a disembodied spirit than a mortal, so light and free and joyous were my very movements—so entirely in unison was I with everything in Nature. The sunset bathed me in its ruby and purple magnificence,—I lifted my eyes to the heavens and murmured almost unconsciously— "Thank God for Life! Thank God for Love! Thank God for all that Life and Love must bring to me!"

A sea-gull soaring inland flew over my head with a little cry—its graceful poise reminded me of the days I had passed in Morton Harland's yacht, when I had watched so many of these snow-white creatures dipping into the waves, and soaring up again to the skies- -and on a sudden impulse I stretched out my hand, determining to stay the bird's flight if I could and bring it down to me. The effort succeeded,—slowly, and as if checked by some obstacle it felt but could not see, the lovely winged thing swept round and round in an ever descending circle and finally alighted on my wrist. I held it so for a moment—it turned its head towards me, its ruby- brown eyes sparkling in the sun—then I tossed it off again into the air of its own freedom, where after another circling sweep or two it disappeared, and I walked on in a happy reverie, realising that what I could do with the visible things of Nature I could do as easily with the invisible. A sense of power vibrated through me [Footnote: The philosophy of Plato teaches that Man originally by the power of the Divine Image within him could control all Nature, but gradually lost this power through his own fault.]—power to command, and power to resist,—power that forbade all hesitation, vacillation or uncertainty— power which being connected by both physical and spiritual currents with this planet, the Earth, and the atmosphere by which it is surrounded, lifts all that it desires towards itself, as it rejects what it does not need.

Returning slowly through the garden, and lingering by the beds of flowers that adorned it, I noticed how when I bent over any particular blossom, it raised itself towards me as though drawn upward by a magnet. I was not inclined to gather a single one for my own pleasure—some occult sympathy had become established between me and these beautiful creations—and I could no more sever a rose from its stem than I could kill a bird that sang its little song to me. On re-entering my room I found the usual refection prepared for me— fresh fruit and bread and water—the only kind of food I was allowed. It was quite sufficient for me,—in fact I had not felt at any time the sensation of hunger. I began to wonder how long I had been a 'probationer' in the House of Aselzion? Days or weeks? I could not tell. I was realising the full truth that with the things of the infinite time has no existence, and I recalled the verse of the ancient psalm:

"A thousand ages in Thy sight Are like an evening gone, Short as the watch that ends the night Before the rising sun."

And while my thoughts ran in this groove, I opened the book of the 'Secret of Life'—and as if in answer to my inward communing, found the following:

THE DELUSION OF TIME

"Time has no existence outside this planet. Humanity counts its seasons, its days and hours by the Sun—but beyond the Sun there are millions and trillions of other and larger suns, compared with which our guiding orb is but a small star. Out in the infinitude of space there is no Time, but only Eternity. Therefore the Soul which knows itself to be eternal should associate Itself with eternal things, and should never count its existence by years. To its Being there can be no end—therefore it never ages and never dies. It is only the sham religionists who talk of death,—it is only the inefficient and unspiritual who talk of age. The man who allows himself to sink into feebleness and apathy merely because of the passing of years has some mental or spiritual weakness in him which he has not the Will to overcome—the woman who suffers her beauty and freshness to wane and fade on account of what she or her 'dearest' friends are pleased to call 'age,' shows that she is destitute of spiritual self-control. The Soul is always young, and its own radiation can preserve the youth of the Body in which it dwells. Age and decrepitude come to those with whom the Soul is 'an unknown quantity.' The Soul is the only barrier against the forces of disintegration which break down effete substances in preparation for the change which humanity calls 'Death.' If the barrier is not strong enough, the enemy takes the city. These facts are simple and true; too simple and too true to be accepted by the world. The world goes to church and asks a Divinity to save its soul, practically showing in all its ways of society and government an utter disbelief in the Soul's existence. Men and women die when they might as well have lived. If we examine into the cause of their deaths we shall find it in the manner of their lives. Obstinacy and selfishness have murdered more human beings than any other form of plague. The blasphemy of sham religion has insulted the majesty of the Creator more than any other form of sin, and He has answered it by His Supreme Silence. The man who attends a ritual of prayer which he does not honestly believe in, merely for the sake of social custom and observance, is openly deriding his Maker and the priests who gain their living out of such ritual are trading on the Divine. Let the people of this Earth be taught that they live not in Time but Eternity,—that their thoughts, words and deeds are recorded minutely and accurately—and that each individual human unit is expected to contribute towards the general beauty and adornment of God's scheme of Perfection. Every man, every woman, must give of his or her best. The artist must give his noblest art, not for what it brings to him personally of gain or renown, but for what it does to others in the way of uplifting;—the poet must give his highest thought, not for praise, but for love;—the very craftsman must do his best and strongest work not for the coin paid, but for the fact that it is work, and as such must be done well—and none must imagine that they can waste the forces wherewith they have been endowed. For no waste and no indolence is permitted, and in the end no selfishness. The attitude of the selfish human being is pure disintegration,—a destroying microbe which crumbles and breaks down the whole constitution, not only ruining the body but the mind, and frequently making havoc of the very wealth that has been too selfishly guarded. For wealth is ephemeral as fame—only Love and the Soul are the lasting things of God, the Makers of Life and the Rulers of Eternity."

So far I read—then laying down my book I listened. Music, solemn and exquisitely beautiful, stole on my ears from the far distance— it seemed to float through the open window as though in a double chorus—rising from the sea and falling from the heavens. Delicious harmonies trembled through the air, soft as fine rain falling on roses,—and with their penetrating tenderness a thousand suggestions, a thousand memories came to me, all infinitely sweet. I began to think that even if Rafel Santoris were separated from me by some mischance, or changed to me in any way, it need not affect me over-much so long as I cherished the love I had for him in my own soul. Our passion was of a higher quality than the merely material,- -it was material and spiritual together, the spiritual predominating, thus making of it the only passion that can last. What difference could a few years more or less bring, if we were bound, by the eternal laws governing us, to become united in the end? The joy of life is to love rather than to be loved,—and the recipient of love is never so fully conscious of perfect happiness as the giver.

The music went on in varying moods of lovely harmony, and my mind, like a floating cloud, drifted lazily above the waves of sound. I thought compassionately of the unrest and discontent of thousands who devote themselves to the smallest and narrowest aims in life,— people with whom the loss of a mere article of wearing apparel is more important than a national difficulty—people who devote all their faculties to social schemes of self-aggrandisement—people who discuss trifles till discussion is worn threadbare, and ears are tired and brain is weary— people who, assuming to be religious and regular church-goers, yet do the mean-est things, and have no scruple in playing the part of tale-bearer and mischief-maker, setting themselves deliberately to break friendships and destroy love— people who talk of God as though He were their intimate, and who have by their very lives drawn everything of God out of them—I thought of all these, I say— and I thought how different this world would be if men would hold by the noblest ideals, and suffer the latent greatness in them to have its way—if they would truly rule their own universe and not allow its movements to fall into chaos— how fair life would become!—how replete with health and joy!—what a paradise would be created around us!—and what constant benediction we should draw down upon us from the Most High! And gradually as I sat absorbed in my own reveries the afternoon waned into twilight, and twilight into dusk—one star brilliant as a great diamond, flashed out suddenly above a rift of cloud—and a soft darkness began to creep stealthily over sky and sea. I moved away from the win-dow and paced slowly up and down the room, waiting and wondering. The music still continued,—but it had now grown slower and more solemn, and founded like a great organ being played in a cathedral. It impressed me with a sense of prayer and praise—more of praise than prayer, for I had nothing to pray for, God having given me my own Soul, which was all!

As the darkness deepened, a soft suffused light illumined the room— and I now noticed that it was the surface of the walls that shone in this delicate yet luminous way. I put my hand on the wall nearest to me—it was quite cold to the touch, yet bright to the eyes, and was no more fatiguing to look at than the sunshine on a landscape. I could not understand how the light was thus arranged and used, but its effect was beautiful. As I walked to and fro, looking at the various graceful and artistic objects which adorned the room, I perceived an easel, on which a picture was placed with a curtain of dark velvet drawn across it. Moved by curiosity, I drew the curtain aside,—and my heart gave a quick bound of delight,—it was an admirably painted portrait of Rafel Santoris. The grave blue eyes looked into my own,—a smile rested on the firm, handsome mouth—the whole picture spoke to me and seemed to ask 'Wherefore didst thou doubt?' I stood gazing at it for sev-eral minutes, enrapt,—realising how much even the 'counterfeit presentment' of a beloved face may mean. And then I began to think how strange it is that we never seem ready to admit the strong insistence of Nature on individuality and personality. Up at a vast height above the Earth, and looking down upon a crowd of people from the car of a balloon, or from an aeroplane, all human beings look the same—just one black mass of tiny moving units; but, in descending among them, we find every face and figure wholly different, and though all are made on the same model there are no two alike. Yet there are many who argue and maintain that though individual personality in bodies may be strongly marked, there is no individual personality in souls—ergo, that Nature thinks so little of the intelligent Spirit inhabiting a mortal form that she limits individuality to that which is subject to change and has no care for it in that which is eternal! Such an hypothesis is absurd on the face of it, since it is the Soul that gives individuality to the Body. The individual personality of Rafel Santoris, expressed even in his painted portrait, appealed to me as being that of one I had loved long and tenderly,—there was no strangeness in his features but only an adorable familiarity. Long long ago, in centuries that had proved like mere days down the vista of time, the Soul in those blue eyes had looked love into mine! I recognised their tender, half-entreating, half-commanding gaze,—I knew the little fleeting, wistful smile which said so little and yet so much—I felt that the striving, ambitious spirit of this man had sought mine as the help and completion of his own uplifting, and that I had misunderstood him and turned from him at the crucial moment when all might have been well. And I studied his picture long and earnestly, so moved by its aspect that I found myself talking to it softly as though it were a living thing.

"I wonder if I shall ever meet you again?" I murmured—"Will you come to me?—or shall I go to you? How shall we find each other? When shall I be able to tell you that I know you now to be the only Beloved!—the one centre of my life round which all other things must for evermore revolve,—the very mainspring of my best thought and action,—the god of my universe from whose love and pleasure spring the light and splendour of creation! When shall I see you again to tell you all that my heart longs to express?—when may I fold myself in your arms as a bird folds its wings in a nest, and be at peace, knowing that I have gained the summit of all ambition and desires in love's perfect union? When shall we attune our lives together in that harmonious chord which shall sound its music sweetly through eternity? When shall our Souls make a radiant ONE, through which God's power and benediction shall vibrate like living fire, creating within us all beauty, all wisdom, all courage, all supernal joy?—For this is bound to be our future—but—when?"

Moved by my own imagining, I stretched out my arms to the picture of my love, and tears filled my eyes. I was nothing but the weakest of mortals in the sudden recollection of the happiness I might have won long ago had I been wise in time!

A door opened quietly behind me, and I turned round quickly. Aselzion's messenger, Honorius, stood before me—and I greeted him with a smile, though my eyes were wet.

"Have you come to fetch me?"—I asked—"I am ready."

He inclined his head a little.

"You are not quite ready"—he said—and with the word he gave into my hands a folded garment and veil—"You must attire yourself in these. I will wait for you outside."

He retired and left me, and I quickly changed my own things for those which had been brought. They were easily put on, as they consisted simply of one long white robe of a rather heavy make of soft silk, and a white veil which covered me from head to foot. My attiring took me but a few minutes, and when all was done I touched the bell by which I had previously summoned Aselzion. Honorius entered at once—his looks were grave and preoccupied.

"If you should not return to this room,"—he said, slowly—"is there any message—any communication you would like me to convey to your friends?"

My heart gave a quick bound. There was some actual danger in store for me, then? I thought for a moment—then smiled.

"None!" I answered—"I shall be able to attend to all such personal matters myself—afterwards!"

Honorius looked at me, and his handsome but rather stern face was grave even to melancholy.

"Do not be too sure!"—he said, in a low tone—"It is not my place to speak, but few pass the ordeal to which you are about to be subjected. Only two have passed it in ten years."

"And one of these two was—?"

For answer, he pointed to the portrait of Santoris, thus confirming my instinctive hope and confidence.

"I am not afraid!" I said—"And I am ready to follow you now wherever you wish me to go."

He made no further remark and, turning round, led the way out of the apartment.

We went down many stairs and through many corridors,—some dimly lit, some scarcely illumined at all. The night had now fully come,— and through one of two of the windows we passed I could see the dark sky patterned with stars. We came to the domed hall where the fountain played, and this was illumined by the same strange all- penetrating light I had previously noticed,—the lovely radiance played on the spray of the fountain, making the delicate frondage of ferns and palms and the hues of flowers look like a dream of fairyland. Passing through the hall, I followed my guide down a dark narrow passage—then I found myself suddenly alone. Guided by the surging sound of organ music, I went on,—and all at once saw a broad stream of light pouring out from the open door of the chapel. Without a moment's hesitation, I entered—then paused—the symbol of the Cross and Star flamed opposite to me—and on every side wherever I looked there were men in white robes with cowls thrown back on their shoulders, all standing in silent rows, watching me as I came. My heart beat quickly,—my nerves thrilled—I trembled as I walked, thankful for the veil that partially protected me from that multitude of eyes!—eyes that looked at me in wonder, but not unkindly—eyes that mutely asked questions never to be answered— eyes that said as plainly as though in actual speech—"Why are you among us?—you, a woman? Why should you have conquered difficulties which we have still to overcome? Is it pride, defiance, or ambition with you?—or is it all love?"

I felt a thousand influences moving around me—the power of many brains at work silently cross-examined my inner spirit as though it were a witness in defence of some great argument—but I made up my mind not to yield to the overpowering nervousness and sudden alarm of my own position which threatened to shake my self-control. I fixed my eyes on the glittering symbol of the Cross and Star and moved on slowly—I must have looked a strangely solitary creature, draped in white like a victim for sacrifice and walking all alone towards those burning, darting rays of light which enveloped the whole of the chapel in a flood of almost blinding splendour. The music still thundered on round me—and I thought I heard voices far off singing—I could distinguish words that came falling through the music, like blossoms falling through rain:

> Into the Light,
> Into the heart of the fire!
> To the innermost core of the deathless flame
> I ascend—I aspire!
> Under me rolls the whirling Earth,
> With the noise of a myriad wheels that run
> Ever round and about the Sun,—
> Over me circles the splendid heaven,

Strewn with the stars of morn and even,
 And I, the queen
 Of my soul serene,
Float with my rainbow wings unfurled,
Alone with Love, 'twixt God and the world!

My heart beat rapidly; every nerve in me trembled—yet I went on resolvedly, not allowing myself to even think of danger.

And then I saw Aselzion—Aselzion, transfigured into an almost supernatural beauty of aspect by the radiance which bathed him in its lustrous glory!—Aselzion, with outstretched hands beckoning me towards him—and as I approached I instinctively sank on my knees. The music died away suddenly, and there was a profound silence. I felt, though I could not see, that the eyes of all present were fixed upon me. And Aselzion spoke:

"Rise!" he said—and his voice was clear and imperative—"Not here must thou kneel—not here must thou rest! Rise and go onward!—thou hast gone far, but the way is still beyond! The gate of the Last Probation stands open—enter!—and may God be thy Guide!"

I rose as he commanded me,—and a dazzling flash of light struck my eyes as though the heavens had opened. The blazing Cross and Star became suddenly severed in two separate portions, dividing asunder and disclosing what seemed to be a Hall of living fire! Flames of every colour burned vividly, leaping and falling without pause or cessation,—it was a kind of open furnace in which surely everything must be consumed! I looked at Aselzion in silent enquiry—not in fear—and in equally silent answer he pointed to the glowing vault. I understood—and without another moment's hesitation I advanced towards it. As in a dream I heard a kind of murmuring behind me—and suppressed exclamations from the students or disciples of Aselzion who were all assembled in the chapel—but I paid no heed to this—my whole soul was set on fulfilling the last task demanded of me. Step by step I went on—I passed Aselzion with a smile—

"Good-bye!" I murmured—"We shall meet again!"

And then I advanced towards the leaping flames. I felt their hot breath on my cheeks—the scorching wind of them lifted my hair through the folds of my veil—an idea came upon me that for some cause or other I was now to experience that 'Change which men call Death'—and that through this means I should meet my Beloved on the other side of life—and with his name on my lips, and a passionate appeal to him in my heart, I stepped into the glowing fire.

As I did so, I lost sight of Aselzion—of the chapel and of all those who watched my movements, and found myself surrounded on all sides by darting points of light which instead of scorching and withering me like a blown leaf in a storm, were like cool and fragrant showers playing all over me! Amazed, I went on—and as I went grew bolder. At one step I was bathed in a rain of delicate rays like sparkling diamond and topaz—at another a lovely violet light shrouded me in its rich hues—at another I walked in melting azure, like the hues of a summer sky— and the farther in I went the deeper and more glowing was the light about me. I felt it penetrating every pore of my skin—I held my hands out to it, and saw them look transparent in the fine luminance,—and presently, gaining courage, I threw back my veil and breathed in the radiance, as one breathes the air! My whole body grew light, and moved as though it floated rather than walked—I looked with unfatigued, undazzled eyes at the glittering flames that sparkled harmlessly about me and which changed to lovely shapes of flowers and leaves beneath my feet, and arched themselves over my head like branches of shading trees—and then all at once, down the long vista I caught sight of a Shape like that of an Angel!—an angel that waited for me with watchful eyes and outstretched arms!—it was but a moment that I saw this vision, and yet I knew what it meant, and I pressed on and on with all my Soul rising in me as it were, to go forth and reach that Companion of itself which stood waiting with such tender patience! The light around me now changed to waves of intense luminance which swept upon me like waves of the sea—and I allowed myself to be borne along with them, I knew not whither. All at once I saw a vast Pillar of Fire which seemed to block my way,—pausing a moment, I looked and saw it break asunder and form the Cross and Star!—I gazed upward, wondering—its rays descending seemed to pierce my eyes, my brain, my very soul!—I sprang forward, dazed and dazzled, murmuring, "Let this be the end!"

Someone caught me in his arms—someone drew me to his breast, holding me there as if I were the dearest possession of all the world or life or time could give— and a voice, infinitely tender, answered me—

"Not the end, but the Endless, my beloved!—Mine at last, and mine for ever!— in triumph, in victory, in perfect joy!"

And then I knew!—I knew that I had found my love!—that it was Rafel Santoris who thus held me in his close embrace,—that I had fulfilled my own desire, which was to prove my faith if not my worthiness—that I had won all I wanted in this world and the next, and that nothing could ever separate our Souls, one from the other again! This is the deep eternal ecstasy of a knowledge divinely shared by the very angels of God, and of such supernal happiness nothing can be said or written!

* * *
* *
*

I pen these last words on the deck of the 'Dream' with my Beloved beside me. The sun is sinking in a glory of crimson—we are about to anchor in still waters. A rosy light flashes on our wonderful white sails, which will be presently furled; and we shall sit together, Rafel and I, watching the night draw its soft dark curtain around us, and the stars come out in the sky like diamonds embroidered on deep purple velvet, and listening to the gentle murmur of the little waves breaking into a rocky corner of the distant shore. And the evening will close on a day of peace and happiness,—one of the many unwearying, beautiful days which, like a procession of angels, bring us new and ever more perfect joy!

More than a year has elapsed since my 'Probation' in the House of Aselzion,—since we, my Beloved and I, knelt before the Master and received his blessing on our eternal union. In that brief time I have lost all my 'worldly' friends and acquaintances,—who have, if I may so express it, become afraid of me. Afraid, chiefly, because I possess all that the world can give me without their advice and assistance—and not only afraid, but offended, because I have found the Companion of my Soul with whom they have nothing in common. They look upon me as 'lost to society' and cannot realise how much such loss is gain! Meanwhile we, Rafel and I, live our own radiant and happy lives, in full possession of all that makes life sweet and valuable, and wanting nothing that our own secret forces cannot supply. Wealth is ours—one of the least among the countless gifts Nature provides for those among her children who know where to find her inexhaustible riches—and we also enjoy the perfect health which accompanies the constant inflowing of an exhaustless vitality. And though the things we attain seem 'miraculous' to others, so that even while accepting help and benefit at our hands, they frown and shake their heads at the attitude we assume towards social hypocrisies and conventions, we are nevertheless able to create such 'influences' around us, that none come near as without feeling stronger, better and more content,—and this is the utmost we are permitted to do for our fellow-creatures, inasmuch as none will listen to argument, and none will follow advice. The most ardent soul that ever dwelt in human form cannot lead another soul in the way of lasting life or lasting happiness if it refuses to go,—and there is no more absolute truth than this—That each man and each woman must make his or her own destiny both here and hereafter. This is the Law which changes not and which can never be subject to the slightest variation. Forgiveness of sins there is none—since every trespass against law carries its own punishment. Necessity for prayer there is none,—since every faithful wish and desire of the Soul is granted without parley. Necessity for praise there is much!- -since the Soul lives and grows in the glory of its Creator. And the whole Secret of Everlasting Life and Happiness is contained in the full possession and control of the Divine Centre of ourselves—this 'Radia' or living flame, which must be DUAL in order to be perfect, and which in its completed state, is an eternal Force which nothing can destroy and nothing can resist. All Nature harmonises with its action, and from Nature it draws its perpetual sustenance and increasing power.

To me, and my Beloved, the world is a garden of paradise—rich with beauty and delight. We live in it as a part of its loveliness—we draw into our own organisations the warmth of the sunlight, the glory of colour, the songs of sweet birds, the fragrance of flowers, and the exquisite vibrations of the light and air. Like two notes of a perfect chord we sound our lives on the keyboard of the Infinite— and we know that the music will become fuller and sweeter as the eternal seasons roll on. If it is asked why there should have been any necessity to pass through the psychic ordeal imposed on me by Aselzion, I reply—Look at the world in which men and women generally live, and say frankly whether its ways are such as to engender happiness! Look at society—look at politics—look at commerce—all mere schemes for self-aggrandisement! And more than all, look at the Sham of modern religion! Is it not too often a mere blasphemy and affront to the majesty of the Divine? And are not many, if not all these mistakes against Nature,—these offences against eternal Law,—the result of Man's own 'influence' working in opposition to the very decrees of God, which he disobeys even while recognising that they exist?

The chief point of Aselzion's instruction was the test of the Brain and Soul against 'influences'—the opposing influences of others— and this is truly the chief hindrance to all spiritual progress. The coward sentiment of fear itself is born in us through the influence of timorous persons—and it is generally the dread of what 'other people will say' or what 'other people will think' that holds us back from performing many a noble action. It should be thoroughly understood that in the eternal advancement of one's own Soul 'other people' and their influences are hindrances to progress. It does not matter a jot what anybody thinks or says, provided the central altar of one's own Spirituality is clear and clean for the steadfast burning of the dual flame of Life and Love. All opinion, all criticism becomes absurd in such matters as these and absolutely worthless.

It does not affect me that anyone outside my sphere of thought should be incredulous of my beliefs,—nor can it move me from my happiness to know that persons who live their lives on a lower plane consider me a fool for electing to live mine on the highest. I take joy in the fact that even in so selfish and material an age as this, Aselzion still has his students and disciples,—a mere handful out of the million, it is true, but still sufficient to keep the beautiful truth of the Soul's power alive and helpful to the chosen few. For such who have studied these truths and have mastered them sufficiently to practise them in the ordinary round of existence, Life presents an ever living happiness—and offers daily proof that there is no such thing as Death. Youth remains where Love is, and Beauty stays with health and vitality. Decay and destruction are changes which are brought about by apathy of the Will and indifference to the Soul's existence, and the same Law which gives the Soul its supreme sovereignty equally works for its release from effete and inactive substances.

To those who would ask me how I am able to hold and keep the treasures of life, love and youth, which the majority of mankind are for ever losing, I answer that I can say no more than I have said, and the lesson which all may learn is contained in what I have written. It is no use arguing with those whom no argument will convince, or trying to teach those who will not be taught. We—my Beloved and I—can only prove the truth of the Soul's absolute command over all spiritual, material and elemental forces by our One life and the way we live it—we, to whom everything that is necessary and desirable for our progress, comes on demand,—we, whom Science serves as an Aladdin's lamp, realising every imaginable delight—we, with whom Love, which with many human beings is judged the most variable and transitory of emotions, is the very Principle of Life, the very essence of the waves of the air through which we move and have our being. The attainment of such happiness as ours is possible to all, but there is only One Way of Attainment, and the clue to that Way is in the Soul of each individual human being. Each one must find it and follow it, regardless of all 'influences' which may be brought to bear on his or her actions,—each one must discover the Centre-poise of Life's movement, and firmly abide by it. It is the Immortal Creature in each one of us whose destiny is to make eternal progress and advancement through endless phases of life, love and beauty, and when once we know and admit the actual existence of this Immortal Centre we shall realise that with it all things are possible, save Death. Radiating outward from itself, it can preserve the health and youth of the body it inhabits indefinitely, till of its own desire it seeks a higher plane of action,—radiating inwardly, it is an irresistible attractive force drawing to itself the powers and virtues of the planet on which it dwells, and making all the forces of visible and invisible Nature subject to its will and command. This is one of those great Truths which the world denies, but which it is destined to learn within the next two thousand years.

If anyone should desire to know the fate of Motion Harland and his daughter, that fate has been precisely what they themselves brought about by their way of life and action. Morton Harland himself 'died,' as the world puts it, of a painful and lingering disease which could have been cured had he chosen to take the means offered to him through Rafel Santoris. He did not choose,—therefore the end was inevitable. Catherine married Dr. Brayle, and they two now live a sufficiently wretched life together,—she, a moping, querulous invalid, and he as a 'society' physician, possessed of great wealth and the position wealth brings. We never meet,—our ways are now for ever sundered. Mine is the upward and onward path—and with my Beloved I ascend the supernal heights where the Shadow of Evil never falls, and where the Secret of Life is centred in the Spirit of Love.

Printed in the United States
22320LVS00003B/155